THE SCOTTISH LIBRARY

The Scottish Library

In the same series:

THE SCOTTISH LIBRARY
General Editor: Alexander Scott

SCOTTISH SHORT STORIES

1800-1900

Edited by

DOUGLAS GIFFORD

CALDER & BOYARS · LONDON

First published in Great Britain in 1971
by Calder and Boyars Ltd
18 Brewer Street London W1

ISBN 0 7145 0656 7 Cloth edition
ISBN 0 7145 0657 5 Paper edition

This volume has been produced with the
assistance of the Scottish Arts Council and
the publishers wish to acknowledge with
thanks the substantial help given not only
by the Council itself but by its Literature
Committee without which this volume and
others in the series could not be viably
published.

Printed in Great Britain by
Northumberland Press Limited
Gateshead

✓ = awreidy excerpt.t

CONTENTS

INTRODUCTION

IN THESE nineteenth-century Scottish short stories, and in Scottish fiction of the same period,[1] one can see that the pattern of cultural and social division of the eighteenth century, with all the attendant religious and political divisions to re-inforce polarisation, still operate; but with changing emphases. With the added complexities of economic and industrial change, the more obvious divisions of the eighteenth century, between the vernacular tradition in poetry and the polite "enclave" culture of the literati of Edinburgh, between a factual culture, the scientific culture of the "head" and the irresponsible sentimental Edinburgh culture of the "heart", oppositions taking place on geographical, linguistic or class grounds, give way to an increasing awareness on the serious writer's part of division *within* the Scottish mind; internal rather than external. Now the major fiction tries to express uneasy tensions between two kinds of Scotland, and two opposing ways of looking at Scotland.[2] Scott sets ancient Disorder, romance, imagination and feeling against new, rational Order, with its Baillie Nicol Jarvie desire for commercial rather than romantic attributes. This "characteristic tension"[3] runs through all his major fiction; so much so that the novels are best seen as extended metaphors for the dissociation in Scotland of thought and feeling, materialism and imagination, repression and sensitivity. Scott does this by opposing groups, in *Waverley* (1814) or *Redgauntlet* (1824), each representing a side of the dissociation; or *via* his "insipid" heroes, each torn between the warring aspects of Scotland and Scottish character.

Just as Scott often presents his division in the "divided family" metaphor, as in the *Heart of Midlothian*, in the division within the family Deans, or in the fact that Jarvie and Rob Roy are related,

so James Hogg's *Private Memoirs ... of a Justified Sinner* (1824) is
organised in terms of the divided family within a divided Scotland.
An intolerant and intensely selfish religious group is set against a
warmer, natural group, Wringhims against Dalcastles, brother
against brother—with the final movement of division being into the
diseased mind of the sinner himself.[4] And with John Galt's *Entail*
(1823) the "divided family" metaphor expresses itself in the form
which persists to the present day.

   This opposition of authority, materialism, religious repression,
brutal lack of sympathy against vulnerability, imagination and sensitivity, is presented with different family groupings, or *via* an
exceptionally close link between friends, which often amounts to a
love-hate relationship. Probably the best examples are found in
Stevenson's Scottish novels. *The Master of Ballantrae* (1889)
opposes the stay-at-home, estate-and-finance-watching brother
Henry with the demoniac, Jacobite and romantic James. Even
Kidnapped (1886) brings the cautious, unwilling adventurous David
Balfour into almost brotherly love (and hate) with the intrinsically
different, romantic Alan Breck.[5] *Weir of Hermiston* (1896) stands
between Galt's *Entail* and George Douglas Brown's *House with the
Green Shutters* (1901) as the broad division of the Scottish character seen yet again in terms of the father-son opposition; while *Dr.
Jekyll and Mr. Hyde* (1886) implicitly states the same theme. It
seems that creative and imaginative Scots, when expressing their
deepest-felt and most personal reactions to their own back-ground,
are compelled to come to the same basic conclusion that there are
darker forces of religion or materialism warring with the more
humane aspects of the Scottish character. At times, the darker
aspects of religion transcend the "family division" theme, so that
instead of merely representing materialism or repressive authori-
tarianism, one of the characters in the conflict takes on demoniac
proportions; thus Redgauntlet; thus Gilmartin or even Robert
Wringhim himself in the *Justified Sinner*; thus the *Master of
Ballantrae* and, *par excellence* John Gourlay senior, of the *House
with the Green Shutters*. This symbolic demonism is found in
several stories in this collection, the outstanding example being
The Merry Men.

Thus two major forces shape the major fiction; protestantism and profit; and the compound delayed effects of these on Scottish life are the themes of all the really serious writers. Where Baillie Nicol Jarvie or Galt's Provost are men of the new economic age, there exist in the great father or demoniac figures of nineteenth-century Scottish fiction, superb "extended metaphors" for *both* these forces. Claud Walkinshaw of the *Entail*, Weir of Hermiston, or John Gourlay senior of *The House with the Green Shutters*, are not to be assessed merely as wither the embodiments of Scottish Greed or simple Calvinism—they are a profound merging of these forces.

This major fiction, the serious attempt to work imaginatively with the real divisions and problems within Scottish life and character, is that which is represented most fully—with one major qualification. A short, even long-short story cannot express the author's full sense of the polarities of Scottish life in the same way that, say, *Redgauntlet* or *Weir of Hermiston* can. What the stories here do is *relate* in theme and design to the major novels. The unity of the short story excludes development of several aspects or themes; so we find that Hogg's *Brownie of the Black Haggs* will stress the demoniac element of the *Justified Sinner*, instead of bringing in the "divided family" theme; or Stevenson's *Merry Men* will likewise stress the theme of guilt and retribution which is almost pre-destined to fall on Gordon Darnaway when he murders the survivor in the *Merry Men*, rather than completing a more complex opposition like the father-son conflict of *Weir of Hermiston*. Nevertheless, the themes are obviously drawn from that major pattern in the novels—guilt, the result of torn and divided conscience, which consumes and destroys; awareness of dark forces only slightly beneath the surface; love-hate relationships like Hogg's Lady and her Merodach; and the tradition not just in the major fiction, but in *Holy Willie's Prayer* as well as *The Justified Sinner*, of oblique comment through dramatic monologue or ambiguity, or sheer symbolic fantasy, on Victorian society where religion and materialism have created the "dissociation of sensibility" between the imagination and the intellect, causing repression with greed to dominate finer feelings, or forcing imagination into fanaticism or undisciplined sensitivity.

The Two Drovers is not quite the pattern of Scott's Scottish fiction, where *inside* Scotland, groups representing Order and Disorder, Past and Present, Imagination and Reason, Repression and Freedom, battle it out with a trapped "hero" in the middle, like Scott himself. But one can see the connection. To a certain extent, the tragedy depends on the typical Scott juxtaposition of the figure from the older society, less ordered, more romantic and wilder in imagination with the figure from civilised, calmer, more prosaic Lowland—English society. Here too are the almost family ties of love becoming hate; yet always there is the strong bond between the two men, as later in the brothers theme of the *Justified Sinner*, or in Stevenson's repeated theme of friends or brothers totally different, yet so linked that their destinies are inextricable.

But the supernatural elements here, while certainly giving shape and tragic anticipation to the story, are limited by Scott's views on the kind of supernatural he sees as permissible for a serious writer, which consists of secret intimations of futurity coming through dreams or second sight.[6] His separation of the folk tale, the vulgar superstition of the peasant, from the permissible strange insight of the sybil or gentleman, seems to me almost to be a watershed in Scottish culture between an older and richer world of Brownies and witches and kelpies, and a world which after Hogg, is sadly reduced in this diversity—the devil, of course, stays, used by Scott himself in *Wandering Willie's Tale*, but Hogg is the last to be naturally at home in this world. In his *Justified Sinner*, his neglected *Three Perils of Man* (1822), in his *Shepherd's Calendar* (1829), from which the story here is selected, Hogg writes with racy economy and vivid detail as the last representative of ballad tradition. It's ironic that Scott preferred a kind of supernatural which is dangerously close to Gothic melodrama, while Hogg's is sure and authentic. And the figure of Merodach in the *Brownie of the Black Haggs* is an oblique way of stating the theme of guilt; the lady has brought retribution upon herself, the devil has sent "Merodach of Babylon" to collect his own. Notice the closeness of this story to the *Justified Sinner*; Merodach is the counterpart of Gilmartin, the devil; they have become "familiars", tied by love-hate bonds, to those who deserve them. And just as in the novel Hogg leaves deliberate ambiguity about the existence of the devil—is the devil real, or only in the imagination of Robert Wringhim?—so here, it is left open whether Merodach is real or supernatural.

This kind of use of the supernatural allows a depth of meaning, in ambiguity and symbolism, beyond the kind Scott advocates. Luckily, Scott's advice is only half taken by later writers like Oliphant and Stevenson. And it is not taken at all in another, totally different kind of "extravagant diablerie" (which was to be attacked in much the same way as Scott attacked Hogg's rich usage of folk elements in his supernatural tales) in George MacDonald's symbolic fantasy.[7] The ambiguity is of another kind; the implications are even further reaching. Like Stevenson's *Will o' the Mill* (1878), or Margaret Oliphant's *Little Pilgrim in the Unseen* (1882), MacDonald's *The Golden Key* is a sort of pilgrim's progress through life, an allegory which stresses the need for charity and love, qualities too lacking in nineteenth-century Scottish life. This use of the short parable, or fantasy, is frequent at this time in Scottish fiction—*Dr. Jekyll and Mr. Hyde* being an outstanding example—and it seems to be yet another oblique method whereby the Scottish writer expresses his hunger for imaginative freedom and human warmth and, by implication, comments on the society which lacks these qualities.

While there is no simple allegorical method by which we can unravel the meaning of *The Golden Key*, there are certain general guides; the key broadly represents faith, the Grandmother imagination and compassion, a sort of religion which defies dogma and creed; a church into which all can enter. And without going too deep into the meaning of the three old men of Sea, Earth and Fire, it helps to realise that Mossy and Tangle are progressing or evolving up an ascending scale of being, stages of which are marked by these elemental figures. Thus when the airfish (conscience?) guide Mossy and Tangle to the starting point, the Grandmother (who is also the finishing point as well), they (being both the airfish and the children) are recreated after a kind of communion, as higher beings one step further on their journey. And although to some, the Old Man of the Sea appears frightening, a devil walking by the shore, to the children (who age fully through the story) he is neither devil or God, but the next stage on their progress to Per-fection. For MacDonald, creeds with the Devil and Hell don't apply; there are only consciences or souls (fish) waiting to be let loose by the Old Man of the Sea from the source of life, the sea, to begin their journey through the other elements of earth and fire—"evildoers" are those whose consciences aren't ready to be let loose. Mossy and Tangle move in stages to become purer, more perceptive; death separates them, but doesn't stop the journey. Nevertheless, for all that MacDonald seems not to refer to the torment and division central to the major Scottish fiction, he makes his own kind of oblique comment; constructive, rather than destruc-tive, criticism. For his central figure, the Grandmother, is obviously Charity in its broadest sense—a mixture, as Brown implies in the *House with the Green Shutters*, of love, imagination and all the other humane qualities lacking in the Scottish scene.

Margaret Oliphant's *The Library Window* is a deceptively slight story. At first it seems close to James's *Turn of the Screw* in method; but it becomes even more disturbing and demoniac on reflection, and its links are rather with the ambiguity of *Wander-ing Willie's Tale* or Hogg's frequent tales with dual interpretations.

On one level, it is almost a modern version of the good fairy, bad fairy tales; with Aunt Mary set against Lady Carnbee. There is an implication that Lady Carnbee, while ironically protesting her youthful virtue, is that evil woman who has caused the death of the young man who now haunts the library. And Lady Carnbee is frequently alluded to by the girl as a witch; she has darker know-ledge of the window's history, she "bewitches" the girl, and her diamond stings, or blazes in malediction. At this level, the story takes place "between the night and the day, when the fairy folk have power", and Lady Carnbee passes on the curse of her guilt to the girl. But Aunt Mary too has deeper knowledge than she reveals, and shares the girl's pain, bonding them in the phrase "women of our blood", recognising the spell, banishing it tempor-arily with her murmured "like a dream when one awaketh", which turns the window blank again. And to round out this fairy-tale aspect, the girl herself, being pure in her love, awakes the writing figure and by communicating with him, breaks the curse and sees him no more. Only the ring, malignant, remains. And on this level, the theme of guilt, together with a slighter demonism, runs through the story.

But on another level, the story is about a feverish and over-imaginative young girl who *creates* her dream world—the figure of the poet is obviously an idealisation of an unattainable love. The older folk are thus merely people who remember or don't remember the heartsickness of youth; who sympathise with the delusions of a sick girl. Thus the story is exactly like Hogg's *Justified Sinner* where the sinner may actually meet the devil, or may merely create him.

Whatever the interpretation we put on the story—and I think both are intended—the relationship with the themes of the major Scottish fiction is still apparent. Excessive imagination and sensitivity, demonism, and on the other hand worldly folk who refuse to share dreams but, like Aunt Mary or Mr. Pitmilly, retreat behind the *Times* to forget them for the news of the world—however slightly presented, these are the elements of the major fiction.

The Penance of John Logan is a more straightforward study of guilt; a sympathetic and compassionate study of the consciousness of age that avoids kailyard sentiment and indeed seems to have more in common with George MacKay Brown's stories today or Iain Crichton Smith's *Consider the Lilies* (1968). But the guilt is still the result of greed; the island seems to the old man to watch him at the moment of theft.

Similar in setting, but deepening the central character in his materialism and guilt, is *The Merry Men*. Again, at first it seems very representative of Stevenson, with its *Kidnapped* setting, the warped uncle, the *Treasure Island* world of treasure and sunken ships, and the *Jekyll and Hyde* figure of the mysterious negro; but it is soon apparent that it is oblique comment, with familiar demonic figures, on Calvinism and materialism. Gordon Darnaway is, like so many central figures in the recurrent pattern of this kind of fiction, psychologically unbalanced, motivated by greed and guilt. At first it seems that the opposition of *Weir of Hermiston* is to be repeated, with the repressed and materialist Gordon set against his college-educated nephew who is almost a son to him. But the nephew recedes into the role of commentator; though he's actively involved, the study of character centres on Gordon Darnaway, whose fate is almost an allegory for the fate of older Scottish Calvinism. Like Gourlay senior, his faith has become "inverted", replacing love with greed and murder. Like that sunken treasure ship, "Espirito Santo", Gordon's *own* "holy spirit" and charity is sunk, buried deep—he is an alien in Aros Jay, which Stevenson tells us is Gaelic for "the House of God".[8] And he takes on demoniac proportions, "set upon a damnatory creed" admitting that evil has become his good, and entering into unholy communion with the hellish dance of the waters called the Merry Men.

The very sea, source of life and open, sparkling to the healthy nephew, becomes hostile to him—but again we find the traditional ambiguity here. The madness may be in Gordon's mind, though it is significant that his nephew experiences a slighter version of the same change when, in *his* greed, the sea darkens and threatens at his invasion of the sunken peace of the "Espirito Santo". (This is a skilful parallel and anticipation of the main theme and climax of the book; the nephew's grisly discovery of human bones relates to Darnaway's murder.) And the nephew and Rorie are aware of the sinister shape, the waiting great fish which follows Darnaway's boat. And in Darnaway's explicit rejection of Christianity and its values, in his hatred of God's ocean and his offences against God's creatures, we reach a climax which takes its place in that long line from *Holy Willie's Prayer* to Galt's *Entail*, from Hogg's *Sinner* to the *House with the Green Shutters*, where the revelation breaks that these central figures are in fact disciples of the devil. Darnaway's destruction, as so often before, proceeds through his own madness. Stevenson uses the majestic negro as the agent-mysterious, possibly satanic—of his doom, fittingly ending the story with a survivor from the sea claiming retribution for that other murdered survivor; ambiguous to the last, the agent possibly for the devil. And the Merry Men, the waters of destruction, are savage irony on the central theme; but they also conceal the monstrous rocks of destruction in the mind itself.

But this ambitious and deeper fiction is limited; outside of this

fairly narrow line of a few writers trying to say something about
the quality of Scottish imagination and character, there were thousands of popular "scotch novels" from Scott onward, broadly
dividing into two schools.

From Galt—but from *Sir Andrew Wylie* (1822) rather than from
Annals of the Parish (1821) descends the domestic or "kailyard
school" aided by political encouragement and publication of "suit-
able" material by the Tory *Blackwood's Magazine* and abetted by
the successor to the crown of Scottish literature after Scott,
"Christopher North"—one of Blackwood's original editors, whose
own novels helped sustain that anecdotal and episodic sentimental
exploitation and distortion of Scottish Life and Character for a
bigger British audience.[9] Only when it is realised how strong a
hold this distorted and debased image of Scottish rural life had on
British, let alone Scottish, audiences, can the peculiar integrity and
honesty of view of William Alexander's *Johnny Gibb of Gushet-
neuk* (1871) be appreciated. Here Alexander is represented by
Baubie Huie's Bastard Geet. While still retaining the moral position
of Victorian Scotland, curious in its gulf between standard English
comment and magnificent Aberdeenshire dialect, yet the story cap-
tures the reality and ability of the peasants to "grow over" and
around the bastard, to accept him, however crudely, into genuine
affection—where "Christopher North" would have used a similar
situation as reason for the degradation of an entire family and for
maximum sentimental exploitation.[10] The tradition still continues
today, handed down to us by Barrie, Crockett and McLaren in
novels like *A Window in Thrums* (1889) or *The Stickit Minister*
(1893).

Galt's *Gudewife* and Aytoun's *Glenmutchkin Railway* are not
"kailyard" or sentimental; but they do have one quality shared by
the kailyard writers, that exploitation *via* skilful and slightly dis-
torting or reducing humour, of local and parochial Scottish charac-
teristics. Galt in the *Entail* shows himself aware of the darker
aspects of materialism and religion; here he confines himself, as
in *Sir Andrew Wylie* or *The Steamboat* (1822) Scottish stories,
to making fun and money of Scottish eccentricity; even manufactur-
ing his own eccentricities where they don't exist. Highlanders

and city capitalists get similar treatment from Aytoun. Pushed any further, with sentiment added, the result *would* be kailyard writing; these stories take comic creative writing to the verge.

On the other hand, there is that line of historical and romantic fiction, from Scott on, which, while still pre-occupied with "Scottland", at least does not involve an exploitation of the present, but rather escapes from it. Without Scott's deeper meaning and metaphor for divided Scotland and divided mind within Scotland, yet the level of achievement within the smaller range is impressive. The Scottish historical fiction seems nearer its source material than its English counterpart; and the wealth of choice here is bewildering, from Thomas Dick Lauder, Hogg, Galt, many of the tales in *Wilson's Tales of the Borders*, to George Whyte-Melville and James Grant.[11]

Of this school, there are two, possibly three, examples; while not historical, Hugh Miller's *Widow of Dunskaith*, from *Wilson's Tales of the Borders*, is not a domestic tale; its locality is far from homely, but is chosen for its dramatic enhancement of the action, which indeed comes close to melodrama. But it is very typical both of the kind of story the *Tales* abound in, and Miller's own descriptive strength and Victorian weakness for stock character and situation. Similarly, James Grant's *Story of Farquhar Shaw* suffers from melodrama and windiness; but nevertheless both stories do have the typical Scottish descriptive strength in setting, a good grasp of narrative and of tragic necessity—both ultimately owe much to the inevitability of Scott's *Two Drovers*, and illustrate the strength and weakness of the historical tradition after Scott.

Finally, a word about the order and range of the stories: The order is not chronological—both the Oliphant and Black stories are later than the Stevenson, though placed before. But as the centre of their fiction *in toto* antedates Stevenson, I have placed them in this way; the range thus excludes those authors whose "centre" lies beyond Stevenson.

I have also deliberately chosen a smaller number of long-short stories, rather than many short stories; for the two reasons that Scott's *Wandering Willie's Tale* or Stevenson's *Thrawn Janet*, for example, are readily accessible elsewhere, and because I feel that the long-short story is peculiarly characteristic of many nineteenth-century writers.[12]

FOOTNOTES

1. For some account of this nineteenth-century fiction, see Part II of David Craig's *Scottish Literature and the Scottish People, 1680-1830;* 1961.
2. For an understanding of these cultural and social divisions, see the following important studies: Edwin Muir: *Scott and Scotland*, 1936. David Craig: *Scottish Literature and the Scottish People, 1680-1830,* 1961. David Daiches: *The Paradox of Scottish Culture*, 1964.
3. The phrase is David Daiches's from his essay "Scott's Achievement as a Novelist", written in 1951, but now available along with other major essays in *Walter Scott*, 1968, collected and edited by D. D. Devlin (in the Macmillan "Modern Judgements" series).
4. It is a characteristic of the fiction of Scott, Galt, Hogg and John Gibson Lockhart, that it takes a much greater interest than hitherto found in the English novel in psychological study and mental disorder. See George Kitchin's essay on John Galt in *Edinburgh Essays on Scots Literature*, 1933, p. 115.
5. It is interesting to find the Balfour-Breck division between canny practicality and wild impetuosity repeated again and again in the romantic fiction of Neil Munro (see especially *The New Road* (1914)) and S. R. Crockett (see *Men of the Moss Haggs* (1895)). To a lesser extent, this is the same opposition as in darker novels like *Weir of Hermiston*.
6. See *Witchcraft and Demonology in Scott's Fiction*, by Coleman O. Parsons, 1964; and Scott's own review of John Galt's *Omen* in *Blackwood's Magazine*, vol. XX, July 1826.
7. For example, J. H. Millar, who in his *Literary History of Scotland*, 1903, attacks MacDonald's *Lilith* (1895) and *Phantastes* (1858) as tedious and unintelligible, whereas to twentieth-century critics like C. S. Lewis, they are his major works.
8. The ship he has salvaged from, and murdered a survivor of, is the "Christ-Anna"; Darnaway dwells on the *first* part of the name, finding it "awful" and shortly thereafter admits he is tempted to believe that it wasn't the Lord created the sea, but "the muckle black de'il".
9. Really John Wilson, one of the "Blackwood Group" who began *Blackwood's Magazine* in 1817; contributed most of the "Noctes Ambrosianae" to that magazine and, in 1822, produced *Lights and Shadows of Scottish Life*, short stories and sketches, which along with his *Trials of Margaret Lyndsay* (1822) or Moir's *Mansie Waugh* (1828) mark the beginning of that nineteenth-century flowering of excessive sentiment and preoccupation with affairs of the parish.
10. In his *Trials of Margaret Lyndsay* (1823) "North" punishes the

sexual and political misdemeanours of Walter, the father, with the degradation of his innocent wife and daughters. It is interesting to note here that so strong is the Blackwood and "North" antagonism to radical agitation that in fact Walter's reading of Tom Paine's *Age of Reason* is seen as a greater sin than his "Scarlet Woman" association, and there is a ceremonial burning of the offending book by his wife! (ch. 3, *Trials*).

11. The tradition of good historical-romantic fiction persists beyond this period in the work of this *genre* by Neil Munro, S. R. Crockett and John Buchan.

12. Most recent collections of Scottish Short Stories tend to stick to the twentieth century; or to select shorter examples of earlier writers. Still available are: *Scottish Short Stories*, ed. Fred Urquhart, 1932; *Scottish Short Stories*, ed. J. M. Reid, 1963.

WALTER SCOTT

THE TWO DROVERS

I

IT WAS the day after Doune Fair when my story commences. It had been a brisk market, several dealers had attended from the northern and midland counties in England, and English money had flown so merrily about as to gladden the hearts of the Highland farmers. Many large droves were about to set off for England, under the protection of their owners, or of the topsmen whom they employed in the tedious, laborious, and responsible office of driving the cattle for many hundred miles, from the market where they had been purchased, to the fields or farm-yards where they were to be fattened for the shambles.

The Highlanders, in particular, are masters of this difficult trade of driving, which seems to suit them as well as the trade of war. It affords exercise for all their habits of patient endurance and active exertion. They are required to know perfectly the drove-roads, which lie over the wildest tracts of the country, and to avoid as much as possible the highways, which distress the feet of the bullocks, and the turnpikes, which annoy the spirit of the drover; whereas, on the broad green or grey track, which leads across the pathless moor, the herd not only move at ease and without taxation, but, if they mind their business, may pick up a mouthful of food by the way. At night, the drovers usually sleep along with their cattle, let the weather be what it will, and many of these hardy men do not once rest under a roof during a journey on foot from Lochaber to Lincolnshire. They are paid very highly, for the trust reposed is of the last importance, as it depends on their prudence, vigilance, and honesty, whether the cattle reach the final market in good order, and afford a profit to the grazier. But as they maintain themselves at their own expense, they are especially economical in that particular. At the period we speak of, a Highland drover was victualled for his long and toilsome journey with a few handfuls of oatmeal, and two or three onions, renewed from time to time, and a ram's horn filled with whisky, which he used regularly, but sparingly, every night and morning. His dirk, or *skene-dhu* (i.e. black-knife), so worn as to be concealed beneath the arm, or by the folds of the plaid, was his only weapon, excepting the cudgel with which he directed the movements of the cattle. A Highlander was never so happy as on these occasions. There was a variety in the whole journey, which exercised the Celt's natural curiosity and love of motion; there were the constant change of place and scene, the petty adventures incidental to the traffic, and the intercourse with the various farmers, graziers, and traders, intermingled with occasional merry-makings, not the less acceptable to Donald that they were void of expense—and there was the consciousness of superior skill; for the Highlander, a child amongst flocks, is a prince amongst herds, and his natural habits induce him to disdain the shepherd's slothful life, so that he feels himself nowhere more at home than when following a gallant drove of his country cattle in the character of their guardian.

Of the number who left Doune in the morning, and with the purpose we described, not a *Glunamie* of them all cocked his bonnet more briskly, or gartered his tartan hose under knee over a pair of more promising *spiogs* (legs) than did Robin Oig M'Combich, called familiarly Robin Oig, that is, Young, or the Lesser, Robin. Though small of stature as the epithet Oig implies, and not very strongly limbed, he was as light and alert as one of the deer of his mountains. He had an elasticity of step which, in the course of a long march, made many a stout fellow envy him; and the manner in which he busked his plaid and adjusted his bonnet, argued a consciousness that so smart a John Highlandman as himself would not pass unnoticed among the Lowland lasses. The ruddy cheek, red lips, and white teeth, set off a countenance which had gained by exposure to the weather a healthful and hardy rather than a rugged hue. If Robin Oig did not laugh, or even smile frequently, as indeed is not the practice among his countrymen, his bright eyes usually gleamed from under his bonnet with an expression of cheerfulness ready to be turned into mirth.

The departure of Robin Oig was an incident in the little town, in and near which he had many friends, male and female. He was a topping person in his way, transacted considerable business on his own behalf, and was entrusted by the best farmers in the Highlands in preference to any other drover in that district. He might have increased his business to any extent had he condescended to manage it by deputy; but except a lad or two, sister's sons of his own, Robin rejected the idea of assistance, conscious, perhaps, how much his reputation depended upon his attending in person to the practical discharge of his duty in every instance. He remained, therefore, contented with the highest premium given to persons of his description, and comforted himself with the hopes that a few journeys to England might enable him to conduct business on his own account, in a manner becoming his birth. For Robin Oig's father, Lachlan M'Combich (or *son of my friend*, his actual clan-surname being M'Gregor), had been so called by the celebrated Rob Roy, because of the particular friendship which had subsisted between the grandsire of Robin and that renowned cateran. Some people even say that Robin Oig derived his Christian name from one as renowned in the wilds of Loch Lomond as ever was his namesake Robin Hood, in the precincts of merry Sherwood. "Of such ancestry", as James Boswell says, "who would not be proud?" Robin Oig was proud accordingly; but his frequent visits to England and to the Lowlands had given him tact enough to know that pretensions, which still gave him a little right to distinction in his own lonely glen, might be both obnoxious and ridiculous if preferred elsewhere. The pride of birth, therefore, was like the miser's treasure, the secret subject of his contemplation, but never exhibited to strangers as a subject of boasting.

Many were the words of gratulation and good luck which were bestowed on Robin Oig. The judges commended his drove, especially Robin's own property, which were the best of them. Some thrust out their snuff-mulls for the parting pinch—others tendered the *doch-an-dorrach* or parting cup. All cried—"Good luck travel out with you and come home with you.—Give you luck

in the Saxon market—brave notes in the *leabhar-dhu*" (black
pocket-book) "and plenty of English gold in the *sporran*" (pouch
of goatskin).

The bonny lasses made their adieus more modestly, and more
than one, it was said, would have given her best brooch to be
certain that it was upon her that his eye last rested as he turned
towards the road.

Robin Oig had just given the preliminary "*Hoo-hoo!*" to urge
forward the loiterers of the drove, when there was a cry behind
him.

"Stay, Robin—bide a blink. Here is Janet of Tomahourich—
auld Janet, your father's sister."

"Plague on her, for an auld Highland witch and spaewife," said
a farmer from the Carse of Stirling; "she'll cast some of her cantrips on the cattle."

"She canna do that," said another sapient of the same profession—"Robin Oig is no the lad to leave any of them without tying
St. Mungo's knot on their tails, and that will put to her speed
the best witch that ever flew over Dimayet upon a broomstick."

It may not be indifferent to the reader to know that the Highland cattle are peculiarly liable to be *taken*, or infected, by spells
and witchcraft; which judicious people guard against by knitting
knots of peculiar complexity on the tuft of hair which terminates
the animal's tail.

But the old woman who was the object of the farmer's suspicion
seemed only busied about the drover, without paying any attention to the drove. Robin, on the contrary, appeared rather impatient
of her presence.

"What auld-world fancy," he said, "has brought you so early
from the ingle-side this morning, Muhme? I am sure I bid you
good-even, and had your God-speed, last night."

"And left me more siller than the useless old woman will use
till you come back again, bird of my bosom," said the sibyl. "But
it is little I would care for the food that nourishes me, or the fire
that warms me, or for God's blessed sun itself, if aught but weel
should happen to the grandson of my father. So let me walk the
deasil round you, that you may go safe out into the foreign land,

and come safe home."

Robin Oig stopped, half embarrassed, half laughing, and signing to those near that he only complied with the old woman to
soothe her humour. In the meantime she traced around him, with
wavering steps, the propitiation, which some have thought has
been derived from the Druidical mythology. It consists, as is well
known, in the person who makes the *deasil* walking three times
round the person who is the object of the ceremony, taking care
to move according to the course of the sun. At once, however, she
stopped short, and exclaimed, in a voice of alarm and horror,
"Grandson of my father, there is blood on your hand."

"Hush, for God's sake, aunt," said Robin Oig; "you will bring
more trouble on yourself with this Taishataragh" (second sight)
"than you will be able to get out of for many a day."

The old woman only repeated, with a ghastly look, "There is
blood on your hand, and it is English blood. The blood of the
Gael is richer and redder. Let us see—let us—"

Ere Robin Oig could prevent her, which, indeed, could only
have been done by positive violence, so hasty and peremptory were
her proceedings, she had drawn from his side the dirk which
lodged in the folds of his plaid, and held it up, exclaiming, although
the weapon gleamed clear and bright in the sun, "Blood, blood—
Saxon blood again. Robin Oig M'Combich, go not this day to
England!"

"Prutt, trutt," answered Robin Oig, "that will never do neither
—it would be next thing to running the country. For shame,
Muhme—give me the dirk. You cannot tell by the colour the
difference betwixt the blood of a black bullock and a white one,
and you speak of knowing Saxon from Gaelic blood. All men have
their blood from Adam, Muhme. Give me my skene-dhu, and let
me go on my road. I should have been half-way to Stirling Brig
by this time.—Give me my dirk, and let me go."

"Never will I give it to you," said the old woman.—"Never will
I quit my hold on your plaid, unless you promise me not to wear
that unhappy weapon."

The women around him urged him also, saying few of his aunt's
words fell to the ground; and as the Lowland farmers continued

to look moodily on the scene, Robin Oig determined to close it at any sacrifice.

"Well, then," said the young drover, giving the scabbard of the weapon to Hugh Morrison, "you Lowlanders care nothing for these freats. Keep my dirk for me. I cannot give it to you, because it was my father's; but your drove follows ours, and I am content it should be in your keeping, not in mine.—Will this do, Muhme?"

"It must," said the old woman—"that is, if the Lowlander is mad enough to carry the knife."

The strong westlandman laughed aloud.

"Goodwife," said he, "I am Hugh Morrison from Glenae, come of the Manly Morrisons of auld langsyne, that never took short weapon against a man in their lives. And neither needed they. They had their broadswords, and I have this bit supple," showing a formidable cudgel—"for dirking ower the board, I leave that to John Highlandman.—Ye needna snort, none of you Highlanders, and you in especial, Robin. I'll keep the bit knife, if you are feared for the auld spaewife's tale, and give it back to you whenever you want it."

Robin was not particularly pleased with some part of Hugh Morrison's speech; but he had learned in his travels more patience than belonged to his Highland constitution originally, and he accepted the service of the descendant of the Manly Morrisons without finding fault with the rather depreciating manner in which it was offered.

"If he had not had his morning in his head, and been but a Dumfriesshire hog into the boot, he would have spoken more like a gentleman. But you cannot have more of a sow than a grumph. It's shame my father's knife should ever slash a haggis for the like of him."

Thus saying (but saying it in Gaelic) Robin drove on his cattle, and waved farewell to all behind him. He was in the greater haste, because he expected to join at Falkirk a comrade and brother in profession, with whom he proposed to travel in company.

Robin Oig's chosen friend was a young Englishman, Harry Wakefield by name, well known at every northern market, and in his way as much famed and honoured as our Highland driver of bullocks. He was nearly six feet high, gallantly formed to keep the rounds at Smithfield, or maintain the ring at a wrestling match; and although he might have been overmatched, perhaps, among the regular professors of the Fancy, yet, as a yokel, or rustic, or a chance customer, he was able to give a bellyful to any amateur of the pugilistic art. Doncaster races saw him in his glory, betting his guinea, and generally successfully; nor was there a main fought in Yorkshire, the feeders being persons of celebrity, at which he was not to be seen, if business permitted. But though a *sprack* lad, and fond of pleasure and its haunts, Harry Wakefield was steady, and not the cautious Robin Oig M'Combich himself was more attentive to the main chance. His holidays were holidays indeed; but his days of work were dedicated to steady and persevering labour. In countenance and temper, Wakefield was the model of old England's merry yeomen, whose clothyard shafts, in so many hundred battles, asserted her superiority over the nations, and whose good sabres in our own time are her cheapest and most assured defence. His mirth was readily excited; for, strong in limb and constitution, and fortunate in circumstances, he was disposed to be pleased with everything about him; and such difficulties as he might occasionally encounter were, to a man of his energy, rather matter of amusement than serious annoyance. With all the merits of a sanguine temper, our young English drover was not without his defects. He was irascible, sometimes to the verge of being quarrelsome; and perhaps not the less inclined to bring his disputes to a pugilistic decision, because he found few antagonists able to stand up to him in the boxing ring.

It is difficult to say how Harry Wakefield and Robin Oig first became intimates; but it is certain a close acquaintance had taken place betwixt them, although they had apparently few common subjects of conversation or of interest, so soon as their talk ceased to be of bullocks. Robin Oig, indeed, spoke the English language rather imperfectly upon any other topics but stots and kyloes, and Harry Wakefield could never bring his broad Yorkshire tongue to utter a single word of Gaelic. It was in vain Robin spent a whole morning, during a walk over Minch Moor in attempting to teach his companion to utter, with true precision, the shibboleth *Llhu*, which is the Gaelic for a calf. From Traquair to Murdercairn, the hill rang with the discordant attempts of the Saxon upon the unmanageable monosyllable, and the heartfelt laugh which followed every failure. They had, however, better modes of awakening the echoes; for Wakefield could sing many a ditty to the praise of Moll, Susan, and Cicely, and Robin Oig had a particular gift at whistling interminable pibrochs through all their involutions, and what was more agreeable to his companion's southern ear, knew many of the northern airs, both lively and pathetic, to which Wakefield learned to pipe a bass. This, though Robin could hardly have comprehended his companion's stories about horse-racing, and cock-fighting or fox-hunting, and although his own legends of clan-fights and *creaghs*, varied with talk of Highland goblins and fairy folk, would have been caviare to his companion, they contrived nevertheless to find a degree of pleasure in each other's company, which had for three years back induced them to join company and travel together, when the direction of their journey permitted. Each, indeed, found his advantage in this companionship; for where could the Englishman have found a guide through the Western Highlands like Robin Oig M'Combich? and when they were on what Harry called the *right* side of the Border, his patronage, which was extensive, and his purse, which was heavy, were at all times in the service of his Highland friend, and on many occasions his liberality did him genuine yeoman's service.

II

Were ever two such loving friends!—
How could they disagree?
O thus it was, he loved him dear,
And thought how to requite him,
And having no friend left but he,
He did resolve to fight him.

Duke upon Duke

THE PAIR of friends had traversed with their usual cordiality the grassy wilds of Liddesdale, and crossed the opposite part of

Cumberland, emphatically called The Waste. In these solitary regions, the cattle under the charge of our drovers derived their subsistence chiefly by picking their food as they went along the drove-road, or sometimes by the tempting opportunity of a *start and owerloup*, or invasion of the neighbouring pasture, where an occasion presented itself. But now the scene changed before them; they were descending towards a fertile and enclosed country, where no such liberties could be taken with impunity, or without a previous arrangement and bargain with the possessors of the ground. This was more especially the case, as a great northern fair was upon the eve of taking place, where both the Scotch and English drover expected to dispose of a part of their cattle, which it was desirable to produce in the market, rested and in good order. Fields were therefore difficult to be obtained, and only upon high terms. This necessity occasioned a temporary separation betwixt the two friends, who went to bargain, each as he could, for the separate accommodation of his herd. Unhappily it chanced that both of them, unknown to each other, thought of bargaining for the ground they wanted on the property of a country gentleman of some fortune, whose estate lay in the neighbourhood. The English drover applied to the bailiff on the property, who was known to him. It chanced that the Cumbrian squire, who had entertained some suspicions of his manager's honesty, was taking occasional measures to ascertain how far they were well founded, and had desired that any inquiries about his enclosures, with a view to occupy them for a temporary purpose, should be referred to himself. As, however, Mr. Ireby had gone the day before upon a journey of some miles' distance to the northward, the bailiff chose to consider the check upon his full powers as for the time removed, and concluded that he should best consult his master's interest, and perhaps his own, in making an agreement with Harry Wakefield. Meanwhile, ignorant of what his comrade was doing, Robin Oig, on his side, chanced to be overtaken by a good-looking smart little man upon a pony, most knowingly hogged and cropped, as was then the fashion, the rider wearing tight leather breeches and long-necked bright spurs. This cavalier asked one or two pertinent

questions about markets and the price of stock. So Robin, seeing
him a well-judging civil gentleman, took the freedom to ask him
whether he could let him know if there was any grass-land to be
let in that neighbourhood, for the temporary accommodation of
his drove. He could not have put the question to more willing
ears. The gentleman of the buckskin was the proprietor with
whose bailiff Harry Wakefield had dealt or was in the act of dealing.

"Thou art in good luck, my canny Scot," said Mr. Ireby, "to
have spoken to me, for I see thy cattle have done their day's work,
and I have at my disposal the only field within three miles that is
to be let in these parts."

"The drove can pe gang two, three, four miles very pratty weel
indeed," said the cautious Highlander; "put what would his honour
be axing for the peasts pe the head, if she was to tak the park for
twa or three days?"

"We won't differ, Sawney, if you let me have six stots for
winterers, in the way of reason."

"And which peasts wad your honour pe for having?"

"Why—let me see—the two black—the dun one—yon doddy—
him with the twisted horn—the brockit—How much by the head?"

"Ah," said Robin, "your honour is a shudge—a real shudge—
I couldna have set off the pest six peasts petter mysell, me that
ken them as if they were my pairns, puir things."

"Well, how much per head, Sawney?" continued Mr. Ireby.

"It was high markets at Doune and Falkirk," answered Robin.

And thus the conversation proceeded, until they had agreed on
the *prix juste* for the bullocks, the squire throwing in the temporary accommodation of the enclosure for the cattle into the
boot, and Robin making, as he thought, a very good bargain, provided the grass was but tolerable. The squire walked his pony
alongside of the drove, partly to show him the way, and see him
put into possession of the field, and partly to learn the latest news
of the northern markets.

They arrived at the field, and the pasture seemed excellent. But
what was their surprise when they saw the bailiff quietly inducting

the cattle of Harry Wakefield into the grassy Goshen which had just been assigned to those of Robin Oig M'Combich by the proprietor himself! Squire Ireby set spurs to his horse, dashed up to his servant, and learning what had passed between the parties, briefly informed the English drover that his bailiff had let the ground without his authority, and that he might seek grass for his cattle wherever he would, since he was to get none there. At the same time he rebuked his servant severely for having transgressed his commands, and ordered him instantly to assist in ejecting the hungry and weary cattle of Harry Wakefield, which were just beginning to enjoy a meal of unusual plenty, and to introduce those of his comrade, whom the English drover now began to consider as a rival.

The feelings which arose in Wakefield's mind would have induced him to resist Mr. Ireby's decision; but every Englishman has a tolerably accurate sense of law and justice, and John Fleecebumpkin, the bailiff, having acknowledged that he had exceeded his commission, Wakefield saw nothing else for it than to collect his hungry and disappointed charge, and drive them on to seek quarters elsewhere. Robin Oig saw what had happened with regret, and hastened to offer to his English friend to share with him the disputed possession. But Wakefield's pride was severely hurt, and he answered disdainfully, "Take it all, man—take it all—never make two bites of a cherry—thou canst talk over the gentry, and blear a plain man's eye—Out upon you, man—I would not kiss any man's dirty latchets for leave to bake in his oven.'

Robin Oig, sorry but not surprised at his comrade's displeasure, hastened to entreat his friend to wait but an hour till he had gone to the squire's house to receive payment for the cattle he had sold, and he could come back and help him to drive the cattle into some convenient place of rest, and explain to him the whole mistake they had both of them fallen into. But the Englishman continued indignant: "Thou hast been selling, hast thou? Ay, ay—thou is a cunning lad for kenning the hours of bargaining. Go to the devil with thyself, for I will ne'er see thy fause loon's visage again—thou should be ashamed to look me in the face."

"I am ashamed to look no man in the face," said Robin Oig,

something moved; "and, moreover, I will look you in the face this blessed day, if you will bide at the clachan down yonder."

"Mayhap you had as well keep away," said his comrade; and turning his back on his former friend, he collected his unwilling associates, assisted by the bailiff, who took some real and some affected interest in seeing Wakefield accommodated.

After spending some time in negotiating with more than one of the neighbouring farmers, who could not, or would not, afford the accommodation desired, Henry Wakefield at last, and in his necessity, accomplished his point by means of the landlord of the alehouse at which Robin Oig and he had agreed to pass the night, when they first separated from each other. Mine host was content to let him turn his cattle on a piece of barren moor, at a price little less than the bailiff had asked for the disputed enclosure; and the wretchedness of the pasture, as well as the price paid for it, were set down as exaggerations of the breach of faith and friendship of his Scottish crony. This turn of Wakefield's passions was encouraged by the bailiff (who had his own reasons for being offended against poor Robin, as having been the unwitting cause of his falling into disgrace with his master), as well as by the innkeeper, and two or three chance guests, who stimulated the drover in his resentment against his quondam associate,—some from the ancient grudge against the Scots which, when it exists anywhere, is to be found lurking in the Border counties, and some from the general love of mischief, which characterizes mankind in all ranks of life, to the honour of Adam's children be it spoken. Good John Barleycorn also, who always heightens and exaggerates the prevailing passions, be they angry or kindly, was not wanting in his offices on this occasion; and confusion to false friends and hard masters was pledged in more than one tankard.

In the meanwhile Mr. Ireby found some amusement in detaining the northern drover at his ancient hall. He caused a cold round of beef to be placed before the Scot in the butler's pantry, together with a foaming tankard of home-brewed, and took pleasure in seeing the hearty appetite with which these unwonted edibles were discussed by Robin Oig M'Combich. The squire himself lighting his pipe, compounded between his patrician dignity and his love of agricultural gossip, by walking up and down while he conversed with his guest.

"I passed another drove," said the squire, "with one of your countrymen behind them—they were something less beasts than your drove, doddies most of them—a big man was with them—none of your kilts though, but a decent pair of breeches—D'ye know who he may be?"

"Hout aye—that might, could, and would be Hughie Morrison—I didna think he could hae peen sae weel up. He has made a day on us; but his Argyleshires will have wearied shanks. How far was he pehind."

"I think about six or seven miles," answered the squire, "for I passed them at the Christenbury Crag, and I overtook you at the Hollan Bush. If his beasts be leg-weary, he will maybe be selling bargains."

"Na, na, Hughie Morrison is no the man for pargains—ye maun come to some Highland body like Robin Oig hersell for the like of these—put I maun pe wishing you goot night, and twenty of them let alane ane, and I maun down to the clachan to see if the lad Harry Waakfelt is out of his humdudgeons yet."

The party at the alehouse was still in full talk, and the treachery of Robin Oig still the theme of conversation, when the supposed culprit entered the apartment. His arrival, as usually happens in such a case, put an instant stop to the discussion of which he had furnished the subject, and he was received by the company assembled with that chilling silence which, more than a thousand exclamations, tells an intruder that he is unwelcome. Surprised and offended, but not appalled by the reception which he experienced, Robin entered with an undaunted and even a haughty air, attempted no greeting as he saw he was received with none, and placed himself by the side of the fire, a little apart from a table at which Harry Wakefield, the bailiff, and two or three other persons were seated. The ample Cumbrian kitchen would have afforded plenty of room, even for a larger separation.

Robin, thus seated, proceeded to light his pipe, and call for a pint of twopenny.

"We have no twopence ale," answered Ralph Heskett, the landlord; "but as thou findest thy own tobacco, it's like thou mayest find thy own liquor too—it's the wont of thy country, I wot."

"Shame, goodman," said the landlady, a blithe bustling house-wife, hastening herself to supply the guest with liquor—"Thou knowest well enow what the strange man wants, and it's thy trade to be civil, man. Thou shouldst know, that if the Scot likes a small pot, he pays a sure penny."

Without taking any notice of this nuptial dialogue, the High-lander took the flagon in his hand, and addressing the company generally, drank the interesting toast of "Good markets", to the party assembled.

"The better that the wind blew fewer dealers from the north," said one of the farmers, "and fewer Highland runts to eat up the English meadows."

"Saul of my pody, put you are wrang there, my friend," answered Robin, with composure, "it is your fat Englishmen that eat up our Scots cattle, puir things."

"I wish there was a summat to eat up their drovers," said another; "a plain Englishman canna make bread within a kenning of them."

"Or an honest servant keep his master's favour, but they will come sliding in between him and the sunshine," said the bailiff.

"If these pe jokes," said Robin Oig, with the same composure, "there is ower mony jokes upon one man."

"It is no joke, but downright earnest," said the bailiff. "Harkye, Mr. Robin Ogg, or whatever is your name, it's right we should tell you that we are all of one opinion, and that is that you, Mr. Robin Ogg, have behaved to our friend Mr. Harry Wakefield here, like a raff and a blackguard."

"Nae doubt, nae doubt," answered Robin, with great composure; "and you are a set of very pretty judges, for whose prains or pehaviour I wad not gie a pinch of sneeshing. If Mr. Harry Waak-felt kens where he is wranged, he kens where he may be righted."

"He speaks truth," said Wakefield, who had listened to what passed, divided between the offence which he had taken at Robin's late behaviour, and the revival of his habitual feelings of regard.

He now arose, and went towards Robin, who got up from his

seat as he approached, and held out his hand.

"That's right, Harry—go it—serve him out," resounded on all sides—"tip him the nailer—show him the mill."

"Hold your peace all of you, and be—," said Wakefield; and then addressing his comrade, he took him by the extended hand, with something alike of respect and defiance. "Robin," he said, "thou hast used me ill enough this day; but if you mean, like a frank fellow, to shake hands, and make a tussle for love on the sod, why I'll forgie thee, man, and we shall be better friends than ever."

"And would it not pe petter to pe cood friends without more of the matter?" said Robin; "we will be much petter friendships with our panes hale than proken."

Harry Wakefield dropped the hand of his friend, or rather threw it from him.

"I did not think I had been keeping company for three years with a coward."

"Coward pelongs to none of my name," said Robin, whose eyes began to kindle, but keeping the command of his temper. "It was no coward's legs or hands, Harry Waakfelt, that drew you out of the fords of Frew, when you was drifting ower the plack rock, and every eel in the river expected his share of you."

"And that is true enough, too," said the Englishman, struck by the appeal.

"Adzooks!" exclaimed the bailiff—"sure Harry Wakefield, the nattiest lad at Whitson Tryste, Wooler Fair, Carlisle Sands, or Stagshaw Bank, is not going to show white feather? Ah, this comes of living so long with kilts and bonnets—men forget the use of their daddles."

"I may teach you, Master Fleecebumpkin, that I have not lost the use of mine," said Wakefield, and then went on. "This will never do, Robin. We must have a turn-up, or we shall be the talk of the country-side. I'll be d—d if I hurt thee—I'll put on the gloves gin thou like. Come, stand forward like a man."

"To pe peaten like a dog," said Robin; "is there any reason in that? If you think I have done you wrong, I'll go before your shudge, though I neither know his law nor his language."

A general cry of "No, no—no law, no lawyer! a bellyful and be friends," was echoed by the bystanders.

"But," continued Robin, "if I am to fight, I've no skill to fight like a jackanapes, with hands and nails."

"How would you fight, then?" said his antagonist; "though I am thinking it would be hard to bring you to the scratch anyhow."

"I would fight with proadswords, and sink point on the first plood drawn, like a gentleman."

A loud shout of laughter followed the proposal, which indeed had rather escaped from poor Robin's swelling heart, than been the dictate of his sober judgement.

"Gentleman, quotha!" was echoed on all sides, with a shout of unextinguishable laughter; "a very pretty gentleman, God wot—Canst get two swords for the gentlemen to fight with, Ralph Heskett?"

"No, but I can send to the armoury at Carlisle, and lend them two forks, to be making shift with in the meantime."

"Tush, man," said another, "the bonny Scots come into the world with the blue bonnet on their heads, and dirk and pistol at their belt."

"Best send post," said Mr. Fleecebumpkin, "to the squire of Corby Castle, to come and stand second to the *gentleman*."

In the midst of this torrent of general ridicule, the Highlander instinctively griped beneath the folds of his plaid.

"But it's better not," he said in his own language. "A hundred curses on the swine-eaters, who know neither decency nor civility!"

"Make room, the pack of you," he said, advancing to the door.

But his former friend interposed his sturdy bulk, and opposed his leaving the house; and when Robin Oig attempted to make his way by force, he hit him down on the floor, with as much ease as a boy bowls down a nine-pin.

"A ring, a ring!" was now shouted, until the dark rafters, and the hams that hung on them, trembled again, and the very platters on the *bink* clattered against each other. "Well done, Harry"—"Give it him home, Harry"—"Take care of him now—he sees his own blood!"

Such were the exclamations, while the Highlander, starting from the ground, all his coldness and caution lost in frantic rage, sprang at his antagonist with the fury, the activity, and the vindictive purpose of an incensed tiger-cat. But when could rage encounter science and temper? Robin Oig again went down in the unequal contest; and as the blow was necessarily a severe one, he lay motionless on the floor of the kitchen. The landlady ran to offer some aid, but Mr. Fleecebumpkin would not permit her to approach.

"Let him alone," he said, "he will come to within time, and come up to the scratch again. He has not got half his broth yet."

"He has got all I mean to give him, though," said his antagonist, whose heart began to relent towards his old associate; "and I would rather by half give the rest to yourself, Mr. Fleecebumpkin, for you pretend to know a thing or two, and Robin had not art enough even to peel before setting to, but fought with his plaid dangling about him.—Stand up, Robin, my man! all friends now; and let me hear the man that will speak a word against you, or your country, for your sake."

Robin Oig was still under the dominion of his passion, and eager to renew the onset; but being withheld on the one side by the peace-making Dame Heskett, and on the other, aware that Wakefield no longer meant to renew the combat, his fury sank into gloomy sullenness.

"Come, come, never grudge so much at it, man," said the brave-spirited Englishman, with the placability of his country, "shake hands, and we will be better friends than ever."

"Friends!" exclaimed Robin Oig, with strong emphasis—"friends!—Never. Look to yourself, Harry Waakfelt."

"Then the curse of Cromwell on your proud Scots stomach, as the man says in the play, and you may do your worst, and be d—; for one man can say nothing more to another after a tussle, than that he is sorry for it."

On these terms the friends parted; Robin Oig drew out, in silence, a piece of money, threw it on the table, and then left the alehouse. But turning at the door, he shook his hand at Wakefield, pointing with his forefinger upwards, in a manner which might imply either a threat or a caution. He then disappeared in the moonlight.

Some words passed after his departure between the bailiff, who piqued himself on being a little of a bully, and Harry Wakefield, who, with generous inconsistency, was now not indisposed to begin a new combat in defence of Robin Oig's reputation, "although he could not use his daddles like an Englishman, as it did not come natural to him." But Dame Heskett prevented this second quarrel from coming to a head by her peremptory interference. "There should be no more fighting in her house," she said; "there had been too much already.—And you, Mr. Wakefield, may live to learn", she added, "what it is to make a deadly enemy out of a good friend."

"Pshaw, dame! Robin Oig is an honest fellow, and will never keep malice."

"Do not trust to that—you do not know the dour temper of the Scots, though you have dealt with them so often. I have a right to know them, my mother being a Scot."

"And so is well seen on her daughter," said Ralph Heskett.

This nuptial sarcasm gave the discourse another turn; fresh customers entered the tap-room or kitchen, and others left it. The conversation turned on the expected markets, and the report of prices from different parts both of Scotland and England—treaties were commenced, and Harry Wakefield was lucky enough to find a chap for a part of his drove, and at a very considerable profit; an event of consequence more than sufficient to blot out all remembrances of the unpleasant scuffle in the earlier part of the day. But there remained one party from whose mind that recollection could not have been wiped away by the possession of every head of cattle betwixt Esk and Eden.

This was Robin Oig M'Combich.—"That I should have had no weapon," he said, "and for the first time in my life!—Blighted be the tongue that bids the Highlander part with the dirk—the dirk—ha! the English blood!—My Muhme's word—when did her word fall to the ground?"

The recollection of the fatal prophecy confirmed the deadly intention which instantly sprang up in his mind.

"Ha! Morrison cannot be many miles behind; and if it were a hundred, what then?"

His impetuous spirit had now a fixed purpose and motive of

action, and he turned the light foot of his country towards the wilds, through which he knew, by Mr. Ireby's report, that Morrison was advancing. His mind was wholly engrossed by the sense of injury —injury sustained from a friend; and by the desire of vengeance on one whom he now accounted his most bitter enemy. The treasured ideas of self-importance and self-opinion—of ideal birth and quality, had become more precious to him (like the hoard to the miser) because he could only enjoy them in secret. But that hoard was pillaged, the idols which he had secretly worshipped had been desecrated and profaned. Insulted, abused, and beaten, he was no longer worthy, in his own opinion, of the name he bore or the lineage which he belonged to—nothing was left to him— nothing but revenge; and, as the reflection added a galling spur to every step, he determined it should be as sudden and signal as the offence.

When Robin Oig left the door of the ale-house, seven or eight English miles at least lay betwixt Morrison and him. The advance of the former was slow, limited by the sluggish pace of his cattle; the last left behind him stubble-field and hedge-row, crag and dark heath, all glittering with frost-rime in the broad November moonlight, at the rates of six miles an hour. And now the distant lowing of Morrison's cattle is heard; and now they are seen creeping like moles in size and slowness of motion on the broad face of the moor; and now he meets them—passes them, and stops their conductor.

"May good betide us," said the Southlander. "Is this you, Robin M'Combich, or your wraith?"

"It is Robin Oig M'Combich," answered the Highlander, "and it is not.—But never mind that, put pe giving me the skene-dhu."

"What! you are for back to the Highlands—The devil!—Have you selt all off before the fair? This beats all for quick markets!"

"I have not sold—I am not going north—May pe I will never go north again.—Give me pack my dirk, Hugh Morrison, or there will pe words petween us."

"Indeed, Robin, I'll be better advised before I gie it back to you —it is a wanchancy weapon in a Highlandman's hand, and I am thinking you will be about some barns-breaking."

"Prutt, trutt! let me have my weapons," said Robin Oig, impatiently.

"Hooly, and fairly," said his well-meaning friend. "I'll tell you what will do better than these dirking doings—Ye ken Highlander, and Lowlander, and Border-men, are a' ae man's bairns when you are over the Scots dyke. See, the Eskdale callants, and fighting Charlie of Liddesdale, and the Lockerby lads, and the four Dandies of Lustruther, and a wheen mair grey plaids, are coming up behind, and if you are wranged, there is the hand of a Manly Morrison, we'll see you righted, if Carlisle and Stanwix baith took up the feud."

"To tell you the truth," said Robin Oig, desirous of eluding the suspicions of his friend, "I have enlisted with a party of the Black Watch, and must march off to-morrow morning."

"Enlisted! Were you mad or drunk?—You must buy yourself off—I can lend you twenty notes, and twenty to that, if the drove sell."

"I thank you—thank ye, Hughie; but I go with good will the gate that I am going,—so the dirk—the dirk!"

"There it is for you then, since less wunna serve. But think on what I was saying.—Waes me, it will be sair news in the braes of Balquidder, that Robin Oig M'Combich should have run an ill gate, and ta'en on."

"Ill news in Balquidder, indeed!" echoed poor Robin. "But Cot speed you, Hughie, and send you good marcats. Ye winna meet with Robin Oig again, either at tryste or fair."

So saying, he shook hastily the hand of his acquaintance, and set out in the direction from which he had advanced, with the spirit of his former pace.

"There is something wrang with the lad," muttered the Morrison to himself, "but we'll maybe see better into the morn's morning."

But long ere the morning dawned, the catastrophe of our tale had taken place. It was two hours after the affray had happened, and it was totally forgotten by almost every one, when Robin Oig returned to Heskett's inn. The place was filled at once by various sorts of men, and with noises corresponding to their character. There were the grave low sounds of men engaged in busy traffic, with the laugh, the song, and the riotous jest of those who had nothing to do but to enjoy themselves. Among the last was Harry Wakefield, who, amidst a grinning group of smock-frocks, hobnailed shoes, and jolly English physiognomies, was trolling forth the old ditty,

> *What though my name be Roger,*
> *Who drives the plough and cart—*

when he was interrupted by a well-known voice saying in a high and stern tone, marked by the sharp Highland accent, "Harry Waakfelt—if you be a man, stand up!"

"What is the matter?—what is it?" the guests demanded of each other.

"It is only a d—d Scotsman," said Fleecebumpkin, who was by this time very drunk, "whom Harry Wakefield helped to his broth the day, who is now come to have *his cauld kail* het again."

"Harry Waakfelt," repeated the same ominous summons, "stand up, if you be a man!"

There is something in the tone of deep and concentrated passion, which attracts attention and imposes awe, even by the very sound. The guests shrank back on every side, and gazed at the Highlander as he stood in the middle of them, his brows bent, and his features rigid with resolution.

"I will stand up with all my heart, Robin, my boy, but it shall be to shake hands with you, and drink down all unkindness. It is not the fault of your heart, man, that you don't know how to clench your hands."

But this time he stood opposite to his antagonist; his open and unsuspecting look strangely contrasted with the stern purpose, which gleamed wild, dark, and vindictive in the eyes of the Highlander.

"'Tis not thy fault, man, that, not having the luck to be an Englishman, thou canst not fight more than a schoolgirl."

"I *can* fight," answered Robin Oig sternly, but calmly, "and you shall know it. You, Harry Waakfelt, showed me to-day how the Saxon churls fight—I show you now how the Highland Dunnièwassel fights."

He seconded the word with the action, and plunged the dagger, which he suddenly displayed, into the broad chest of the English yeoman, with such fatal certainty and force, that the hilt made a hollow sound against the breast-bone, and the double-edged point split the very heart of his victim. Harry Wakefield fell and expired with a single groan. His assassin next seized the bailiff by the collar, and offered the bloody poniard to his throat, whilst dread and surprise rendered the man incapable of defence.

"It were very just to lay you beside him," he said, "but the blood of a base pick-thank shall never mix on my father's dirk with that of a brave man."

As he spoke, he cast the man from him with so much force that he fell on the floor, while Robin, with his other hand, threw the fatal weapon into the blazing turf-fire.

"There," he said, "take me who likes—and let fire cleanse blood if it can."

The pause of astonishment still continuing, Robin Oig asked for a peace-officer, and a constable having stepped out, he surrendered himself to his custody.

"A bloody night's work you have made of it," said the constable.

"Your own fault," said the Highlander. "Had you kept his hands off me twa hours since, he would have been now as well and merry as he was twa minutes since."

"It must be sorely answered," said the peace-officer.

"Never mind that—death pays all debts; it will pay that too."

The horror of the bystanders began now to give way to indignation; and the sight of a favourite companion murdered in the midst of them, the provocation being, in their opinion, so utterly inadequate to the excess of vengeance, might have induced them to kill the perpetrator of the deed even upon the very spot. The constable, however, did his duty on this occasion, and with the assistance of some of the more reasonable persons present, procured horses to guard the prisoner to Carlisle, to abide his doom at the next assizes. While the escort was preparing, the prisoner neither expressed the least interest nor attempted the slightest reply. Only, before he was carried from the fatal apartment, he desired to looked at the dead body, which, raised from the floor, had been deposited upon the large table (at the head of which Harry Wakefield had presided but a few minutes before, full of life, vigour, and animation) until the surgeons should examine the mortal wound. The face of the corpse was decently covered with a napkin. To the surprise and horror of the bystanders, which displayed itself in a general *Ah!* drawn through clenched teeth and half-shut lips, Robin Oig removed the cloth, and gazed with a mournful but steady eye on the lifeless visage, which had been so lately animated that the smile of good-humoured confidence in his own strength, of conciliation at once and contempt towards his enemy, still curled his lip. While those present expected that the wound, which had so lately flooded the apartment with gore, would send forth fresh streams at the touch of the homicide, Robin Oig replaced the covering with the brief exclamation—"He was a pretty man!"

My story is nearly ended. The unfortunate Highlander stood his trial at Carlisle. I was myself present, and as a young Scottish lawyer, or barrister at least, and reputed a man of some quality, the politeness of the Sheriff of Cumberland offered me a place on the bench. The facts of the case were proved in the manner I have related them; and whatever might be at first the prejudice of the audience against a crime so un-English as that of assassination from revenge, yet when the rooted national prejudices of the prisoner had been explained, which made him consider himself as stained with indelible dishonour when subjected to personal violence; when his previous patience, moderation, and endurance were considered, the generosity of the English audience was inclined to regard his crime as the wayward aberration of a false idea of honour rather than as flowing from a heart naturally savage, or perverted by habitual vice. I shall never forget the charge of the venerable judge to the jury, although not at that time liable to be much affected either by that which was eloquent or pathetic.

"We have had", he said, "in the previous part of our duty" (alluding to some former trials) "to discuss crimes which infer disgust and abhorrence, while they call down the well-merited vengeance of the law. It is now our still more melancholy task to apply its salutary though severe enactments to a case of a very singular character, in which the crime (for a crime it is, and a deep one) arose less out of the malevolence of the heart, than the error of the understanding—less from an idea of committing wrong, than from an unhappily perverted notion of that which is right. Here we have two men, highly esteemed, it has been stated, in their rank of life, and attached, it seems, to each other as friends, one of whose lives has been already sacrificed to a punctilio, and the other is about to prove the vengeance of the offended laws; and yet both may claim our commiseration at least, as men acting in ignorance of each other's national prejudices, and unhappily misguided rather than voluntarily erring from the path of right conduct.

"In the original cause of the misunderstanding, we must in justice give the right to the prisoner at the bar. He had acquired possession of the enclosure, which was the object of competition, by a legal contract with the proprietor, Mr. Ireby; and yet, when accosted with reproaches undeserved in themselves, and galling doubtless to a temper at least sufficiently susceptible of passion, he offered notwithstanding to yield up half his acquisition for the sake of peace and good neighbourhood, and his amicable proposal was rejected with scorn. Then follows the scene at Mr. Heskett the publican's, and you will observe how the stranger was treated by the deceased, and, I am sorry to observe, by those around, who seem to have urged him in a manner which was aggravating in the highest degree. While he asked for peace and for composition, and offered submission to a magistrate, or to a mutual arbiter, the prisoner was insulted by a whole company, who seem on this occasion to have forgotten the national maxim of 'fair play'; and while attempting to escape from the place in peace, he was intercepted, struck down, and beaten to the effusion of his blood.

"Gentlemen of the jury, it was with some impatience that I heard my learned brother, who opened the case for the crown, give an unfavourable turn to the prisoner's conduct on this occasion. He said the prisoner was afraid to encounter his antagonist in fair fight, or to submit to the laws of the ring; and that therefore, like a cowardly Italian, he had recourse to his fatal stiletto, to murder the man whom he dared not meet in manly encounter. I observed the prisoner shrink from this part of the accusation with the abhorrence natural to a brave man; and as I would wish to make my words impressive when I point his real crime, I must secure his opinion of my impartiality, by rebutting everything that seems to me a false accusation. There can be no doubt that the prisoner is a man of resolution—too much resolution—I wish to Heaven that he had less, or rather that he had had a better education to regulate it.

"Gentlemen, as to the laws my brother talks of, they may be known in the bull-ring, or the bear-garden, or the cockpit, but they are not known here. Or, if they should be so far admitted as furnishing a species of proof that no malice was intended in this sort of combat, from which fatal accidents do sometimes arise, it can only be so admitted when both parties are *in pari casu*, equally acquainted with, and equally willing to refer themselves to, that species of arbitrament. But will it be contended that a man of superior rank and education is to be subjected, or is obliged to subjet himself, to this coarse and brutal strife, perhaps in opposition to a younger, stronger, or more skilful opponent? Certainly even the pugilistic code, if founded upon the fair play of Merry Old England, as my brother alleges it to be, can contain nothing so preposterous. And, gentlemen of the jury, if the laws would support an English gentleman, wearing, we will suppose, his sword, in defending himself by force against a violent personal aggression of the nature offered to this prisoner, they will not less protect a foreigner and a stranger, involved in the same unpleasing circumstances. If, therefore, gentlemen of the jury, when thus pressed by a *vis major*, the object of obloquy to a whole company, and of direct violence from one at least, and, as he might reasonably apprehend, from more, the panel had produced the weapon which his countrymen, as we are informed, generally carry about their persons, and the same unhappy circumstance had ensued which you have heard detailed in evidence, I could not in my conscience have asked from you a verdict of murder. The prisoner's personal defence might, indeed, even in that case, have gone more or less beyond the *Moderamen inculpatae tutelae*, spoken of by lawyers, but the punishment incurred would have been that of manslaughter, not of murder. I beg leave to add that I should have thought this milder species of charge was demanded in the case supposed, notwithstanding the statute of James I cap. 8, which takes the case of slaughter by stabbing with a short weapon, even without malice prepense, out of the benefit of clergy. For this statute of stabbing, as it is termed, arose out of a temporary cause; and as the real guilt is the same, whether the slaughter be committed by the dagger, or by sword or pistol, the benignity of the modern law places them all on the same, or nearly the same footing.

"But, gentlemen of the jury, the pinch of the case lies in the interval of two hours interposed betwixt the reception of the injury and the fatal retaliation. In the heat of affray and *chaude mêlée*, law, compassionating the infirmities of humanity, makes allowance for the passions which rule such a stormy moment—for the sense of present pain, for the apprehension of further injury, for the difficulty of ascertaining with due accuracy the precise degree of violence which is necessary to protect the person of the individual, without annoying or injuring the assailant more than is absolutely requisite. But the time necessary to walk twelve miles, however speedily performed, was an interval sufficient for the prisoner to have recollected himself; and the violence with so many circumstances of deliberate determination, could neither be induced by the passion of anger, nor that of fear. It was the purpose and the act of predetermined revenge, for which law neither can, will, nor ought to have sympathy or allowance.

"It is true, we may repeat to ourselves, in alleviation of this poor man's unhappy action, that his case is a very peculiar one. The country which he inhabits was, in the days of many now alive, inaccessible to the laws, not only of England, which have not even yet penetrated thither, but to those to which our neighbours of Scotland are subjected, and which must be supposed to be, and no doubt actually are, founded upon the general principles of justice and equity which pervade every civilized country. Amongst their mountains, as among the North American Indians, the various tribes were wont to make war upon each other, so that each man was obliged to go armed for his protection. These men, from the ideas which they entertained of their own descent and of their own consequence, regarded themselves as so many cavaliers or men-at-arms, rather than as the peasantry of a peaceful country. Those laws of the ring, as my brother terms them, were unknown to the race of warlike mountaineers; that decision of quarrels by no other weapons than those which nature has given every man, must to them have seemed as vulgar and as preposterous as to the noblesse of France. Revenge, on the other hand, must have been as familiar to their habits of society as to those of the Cherokees or Mohawks. It is indeed, as described by Bacon, at bottom a kind of wild untutored justice; for the fear of retaliation must withhold the hands of the oppressor where there is no regular law to check daring violence. But though all this may be granted, and though we may allow that, such having been the case of the Highlands in the days of the prisoner's fathers, many of the opinions and sentiments must still continue to influence the present generation, it cannot, and ought not, even in this most painful case, to alter the administration of the law, either in your hands, gentlemen of the jury, or in mine. The first object of civilization is to place the general protection of the law, equally administered, in the room of that wild justice, which every man cut and carved for himself, according to the length of his sword and the strength of his arm. The law says to the subjects, with a voice only inferior to that of the Deity, 'Vengeance is mine.' The instant that there is time for passion to cool, and reason to interpose, an injured party must become aware that the law assumes the exclusive cognizance of the right and wrong betwixt the parties, and opposes her inviolable buckler to every attempt of the private party to right himself. I repeat, that this unhappy man ought personally to be the object rather of our pity than our abhorrence, for he failed in his ignorance, and from mistaken notions of honour. But his crime is not the less that of murder, gentlemen, and, in your high and important office, it is your duty so to find. Englishmen have their angry passions as well as Scots; and should this man's action remain unpunished, you may unsheath, under various pretences, a thousand daggers betwixt the Land's-end and the Orkneys."

The venerable judge thus ended what, to judge by his apparent emotion, and by the tears which filled his eyes, was really a painful task. The jury, according to his instructions, brought in a verdict of Guilty; and Robin Oig M'Combich, *alias* M'Gregor, was sentenced to death and left for execution, which took place accordingly. He met his fate with great firmness, and acknowledged the justice of his sentence. But he repelled indignantly the observations of those who accused him of attacking an unarmed man. "I give a life for the life I took," he said, "and what can I do more?"

JAMES HOGG

THE BROWNIE OF THE BLACK HAGGS

WHEN THE Sprots were Lairds of Wheelhope, which is now a long time ago, there was one of the ladies who was very badly spoken of in the country. People did not just openly assert that Lady Wheelhope (for every landward laird's wife was then styled Lady) was a witch, but every one had an aversion even at hearing her named; and when by chance she happened to be mentioned, old men would shake their heads and say, "Ah! let us alane o' her! The less ye meddle wi' her the better." Old wives would give over spinning, and, as a pretence for hearing what might be said about her, poke in the fire with the tongs, cocking up their ears all the while; and then, after some meaning coughs, hems, and haws, would haply say, "Hech-wow, sirs! An a' be true that's said!" or something equally wise and decisive.

In short, Lady Wheelhope was accounted a very bad woman. She was an inexorable tyrant in her family, quarrelled with her servants, often cursing them, striking them, and turning them away; especially if they were religious, for she could not endure people of that character, but charged them with every thing bad. Whenever she found out that any of the servant men of the Laird's establishment were religious, she gave them up to the military, and got them shot; and several girls that were regular in their devotions, she was supposed to have got rid of by poison. She was certainly a wicked woman, else many good people were mistaken in her character; and the poor persecuted Covenanters were obliged to unite in their prayers against her.

As for the Laird, he was a big, dun-faced, pluffy body, that cared neither for good nor evil, and did not well know the one

from the other. He laughed at his lady's tantrums and barley-
hoods; and the greater the rage that she got into, the Laird thought
it the better sport. One day, when two maid-servants came running
to him, in great agitation, and told him that his lady had felled
one of their companions, the Laird laughed heartily, and said he
did not doubt it.

"Why, sir, how can you laugh?" said they. "The poor girl is
killed."

"Very likely, very likely," said the Laird. "Well, it will teach her
to take care who she angers again."

"And, sir, your lady will be hanged."

"Very likely; well, it will teach her how to strike so rashly again
—Ha, ha, ha! Will it not, Jessy?"

But when this same Jessy died suddenly one morning, the Laird
was greatly confounded, and seemed dimly to comprehend that
there had been unfair play going. There was little doubt that she
was taken off by poison; but whether the lady did it through
jealously or not, was never divulged; but it greatly bamboozled and
astonished the poor Laird, for his nerves failed him, and his whole
frame became paralytic. He seems to have been exactly in the
same state of mind with a colley that I once had. He was extremely
fond of the gun as long as I did not kill any thing with it, (there
being no game laws in Ettrick Forest in those days,) and he got a
grand chase after the hares when I missed them. But there was one
day that I chanced for a marvel to shoot one dead, a few paces
before his nose. I'll never forget the astonishment that the poor
beast manifested. He stared one while at the gun, and another while
at the dead hare, and seemed to be drawing the conclusion, that if
the case stood thus, there was no creature sure of its life. Finally,
he took his tail between his legs and ran away home, and never
would face a gun all his life again.

So was it precisely with Laird Sprot of Wheelhope. As long as
his lady's wrath produced only noise and uproar among the servants, he thought it fine sport; but when he saw what he believed
the dreadful effects of it, he became like a barrel organ out of tune,
and could only discourse one note, which he did to every one he
met. "I wish she mayna hae gotten something she had been the

waur of." This note he repeated early and late, night and day, sleeping and waking, alone and in company, from the moment that Jessy died till she was buried; and on going to the churchyard as chief mourner, he whispered it to her relatives by the way. When they came to the grave, he took his stand at the head, nor would he give place to the girl's father; but there he stood, like a huge post, as though he neither saw nor heard; and when he had lowered her head into the grave and dropped the cord, he slowly lifted his hat with one hand, wiped his dim eyes with the back of the other, and said, in a deep tremulous tone, "Poor lassie! I wish she didna get something she had been the waur of."

This death made a great noise among the common people; but there was little protection for the life of the subject in those days; and provided a man or woman was a real Anti-Covenanter, they might kill a good many without being quarrelled for it. So there was no one to take cognizance of the circumstances relating to the death of poor Jessy.

After this the Lady walked softly for the space of two or three years. She saw that she had rendered herself odious, and had entirely lost her husband's countenance, which she liked worst of all. But the evil propensity could not be overcome; and a poor boy, whom the Laird out of sheer compassion had taken into his service, being found dead one morning, the country people could no longer be restrained; so they went in a body to the Sheriff, and insisted on an investigation. It was proved that she detested the boy, had often threatened him, and had given him brose and butter the afternoon before he died; but notwithstanding of all this, the cause was ultimately dismissed, and the pursuers fined.

No one can tell to what height of wickedness she might now have proceeded, had not a check of a very singular kind been laid upon her. Among the servants that came home at the next term was one who called himself Merodach; and a strange person he was. He had the form of a boy, but the features of one a hundred years old, save that his eyes had a brilliancy and restlessness, which were very extraordinary, bearing a strong resemblance to the eyes of a well-known species of monkey. He was forward and perverse, and disregarded the pleasure or displeasure of any person; but he performed his work well, and with apparent ease. From the moment he entered the house, the Lady conceived a mortal antipathy towards him, and besought the Laird to turn him away. But the Laird would not consent; he never turned away any servant, and moreover, he had hired this fellow for a trivial wage, and he neither wanted activity nor perseverance. The natural consequence of this refusal was, that the Lady instantly set herself to embitter Merodach's life as much as possible, in order to get early quit of a domestic every way so disagreeable. Her hatred of him was not like a common antipathy entertained by one human being against another,—she hated him as one might hate a toad or an adder; and his occupation of jotteryman (as the Laird termed his servant of all work) keeping him always about her hand, it must have proved highly annoying.

She scolded him, she raged at him; but he only mocked her wrath, and giggled and laughed at her, with the most provoking derision. She tried to fell him again and again, but never, with all her address, could she hit him; and never did she make a blow at him, that she did not repent it. She was heavy and unwieldy, and he as quick in his motions as a monkey; besides, he generally contrived that she should be in such an ungovernable rage, that when she flew at him, she hardly knew what she was doing. At one time she guided her blow towards him, and he at the same instant avoided it with such dexterity, that she knocked down the chief-hind, or foresman; and then Merodach giggled so heartily, that, lifting the kitchen poker, she threw it at him with a full design of knocking out his brains; but the missile only broke every article of crockery on the kitchen dresser.

She then hastened to the Laird, crying bitterly, and telling him she would not suffer that wretch Merodach, as she called him, to stay another night in the family.

"Why, then, put him away, and trouble me no more about him," said the Laird.

"Put him away!" exclaimed she; "I have already ordered him away a hundred times, and charged him never to let me see his horrible face again; but he only grins, and answers with some intolerable piece of impertinence."

The pertinacity of the fellow amused the Laird; his dim eyes turned upwards into his head with delight; he then looked two ways at once, turned round his back, and laughed till the tears ran down his dun cheeks; but he could only articulate, "You're fitted now."

The Lady's agony of rage still increasing from this derision, she upbraided the Laird bitterly, and said he was not worthy the name of man, if he did not turn away that pestilence, after the way he had abused her.

"Why, Shusy, my dear, what has he done to you?"

"What done to me! has he not caused me to knock down John Thomson? and I do not know if ever he will come to life again!"

"Have you felled your favourite John Thomson?" said the Laird, laughing more heartily than before; "you might have done a worse deed than that."

"And has he not broken every plate and dish on the whole dresser?" continued the Lady; "and for all this devastation, he only mocks at my displeasure,—absolutely mocks me,—and if you do not have him turned away, and hanged or shot for his deeds, you are not worthy the name of man."

"O alack! What a devastation among the cheena metal!" said the Laird; and calling on Merodach, he said, "Tell me, thou evil Merodach of Babylon, how thou daredst knock down thy Lady's favourite servant, John Thomson?"

"Not I, your honour. It was my Lady herself, who got into such a furious rage at me, that she mistook her man, and felled Mr. Thomson; and the good man's skull is fractured."

"That was very odd," said the laird, chuckling; "I do not comprehend it. But then, what set you on smashing all my Lady's delft and cheena ware?—That was a most infamous and provoking action."

"It was she herself, your honour. Sorry would I be to break one dish belonging to the house. I take all the house servants to witness, that my lady smashed all the dishes with a poker; and now lays the blame on me!"

The Laird turned his dim eyes on his lady, who was crying with vexation and rage, and seemed meditating another personal attack on the culprit, which he did not all appear to shun, but rather to court. She, however, vented her wrath in the most deep and desperate revenge, the creature all the while assuring her that she would be foiled, and that in all encounters and contests with him, she would uniformly come to the worst; he was resolved to do his duty, and there before his master he defied her.

The Laird thought more than he considered it prudent to reveal; he had little doubt that his wife would find some means of wreaking her vengeance on the object of her displeasure; and he shuddered when he recollected one who had taken "something that she had been the waur of."

In a word, the Lady of Wheelhope's inveterate malignity against this one object, was like the rod of Moses, that swallowed up the rest of the serpents. All her wicked and evil propensities seemed to be superseded if not utterly absorbed by it. The rest of the family now lived in comparative peace and quietness; for early and late her malevolence was venting itself against the jotteryman, and against him alone. It was a delirium of hatred and vengeance, on which the whole bent and bias of her inclination was set. She could not stay from the creature's presence, or, in the intervals when absent from him, she spent her breath in curses and execrations; and then, not able to rest, she ran again to seek him, her eyes gleaming with the anticipated delights of vengeance, while, ever and anon, all the ridicule and harm redounded on herself.

Was it not strange that she could not get quit of this sole annoyance of her life? One would have thought she easily might. But by this time there was nothing further from her wishes; she wanted vengeance, full, adequate, and delicious vengeance, on her audacious opponent. But he was a strange and terrible creature, and the means of retaliation constantly came, as it were, to his hand.

Bread and sweet milk was the only fare that Merodach cared for, and having bargained for that, he would not want it, though he often got it with a curse and with ill will. The Lady having, upon one occasion, intentionally kept back his wonted allowance for some days, on the Sabbath morning following, she set him down a bowl of rich sweet milk, well drugged with a deadly poison; and then she lingered in a little ante-room to watch the success of her grand plot, and prevent any other creature from tasting of the potion. Merodach came in, and the housemaid said to him, "There is your breakfast, creature."

"Oho! my landlady has been liberal this morning," said he; "but I am beforehand with her.—Here, little Missie, you seem very hungry to-day—take you my breakfast." And with that he set the beverage down to the Lady's little favourite spaniel. It so happened that the Lady's only son came at that instant into the ante-room seeking her, and teasing his mama about something, which withdrew her attention from the hall table for a space. When she looked again, and saw Missie lapping up the sweet milk, she burst from her hiding place like a fury, screaming as if her head had been on fire, kicked the remainder of its contents against the wall, and lifting Missie in her bosom, retreated hastily crying all the way.

"Ha, ha, ha—I have you now!" cried Merodach, as she vanished from the hall.

Poor Missie died immediately, and very privately; indeed, she would have died and been buried, and never one have seen her, save her mistress, had not Merodach, by a luck that never failed him, looked over the wall of the flower garden, just as his lady was laying her favourite in a grave of her own digging. She, not perceiving her tormentor, plied on at her task, apostrophising the insensate little carcass,—"Ah! poor dear little creature, thou hast had a hard fortune, and hast drank of the bitter potion that was not intended for thee; but he shall drink it three times double for thy sake!"

"Is that little Missie!" said the eldrich vioce of the jotteryman, close at the Lady's ear. She uttered a loud scream, and sunk down on the bank. "Alack for poor Missie!" continued the creature in a tone of mockery, "my heart is sorry for Missie. What has befallen her—whose breakfast cup did she drink?"

"Hence with thee, fiend!" cried the Lady; "what right hast thou to intrude on thy mistress's privacy? Thy turn is coming yet; or may the nature of woman change within me!"

"It is changed already," said the creature, grinning with delight;

"I have thee now, I have thee now! And were it not to show my superiority over thee, which I do every hour, I should soon see thee strapped like a mad cat, or a worrying bratch. What wilt thou try next?"

"I will cut thy throat, and if I die for it, will rejoice in the deed; a deed of charity to all that dwell on the face of the earth."

"I have warned thee before, dame, and I now warn thee again, that all thy mischief meditated against me will fall double on thine own head."

"I want none of your warning, fiendish cur. Hence with your elvish face, and take care of yourself."

It would be too disgusting and horrible to relate or read all the incidents that fell out between this unaccountable couple. Their enmity against each other had no end, and no mitigation; and scarcely a single day passed over on which the Lady's acts of malevolent ingenuity did not terminate fatally for some favourite thing of her own. Scarcely was there a thing, animate or inanimate, on which she set a value, left to her, that was not destroyed; and yet scarcely one hour or minute could she remain absent from her tormentor, and all the while, it seems, solely for the purpose of tormenting him. While all the rest of the establishment enjoyed peace and quietness from the fury of their termagant dame, matters still grew worse and worse between the fascinated pair. The Lady haunted the menial, in the same manner as the raven haunts the eagle,—for a perpetual quarrel, though the former knows that in every encounter she is to come off the loser. Noises were heard on the stairs by night, and it was whispered among the servants, that the Lady had been seeking Merodach's chamber, on some horrible intent. Several of them would have sworn that they had seen her passing and repassing on the stair after midnight, when all was quiet; but then it was likewise well known, that Merodach slept with well-fastened doors, and a companion in another bed in the same room, whose bed, too, was nearest the door. Nobody cared much what became of the jotteryman, for he was an unsocial and disagreeable person; but some one told him what they had seen, and hinted a suspicion of the Lady's intent. But the creature only bit his upper lip, winked with his eyes, and said, "She had better let that alone; she will be the first to rue that."

Not long after this, to the horror of the family and the whole country side, the Laird's only son was found murdered in his bed one morning, under circumstances that manifested the most fiendish cruelty and inveteracy on the part of his destroyer. As soon as the atrocious act was divulged, the Lady fell into convulsions, and lost her reason; and happy had it been for her had she never recovered the use of it, for there was blood upon her hand, which she took no care to conceal, and there was little doubt that it was the blood of her own innocent and beloved boy, the sole heir and hope of the family.

This blow deprived the Laird of all power of action; but the Lady had a brother, a man of the law, who came and instantly proceeded to an investigation of this unaccountable murder. Before the Sheriff arrived, the housekeeper took the Lady's brother aside, and told him he had better not go on with the scrutiny, for she was sure the crime would be brought home to her unfortunate mistress; and after examining into several corroborative circumstances, and viewing the state of the raving maniac, with the blood on her hand and arm, he made the investigation a very short one, declaring the domestics all exculpated.

The Laird attended his boy's funeral, and laid his head in the grave, but appeared exactly like a man walking in a trance, an automaton, without feelings or sensations, oftentimes gazing at the funeral procession, as on something he could not comprehend. And when the death-bell of the parish church fell a-tolling, as the corpse approached the kirk-stile, he cast a dim eye up towards the belfry, and said hastily, "What, what's that? Och ay, we're just in time, just in time." And often was he hammering over the name of "Evil Merodach, King of Babylon," to himself. He seemed to have some far-fetched conception that his unaccountable jotteryman was in some way connected with the death of his only son, and other lesser calamities, although the evidence in favour of Merodach's innocence was as usual quite decisive.

This grievous mistake of Lady Wheelhope can only be accounted for, by supposing her in a state of derangement, or rather under some evil influence, over which she had no control; and to a person in such a state, the mistake was not so very unnatural. The mansion-house of Wheelhope was old and irregular. The stair had four acute turns, and four landing-places, all the same. In the uppermost chamber slept the two domestics—Merodach in the bed farthest in, and in the chamber immediately below that, which was exactly similar, slept the Young Laird and his tutor, the former in the bed farthest in; and thus, in the turmoil of her wild and raging passions, her own hand made herself childless.

Merodach was expelled the family forthwith, but refused to accept of his wages, which the man of law pressed upon him, for fear of farther mischief; but he went away in apparent sullenness and discontent, no one knowing whither.

When his dismissal was announced to the Lady, who was watched day and night in her chamber, the news had such an effect on her, that her whole frame seemed electrified; the horrors of remorse vanished, and another passion, which I neither can comprehend nor define, took the sole possession of her distempered spirit. "He *must* not go!—He *shall* not go!" she exclaimed. "No, no, no— he shall not—he shall not—he shall not!" and then she instantly set herself about making ready to follow him, uttering all the while the most diabolical expressions, indicative of anticipated vengeance.—"Oh, could I but snap his nerves one by one, and birl among his vitals! Could I but slice his heart off piecemeal in small messes, and see his blood lopper, and bubble, and spin away in purple slays; and then to see him grin, and grin, and grin, and grin! Oh—oh—oh—How beautiful and grand a sight it would be to see him grin, and grin, and grin!" And in such a style would she run on for hours together.

She thought of nothing, she spake of nothing, but the discarded jotteryman, who most people now began to regard as a creature that was "not canny." They had seen him eat, and drink, and work, like other people; still he had that about him that was not like other men. He was a boy in form, and an antediluvian in feature. Some thought he was a mongrel, between a Jew and an ape; some a wizard, some a kelpie, or a fairy, but most of all, that he was really and truly a Brownie. What he was I do not know, and therefore will not pretend to say; but be that as it may, in spite of locks and keys, watching and waking, the Lady of Wheelhope soon made her escape, and eloped after him. The attendants, indeed, would have made oath that she was carried away by some invisible hand, for it was impossible, they said, that she could have escaped on foot like other people; and this edition of the story took in the country; but sensible people viewed the matter in another light.

As for instance, when Wattie Blythe, the Laird's old shepherd, came in from the hill one morning, his wife Bessie thus accosted him,—"His presence be about us, Wattie Blythe! have ye heard what has happened at the ha'? Things are aye turning waur and waur there, and it looks like as if Providence had gi'en up our Laird's house to destruction. This grand estate maun now gang frae the Sprots; for it has finished them."

"Na, na. Bessie, it isna the estate that has finished the Sprots, but the Sprots that hae finished the estate, and themsells into the boot. They hae been a wicked and degenerate race, and aye the langer the waur, till they hae reached the utmost bounds o' earthly wickedness; and it's time the deil were looking after his ain."

"Ah, Wattie Blythe, ye never said a truer say. And that's just the very point where your story ends, and mine begins; for hasna the deil, or the fairies, or the brownies, ta'en away our Leddy bodily! and the haill country is running and riding in search o' her; and there is twenty hunder merks offered to the first that can find her, and bring her safe back. They hae ta'en her awa, skin and bane, body and soul, and a', Wattie!"

"Hech-wow! but that is awesome! And where is it thought they have ta'en her to, Bessie?"

"O, they hae some guess at that frae her ain hints afore. It is thought they hae carried her after that Satan of a creature, wha wrought sae muckle wae about the house. It is for him they are a'looking, for they ken weel, that where they get the tane they will get the tither."

"Whew! is that the gate o't, Bessie? Why, then, the awfu' story is nouther mair nor less than this, that the Leddy has made a 'lopement, as they ca't, and away after a blackguard jotteryman. Hech-wow! wae's me for human frailty! But that's just the gate! When aince the deil gets in the point o' his finger, he will soon have in his haill hand. Ay, he wants but a hair to make a tether of, ony day! I hae seen her a braw sonsy lass; but even then I feared she was devoted to destruction, for she aye mockit at religion, Bessie, and that's no a good mark of a young body. And she made a' its servants her enemies; and think you these good men's prayers were a' to blaw away i' the wind, and be nae mair regarded? Na, na, Bessie, my woman, take ye this mark baith o' our ain bairns and other folk's.—If ever ye seen a young body that disregards the Sabbath, and makes a mock at the ordinances o' religion, ye will never see that body come to muckle good.—A braw hand our Leddy has made o' her gibes and jeers at religion, and her mockeries o' the poor persecuted hill-folk!—sunk down by degrees into the very dregs o' sin and misery! run away after a scullion!"

"Fy, fy, Wattie, how can ye say sae? It was weel kenn'd that she hatit him wi' a perfect and mortal hatred, and tried to make away wi' him mae ways nor ane."

"Aha, Bessie; but nipping and scarting is Scots folk's wooing; and though it is but right that we suspend our judgments, there will naebody persuade me if she be found alang wi' the creature, but that she has run away after him in the natural way on her twa shanks, without help either frae fairy or brownie."

"I'll never believe sic a think of ony woman born, let be a leddy weel up in years."

"Od help ye, Bessie! ye dinna ken the stretch o' corrupt nature. The best o' us, when left to oursells, are nae better than strayed sheep, that will never find the way back to their ain pastures; and of a' things made o' mortal flesh, a wicked woman is the warst."

"Alack-a-day! we get the blame o' muckle that we little deserve. But, Wattie, keep ye a geyan sharp lookout about the cleuchs and the caves o' our hope; for the Leddy kens them a' geyan weel; and gin the twenty hunder merks wad come our way, it might gang a waur gate. It wad tocher a' our bonny lasses."

"Ay, weel I wat, Bessie, that's nae lee. And now, when ye bring me amind o't, I'm sair mista'en if I didna hear a creature up in the Brockholes this morning, skirling as if something were cutting its throat. It gars a' the hairs stand on my head when I think it may hae been our Leddy, and the droich of a creature murdering her. I took it for a battle of wulcats, and wished they might pu' out ane anither's thrapples; but when I think on it again, they, war unco like some o' our Leddy's unearthly screams."

"His presence be about us, Wattie! Haste ye—pit on your bonnet—tak' your staff in your hand, and gang and see what it is."

"Shame fa' me, if I daur gang, Bessie."

"Hout, Wattie, trust in the Lord."

"Aweel, sae I do. But ane's no to throw himsell ower a linn, and trust that the Lord will kep him in a blanket. And it's nae muckle safer for an auld stiff man like me to gang away out to a wild remote place, where there is ae body murdering another.—What is that I hear, Bessie? Haud the lang tongue o' you, and rin to the door, and see what noise that is."

Bessie ran to the door, but soon returned, with her mouth wide open, and her eyes set in her head.

"It is them, Wattie! it is them! His presence be about us! What will we do?"

"Them? whaten them?"

"Why, that blackguard creature, coming here, leading our Leddy by the hair o' the head, and yerking her wi' a stick. I am terrified out o' my wits. What will we do?"

"We'll *see* what they *say*," said Wattie, manifestly in as great terror as his wife; and by a natural impulse, or as a last resource, he opened the Bible, not knowing what he did, and then hurried on his spectacles; but before he got two leaves turned over, the two entered,—a frightful-looking couple indeed. Merodach, with his old withered face, and ferret eyes, leading the Lady of Wheelhope by the long hair, which was mixed with grey, and whose face was all bloated with wounds and bruises, and having stripes of blood on her garments.

"How's this!—How's this, sirs?" said Wattie Blythe.

"Close that book, and I will tell you, goodman," said Merodach.

"I can hear what you hae to say wi the beuk open, sir," said Wattie, turning over the leaves, pretending to look for some particular passage, but apparently not knowing what he was doing. "It is a shamefu' business this; but some will hae to answer for't. My leddy, I am unco grieved to see you in sic a plight. Ye hae surely been dooms sair left to yoursel."

The Lady shook her head, uttered a feeble hollow laugh, and fixed her eyes on Merodach. But such a look! It almost frightened the simple aged couple out of their senses. It was not a look of love nor of hatred exclusively; neither was it of desire or disgust, but it was a combination of them all. It was such a look as one fiend would cast on another, in whose everlasting destruction he rejoiced. Wattie was glad to take his eyes from such countenances, and look into the Bible, that firm foundation of all his hopes and all his joy.

"I request that you will shut that book, sir," said the horrible creature; "or if you do not, I will shut it for you with a vengeance"; and with that he seized it, and flung it against the wall. Bessie uttered a scream, and Wattie was quite paralyzed; and although he seemed disposed to run after his best friend, as he called it, the hellish looks of the Brownie interposed, and glued him to his seat.

"Hear what I have to say first," said the creature, "and then pore your fill on that precious book of yours. One concern at a time is enough. I came to do you a service. Here, take this cursed, wretched woman, whom you style your Lady, and deliver her up to the lawful authorities, to be restored to her husband and her place in society. She has followed one that hates her, and never said one kind word to her in his life; and though I have beat her like a dog, still she clings to me, and will not depart, so enchanted is she with the laudable purpose of cutting my throat. Tell your master and her brother, that I am not to be burdened with their maniac. I have scourged—I have spurned and kicked her, afflicting her night and day, and yet from my side she will not depart. Take her. Claim the reward in full, and your fortune is made; and so farewell!"

The creature went away, and the moment his back was turned, the Lady fell a-screaming and struggling, like one in an agony, and, in spite of all the couple's exertions, she forced herself out of their hands, and ran after the retreating Merodach. When he saw better would not be, he turned upon her, and, by one blow with his stick, struck her down; and, not content with that, continued to maltreat her in such a manner, as to all appearance would have killed twenty ordinary persons. The poor devoted dame could do nothing, but now and then utter a squeak like a half-worried cat, and writhe and grovel on the sward, till Wattie and his wife came up, and withheld her tormentor from further violence. He then bound her hands behind her back with a strong cord, and delivered her once more to the charge of the old couple, who contrived to hold her by that means, and take her home.

Wattie was ashamed to take her into the hall, but led her into one of the out-houses, whither he brought her brother to receive her. The man of the law was manifestly vexed at her reappearance, and scrupled not to testify his dissatisfaction; for when Wattie told him how the wretch had abused his sister, and that, had it not been for Bessie's interference and his own, the Lady would have been killed outright, he said, "Why, Walter it is a great pity that he did *not* kill her outright. What good can her life now do to her, or of what value is her life to any creature living? After one has lived to disgrace all connected with them, the sooner they are taken off the better."

The man, however, paid old Walter down his two thousand merks, a great fortune for one like him in those days; and not to dwell longer on this unnatural story, I shall only add, very shortly, that the Lady of Wheelhope soon made her escape once more, and flew, as if drawn by an irresistible charm, to her tormentor. Her friends looked no more after her; and the last time she was seen alive, it was following the uncouth creature up the water of Daur, weary, wounded, and lame, while he was all the way beating her, as a piece of excellent amusement. A few days after that, her body was found among some wild haggs, in a place called Crook-burn, by a party of the persecuted Covenanters that were in hiding there, and some of the very men whom she had exerted herself to destroy, and who had been driven, like David of old, to pray for a curse and earthly punishment upon her. They buried her like a dog at the Yetts of Keppel, and rolled three huge stones upon her grave, which are lying there to this day. When they found her corpse, it was mangled and wounded in a most shocking manner, the fiendish creature having manifestly tormented her to death. He was never more seen or heard of in this kingdom, though all that country-side was kept in terror for him many years afterwards; and to this day, they will tell you of THE BROWNIE OF THE BLACK HAGGS, which title he seems to have acquired after his disappearance.

This story was told to me by an old man named Adam Halliday, whose great-grandfather, Thomas Halliday, was one of those that found the body and buried it. It is many years since I heard it; but, however ridiculous it may appear, I remember it made a dreadful impression on my young mind. I never heard any story like it, save one of an old fox-hound that pursued a fox through the Grampians for a fortnight, and when at last discovered by the Duke of Athole's people, neither of them could run, but the hound was still continuing to walk after the fox, and when the latter lay down, the other lay down beside him, and looked at him steadily all the while, though unable to do him the least harm. The passion of inveterate malice seems to have influenced these two exactly alike. But, upon the whole, I can scarcely believe the tale can be true.

JOHN GALT

THE GUDEWIFE

INTRODUCTION

I AM inditing the good matter of this book for the instruction of
our only daughter when she comes to years of discretion, as she
soon will, for her guidance when she has a house of her own, and
has to deal with the kittle temper of a gudeman in so couthy a
manner as to mollify his sour humour when anything out of doors
troubles him. Thanks be and praise I am not ill qualified! indeed,
it is a clear ordinance that I was to be of such a benefit to the
world; for it would have been a strange thing if the pains taken
with my education had been purposeless in the decrees of Providence.

Mr Desker, the schoolmaster, was my father; and, as he was
reckoned in his day a great teacher, and had a pleasure in opening
my genie for learning, it is but reasonable to suppose that I in a
certain manner profited by his lessons, and made a progress in
parts of learning that do not fall often into the lot of womankind.
This much it behoves me to say, for there are critical persons in
the world that might think it very upsetting of one of my degree
to write a book, especially a book which has for its end the better-
ing of the conjugal condition. If I did not tell them, as I take it
upon me to do, how well I have been brought up for the work,
they might look down upon my endeavours with a doubtful eye;
but when they read this, they will have a new tout to their old
horn, and reflect with more reverence of others who may be in
some things their inferiors, superiors, or equals. It would not
become me to say to which of these classes I belong, though I am
not without an inward admonition on that head.

It fell out, when I was in my twenties, that Mr Thrifter came,

in the words of the song of Auld Robin Gray, "a-courting to me";
and, to speak a plain matter of fact, in some points he was like
that bald-headed carle. For he was a man considering my juven-
ility, well stricken in years; besides being a bachelor, with a natural
inclination (as all old bachelors have) to be dozened, and fond
of his own ayes and nays. For my part, when he first came about
the house, I was as dawty as Jeanie—as I thought myself entitled
to a young man, and did not relish the apparition of him coming
in at the gloaming, when the day's darg was done, and before
candles were lighted. However, our lot in life is not of our own
choosing. I will say—for he is still to the fore—that it could not
have been thought he would have proved himself such a satisfactory gudeman as he has been. To be sure, I put my shoulder to
the wheel, and likewise prayed to Jupiter; for there never was a
rightful head of a family without the concurrence of his wife. These
are words of wisdom that my father taught, and I put in practice.

Mr Thrifter, when he first came about me, was a bein man. He
had parts in two vessels, besides his own shop, and was sponsible
for a nest-egg of lying money; so that he was not, though rather
old, a match to be, as my father thought, discomfited with a flea
in the lug instanter. I therefore, according to the best advice, so
comported myself that it came to pass in the course of time that
we were married; and of my wedded life and experience I intend
to treat in this book.

I

AMONG the last words that my sagacious father said when I took
upon me to be the wedded wife of Mr Thrifter were, that a man
never throve unless his wife would let, which is a text that I have
not forgotten; for though in a way, and in obedience to the customs
of the world, women acknowledge men as their head, yet we all
know in our hearts that this is but diplomatical. Do not we see
that men work for us, which shews that they are our servants?
do we not see that men protect us, are they not therefore our
soldiers? do we not see that they go hither and yon at our bidding,

which shews that they have that within their nature that teaches them to obey? and do not we feel that we have the command of them in all things, just as they had the upper hand in the world till woman was created? No clearer proof do I want that, although in a sense for policy we call ourselves the weaker vessels—and in that very policy there is power—we know well in our hearts that, as the last made creatures, we necessarily are more perfect, and have all that was made before us, by hook or crook, under our thumb. Well does Robin Burns sing of this truth in the song where he has—

> *Her 'prentice hand she tried on man,*
> *And syne she made the lassies oh!*

Accordingly, having a proper conviction of the superiority of my sex, I was not long of making Mr Thrifter, my gudeman, to know into what hands he had fallen, by correcting many of the bad habits of body to which he had become addicted in his bachelor loneliness. Among these was a custom that I did think ought not to be continued after he had surrendered himself into the custody of a wife, and that was an usage with him in the morning before breakfast to toast his shoes against the fender and forenent the fire. This he did not tell me till I saw it with my own eyes the morning after we were married, which, when I beheld, gave me a sore heart, because, had I known it before we were everlastingly made one, I will not say but there might have been a dubiety as to the paction; for I have ever had a natural dislike to men who toasted their shoes, thinking it was a hussie fellow's custom. However, being endowed with an instinct of prudence, I winked at it for some days; but it could not be borne any longer, and I said in a sweet manner, as it were by and by,

"Dear Mr Thrifter, that servant lass we have gotten has not a right notion of what is a genteel way of living. Do you see how the misleart creature sets up your shoes in the inside of the fender, keeping the warmth from our feet? really I'll thole this no longer; it's not a custom in a proper house. If a stranger were accidently coming in and seeing your shoes in that situation, he would not think of me as it is well known he ought to think."

Mr Thrifter did not say much, nor could he; for I had judiciously laid all the wyte and blame of the thing to the servant; but he said, in a diffident manner, that it was not necessary to be so particular.

"No necessary! Mr Thrifter, what do you call a particularity, when you would say that toasting shoes is not one? It might do for you when you were a bachelor, but ye should remember that you're so no more, and it's a custom I will not allow."

"But," replied he with a smile, "I am the head of the house; and to make few words about it, I say, Mrs Thrifter, I will have my shoes warmed anyhow, whether or no."

"Very right, my dear," quo' I; "I'll ne'er dispute that you are the head of the house; but I think that you need not make a poor wife's life bitter by insisting on toasting your shoes."

And I gave a deep sigh. Mr Thrifter looked very solemn on hearing this, and as he was a man not void of understanding, he said to me.

"My dawty," said he, "we must not stand on trifles; if you do not like to see my shoes within the parlour fender, they can be toasted in the kitchen."

I was glad to hear him say this; and, ringing the bell, I told the servant-maid at once to take them away and place them before the kitchen fire, well pleased to have carried my point with such debonair sauvity; for if you get the substance of a thing, it is not wise to make a piece of work for the shadow likewise. Thus it happened I was conqueror in the controversy; but Mr Thrifter's shoes have to this day been toasted every morning in the kitchen; and I daresay the poor man is vogie with the thoughts of having gained a victory; for the generality of men have, like parrots, a good conceit of themselves, and cry "Pretty Poll!" when everybody sees they have a crooked neb.

II

BUT what I have said was nothing to many other calamities that darkened our honeymoon. Mr Thrifter having been a long-keepit bachelor, required a consideration in many things besides his shoes; for men of that stamp are so long accustomed to their own ways that it is not easy to hammer them into docility, far less to make them obedient husbands. So that although he is the best of men, yet I cannot say on my conscience that he was altogether free from an ingrained temper, requiring my canniest hand to manage properly. It could not be said that I suffered much from great faults; but he was fiky, and made more work about trifles that didna just please him than I was willing to conform to. Some excuse, however, might be pleaded for him, because he felt that infirmities were growing upon him, which was the cause that made him think of taking a wife; and I was not in my younger days quite so thoughtful, maybe, as was necessary: for I will take blame to myself, when it would be a great breach of truth in me to deny a fault that could be clearly proven.

Mr Thrifter was a man of great regularity; he went to the shop and did his business there in a most methodical manner; he returned to the house and ate his meals like clockwork; and he went to bed every night at half-past nine o'clock, and slept there like a door nail. In short, all he did and said was as orderly as commodities on chandler pins; but for all that he was at times of a crunkly spirit, fractiously making faults about nothing at all: by which he was neither so smooth as oil nor so sweet as honey to me, whose duty it was to govern him.

At the first outbreaking of the original sin that was in him, I was vexed and grieved, watering the plants in the solitude of the room, when he was discoursing on the news of the day with customers in the shop. At last I said to myself, "This will never do; one of two must obey: and it is not in the course of nature that a gudeman should rule a house, which is the province of a wife and becomes her nature to do."

So I set a stout heart to the stey brae, and being near my time with our daughter, I thought it would be well to try how he would put up with a little sample of womanhood. So that day when he came in to his dinner, I was, maybe, more incommoded with my temper than might be, saying to him, in a way as if I could have fought with the wind, that it was very unsettled weather.

"My dawty," said he, "I wonder what would content you! we have had as delightful a week as ever made the sight of the sun heartsome."

"Well, but," said I, "good weather that is to you may not be so to me; and I say again, that this is most ridiculous weather."

"What would you have, my dawty? Is it not known by a better what is best for us?"

"Oh," cried I, "we can never speak of temporal things but you haul in the grace of the Maker by the lug and the horn. Mr Thrifter, ye should set a watch on the door of your lips; especially as ye have now such a prospect before you of being the father of a family."

"Mrs Thrifter," said he, "what has that to do with the state of the weather?"

"Everything," said I. "Isn't the condition that I am in a visibility that I cannot look after the house as I should do? which is the cause of your having such a poor dinner to-day; for the weather wiled out the servant lass, and she has in consequence not been in the kitchen to see to her duty. Doesn't that shew you that, to a woman in the state that I am, fine sunshiny weather is no comfort?"

"Well," said he, "though a shower is at times seasonable, I will say that I prefer days like this."

"What you, Mr Thrifter, prefer, can make no difference to me; but I will uphold, in spite of everything you can allege to the contrary, that this is not judicious weather."

"Really now, gudewife," said Mr Thrifter, "what need we quarrel about the weather? neither of us can make it better or worse."

"That's a truth," said I, "but what need you maintain that dry weather is pleasant weather, when I have made it plain to you that it is a great affliction? And how can you say the contrary? does not both wet and dry come from Providence? Which of them is the evil?—for they should be in their visitations both alike."

"Mrs Thrifter," said he, "what would you be at, summering and wintering on nothing?"

Upon which I said, "Oh, Mr Thrifter, if ye were like me, ye would say anything; for I am not in a condition to be spoken to.

I'll not say that ye're far wrong, but till my time is a bygone ye should not contradict me so; for I am no in a state to be contradicted: it may go hard with me if I am. So I beg you to think, for the sake of the baby unborn, to let me have my way in all things for a season."

"I have no objection," said he, "if there is a necessity for complying; but really, gudewife, ye're at times a wee fashous just now; and this house has not been a corner in the kingdom of heaven for some time."

Thus, from less to more, our argolbargoling was put an end to; and from that time I was the ruling power in our domicile, which has made it the habitation of quiet ever since; for from that moment I never laid down the rod of authority, which I achieved with such a womanly sleight of hand.

III

THOUGH from the time of the conversation recorded in the preceding chapter I was, in a certain sense, the ruling power in our house, as a wedded wife should be, we did not slide down a glassy brae till long after. For though the gudeman in a compassionate manner allowed me to have my own way till my fullness of time was come, I could discern by the tail of my eye that he meditated to usurp the authority again, when he saw a fit time to effect the machination. Thus it came to pass, when I was delivered of our daughter, I had, as I lay on my bed, my own thoughts anent the evil that I saw barming within him; and I was therefore determined to keep the upper hand, of which I had made a conquest with such dexterity, and the breaking down of difficulties.

So when I was some days in a recumbent posture, but in a well-doing way, I said nothing; it made me, however, often grind my teeth in a secrecy when I saw from the bed many a thing that I treasured in remembrance should never be again. But I was very thankful for my deliverance, and assumed a blitheness in my countenance that was far from my heart. In short, I could see that the gudeman, in whose mouth you would have thought sugar would have melted, had from day to day a stratagem in his head subversive of the regency that I had won in my tender state; and as I saw it would never do to let him have his own will, I had recourse to the usual diplomaticals of womankind.

It was a matter before the birth that we settled, him and me, that the child should be baptized on the eighth day after, in order that I might be up and a partaker of the ploy; which, surely, as the mother, I was well entitled to. But from what I saw going on from the bed and jaloused, it occurred to me that the occasion should be postponed, and according as Mr Thrifter should give his consent, or withhold it, I should comport myself; determined, however, I was to have the matter postponed, just to ascertain the strength and durability of what belonged to me.

On the fifth day I, therefore, said to him, as I was sitting in the easy chair by the fire, with a cod at my shoulders and my mother's fur cloak about me—the baby was in a cradle close by, but not rocking, for the keeper said it was yet too young—and sitting, as I have said, Mr Thrifter forenent me, "My dear," said I, "it will never do to have the christening on the day we said."

"What for no?" was the reply; "isn't it a very good day?"

So I, seeing that he was going to be upon his peremptors, replied, with my usual meekness, "No human being, my dear, can tell what sort of day it will be; but be it good or be it bad, the christening is not to be on that day."

"You surprise me!" said he, "I considered it a settled point, and have asked Mr Sweetie, the grocer, to come to his tea."

"Dear me!" quo' I; "ye should not have done that without my consent; for although we set the day before my time was come, it was not then in the power of man to say how I was to get through; and therefore it was just a talk we had on the subject, and by no manner of means a thing that could be fixed."

"In some sort," said Mr Thrifter, "I cannot but allow that you are speaking truth; but I thought that the only impediment to the day was your illness. Now you have had a most blithe time o't, and there is nothing in the way of an obstacle."

"Ah, Mr Thrifter!" said I, "it's easy for you, who have such a barren knowledge of the nature of women, so to speak, but I know that I am in no condition to have such a handling as a christening; and besides, I have a scruple of conscience well worth your attention concerning the same—and it's my opinion, formed in the watches of the night, when I was in my bed, that baby should be christened in the kirk on the Lord's day."

"Oh," said he, "that's but a fashion, and you'll be quite well by the eighth; the howdie told me that ye had a most pleasant time o't, and cannot be ill on the eighth day."

I was just provoked into contumacy to hear this; for to tell a new mother that childbirth is a pleasant thing, set me almost in a passion; and I said to him that he might entertain Mr Sweetie himself, for that I was resolved the christening should not be as had been set.

In short, from less to more, I gained my point; as, indeed, I always settled it in my own mind before broaching the subject: first, by letting him know that I had latent pains, which made me very ill, though I seemed otherwise; and, secondly, that it was very hard, and next to a martyrdom, to be controverted in religion, as I would be if the bairn was baptized anywhere but in the church.

IV

IN DUE time the christening took place in the kirk, as I had made a point of having; and for some time after we passed a very happy married life. Mr Thrifter saw that it was of no use to contradict me, and in consequence we lived in great felicity, he never saying nay to me; and I, as became a wife in the rightful possession of her prerogatives, was most condescending. But still he shewed, when he durst, the bull-horn; and would have meddled with our householdry, to the manifest detriment of our conjugal happiness, had I not continued my interdict in the strictest manner. In truth, I was all the time grievously troubled with nursing Nance, our daughter, and could not take the same pains about things that I otherwise would have done; and it is well known that husbands are like mice, that know when the cat is out of the house or her back turned, they take their own way: and I assure the courteous reader, to say no ill of my gudeman, that he was one of the mice genus.

But at last I had a trial that was not to be endured with such a composity as if I had been a black snail. It came to pass that our daughter was to be weaned, and on the day settled—a Sabbath day—we had, of course, much to do, for it behoved in this ceremony that I should keep out of sight; and keeping out of sight it seemed but reasonable, considering his parentage to the wean, that Mr Thrifter should take my place. So I said to him in the morning that he must do so, and keep Nance for that day; and, to do the poor man justice, he consented at once, for he well knew that it would come to nothing to be contrary.

So I went to the kirk, leaving him rocking the cradle and singing hush, ba! as he saw need. But oh, dule! scarcely had I left the house when the child screamed up in a panic, and would not be pacified. He thereupon lifted it out of the cradle, and with it in his arms went about the house; but it was such a roaring buckie that for a long time he was like to go distracted. Over what ensued I draw the curtain, and must only say that, when I came from the church, there he was, a spectacle, and as sour as a crab apple, blaming me for leaving him with such a devil.

I was really woeful to see him, and sympathised in the most pitiful manner with him, on account of what had happened; but the more I condoled with him the more he would not be comforted, and for all my endeavours to keep matters in a propriety, I saw my jurisdiction over the house was in jeopardy, and every now and then the infant cried out, just as if it had been laid upon a heckle. Oh! such a day as that was for Mr Thrifter, when he heard the tyrant bairn shrieking like mad, and every now and then drumming with its wee feetie like desperation, he cried,

"For the love of God, give it a drop of the breast! or it will tempt me to wring off its ankles or its head."

But I replied composedly that it could not be done, for the wean must be speant, and what he advised was evendown nonsense. *?see*

"What has come to pass, both my mother and other sagacious carlines told me I had to look for; and so we must bow the head of resignation to our lot. You'll just," said I, "keep the bairn this afternoon; it will not be a long fashery."

He said nothing, but gave a deep sigh.

At this moment the bells of the kirk were ringing for the afternoon's discourse, and I lifted my bonnet to put it on and go; but ere I knew where I was, Mr Thrifter was out of the door and away, leaving me alone with the torment in the cradle, which the bells at that moment wakened: and it gave a yell that greatly discomposed me.

Once awa and aye awa, Mr Thrifter went into the fields, and would not come back when I lifted the window and called to him, but walked faster and faster, and was a most demented man; so that I was obligated to stay at home, and would have had my own work with the termagant baby if my mother had not come in and advised me to give it sweetened rum and water for a pacificator.

V

MR THRIFTER began in time to be a very complying husband, and we had, after the trial of the weaning, no particular confabulation; indeed he was a very reasonable man, and had a rightful instinct of the reverence that is due to the opinion of a wife of discernment. I do not think, to the best of my recollection, that between the time Nance was weaned till she got her walking shoes and was learning to walk, that we had a single controversy; nor can it be said that we had a great ravelment on that occasion. Indeed, saving our daily higling about trifles not worth remembering, we passed a pleasant life. But when Nance came to get her first walking shoes, that was a catastrophe well worthy of being rehearsed for her behoof now.

It happened that for some months before, she had, in place of shoes, red worsted socks; but as she began, from the character of her capering, to kithe that she was coming to her feet, I got a pair of yellow slippers for her; and no mother could take more pains than I did to learn her how to handle her feet. First, I tried to teach her to walk by putting a thimble or an apple beyond her reach, at least a chair's breadth off, and then I endeavoured to make the cutty run from me to her father, across the hearth, and he held out his hands to catch her.

This, it will be allowed, was to us pleasant pastime. But it fell out one day, when we were diverting ourselves by making Nance run to and fro between us across the hearth, that the glaiket baudrons chanced to see the seal of her father's watch glittering, and, in coming from him to me, she drew it after her, as if it had been a turnip. He cried, "Oh, Christal and—" I lifted my hands in wonderment; but the tottling creature, with no more sense than a sucking turkey, whirled the watch—the Almighty knows how!— into the fire, and giggled as if she had done an exploit.

"Take it out with the tongs," said I.

"She's an ill-brought-up wean," cried he.

The short and the long of it was, before the watch could be got out, the heat broke the glass and made the face of it dreadful; besides, he wore a riband chain—that was in a blaze before we could make a redemption.

When the straemash was over, I said to him that he could expect no better by wearing a watch in such a manner.

"It is not," said he, "the watch that is to blame, but your bardy bairn that ye have spoiled in the bringing up."

"Mr Thrifter," quo' I, "this is not a time for upbraiding; for if ye mean to insinuate anything to my disparagement, it is what I will not submit to."

"E'en as you like, my dawty," said he; "but what I say is true —that your daughter will just turn out a randy like her mother."

"What's that ye say?" quo' I, and I began to wipe my eyes with the corner of my shawl—saying in a pathetic manner, "If I am a randy, I ken who has made me one."

"Ken," said he, "Ken! everybody kens that ye are like a clubby foot, made by the hand of God, and passed the remede of doctors."

Was not this most diabolical to hear? Really my corruption rose at such blasphemy; and starting from my seat, I put my hands on my haunches, and gave a stamp with my foot that made the whole house dirl; "What does the man mean?" said I.

But he replied with a composity as if he had been in liquor, saying, with an ill-faured smile, "Sit down, my dawty; you'll do

yourself a prejudice if ye allow your passion to get the better of
you."

Could mortal woman thole the like of this; it stunned me speechless, and for a time I thought my authority knocked on the head.
But presently the spirit that was in my nature mustered courage,
and put a new energy within me, which caused me to say nothing,
but to stretch out my feet, and stiffen back, with my hands at
my sides, as if I was a dead corpse. Whereupon the good man ran
for a tumbler of water to jaup on my face; but when he came near
me in this posture, I dauded the glass of water in his face, and
drummed with my feet and hands in a delirious manner, which
convinced him that I was going by myself. Oh, but he was in an
awful terrification! At last, seeing his fear and contrition, I began
to moderate, as it seemed; which made him as softly and kindly
as if I had been a true frantic woman; which I was not, but a
practiser of the feminine art, to keep the ruling power.

Thinking by my state that I was not only gone daft, but not
without the need of soothing, he began to ask my pardon in a
proper humility, and with a most pitiful penitence. Whereupon
I said to him, that surely he had not a rightful knowledge of my
nature: and then he began to confess a fault, and was such a
dejected man that I took the napkin from my eyes and gave a
great guffaw, telling him that surely he was silly daft and gi'en
to pikery, if he thought he could daunton me. "No, no, Mr
Thrifter," quo' I, "while I live, and the iron tongs are by the
chumly leg, never expect to get the upper hand of me."

From that time he was as bidable a man as any reasonable woman
could desire; but he gave a deep sigh, which was a testificate to
me that the leaven of unrighteousness was still within him, and
might break out into treason and rebellion if I was not on my
guard.

HUGH MILLER

THE WIDOW OF DUNSKAITH

> *Oh, mony a shriek, that waefu' night,*
>   *Rose frae the stormy main;*
> *An' mony a bootless vow was made,*
>   *An' mony a prayer vain;*
> *An' mithers wept, an' widows mourned*
>   *For mony a weary day;*
> *An' maidens, ance o' blithest mood,*
>   *Grew sad, and pined away.*

THE NORTHERN Sutor of Cromarty is of a bolder character than even the southern one, abrupt, and stern, and precipitous as that is. It presents a loftier and more unbroken wall of rock; and, where it bounds on the Moray Firth, there is a savage magnificence in its cliffs and caves, and in the wild solitude of its beach, which we find nowhere equalled on the shores of the other. It is more exposed, too, in the time of tempest. The waves often rise, during the storms of winter, more than a hundred feet against its precipices, festooning them, even at that height, with wreaths of kelp and tangle; and, for miles within the bay, we may hear, at such seasons, the savage uproar that maddens amid its cliffs and caverns, coming booming over the lashings of the nearer waves, like the roar of artillery. There is a sublimity of desolation on its shores, the effects of a conflict maintained for ages, and on a scale so gigantic. The isolated, spire-like crags that rise along its base, are so drilled and bored by the incessant lashings of the surf, and are ground down into shapes so fantastic, that they seem but the wasted skeletons of their former selves; and we find almost every natural fissure in the solid rock hollowed into an immense cavern, whose very ceiling, though the head turns as we look up to it, owes evidently its comparative smoothness to the action of the waves. One of the most remarkable of these recesses occupies what we may term the apex of a lofty promontory. The entrance, unlike that of most of the others, is narrow and rugged, though of great height; but it widens within into a shadowy chamber, perplexed, like the nave of a cathedral, by uncertain cross lights, that come glimmering into it through two lesser openings, which perforate the opposite sides of the promontory. It is a strange, ghostly-looking place: there is a sort of moonlight greenness in the twilight which forms its noon, and the denser shadows which rest along its sides; a blackness, so profound that it mocks the eye, hangs over a lofty passage which leads from it, like a corridor, still deeper into the bowels of the hill; the light falls on a sprinkling of half-buried bones, the remains of animals that, in the depth of winter, have creeped into it for shelter, and to die; and, when the winds are up, and the hoarse roar of the waves comes reverberated from its inner recesses, or creeps howling along its roof, it needs no over-active fancy to people its avenues with the shapes of beings long since departed from every gayer and softer scene, but which still rise uncalled to the imagination in those by-corners of nature which seem dedicated, like this cavern, to the wild, the desolate, and the solitary.

There is a little rocky bay a few hundred yards to the west, which has been known for ages to all the seafaring men of the place, as the Cova Green. It is such a place as we are sometimes made acquainted with in the narratives of disastrous shipwrecks. First, there is a broad semicircular strip of beach, with a wilderness of insulated piles of rock in front; and so steep and continuous is the wall of precipices which rises behind, that, though we may see directly over head the grassy slopes of the hill, with here and there a few straggling firs, no human foot ever gained the nearer edge. The bay of the Cova Green is a prison to which the sea presents the only outlet; and the numerous caves which open along its sides, like the arches of an amphitheatre, seem but its darker cells. It is, in truth, a wild impressive place, full of beauty and terror, and with none of the squalidness of the mere dungeon about it. There is a puny littleness in our brick and lime receptacles of misery and languor which speaks as audibly of the feebleness of man, as of his crimes or his inhumanity; but here all is great and magnificent—and there is much, too, that is pleasing. Many of the higher cliffs, which rise beyond the influence of the spray, are tapestried with ivy. We may see the heron watching on the ledges beside her bundle of withered twigs, or the blue hawk darting from her cell; there is life on every side of us—life in even the wild tumbling of the waves, and in the stream of pure water which, rushing from the higher edge of the precipice in a long white cord, gradually untwists itself by the way, and spatters ceaselessly among the stones over the entrance of one of the caves. Nor does the scene want its old story to strengthen its hold on the imagination.

I am wretchedly uncertain in my dates; but it must have been some time late in the reign of Queen Anne, that a fishing yawl, after vainly labouring for hours to enter the bay of Cromarty, during a strong gale from the west, was forced, at nightfall, to relinquish the attempt, and take shelter in the Cova Green. The crew consisted of but two persons—an old fisherman and his son. Both had been thoroughly drenched by the spray, and chilled by the piercing wind, which, accompanied by thick snow showers, had blown all day through the opening, from off the snowy top of Ben Wyvis; and it was with no ordinary satisfaction that, as they opened the little bay on their last tack, they saw the red gleam of a fire flickering from one of the caves, and a boat drawn upon the beach.

"It must be some of the Tarbet fishermen," said the old man, "wind-bound like ourselves; but wiser than us, in having made provision for it. I shall feel willing enough to share their fire with them for the night."

"But see," remarked the younger, "that there be no unwillingness on the other side. I am much mistaken if that be not the boat of my cousins the Macinlas, who would so fain have broken my head last Rhorichie Tryst. But, hap what may, father, the night is getting worse, and we have no choice of quarters. Hard up your helm, or we shall barely clear the Skerries; there now; every nail

an anchor." He leaped ashore, carrying with him the small hawser
attached to the stern, which he wound securely round a jutting
crag, and then stood for a few seconds until the old man, who
moved but heavily along the thwarts, had come up to him. All
was comparatively calm under the lee of the precipices; but the
wind was roaring fearfully in the woods above, and whistling amid
the furze and ivy of the higher cliff; and the two boatmen, as they
entered the cave, could see the flakes of a thick snow shower, that
had just begun to descend, circling round and round in the eddy.

The place was occupied by three men, who were sitting beside
the fire, on blocks of stone which had been rolled from the beach.
Two of them were young, and comparatively commonplace-look-
ing persons; the third was a grey-headed old man, apparently of
great muscular strength, though long past his prime, and of a
peculiarly sinister cast of countenance. A keg of spirits, which was
placed end up in front of them, served as a table; there were little
drinking measures of tin on it, and the mask-like, stolid expressions of the two younger men showed that they had been indulg-
ing freely. The elder was apparently sober. They all started to
their feet on the entrance of the fishermen, and one of the younger,
laying hold of the little cask, pitched it hurriedly into a dark corner
of the cave.

"HIS peace be here!" was the simple greeting of the elder
fisherman, as he came forward. "Eachen Macinla," he continued,
addressing the old man, "we have not met for years before—not,
I believe, since the death o' my puir sister, when we parted such ill
friends; but we are short-lived creatures ourselves, Eachen—surely
our anger should be short-lived too; and I have come to crave from
you a seat by your fire."

"William Beth," replied Eachen, "it was no wish of mine we
should ever meet; but to a seat by the fire you are welcome."

Old Macinla and his sons resumed their seats, the two fishermen took their places fronting them, and for some time neither
party exchanged a word.

A fire, composed mostly of fragments of wreck and driftwood,
threw up its broad cheerful flame towards the roof, but so spacious
was the cavern that, except where here and there a whiter mass of

stalactites, or bolder projection of cliff stood out from the darkness, the light seemed lost in it. A dense body of smoke, which stretched its blue level surface from side to side, and concealed the roof went rolling outwards like an inverted river.

"This is but a gousty lodging-place," remarked the old fisher-man, as he looked round him; "but I have seen a worse. I wish the folk at home kent we were half sae snug; and then the fire, too— I have always felt something companionable in a fire, something consolable, as it were; it appears, somehow, as if it were a creature like ourselves, and had life in it." The remark seemed directed to no one in particular, and there was no reply. In a second attempt at conversation, the fisherman addressed himself to the old man.

"It has vexed me," he said, "that our young folk shouldna, for my sister's sake, be on more friendly terms, Eachen. They hae been quarrelling, an' I wish to see the quarrel made up." The old man, without deigning a reply, knit his grey shaggy brows, and looked doggedly at the fire.

"Nay, now," continued the fisherman, "we are getting auld men, Eachen, an' wauld better bury our hard thoughts o' ane anither afore we come to be buried ourselves. What if we were sent to the Cova Green the night, just that we might part friends!"

Eachen fixed his keen scrutinizing glance on the speaker;—it was but for a moment; there was a tremulous motion of the under lip as he withdrew it, and a setting of the teeth—the expression of mingled hatred and anger; but the tone of his reply savoured more of sullen indifference than of passion.

"William Beth," he said, "ye hae tricked my boys out o' the bit property that suld hae come to them by their mother; it's no lang since they barely escaped being murdered by your son. What more want you? But ye perhaps think it better that the time should be passed in making hollow lip professions o' good will, than that it suld be employed in clearing off an old score."

"Ay," hiccuped out the elder of the two sons, "the houses might come my way, then; an', besides, gin Helen Henry were to lose her a'e joe, the ither might hae a better chance. Rise, brither— rise, man, an' fight for me an' your sweetheart." The younger lad, who seemed verging towards the last stage of intoxication, struck his clenched fist against his palm, and attempted to rise.

"Look ye, uncle," exclaimed the younger fisherman, a power-ful-looking and very handsome stripling, as he sprang to his feet, "your threat might be spared. Our little property was my grand-father's, and naturally descended to his only son; and, as for the affair at Rhorichie, I dare either of my cousins to say the quarrel was of my seeking. I have no wish to raise my hand against the sons or the husband of my aunt; but, if forced to it, you will find that neither my father nor myself are wholly at your mercy."

"Whisht, Earnest," said the old fisherman, laying his hand on the hand of the young man; "sit down—your uncle maun hae ither thoughts. It is now fifteen years, Eachen," he continued, "since I was called to my sister's deathbed. You yourself canna forget what passed there. There had been grief, an' cauld, an' hunger, beside that bed. I'll no say you were willingly unkind—few folk are that but when they hae some purpose to serve by it, an' you could have none; but you laid no restraint on a harsh temper, and none on a craving habit that forgets everything but itsel; and so my puir sister perished in the middle o' her days—a wasted, heart-broken thing. It's no that I wish to hurt you. I mind how we passed our youth thegither, among the wild Buccaneers; it was a bad school, Eachen; an' I owre often feel I havena unlearned a' my ain lessons, to wonder that you shouldna hae unlearned a' yours. But we're getting old men, Eachen, an' we have now what we hadna in our young days, the advantage o' the light. Dinna let us die fools in the sight o' Him who is so willing to give us wisdom—dinna let us die enemies. We have been early friends, though maybe no for good; we have fought afore now at the same gun; we have been united by the luve o' her that's now in the dust; an' there are our boys—the nearest o' kin to ane anither that death has spared. But, what I feel as strongly as a' the rest, Eachen—we hae done meikle ill thegither. I can hardly think o' a past sin without thinking o' you, an thinking too, that, if a creature like me may hope he has found pardon, you shouldna despair. Eachen, we maun be friends."

The features of the stern old man relaxed. "You are perhaps right, William," he at length replied; "but ye were aye a luckier man than me,—luckier for this world, I'm sure, an' maybe for the next. I had aye to seek, an' aften without finding, the good that came in your gate o' itsel. Now that age is coming upon us, ye get a snug rental frae the little houses, an' I hae naething; an' ye hae character an' credit, but wha would trust me, or cares for me? Ye hae been made an elder o' the kirk, too, I hear, an' I am still a reprobate; but we were a' born to be just what we are, an' sae maun submit. An' your son, too, shares in your luck; he has heart an' hand, an' my whelps hae neither; an' the girl Henry, that scouts that sot there, likes him—but what wonder o' that? But you are right, William—we maun be friends. Pledge me." The little cask was produced; and, filling the measures, he nodded to Earnest and his father. They pledged him; when, as if seized by a sudden frenzy, he filled his measure thrice in hasty succession, draining it each time to the bottom, and then flung it down with a short hoarse laugh. His sons, who would fain have joined with him, he repulsed with a firmness of manner which he had not before exhibited. "No, whelps," he said, "get sober as fast as ye can."

"We had better," whispered Earnest to his father, "not sleep in the cave to-night."

"Let me hear now o' your quarrel, Earnest," said Eachen—"your father was a more prudent man than you; and, however much he wronged me, did it without quarrelling."

"The quarrel was none of my seeking," replied Earnest. "I was insulted by your sons, and would have borne it for the sake of what they seemed to forget; but there was another whom they also insulted, and that I could not bear."

"The girl Henry—and what then?"

"Why, my cousins may tell the rest. They were mean enough to take odds against me, and I just beat the two spiritless fellows that did so."

But why record the quarrels of this unfortunate evening? An hour or two passed away in disagreeable bickerings, during which the patience of even the old fisherman was worn out, and that of Earnest had failed him altogether. They both quitted the cave, boisterous as the night was, and it was now stormier than ever; and, heaving off their boat, till she rode at the full length of her swing from the shore, sheltered themselves under the sail. The

Macinlas returned next evening to Tarbet; but, though the wind moderated during the day, the yawl of William Beth did not enter the bay of Cromarty. Weeks passed away, during which the clergymen of the place corresponded, regarding the missing fishermen, with all the lower parts of the Frith; but they had disappeared, as it seemed, for ever.

Where the northern Sutor sinks into the low sandy tract that nearly fronts the town of Cromarty, there is a narrow grassy terrace raised but a few yards over the level of the beach. It is sheltered behind by a steep undulating bank; for, though the rock here and there juts out, it is too rich in vegetation to be termed a precipice. To the east, the coast retires into a semicircular rocky recess, terminating seawards in a lofty, dark-browed precipice, and bristling, throughout all its extent, with a countless multitude of crags, that, at every heave of the wave, break the surface into a thousand eddies. Towards the west, there is a broken and somewhat dreary waste of sand. The terrace itself, however, is a sweet little spot, with its grassy slopes, that recline towards the sun, partially covered with thickets of wild-rose and honeysuckle, and studded, in their season, with violets, and daisies, and the delicate rock geranium. Towards its eastern extremity, with the bank rising immediately behind, and an open space in front, which seemed to have been cultivated at one time as a garden, there stood a picturesque little cottage. It was that of the widow of William Beth. Five years had now elapsed since the disappearance of her son and husband, and the cottage bore the marks of neglect and decay. The door and window, bleached white by the sea winds, shook loosely to every breeze; clusters of chickweed luxuriated in the hollows of the thatch, or mantled over the eaves; and a honeysuckle that had twisted itself round the chimney, lay withering in a tangled mass at the foot of the wall. But the progress of decay was more marked in the widow herself than in her dwelling. She had had to contend with grief and penury: a grief not the less undermining in its effects, from the circumstance of its being sometimes suspended by hope—a penury so extreme that every succeeding day seemed as if won by some providential interference from absolute want. And she was now, to all appearance, fast sinking in the struggle. The autumn was well nigh over. She had been weak and ailing for months before, and had now become so feeble as to be confined for days together to her bed. But, happily, the poor solitary woman had, at least, one attached friend in the daughter of a farmer of the parish, a young and beautiful girl, who, though naturally of no melancholy temperament, seemed to derive almost all she enjoyed of pleasure from the society of the widow. Helen Henry was in her twenty-third year; but she seemed older in spirit than in years. She was thin and pale, though exquisitely formed; there was a drooping heaviness in her fine eyes, and a cast of pensive thought on her forehead, that spoke of a longer experience of grief than so brief a portion of life might be supposed to have furnished. She had once lovers; but they had gradually dropped away in the despair of moving her, and awed by a deep and settled pensiveness which, in the gayest season of youth, her character had suddenly but permanently assumed. Besides, they all knew her affections were already engaged, and had come to learn, though late and unwillingly, that there are cases in which no rival can be more formidable than a dead one.

Autumn, I have said, was near its close. The weather had given indications of an early and severe winter; and the widow, whose worn-out and delicate frame was affected by every change of atmosphere, had for a few days been more than usually indisposed. It was now long past noon, and she had but just risen. The apartment, however, bore witness that her young friend had paid her the accustomed morning visit; the fire was blazing on a clean comfortable-looking hearth, and every little piece of furniture it contained was arranged with the most scrupulous care. Her devotions were hardly over, when the well-known tap was again heard at the door.

"Come in, my lassie," said the widow, and then lowering her voice, as the light foot of her friend was heard on the threshold, "God," she said, "has been ever kind on me—far, very far aboon my best deservings; and, oh, may He bless and reward her who has done so meikle, meikle for me!" The young girl entered and took her seat beside her.

"You told me, mother," she said, "that to-morrow is Earnest's birthday. I have been thinking of it all last night, and feel as if my heart were turning into stone. But when I am alone, it is always so. There is a cold death-like weight at my breast that makes me unhappy, though, when I come to you, and we speak together, the feeling passes away, and I become cheerful."

"Ah, my bairn," replied the old woman; "I fear I'm no your friend, meikle as I love you. We speak owre, owre often o' the lost; for our foolish hearts find mair pleasure in that than in any-thing else; but ill does it fit us for being alone. Weel do I ken your feeling—a stone deadness o' the heart, a feeling there are no words to express, but that seems as it were insensibility itself turning into pain; an' I ken, too, my lassie, that it is nursed by the very means ye take to flee from it. Ye maun learn to think mair o' the living and less o' the dead. Little, little does it matter, how a puir worn-out creature like me passes the few broken days o' life that remains to her; but ye are young, my Helen, an' the world is a' before you; an' ye maun just try an' live for it."

"To-morrow," rejoined Helen, "is Earnest's birthday. Is it no strange that, when our minds make pictures o' the dead, it is always as they looked best, an' kindest, an' maist life-like. I have been seeing Earnest all night long, as when I saw him on his last birthday; an', Oh, the sharpness o' the pang, when, every now an' then, the back o' the picture is turned to me, an' I see him as he is —dust!"

The widow grasped her young friend by the hand. "Helen," she said, "you will get better when I am taken from you; but, so long as we continue to meet, our thoughts will aye be running the one way. I had a strange dream last night, an' must tell it you. You see yon rock to the east, in the middle o' the little bay, that now rises through the back draught o' the sea, like the hull o' a ship, an' is now buried in a mountain o' foam. I dreamed I was sitting on that rock, in what seemed a bonny summer's morning; the sun was glancin' on the water; an' I could see the white sand far down at the bottom, wi' the reflection o' the little wavies run-ning o'er it in long curls o' goud. But there was no way o' leaving the rock, for the deep waters were round an' round me; an' I saw the tide covering one wee bittie after another, till at last the whole was covered. An' yet I had but little fear; for I remembered that baith Earnest an' William were in the sea afore me; an' I had the feeling that I could hae rest nowhere but wi' them. The water at last closed o'er me, an' I sank frae aff the rock to the sand at the bottom. But death seemed to have no power given him to hurt me; an' I walked as light as ever I hae done on a gowany brae, through the green depths o' the sea. I saw the silvery glitter o' the trout an' the salmon, shining to the sun, far far aboon me, like white pigeons in the lift; an' around me there were crimson starfish, an' sea-flowers, an' long trailing plants that waved in the tide like streamers; an' at length I came to a steep rock wi' a little cave like a tomb in it. 'Here,' I said, 'is the end o' my journey—William is here, an' Earnest.' An', as I looked into the cave, I saw there were bones in it, an' I prepared to take my place beside them. But, as I stooped to enter, some one called me, an' on looking up, there was William. 'Lillias,' he said, 'it is not night yet, nor is that your bed; you are to sleep, not with me, but with Earnest—haste you home, for he is waiting you.' 'Oh, take me to him!' I said; an' then all at once I found myself on the shore, dizzied an' blinded wi' the bright sunshine; for, at the cave, there was a darkness like that o' a simmer's gloamin; an', when I looked up for William, it was Earnest that stood before me, life-like an' handsome as ever; an' you were beside him."

The day had been gloomy and lowering, and, though there was little wind, a tremendous sea, that, as the evening advanced, rose higher and higher against the neighbouring precipice, had been rolling ashore since morning. The wind now began to blow in long hollow gusts among the cliffs, and the rain to patter against the widow's casement.

"It will be a storm from the sea," she said; "the scarts an' gulls hae been flying landward sin' daybreak, an' I hae never seen the ground swell come home heavier against the rocks. Wae's me for the puir sailors!"

"In the lang stormy nights," said Helen, "I canna sleep for thinking o' them, though I have no one to bind me to them now. Only look how the sea rages among the rocks, as if it were a thing o' life an' passion!—that last wave rose to the crane's nest. An', look, yonder is a boat rounding the rock wi' only one man in it. It dances on the surf as if it were a cork, an' the wee bittie o' sail, sae black an' weet, seems scarcely bigger than a napkin. Is it no bearing in for the boat haven below?"

"My poor old eyes," replied the widow, "are growing dim, an' surely no wonder; but yet I think I should ken that boatman. Is it no Eachen Macinla o' Tarbet?"

"Hard-hearted, cruel old man," exclaimed the maiden, "what can be takin' him here? Look how his skiff shoots in like an arrow on the long roll o' the surf!—an' now she is high on the beach. How unfeeling it was o' him to rob you o' your little property in the very first o' your grief! But, see, he is so worn out that he can hardly walk over the rough stones. Ah, me, he is down: wretched old man, I must run to his assistance.—But no, he has risen again. See he is coming straight to the house; an' now he is at the door." In a moment after, Eachen entered the cottage.

"I am perishing, Lillias," he said, "with cold an' hunger, an' can gang nae further; surely ye'll no shut your door on me in a night like this."

The poor widow had been taught in a far different school. She relinquished to the worn-out fisherman her seat by the fire, now hurriedly heaped with fresh fuel, and hastened to set before him the simple viands which her cottage afforded.

As the night darkened, the storm increased. The wind roared among the rocks like the rattling of a thousand carriages over a paved street; and there were times when, after a sudden pause, the blast struck the cottage, as if it were a huge missile flung against it, and pressed on its roof and walls till the very floor rocked, and the rafters strained and shivered like the beams of a stranded vessel. There was a ceaseless patter of mingled rain and snow,— now lower, now louder; and the fearful thunderings of the waves, as they raged among the pointed crags, was mingled with the hoarse roll of the storm along the beach. The old man sat beside the fire, fronting the widow and her companion, with his head reclined nearly as low as his knee, and his hands covering his face. There was no attempt at conversation. He seemed to shudder every time the blast yelled along the roof; and, as a fiercer gust burst open the door, there was a half-muttered ejaculation.

"Heaven itsel hae mercy on them! for what can man do in a night like this?"

"It is black as pitch," exclaimed Helen, who had risen to draw the bolt; "an' the drift flies sae thick that it feels to the hand like a solid snaw wreath. An,' Oh, how it lightens!"

"Heaven itsel' hae mercy on them!" again ejaculated the old man. "My two boys," said he, addressing the widow, "are at the far Frith; an' how can an open boat live in a night like this?"

There seemed something magical in the communication—something that awakened all the sympathies of the poor bereaved woman; and she felt she could forgive him every unkindness.

"Wae's me!" she exclaimed, "it was in such a night as this, an' scarcely sae wild, that my Earnest perished."

The old man groaned and wrung his hands.

In one of the pauses of the hurricane, there was a gun heard from the sea, and shortly after a second. "Some puir vessel in distress," said the widow; "but alas! where can succour come frae in sae terrible a night? There is help only in Ane. Wae's me! would we no better light up a blaze on the floor, an', dearest Helen, draw aff the cover frae the window. My puir Earnest has told me that my light has aften shewed him his bearing frae the deadly bed o' Dunskaith. That last gun"—for a third was now heard booming over the mingled roar of the sea and the wind—"that last gun came frae the very rock edge. Wae's me, wae's me! maun they perish, an' sae near!" Helen hastily lighted a bundle of more fir, that threw up its red, spluttering blaze half-way to the roof, and, dropping the covering, continued to wave it opposite the window. Guns were still heard at measured intervals, but apparently from a safer offing; and the last, as it sounded faintly against the wind, came evidently from the interior of the bay.

"She has escaped," said the old man; "it's a feeble hand that canna do good when the heart is willing—but what has mine been doing a' life long?" He looked at the widow and shuddered.

Towards morning, the wind fell, and the moon, in her last quarter, rose red and glaring out of the Frith, lighting the melancholy roll of the waves, that still came like mountains, and

the broad white belt of surf that skirted the shores. The old fisherman left the cottage, and sauntered along the beach. It was heaped
with huge wreaths of kelp and tangle uprooted by the storm, and
in the hollow of the rocky bay lay the scattered fragments of a
boat. Eachen stooped to pick up a piece of the wreck, in the fearful
expectation of finding some known mark by which to recognise it,
when the light fell full on the swollen face of a corpse that seemed
to be staring at him from out a wreath of weed. It was that of his
eldest son. The body of the younger, fearfully gashed and mangled
by the rocks, lay a few yards farther to the east.

The morning was as pleasant as the night had been boisterous;
and; except that the distant hills were covered with snow, and that
a heavy swell still continued to roll in from the sea, there remained
scarce any trace of the recent tempest. Every hollow of the neighbouring hill had its little runnel, formed by the rains of the previous
night, that now splashed and glistened to the sun. The bushes
round the cottage were well nigh divested of their leaves; but their
red berries—hips and haws, and the juicy fruit of the honeysuckle
—gleamed cheerfully to the light; and a warm steam of vapour,
like that of a May morning, rose from the roof and the little mossy
platform in front. But the scene seemed to have something more
than merely its beauty to recommend it to a young man, drawn
apparently to the spot, with many others, by the fate of the two
unfortunate fishermen, and who now stood gazing on the rocks,
and the hills, and the cottage, as a lover on the features of his
mistress. The bodies had been carried to an old storehouse, which
may still be seen a short mile to the west; and the crowds that,
during the early part of the morning, had been perambulating the
beach, gazing at the wreck, and discussing the various probabilities
of the accident, had gradually dispersed. But this solitary
individual, whom no one knew, remained behind. He was a tall
and swarthy, though very handsome man, of about five-and-
twenty, with a slight scar on his left cheek; his dress, which was
plain and neat, was distinguished from that of the common seaman by three narrow stripes of gold lace on the upper part of one
of the sleeves. He had twice stepped towards the cottage door,
and twice drawn back, as if influenced by some unaccountable feel-

ing—timidity, perhaps, or bashfulness; and yet the bearing of the man gave little indication of either. But, at length, as if he had gathered heart, he raised the latch and went in.

The widow, who had had many visitors that morning seemed to be scarcely aware of his entrance; she was sitting on a low seat beside the fire, her face covered with her hands, while the tremulous rocking motion of her body showed that she was still brooding over the distresses of the previous night. Her companion, who had thrown herself across the bed, was fast asleep. The stranger seated himself beside the fire, which seemed dying amid its ashes, and, turning sedulously from the light of the window, laid his hand gently on the widow's shoulder. She started, and looked up.

"I have strange news for you," he said. "You have long mourned for your husband and your son; but, though the old man has been dead for years, your son, Earnest, is still alive, and is now in the harbour of Cromarty. He is lieutenant of the vessel whose guns you must have heard during the night."

The poor woman seemed to have all power of reply.

"I am a friend of Earnest's," continued the stranger; "and have come to prepare you for meeting with him. It is now five years since his father and he were blown off to sea by a strong gale from the land. They drove before it for four days, when they were picked up by an armed vessel then cruising in the North Sea, and which soon after sailed for the coast of Spanish America. The poor old man sank under the fatigues he had undergone; though Earnest, better able from his youth to endure hardship, was little affected by them. He accompanied us on our Spanish expedition; indeed, he had no choice, for we touched at no British port after meeting with him; and, through good fortune, and what his companions call merit, he has risen to be the second man aboard; and has now brought home with him gold enough, from the Spaniards, to make his old mother comfortable. He saw your light yester-evening, and steered by it to the roadstead, blessing you all the way. Tell me, for he anxiously wished me to inquire of you, whether Helen Henry is yet unmarried."

"It is Earnest,—it is Earnest himself!" exclaimed the maiden, as she started from the widow's bed. In a moment after she was locked in his arms. But why dwell on a scene which I feel myself unfitted to describe?

It was ill, before evening, with old Eachen Macinla. The fatigues of the previous day, the grief and horror of the following night, had prostrated his energies, bodily and mental, and he now lay tossing, in a waste apartment of the storehouse, in the delirium of a fever. The bodies of his two sons occupied the floor below. He muttered, unceasingly, in his ravings, of William and Earnest Beth. They were standing beside him, he said, and every time he attempted to pray for his poor boys and himself, the stern old man laid his cold swollen hands on his lips.

"Why trouble me?" he exclaimed. "Why stare with your white dead eyes on me? Away, old man! the little black shells are sticking in your gray hairs; away to your place! Was it I who raised the wind on the sea?—was it I?—was it I? Uh, u!—no—no, you were asleep—you were fast asleep, and could not see me cut the *swing*; and, besides, it was only a piece of rope. Keep away; touch me not; I am a free man, and will plead for my life. Please your honour, I did not murder these two men; I only cut the rope that fastened their boat to the land. Ha! ha! ha! he has ordered them away, and they have both left me unskaithed." At this moment Earnest Beth entered the apartment, and approached the bed. The miserable old man raised himself on his elbow, and, regarding him with a horrid stare, shrieked out—"Here is Earnest Beth come for me a second time!" and, sinking back on the pillow, instantly expired.

W. E. AYTOUN

HOW WE GOT UP THE
GLENMUTCHKIN RAILWAY AND
HOW WE GOT OUT OF IT

I WAS confoundedly hard up. My patrimony, never of the largest, had been for the last year on the decrease—a herald would have emblazoned it, "ARGENT, a moneybag improper, in detriment"—and though the attenuating process was not excessively rapid, it was, nevertheless, proceeding at a steady ratio. As for the ordinary means and appliances by which men contrive to recruit their exhausted exchequers, I knew none of them. Work I abhorred with a detestation worthy of a scion of nobility; and, I believe, you could just as soon have persuaded the lineal representative of the Howards or Percys to exhibit himself in the character of a mountebank, as have got me to trust my person on the pinnacle of a three-legged stool. The rule of three is all very well for base mechanical souls; but I flatter myself I have an intellect too large to be limited to a ledger. "Augustus," said my poor mother to me, while stroking my hyacinthine tresses, one fine morning, in the very dawn and budding-time of my existence—"Augustus, my dear boy, whatever you do, never forget that you are a gentleman." The maternal maxim sunk deeply into my heart, and I never for a moment have forgotten it.

Notwithstanding this aristocratical resolution, the great practical question "How am I to live!" began to thrust itself unpleasantly before me. I am one of that unfortunate class who have neither uncles nor aunts. For me, no yellow liverless individuals, with characteristic bamboo and pigtail—emblems of half-a-million—returned to his native shores from Ceylon or remote Penang. For me, no venerable spinster hoarded in the Trongate, permitting herself few luxuries during a long-protracted life, save a lass and a lanthorn, a parrot, and the invariable baudrons of antiquity. No such luck was mine. Had all Glasgow perished by some vast epidemic, I should not have found myself one farthing the richer. There would have been no golden balsam for me in the accumulated woes of Tradestown, Shettleston, and Camlachie. The time has been when—according to Washington Irving and other veracious historians—a young man had no sooner got into difficulties than a guardian angel appeared to him in a dream, with the information that at such and such a bridge, or under such and such a tree, he might find, at a slight expenditure of labour, a gallipot secured with bladder, and filled with glittering tomauns; or in the extremity of despair, the youth had only to append himself to a cord, and straightaway the other end thereof, forsaking its staple in the roof, would disclose amidst the fractured ceiling the glories of a profitable pose. These blessed days have long since gone by—at any rate, no such luck was mine. My guardian angel was either woefully ignorant of metallurgy or the stores had been surreptitiously ransacked; and as to the other expedient, I frankly confess I should have liked some better security for its result, than the precedent of the 'Heir of Lynn.'

It is a great consolation amidst all the evils of life, to know that, however bad your circumstances may be, there is always somebody else in nearly the same predicament. My chosen friend and ally, Bob M'Corkindale, was equally hard up with myself, and, if possible, more averse to exertion. Bob was essentially a speculative man—that is, in a philosophical sense. He had once got hold of a stray volume of Adam Smith, and muddled his brains for a whole week over the intricacies of the *Wealth of Nations*. The result was a crude farrago of notions regarding the true nature of money, the soundness of currency, and relative value of capital, with which he nightly favoured an admiring audience at 'The Crow'; for Bob was by no means—in the literal acceptation of the word—a dry philosopher. On the contrary, he perfectly appreciated the merits of each distinct distillery; and was understood to be the compiler of a statistical work entitled, *A Tour through the Alcoholic Districts of Scotland*. It had very early occurred to me, who knew as much of political economy as of the bagpipes, that a gentleman so well versed in the art of accumulating national wealth, must have some remote ideas of applying his principles profitably on a smaller scale. Accordingly, I gave M'Corkindale an unlimited invitation to my lodgings; and, like a good hearty fellow as he was, he availed himself every evening of the license; for I had laid in a fourteen-gallon cask of Oban whisky, and the quality of the malt was undeniable.

These were the first glorious days of general speculation. Railroads were emerging from the hands of the greater into the fingers of the lesser capitalists. Two successful harvests had given a fearful stimulus to the national energy; and it appeared perfectly certain that all the populous towns would be united, and the rich agricultural districts intersected, by the magical bands of iron. The columns of the newspapers teemed every week with the parturition of novel schemes; and the shares were no sooner announced than they were rapidly subscribed for. But what is the use of my saying anything more about the history of last year? Every one of us remembers it perfectly well. It was a capital year on the whole, and put money into many a pocket. About that time, Bob and I commenced operations. Our available capital, or negotiable bullion, in the language of my friend, amounted to about three hundred pounds, which we set aside as a joint fund for speculation. Bob, in a series of learned discourses, had convinced me that it was not only folly, but a positive sin, to leave this sum lying in the bank at a pitiful rate of interest, and otherwise unemployed, whilst every one else in the kingdom was having a pluck at the public pigeon. Somehow or other, we were unlucky in our first attempts. Speculators are like wasps; for when they have once got hold of a ripening and peach-like project, they keep it rigidly for their own swarm, and repel the approach of interlopers. Notwithstanding all our efforts, and very ingenious ones they were, we never, in a single instance, succeeded in procuring an allocation of original shares; and though we did now and then make a hit by purchase, we more frequently bought at a premium, and parted with our scrip at a discount. At the end of six months, we were not twenty pounds richer than before.

"This will never do," said Bob, as he sat one evening in my

rooms compounding his second tumbler. "I thought we were living in an enlightened age; but I find I was mistaken. That brutal spirit of monopoly is still abroad and uncurbed. The principles of free-trade are utterly forgotten, or misunderstood. Else how comes it that David Spreul received but yesterday an allocation of two hundred shares in the Westermidden Junction; whilst your application and mine, for a thousand each, were overlooked? Is this a state of things to be tolerated? Why should he, with his fifty thousand pounds, receive a slapping premium, whilst our three hundred of available capital remains unrepresented? The fact is monstrous, and demands the immediate and serious interference of the legislature."

"It is a bloody shame," I said, fully alive to the manifold advantages of a premium.

"I'll tell you what, Dunshunner," rejoined M'Corkindale. "It's no use going on in this way. We haven't shown half pluck enough. These fellows consider us as snobs, because we don't take the bull by the horns. Now's the time for a bold stroke. The public are quite ready to subscribe for anything—and we'll start a railway for ourselves."

"Start a railway with three hundred pounds of capital!"

"Pshaw, man! you don't know what you're talking about—we've a great deal more capital than that. Have not I told you seventy times over, that everything a man has—his coat, his hat, the tumblers he drinks from, nay, his very corporeal existence—is absolute marketable capital? What do you call that fourteen-gallon cask, I should like to know?"

"A compound of hoops and staves, containing about a quart and a half of spirits—you have effectually accounted for the rest."

"Then it has gone to the fund of profit and loss, that's all. Never let me hear you sport those old theories again. Capital is indestructible, as I am ready to prove to you any day, in half an hour. But let us sit down seriously to business. We are rich enough to pay for the advertisements, and that is all we need care for in the mean time. The public is sure to step in, and bear us out handsomely with the rest."

"But where in the face of the habitable globe shall the railway be? England is out of the question, and I hardly know of a spot in the Lowlands that is not occupied already."

"What do you say to a Spanish scheme—the Alcantara Union? Hang me if I know whether Alcantara is in Spain or Portugal; but nobody else does, and the one is quite as good as the other. Or what would you think of the Palermo Railway, with a branch to the sulphur mines?—that would be popular in the North—or the Pyrenees Direct? They would all go to a premium."

"I must confess I should prefer a line at home."

"Well, then, why not try the Highlands? There must be lots of traffic there in the shape of sheep, grouse, and Cockney tourists, not to mention salmon and other et-ceteras. Couldn't we tip them a railway somewhere in the west?"

"There's Glenmutchkin, for instance—"

"Capital, my dear fellow! Glorious? By Jove, first-rate!" shouted Bob in an ecstasy of delight. "There's a distillery there, you know, and a fishing-village at the foot—at least there used to be six years ago, when I was living with the exciseman. There may be some bother about the population, though. The last laird shipped every mother's son of the aboriginal Celts to America; but, after all, that's not of much consequence. I see the whole thing! Unrivalled scenery—stupendous waterfalls—herds of black cattle—spot where Prince Charles Edward met Macgrugar of Glengrugar and his clan! We could not possibly have lighted on a more promising place. Hand us over that sheet of paper, like a good fellow, and a pen. There is no time to be lost, and the sooner we get out the prospectus the better."

"But, heaven bless you, Bob, there's a great deal to be thought of first. Who are we to get for a provisional committee?"

"That's very true," said Bob, musingly. "We *must* treat them to some respectable names, that is, good sounding ones. I'm afraid there is little chance of our producing a Peer to begin with?"

"None whatever—unless we could invent one, and that's hardly safe—*Burke's Peerage* has gone through too many editions. Couldn't we try the Dormants?"

"That would be rather dangerous in the teeth of the standing orders. But what do you say to a baronet? There's Sir Polloxfen

Tremens. He got himself served the other day to a Nova Scotia baronetcy, with just as much title as you or I have; and he has sported the riband, and dined out on the strength of it ever since. He'll join us at once, for he has not a sixpence to lose."

"Down with him, then," and we headed the Provisional list with the pseudo Orange-tawny.

"Now," said Bob, "it's quite indispensable, as this is a Highland line, that we should put forward a Chief or two. That has always a great effect upon the English, whose feudal notions are rather of the mistiest, and principally derived from Waverley."

"Why not write yourself down as the Laird of M'Corkindale?" said I. "I daresay you would not be negatived by a counter-claim."

"That would hardly do," replied Bob, "as I intend to be Secretary. After all, what's the use of thinking about it? Here goes for an extempore Chief"; and the villain wrote down the name of Tavish M'Tavish of Invertavish.

"I say, though," said I, "we must have a real Highlander on the list. If we go on this way, it will become a Justiciary matter."

"You're devilish scrupulous, Gus," said Bob, who, if left to himself, would have stuck in the names of the heathen gods and goddesses, or borrowed his directors from the Ossianic chronicles, rather than have delayed the prospectus. "Where the mischief are we to find the men? I can think of no others likely to go the whole hog, can you?"

"I don't know a single Celt in Glasgow except old M'Closkie, the drunken porter at the corner of Jamaica Street."

"He's the very man! I suppose, after the manner of his tribe, he will do anything for a pint of whisky. But what shall we call call him? Jamaica Street, I fear, will hardly do for a designation."

"Call him THE M'CLOSKIE. It will be sonorous in the ears of the Saxon!"

"Bravo!" and another Chief was added to the roll of the clans.

"Now," said Bob, "we must put you down. Recollect, all the management—that is, the allocation—will be intrusted to you. Augustus—you haven't a middle name, I think?—well, then, suppose we interpolate 'Reginald', it has a smack of the Crusades.

Augustus Reginald Dunshunner, Esq. of—where, in the name of Munchausen?"

"I'm sure I don't know. I never had any land beyond the contents of a flower-pot. Stay—I rather think I have a superiority somewhere about Paisley."

"Just the thing," cried Bob. "It's heritable property, and therefore titular. What's the denomination?"

"St. Mirrens."

"Beautiful! Dunshunner of St. Mirrens, I give you joy! Had you discovered that a little sooner—and I wonder you did not think of it—we might both of us have had lots of allocations. These are not the times to conceal hereditary distinctions. But now comes the serious work. We must have one or two men of known wealth upon the list. The chaff is nothing without a decoy-bird. Now, can't you help me with a name?"

"In that case," said I, "the game is up, and the whole scheme exploded. I would as soon undertake to evoke the ghost of Croesus."

"Dunshunner," said Bob very seriously, "to be a man of information, you are possessed of marvellous few resources. I am quite ashamed of you. Now listen to me. I have thought deeply upon this subject, and am quite convinced that, with some little trouble, we may secure the co-operation of a most wealthy and influential body—one, too, that is generally supposed to have stood aloof from all speculation of the kind, and whose name would be a tower of strength in the moneyed quarters. I allude," continued Bob, reaching across for the kettle, "to the great Dissenting Interest."

"The what?" cried I, aghast.

"The great Dissenting Interest. You can't have failed to observe the row they have lately been making about Sunday travelling and education. Old Sam Sawley, the coffin-maker, is their principal spokesman here; and wherever he goes the rest will follow, like a flock of sheep bounding after a patriarchal ram. I propose, therefore, to wait upon him to-morrow, and request his co-operation in a scheme which is not only to prove profitable, but to make head against the lax principles of the present age. Leave me alone to tickle him. I consider his name, and those of one or two others belonging to the same meeting-house—fellows with bank-stock, and all sorts of tin, as perfectly secure. These dissenters smell a premium from an almost incredible distance. We can fill up the rest of the committee with ciphers, and the whole thing is done."

"But the engineer—we must announce such an officer as a matter of course."

"I never thought of that," said Bob. "Couldn't we hire a fellow from one of the steamboats?"

"I fear that might get us into trouble. You know there are such things as gradients and sections to be prepared. But there's Watty Solder, the gas-fitter, who failed the other day. He's a sort of civil engineer by trade, and will jump at the proposal like a trout at the tail of a May fly."

"Agreed. Now, then, let's fix the number of shares. This is our first experiment, and I thing we ought to be moderate. No sound political economist is avaricious. Let us say twelve thousand, at twenty pounds a-piece."

"So be it."

"Well, then, that's arranged. I'll see Sawley and the rest to-morrow; settle with Solder, and then write out the prospectus. You look in upon me in the evening, and we'll revise it together. Now, by your leave, let's have in the Welsh rabbit and another tumbler to drink success and prosperity to the Glenmutchkin Railway."

I confess that, when I rose on the morrow, with a slight headache and a tongue indifferently parched, I recalled to memory, not without perturbation of conscience, and some internal qualms, the conversation of the previous evening. I felt relieved, however, after two spoonfuls of carbonate of soda, and a glance at the newspaper, wherein I perceived the announcement of no less than four other schemes equally preposterous with our own. But, after all, what right had I to assume that the Glenmutchkin project would prove an ultimate failure? I had not a scrap of statistical information that might entitle me to form such an opinion. At any rate, Parliament, by substituting the Board of Trade as an initiating body of inquiry, had created a responsible tribunal, and freed us from the chance of obloquy. I saw before me a vision of six months' steady gambling,

at manifest advantage, in the shares, before a report could possibly
be pronounced, or our proceedings be in any way overhauled. Of
course I attended that evening punctually at my friend M'Corkindale's. Bob was in high feather; for Sawley no sooner heard of the
principles upon which the railway was to be conducted, and his
own nomination as a director, than he gave in his adhesion, and
promised his unflinching support to the uttermost. The Prospectus ran as follows:

DIRECT GLENMUTCHKIN RAILWAY
In 12,000 Shares of £20 each. Deposit £1 per Share.
Provisional Committee

SIR POLLOXFEN TREMENS, Bart. of Toddymains.

TAVISH M'TAVISH of Invertavish.

THE M'CLOSKIE.

AUGUSTUS REGINALD DUNSHUNNER, Esq., of St. Mirrens.

SAMUEL SAWLEY, Esq., Merchant.

MHIC-MHAC-VICH-INDUIBH.

PHELIM O'FINLAN, Esq., of Castle-rook, Ireland.

THE CAPTAIN of M'ALCOHOL.

FACTOR for GLENTUMBLERS.

JOHN JOB JOBSON, Esq., Manufacturer.

EVAN M'CLAW of Glenscart and Inveryewky.

JOSEPH HECKLES, Esq.

HABBAKUK GRABBIE, Portioner in Ramoth-Drumclog.

Engineer—WALTER SOLDER, Esq.
Interim-Secretary—ROBERT M'CORKINDALE, Esq.

"The necessity of a direct line of Railway communication
through the fertile and populous district known as the VALLEY of
GLENMUTCHKIN, has been long felt and universally acknowledged.
Independently of the surpassing grandeur of its mountain scenery,
which shall immediately be referred to, and other considerations
of even greater importance, GLENMUTCHKIN is known to the capita-
list as the most important BREEDING STATION in the Highlands of
Scotland, and indeed as the great emporium from which the
southern markets are supplied. It has been calculated by a most

eminent authority, that every acre in the strath is capable of rear-
ing twenty head of cattle; and, as has been ascertained after a careful admeasurement, that there are not less than TWO HUNDRED
THOUSAND improvable acres immediately contiguous to the proposed line of Railway, it may confidently be assumed that the number of cattle to be conveyed along the line will amount to FOUR
MILLIONS annually, which, at the lowest estimate, would yield a
revenue larger, in proportion to the capital subscribed, than that
of any Railway as yet completed within the United Kingdom. From
this estimate the traffic in Sheep and Goats, with which the mountains are literally covered, has been carefully excluded, it having
been found quite impossible (from its extent) to compute the actual
revenue to be drawn from that most important branch. It may,
however, be roughly assumed as from seventeen to nineteen *per
cent* upon the whole, after deduction of the working expenses.

"The population of Glenmutchkin is extremely dense. Its situation on the west coast has afforded it the means of direct communication with America, of which for many years the inhabitants
have actively availed themselves. Indeed, the amount of exportation
of live stock from this part of the Highlands to the Western continent, has more than once attracted the attention of Parliament.
The Manufacturers are large and comprehensive, and include the
most famous distilleries in the world. The Minerals are most
abundant, and amongst these may be reckoned quartz, porphyry,
felspar, malachite, manganese, and basalt.

"At the foot of the valley, and close to the sea, lies the important
village known as the CLACHAN of INVERSTARVE. It is supposed by
various eminent antiquaries to have been the capital of the Picts,
and, amongst the busy inroads of commercial prosperity, it still
retains some interesting traces of its former grandeur. There is a
large fishing station here, to which vessels from every nation resort,
and the demand for foreign produce is daily and steadily increasing.

"As a sporting country Glenmutchkin is unrivalled; but it is by
the tourists that its beauties will most greedily be sought. These
consist of every combination which plastic nature can afford—
cliffs of unusual magnitude and grandeur—waterfalls only second
to the sublime cascades of Norway—woods, of which the bark is a

remarkably valuable commodity. It need scarcely be added, to rouse the enthusiasm inseparable from this glorious glen, that here, in 1745, Prince Charles Edward Stuart, then in the zenith of his hopes, was joined by the brave Sir Grugar M'Grugar at the head of his devoted clan.

"The Railway will be twelve miles long, and can be completed within six months after the Act of Parliament is obtained. The gradients are easy, and the curves obtuse. There are no viaducts of any importance, and only four tunnels along the whole length of the line. The shortest of these does not exceed a mile and a half.

"In conclusion, the projectors of this Railway beg to state that they have determined, as a principle, to set their face AGAINST ALL SUN-DAY TRAVELLING WHATSOEVER, and to oppose EVERY BILL which may hereafter be brought into Parliament, unless it shall contain a clause to that effect. It is also their intention to take up the cause of the poor and neglected STOKER, for whose accommodation, and social, moral, religious, and intellectual improvement, a large stock of evangelical tracts will speedily be required. Tenders of these, in quantities of not less than 12,000 may be sent in to the Interim Secretary. Shares must be applied for within ten days from the present date.

By order of the Provisional Committee,
ROBT. M'CORKINDALE, *Secretary.*

"There!" said Bob, slapping down the prospectus on the table, with the jauntiness of a Cockney vouchsafing a Pint of Hermitage to his guests—"What do you think of that? If it doesn't do the business effectually, I shall submit to be called a Dutchman. That last touch about the stoker will bring us in the subscriptions of the old ladies by the score."

"Very masterly, indeed?" said I. "But who the deuce is Mhic-Mhac-vich-Induibh?"

"A *bona fide* chief, I assure you, though a little reduced: I picked him up upon the Broomielaw. His grandfather had an island somewhere to the west of the Hebrides; but it is not laid down in the maps."

"And the Captain of M'Alcohol?"

"A crack distiller."

"And the Factor for Glentumblers?"

"His principal customer. But, bless you, my dear St. Mirrens! don't bother yourself any more about the committee. They are as respectable a set—on paper at least—as you would wish to see of a summer's morning, and the beauty of it is that they will give us no manner of trouble. Now about the allocation. You and I must restrict ourselves to a couple of thousand shares a-piece. That's only a third of the whole, but it won't do to be greedy."

"But, Bob, consider! Where on earth are we to find the money to pay up the deposits?"

"Can you, the principal director of the Glenmutchkin Railway, ask me, the secretary, such a question? Don't you know that any of the banks will give us tick to the amount 'of half the deposits.' All that is settled already, and you can get your two thousand pounds whenever you please merely for the signing of a bill. Sawley must get a thousand according to stipulation—Jobson, Heckles, and Grabbie, at least five hundred a-piece, and another five hundred, I should think, will exhaust the remaining means of the committee. So that, out of our whole stock, there remain just five thousand shares to be allocated to the speculative and evangelical public. My eyes! won't there be a scramble for them!"

Next day our prospectus appeared in the newspapers. It was read, canvassed, and generally approved of. During the afternoon, I took an opportunity of looking into the Tontine, and whilst under shelter of the *Glasgow Herald*, my ears were solaced with such ejaculations as the following:—

"I say, Jimsy, hae ye seen this grand new prospectus for a railway tae Glenmutchkin?"

"Ay—it looks no that ill. The Hieland lairds are pitting their best fit foremost. Will ye apply for shares?"

"I think I'll tak' twa hundred. Wha's Sir Polloxfen Tremens?"

"He'll be yin o' the Ayrshire folk. He used to rin horses at the Paisley races."

("The devil he did!" thought I.)

"D'ye ken ony o' the directors, Jimsy?"

"I ken Sawley fine. Ye may depend on't, it's a gude thing if he's in't, for he's a howkin' body."

"Then it's sure to gae up. What prem. d'ye think it will bring?"

"Twa pund a share, and maybe mair."

"'Od, I'll apply for three hundred!"

"Heaven bless you, my dear countrymen!" thought I as I sallied forth to refresh myself with a basin of soup, "do but maintain this liberal and patriotic feeling—this thirst for national improvement, internal communication, and premiums—a short while longer, and I know whose fortune will be made."

On the following morning my breakfast-table was covered with shoals of letters, from fellows whom I scarcely ever had spoken to —or who, to use a franker phraseology, had scarcely ever condescended to speak to me—entreating my influence as a director to obtain them shares in the new undertaking. I never bore malice in my life, so I chalked them down, without favouritism, for a certain proportion. Whilst engaged in this charitable work, the door flew open, and M'Corkindale, looking utterly haggard with excitement, rushed in.

"You may buy an estate whenever you please, Dunshunner," cried he, "the world's gone perfectly mad! I have been to Blazes the broker, and he tells me that the whole amount of the stock has been subscribed for four times over already, and he has not yet got in the returns from Edinburgh and Liverpool!"

"Are they good names though, Bob—sure cards—none of your M'Closkies, and M'Alcohols?"

"The first names in the city, I assure you, and most of them holders for investment. I wouldn't take ten millions for their capital."

"Then the sooner we close the list the better."

"I think so too. I suspect a rival company will be out before long. Blazes says the shares are selling already conditionally on allotment, at seven-and-sixpence premium."

"The deuce they are! I say, Bob, since we have the cards in our hands, would it not be wise to favour them with a few hundred at that rate? A bird in the hand, you know, is worth two in the bush, eh?"

"I know no such maxim in political economy," replied the secretary. "Are you mad, Dunshunner? How are the shares ever to go up, if it gets wind that the directors are selling already? Our business just now, is to *bull* the line, not to *bear* it; and if you will trust me, I shall show them such an operation on the ascending scale, as the Stock Exchange has not witnessed for this long and many a day. Then, to-morrow, I shall advertise in the papers that the committee, having received applications for ten times the amount of stock, have been compelled, unwillingly, to close the lists. That will be a slap in the face to the dilatory gentlemen, and send up the shares like wildfire."

Bob was right. No sooner did the advertisement appear, than a simultaneous groan was uttered by some hundreds of disappointed speculators, who with unwonted and unnecessary caution had been anxious to see their way a little before committing themselves to our splendid enterprise. In consequence, they rushed into the market, with intense anxiety to make what terms they could at the earliest stage, and the seven-and-sixpence of premium was doubled in the course of a forenoon.

The allocation passed over very peaceably. Sawley, Heckles, Jobson, Grabbie, and the Captain of M'Alcohol, besides myself, attended, and took part in the business. We were also threatened with the presence of the M'Closkie and Vich-Induibh; but M'Corkindale, entertaining some reasonable doubts as the effect which their corporeal appearance might have upon the representatives of the dissenting interest, had taken the precaution to get them snugly housed in a tavern, where an unbounded supply of gratuitous Ferintosh deprived us of the benefit of their experience. We, however, allotted them twenty shares a-piece. Sir Polloxfen Tremens sent a handsome, though rather illegible letter of apology, dated from an island in Lochlomond, where he was said to be detained on particular business.

Mr Sawley, who officiated as our chairman, was kind enough, before parting, to pass a very flattering eulogium upon the excellence and candour of all the preliminary arrangements. It would now, he said, go forth to the public that this line was not, like some others he could mention, a mere bubble, emanating from the stank of private interest, but a solid, lasting superstructure, based upon the principles of sound return for capital, and serious evangelical truth (hear, hear). The time was fast approaching, when the gravestone, with the words 'HIC OBIIT' chiselled upon it, would be placed at the head of all the other lines which rejected the grand opportunity of conveying education to the stoker. The stoker, in his (Mr Sawley's) opinion, had a right to ask the all-important question, "Am I not a man and a brother?" (Cheers). Much had been said and written lately about a work called *Tracts for the Times*. With the opinions contained in that publication he was not conversant, as it was conducted by persons of another community from that to which he (Mr Sawley) had the privilege to belong. But he hoped very soon, under the auspices of the Glenmutchkin Railway Company, to see a new periodical established, under the title of *Tracts for the Trains*. He never for a moment would relax his efforts to knock a nail into the coffin, which, he might say, was already made, and measured, and cloth-covered for the reception of all establishments; and with these sentiments, and the conviction that the shares must rise, could it be doubted that he would remain a fast friend to the interests of this Company for ever? (much cheering).

After having delivered this address, Mr Sawley affectionately squeezed the hands of his brother directors, leaving several of us much overcome. As, however, M'Corkindale had told me that every one of Sawley's shares had been disposed of in the market the day before, I felt less compunction at having refused to allow that excellent man an extra thousand beyond the amount he had applied for, not withstanding of his broadest hints, and even private entreaties.

"Confound the greedy hypocrite!" said Bob; "does he think we shall let him Burke the line for nothing? No—no! let him go to the brokers and buy his shares back, if he thinks they are likely to rise. I'll be bound he has made a cool five hundred out of them already."

On the day which succeeded the allocation, the following entry appeared in the Glasgow share-lists. 'Direct Glenmutchkin Railway 15s. 15s. 6d. 15s. 6d. 16s. 15s. 6d. 16s. 16s. 6d. 16s. 6d. 16s.

17s. 18s. 18s. 19s. 6d. 21s. 21s. 22s. 6d. 24s. 25s. 6d. 27s. 29s. 29s. 6d. 30s. 31s. pm.'

"They might go higher, and they ought to go higher," said Bob musingly; "but there's not much more stock to come and go upon, and these two share-sharks, Jobson and Grabbie, I know, will be in the market to-morrow. We must not let them have the whip-hand of us. I think upon the whole, Dunshunner, though it's letting them go dog cheap, that we ought to sell half our shares at the present premium, whilst there is a certainty of getting it."

"Why not sell the whole? I'm sure I have no objections to part with every stiver of the scrip on such terms."

"Perhaps," said Bob, "upon general principles you might be right; but then remember that we have a vested interest in the line."

"Vested interest be hanged!"

"That's very well—at the same time it is no use to kill your salmon in a hurry. The bulls have done their work pretty well for us, and we ought to keep something on hand for the bears; they are snuffing at it already. I could almost swear that some of those fellows who have sold to-day are working for a time-bargain."

We accordingly got rid of a couple of thousand shares, the proceeds of which not only enabled us to discharge the deposit loan, but left us a material surplus. Under these circumstances, a two-hand banquet was proposed and unanimously carried, the commencement of which I distinctly remember, but am rather dubious as to the end. So many stories have lately been circulated to the prejudice of railway directors, that I think it my duty to state that this entertainment was scrupulously defrayed by ourselves, and *not* carried to account, either of the preliminary survey, or the expense of the provisional committee.

Nothing effects so great a metamorphosis in the bearing of the outer man as a sudden change of fortune. The anemone of the garden differs scarcely more from its unpretending prototype of the woods, than Robert M'Corkindale, Esq., Secretary and Projector of the Glenmutchkin Railway, differed from Bob M'Corkindale, the seedy frequenter of 'The Crow'. In the days of yore, men eyed the surtout—napless at the velvet collar, and preternaturally

white at the seams—which Bob vouchsafed to wear, with looks of
dim suspicion, as if some faint reminiscence, similar to that which is
said to recall the memory of a former state of existence, suggested
to them a notion that the garment had once been their own. Indeed,
his whole appearance was then wonderfully second-hand. Now he
had cast his slough. A most undeniable Taglioni, with trimmings
just bordering upon frogs, gave dignity to his demeanour and two-
fold amplitude to his chest. The horn eyeglass was exchanged for
one of purest gold, the dingy high-lows for well-waxed Wellingtons,
the Paisley fogle for the fabric of the China loom. Moreover, he
walked with a swagger, and affected in common conversation a
peculiar dialect which he opined to be the purest English, but
which no one—except a bagman—could be reasonably expected to
understand. His pockets were invariably crammed with share-lists;
and he quoted, if he did not comprehend, the money article from
the *Times*. This sort of assumption, though very ludicrous in itself,
goes down wonderfully. Bob gradually became a sort of authority,
and his opinions got quoted on 'Change. He was no ass, notwithstanding his peculiarities, and made good use of his opportunity.

For myself, I bore my new dignities with an air of modest
meekness. A certain degree of starchness is indispensable for a
railway director, if he means to go forward in his high calling and
prosper; he must abandon all juvenile eccentricities, and aim at the
appearance of a decided enemy to free trade in the article of Wild
Oats. Accordingly, as the first step towards respectability, I
eschewed coloured waistcoats, and gave out that I was a marrying
man. No man under forty, unless he is a positive idiot, will stand
forth as a theoretical bachelor. It is all nonsense to say that there
is anything unpleasant in being courted. Attention, whether from
male or female, tickles the vanity; and although I have a reasonable,
and I hope, not unwholesome regard for the gratification of my
other appetites, I confess that this same vanity is by far the most
poignant of the whole. I therefore surrendered myself freely to the
soft allurements thrown in my way by such matronly denizens of
Glasgow as were possessed of stock in the shape of marriageable
daughters; and walked the more readily into their toils, because
every party, though nominally for the purposes of tea, wound up

with a hot supper, and something hotter still by way of assisting the digestion.

I don't know whether it was my determined conduct at the allocation, my territorial title, or a most exaggerated idea of my circumstances, that worked upon the mind of Mr Sawley. Possibly it was a combination of the three; but sure enough few days had elapsed before I received a formal card of invitation to a tea and serious conversation. Now serious conversation is a sort of thing that I never shone in, possibly because my early studies were framed in a different direction; but as I really was unwilling to offend the respectable coffin-maker, and as I found that the Captain of M'Alcohol—a decided trump in his way—had also received a summons, I notified my acceptance.

M'Alcohol and I went together. The Captain, an enormous browny Celt, with superhuman whiskers, and a shock of the fieriest hair, had figged himself out, *more majorum*, in the full Highland costume. I never saw Rob Roy on the stage look half so dignified or ferocious. He glittered from head to foot, with dirk, pistol, and skean-dhu, and at least a hundredweight of cairngorms cast a prismatic glory around his person. I felt quite abashed beside him.

We were ushered into Mr Sawley's drawing-room. Round the walls, and at considerable distances from each other, were seated about a dozen characters, male and female, all of them dressed in sable, and wearing countenances of woe. Sawley advanced, and wrung me by the hand with so piteous an expression of visage, that I could not help thinking some awful catastrophe had just befallen his family.

"You are welcome, Mr Dunshunner—welcome to my humble tabernacle. Let me present you to Mrs Sawley"—and a lady, who seemed to have bathed in the Yellow Sea, rose from her seat, and favoured me with a profound curtsy.

"My daughter—Miss Selina Sawley."

I felt in my brain the scorching glance of the two darkest eyes it ever was my fortune to behold, as the beauteous Selina looked up from the perusal of her handkerchief hem. It was a pity that the other features were not corresponding; for the nose was flat, and the mouth of such dimensions, that Harlequin might have jumped down it with impunity—but the eyes *were* splendid.

In obedience to a sign from the hostess, I sank into a chair beside Selina; and not knowing exactly what to say, hazarded some observation about the weather.

"Yes, it is indeed a suggestive season. How deeply, Mr Dunshunner, we ought to feel the pensive progress of autumn towards a soft and premature decay! I always think, about this time of the year, that nature is falling into a consumption!"

"To be sure, ma'am," said I, rather taken aback by this style of colloquy, "the trees are looking devilishly hectic."

"Ah, you have remarked that too! Strange! it was but yesterday that I was wandering through Kelvin Grove, and as the phantom breeze brought down the withered foliage from the spray, I thought how probable it was that they might ere long rustle over young and glowing hearts deposited prematurely in the tomb!"

This, which struck me as a very passable imitation of Dickens's pathetic writings, was a poser. In default of language, I looked Miss Sawley straight in the face, and attempted a substitute for a sigh. I was rewarded with a tender glance.

"Ah!" said she, "I see you are a congenial spirit. How delightful, and yet how rare it is to meet with any one who thinks in unison with yourself! Do you ever walk in the Necropolis, Mr Dunshunner? It is my favourite haunt of a morning. There we can wean ourselves, as it were, from life, and, beneath the melancholy yew and cypress, anticipate the setting star. How often there have I seen the procession—the funeral of some very, *very* little child"—

"Selina, my love," said Mrs Sawley, "have the kindness to ring for the cookies."

I, as in duty bound, started up to save the fair enthusiast the trouble, and was not sorry to observe my seat immediately occupied by a very cadaverous gentleman, who was evidently jealous of the progress I was rapidly making. Sawley, with an air of great mystery, informed me that this was a Mr Dalgleish of Raxmathrapple, the representative of an ancient Scottish family who claimed an important heritable office. The name, I thought, was familiar to me, but there was something in the appearance of Mr Dalgleish which, notwithstanding the smiles of Miss Selina, rendered a rival-ship in that quarter utterly out of the question.

I hate injustice, so let me do due honour in description to the Sawley banquet. The tea-urn most literally corresponded to its name. The table was decked out with divers platters, containing seed-cakes cut into rhomboids, almond biscuits, and ratafia drops. Also, on the sideboard, there were two salvers, each of which con-tained a congregation of glasses, filled with port and sherry. The former fluid, as I afterwards ascertained, was of the kind adver-tised as 'curious,' and proffered for sale at the reasonable rate of sixteen shillings per dozen. The banquet, on the whole, was rather peculiar than enticing; and, for the life of me, I could not divest myself of the idea that the selfsame viands had figured, not long before, as funeral refreshments at a dirige. No such suspicion seemed to cross the mind of M'Alcohol, who hitherto had remained uneasily surveying his nails in a corner, but at the first symptom of food started forwards, and was in the act of making a clean sweep of the china, when Sawley proposed the singular preliminary of a hymn.

The hymn was accordingly sung. I am thankful to say it was such a one as I never heard before, or expect to hear again; and unless it was composed by the Reverend Saunders Peden in an hour of paroxysm on the moors, I cannot conjecture the author. After this original symphony, tea was discussed, and after tea, to my amazement, more hot brandy-and-water that I ever remember to have seen circulated at the most convivial party. Of course this effected a radical change in the spirits and coversation of the circle. It was again my lot to be placed by the side of the fascinating Selina, whose sentimentality gradually thawed away beneath the influence of sundry sips, which she accepted with a delicate reluctance. This time Dalgleish of Raxmathrapple had not the remotest chance. M'Alcohol got furious, sang Gaelic songs, and even delivered a sermon in genuine Erse, without incurring a rebuke; whilst, for my own part, I must needs confess that I waxed unnecessarily amorous, and the last thing I recollect was the pressure of Mr Sawley's hand at the door, as he denominated me his dear boy, and hoped I would soon come back and visit Mrs Sawley and Selina. The recollection of these passages next morning was the surest antidote to my return.

Three weeks had elapsed, and still the Glenmutchkin Railway shares were at a premium, though rather lower than when we sold. Our engineer, Watty Solder, returned from his first survey of the line, along with an assistant who really appeared to have some remote glimmerings of the science and practice of mensuration. It seemed, from a verbal report, that the line was actually practicable; and the survey would have been completed in a very short time— "If," according to the account of Solder, "there had been ae hoos in the glen. But ever sin' the distillery stoppit—and that was twa year last Martinmas—there wasna a hole whaur a Christian could lay his head, muckle less get white sugar to his toddy, forbye the change-house at the clachan; and the auld luckie that keepit it was sair forfochten wi' the palsy, and maist in the dead-thraws. There was naebody else living within twal miles o' the line, barring a tacksman, a lamiter, and a bauldie."

We had some difficulty in preventing Mr Solder from making this report open and patent to the public, which premature disclosure might have interfered materially with the preparation of our traffic tables, not to mention the marketable value of the shares. We therefore kept him steadily at work out of Glasgow, upon a very liberal allowance, to which, apparently, he did not object.

"Dunshunner," said M'Corkindale to me one day, "I suspect that there is something going on about our railway more than we are aware of. Have you observed that the shares are preternaturally high just now?"

"So much the better. Let's sell."

"I did this morning—both yours and mine, at two pounds ten shillings premium."

"The deuce you did! Then we're out of the whole concern."

"Not quite. If my suspicions are correct, there's a good deal more money yet to be got from the speculation. Somebody has been bulling the stock without orders; and, as they can have no information which we are not perfectly up to, depend upon it, it is done for a purpose. I suspect Sawley and his friends. They have never been quite happy since the allocation; and I caught him yesterday pumping our broker in the back shop. We'll see in a day or two. If they are beginning a bearing operation, I know how to catch them."

And, in effect, the bearing operation commenced. Next day, heavy sales were affected for delivery in three weeks; and the stock, as if waterlogged, began to sink. The same thing continued for the following two days, until the premium became nearly nominal. In the mean time, Bob and I, in conjunction with two leading capitalists whom we let into the secret, bought up steadily every share that was offered; and at the end of a fortnight we found that we had purchased rather more than double the amount of the whole original stock. Sawley and his disciples, who, as M'Corkindale suspected, were at the bottom of the whole transaction, having beared to their heart's content, now came into the market to purchase, in order to redeem their engagements. The following extracts from the weekly share-lists will show the results of their endeavours to regain their lost position:—

GLENMUTCHKIN RAIL., £1 paid

Sat.	Mon.	Tues.	Wed.	Thurs.	Frid.	Sat.
$1\frac{1}{8}$	$2\frac{1}{4}$	$4\frac{3}{8}$	$7\frac{1}{2}$	$10\frac{3}{4}$	$15\frac{3}{8}$	17

and Monday was the day of delivery.

I have no means of knowing in what frame of mind Mr Sawley spent the Sunday, or whether he had recourse for mental consolation to Peden; but on Monday morning he presented himself at my door in full funeral costume, with about a quarter of a mile of crape swathed round his hat, black gloves, and a countenance infinitely more doleful than if he had been attending the internment of his beloved wife.

"Walk in, Mr Sawley," said I cheerfully. "What a long time it is since I have had the pleasure of seeing you—too long indeed for brother directors. How are Mrs Sawley and Miss Selina—won't you take a cup of coffee?"

"Grass, sir, grass!" said Mr Sawley, with a sigh like the groan of a furnace-bellows. "We are all flowers of the oven—weak, erring creatures, every one of us. Ah! Mr Dunshunner! you have been a great stranger at Lykewake Terrace!"

"Take a muffin, Mr Sawley. Anything new in the railway world?"

"Ah, my dear sir—my good Mr Augustus Reginald—I wanted to have some serious conversation with you on that very point. I am afraid there is something far wrong indeed in the present state of our stock."

"Why, to be sure it is high; but that, you know, is a token of the public confidence in the line. After all, the rise is nothing compared to that of several English railways; and individually, I suppose, neither of us have any reason to complain."

"I don't like it," said Sawley, watching me over the margin of his coffee-cup. "I don't like it. It savours too much of gambling for a man of my habits. Selina, who is a sensible girl, has serious qualms on the subject."

"Then why not get out of it? I have no objection to run the risk, and if you like to transact with me, I will pay you ready money for every share you have at the present market price."

Sawley writhed uneasily in his chair.

"Will you sell me five hundred, Mr Sawley? Say the word and it is a bargain."

"A time bargain?" quavered the coffin-maker.

"No. Money down, and scrip handed over."

"I—I can't. The fact is, my dear friend, I have sold all my stock already!"

"Then permit me to ask, Mr Sawley, what possible objection you can have to the present aspect of affairs? You do not surely suppose that we are going to issue new shares and bring down the market, simply because you have realised at a handsome premium?"

"A handsome premium! O Lord!" moaned Sawley.

"Why, what did you get for them?"

"Four, three, and two and a half."

"A very considerable profit indeed," said I; "and you ought to be abundantly thankful. We shall talk this matter over at another time, Mr Sawley, but just now I must beg you to excuse me. I have a particular engagement this morning with my broker—rather a heavy transaction to settle—and so—"

"It's no use beating about the bush, any longer," said Mr

Sawley in an excited tone, at the same time dashing down his crape-covered castor on the floor. "Did you ever see a ruined man with a large family? Look at me, Mr Dunshunner—I'm one, and you've done it!"

"Mr Sawley! are you in your senses?"

"That depends on circumstances. Haven't you been buying stock lately?"

"I am glad to say I have—two thousand Glenmutchkins, I think, and this is the day of delivery."

"Well, then—can't you see how the matter stands? It was I who sold them!'

"Well!"

"Mother of Moses, sir! don't you see I'm ruined?"

"By no means—but you must not swear. I pay over the money for your scrip, and you pocket a premium. It seems to me a very simple transaction."

"But I tell you I haven't got the scrip!" cried Sawley, gnashing his teeth, whilst the cold beads of perspiration gathered largely on his brow.

"This is very unfortunate! Have you lost it?"

"No!—the devil tempted me, and I oversold!"

There was a very long pause, during which I assumed an aspect of serious and dignified rebuke.

"Is it possible?" said I in a low tone, after the manner of Kean's offended fathers. "What! you, Mr Sawley—the stoker's friend—the enemy of gambling—the father of Selina—condescend to so equivocal a transaction? You amaze me! But I never was the man to press heavily on a friend"—here Sawley brightened up—"your secret is safe with me, and it shall be your own fault if it reaches the ears of the Session. Pay me over the difference at the present market price, and I release you of your obligation."

"Then I'm in the Gazette, that's all," said Sawley doggedly, "and a wife and nine beautiful babes upon the parish! I had hoped other things from you, Mr Dunshunner—I thought you and Selina—"

"Nonsense, man! Nobody goes into the Gazette just now—it will be time enough when the general crash comes. Out with your cheque-book, and write me an order for four-and-twenty thousand.

Confound fractions! in these days one can afford to be liberal."

"I haven't got it," said Sawley. "You have no idea how bad our trade has been of late, for nobody seems to think of dying. I have not sold a gross of coffins this fortnight. But I'll tell you what—I'll give you five thousand down in cash, and ten thousand in shares—further I can't go."

"Now, Mr Sawley," said I, "I may be blamed by worldly-minded persons for what I am going to do; but I am a man of principle, and feel deeply for the situation of your amiable wife and family. I bear no malice, though it is quite clear that you intended to make me the sufferer. Pay me fifteen thousand over the counter, and we cry quits for ever."

"Won't you take Camlachie Cemetery shares? They are sure to go up."

"No!"

"Twelve Hundred Cowcaddens' Water, with an issue of new stock next week?"

"Not if they disseminated the Ganges!"

"A thousand Ramshorn Gas—four per cent guaranteed until the act?"

"Not if they promised twenty, and melted down the sun in their retort!"

"Blawweary Iron? Best spec. going."

"No, I tell you once for all! If you don't like my offer—and it is an uncommonly liberal one—say so, and I'll expose you this afternoon upon 'Change."

"Well, then—there's a cheque. But may the—"

"Stop, sir! Any such profane expressions, and I shall insist upon the original bargain. So, then—now we're quits. I wish you a very good-morning, Mr Sawley, and better luck next time. Pray remember me to your amiable family."

The door had hardly closed upon the discomfited coffin-maker, and I was still in the preliminary steps of an extempore *pas seul*, intended as the outward demonstration of exceedingly inward joy, when Bob M'Corkindale entered. I told him the result of the morning's conference.

"You have let him off too easily," said the Political Economist.

"Had I been his creditor, I certainly should have sacked the shares into the bargain. There is nothing like rigid dealing between man and man."

"I am contented with moderate profits," said I; "besides, the image of Selina overcame me. How goes it with Jobson and Grabbie?"

"Jobson has paid, and Grabbie compounded. Heckles—may he die an evil death!—has repudiated, become a lame duck, and waddled; but no doubt his estate will pay a dividend."

"So, then, we are clear of the whole Glenmutchkin business, and at a handsome profit."

"A fair interest for the outlay of capital—nothing more. But I'm not quite done with the concern yet."

"How so? not another bearing operation?"

"No; that cock would hardly fight. But you forget that I am secretary of the company, and have a small account against them for services already rendered. I must do what I can to carry the bill through Parliament; and, as you have now sold your whole shares, I advise you to resign from the direction, go down straight to Glenmutchkin, and qualify yourself for a witness. We shall give you five guineas a-day, and pay all your expenses."

"Not a bad notion. But what has become of M'Closkie, and the other fellow with the jaw-breaking name?"

"Vich-Induibh? I have looked after their interests, and in duty bound, sold their shares at a large premium, and despatched them to their native hills on annuities."

"And Sir Polloxfen?"

"Died yesterday of spontaneous combustion."

As the company seemed breaking up, I thought I could not do better than take M'Corkindale's hint, and accordingly betook myself to Glenmutchkin, along with the Captain of M'Alcohol, and we quartered ourselves upon the Factor for Glentumblers. We found Watty Solder very shaky, and his assistant also lapsing into habits of painful inebriety. We saw little of them except of an evening, for we shot and fished the whole day, and made ourselves remarkably comfortable. By singular good-luck, the plans and sections were lodged in time, and the Board of Trade very handsomely reported in our favour, with a recommendation of what they were pleased to call 'the Glenmutchkin system,' and a hope that it might generally be carried out. What this system was, I never clearly understood; but, of course, none of us had any objections. This circumstance gave an additional impetus to the shares, and they once more went up. I was, however too cautious to plunge a second time into Charybdis, but M'Corkindale did, and again emerged with plunder.

When the time came for the parliamentary contest, we all emigrated to London. I still recollect, with lively satisfaction, the many pleasant days we spent in the metropolis at the company's expense. There were just a neat fifty of us, and we occupied the whole of an hotel. The discussion before the committee was long and formidable. We were opposed by four other companies who patronised lines, of which the nearest was at least a hundred miles distant from Glenmutchkin; but as they founded their opposition upon dissent from 'the Glenmutchkin system' generally, the committee allowed them to be heard. We fought for three weeks a most desperate battle, and might in the end have been victorious, had not our last antagonist, at the very close of his case, pointed out no less than seventy-three fatal errors in the parliamentary plan deposited by the unfortunate Solder. Why this was not done earlier, I never exactly understood; it may be, that our opponents, with gentlemanly consideration, were unwilling to curtail our sojourn in London—and their own. The drama was now finally closed, and after all preliminary expenses were paid, sixpence per share was returned to the holders upon surrender of their scrip.

Such is an accurate history of the Origin, Rise, Progress and Fall of the Direct Glenmutchkin Railway. It contains a deep moral, if anybody has sense enough to see it; if not, I have a new project in my eye for next session, of which timely notice shall be given.

JAMES GRANT

THE STORY OF FARQUHAR SHAW

THIS SOLDIER, whose name, from the circumstances connected with his remarkable story, daring courage, and terrible fate, is still remembered in the regiment, in the early history of which he bears so prominent a part, was one of the first who enlisted in Captain Campbell of Finab's independent band of the *Reicudan Dhu*, or Black Watch, when the six separate companies composing this Highland force were established along the Highland Border in 1729, to repress the predatory spirit of certain tribes, and to prevent the levy of black mail. The company were independent, and at that time wore the clan tartan of their captains, who were Simon Frazer, the celebrated Lord Lovat; Sir Duncan Campbell of Lochnell; Grant of Ballindalloch; Alister Campbell of Finab, whose father fought at Darien; Ian Campbell of Carrick, and Deors Monro of Culcairn.

The privates of these companies were all men of a superior station, being mostly cadets of good families—gentlemen of the old Celtic and patriarchal lines, and of baronial proprietors. In the Highlands, the only genuine mark of aristocracy was descent from the founder of the tribe; all who claimed this were styled *uislain*, or gentlemen, and, as such, when off duty, were deemed the equal of the highest chief in the land. Great care was taken by the six captains to secure men of undoubted courage, of good stature, stately deportment, and handsome figure. Thus, in all the old Highland regiments, but more especially the *Reicudan Dhu*, equality of blood and similarity of descent, secured familiarity and regard between the officers and their men—for the latter deemed themselves inferior to no man who breathed the air of heaven. Hence, according to an English engineer officer, who frequently saw these independent companies, "many of those private gentlemen-soldiers have gillies or servants to attend upon them in their quarters, and upon a march, to carry their provisions, baggage, and firelocks."

Such was the composition of the corps, now first embodied among that remarkable people, the Scottish Highlanders—"a people," says the Historian of Great Britain, "untouched by the Roman or Saxon invasions on the south, and by those of the Danes on the east and west skirts of their country—the *unmixed remains* of that vast Celtic empire, which once stretched from the Pillars of Hercules to Archangel."

The Reicudan Dhu were armed with the usual weapons and accoutrements of the line; but, in addition to these, had the arms of their native country—the broadsword, target, pistol, and long dagger, while the sergeants carried the old Celtic *tuagh*, or Lochaber axe. It was distinctly understood by all who enlisted in this new force, that their military duties were to be confined *within* the Highland Border, where, from the wild, predatory spirit of those clans which dwelt next the Lowlands, it was known that they would find more than enough of military service of the most harassing kind. In the conflicts which daily ensued among the mountains—in the sudden marches by night; the desperate brawls among Caterans, who were armed to the teeth, fierce as nature and outlawry could make them, and who dwelt in wild and pathless fastnesses secluded amid rocks, woods, and morasses, there were few who in courage, energy, daring, and activity equalled Farquhar Shaw, a gentleman from the Braes of Lochaber, who was esteemed the *premier* private in the company of Campbell of Finab, which was then quartered in that district; for each company had its permanent cantonment and scene of operations during the eleven years which succeeded the first formation of the Reicudan Dhu.

Farquhar was a perfect swordsman, and deadly shot alike with the musket and pistol; and his strength was such, that he had been known to twist a horse-shoe, and drive his *skene dhu* to the hilt in a pine log; while his activity and power of enduring hunger, thirst, heat, cold and fatigue, became a proverb among the companies of the Watch: for thus he had been reared and trained by his father, a genuine old Celtic gentleman and warrior, whose memory went back to the days when Dundee led the valiant and true to the field of Rinrory, and in whose arms the viscount fell from his horse in the moment of victory, and was borne to the house of Urrard to die. He was a true Highlander of the old school; for an *old school* has existed in all ages and everywhere, even among the Arabs, the children of Ishmael, in the desert; for they, too, have an olden time to which they look back with regret, as being nobler, better, braver, and purer than the present. Thus, the father of Farquhar Shaw was a grim *duinewassal*, who never broke bread or saw the sun rise without uncovering his head and invoking the names of "God, the Blessed Mary, and St. Colme of the Isle;" who never sat down to a meal without opening wide his gates, that the poor and needy might enter freely; who never refused the use of his purse and sword to a friend or kinsman, and was never seen unarmed, even in his own dining-room; who never wronged any man; but who *never* suffered a wrong or affront to pass, without sharp and speedy vengeance; and who, rather than acknowledge the supremacy of the House of Hanover, died sword in hand at the rising in Glenshiel. For this act, his estates were seized by the House of Breadalbane, and his only son, Farquhar, became a private soldier in the ranks of the Black Watch.

It may easily be supposed, that the son of such a father was imbued with all his cavalier spirit, his loyalty and enthusiasm, and that his mind was filled by all the military, legendary, and romantic memories of his native mountains, the land of the Celts, which, as a fine Irish ballad says, was THEIRS

Ere the Roman or the Saxon, the Norman or the Dane,
Had first set foot in Britain, or trampled heaps of slain,
Whose manhood saw the Druid rite, at forest tree and rock—
And savage tribes of Britain round the shrines of Zernebok;
Which for generations witnessed all the glories of the Gael,
Since their Celtic sires sang war-songs round the sacred fires of
Baal.

When it was resolved by Government to form the six independent Highland companies into one regiment, Farquhar Shaw was left on the sick list at the cottage of a widow, named Mhona Cameron, near Inverlochy, having been wounded in a skirmish with Caterans in Glennevis, and he writhed on his sickbed when his comrades, under Finab, marched for the Birks of Aberfeldy, the muster-place of the whole, where the companies were to be united into one battalion, under the celebrated John Earl of Crawford and Lindesay, the last of his ancient race, a hero covered with wounds and honours won in the services of Britain and Russia.

Weak, wan, and wasted though he was (for his wound, a slash from a pole-axe, had been a severe one), Farquhar almost sprang from bed when he heard the notes of their retiring pipes dying away, as they marched through Maryburgh, and round by the margin of Lochiel. His spirit of honour was ruffled, moreover, by a rumour, spread by his enemies the Caterans, against whom he had fought repeatedly, that he was growing faint-hearted at the prospect of the services of the Black Watch being extended beyond the Highland Border. As rumours to this effect were already finding credence in the glens, the fierce, proud heart of Farquhar burned within him with indignation and unmerited shame.

At last, one night, an old crone, who came stealthily to the cottage in which he was residing, informed him that, by the same outlaws who were seeking to deprive him of his honour, a subtle plan had been laid to surround his temporary dwelling, and put him to death, in revenge for certain wounds inflicted by his sword upon their comrades.

The energy and activity of the Black Watch had long since driven the Caterans to despair, and nothing but the anticipation of killing Farquhar comfortably, and chopping him into ounce pieces at leisure, enabled them to survive their troubles with anything like Christian fortitude and resignation.

"And this is their plan, mother?" said Farquhar to the crone.

"To burn the cottage, and you with it."

"Dioul! say you so, Mother Mhona," he exclaimed; "then 'tis time I were betaking me to the hills. Better have a cool bed for a few nights on the sweet-scented heather, than be roasted in a burning cottage, like a fox in its hole."

In vain the cotters besought him to seek concealment elsewhere; or to tarry until he had gained his full strength.

"Were I in the prime of strength, I would stay here," said Farquhar; "and when sleeping on my sword and target, would fear nothing. If these dogs of Caterans came, they should be welcome to my life, if I could not redeem it by the three best lives in their band; but I am weak as a growing boy, and so shall be off to the free mountain side, and seek the path that leads to the Birks of Aberfeldy."

"But the Birks are far from here, Farquhar," urged old Mhona.

"*Attempt*, and *Did-not*, were the worst of Fingal's hounds," replied the soldier. "Farquhar will owe you a day in harvest for all your kindness; but his comrades wait, and go he must! Would it not be a strange thing and a shameful, too, if all the Reicudan Dhu should march down into the flat, bare land of the Lowland clowns, and Farquhar not be with them? What would Finab, his captain, think? and what would all in Brae Lochaber say?"

"Yet pause," continued the crones.

"Pause! Dhia! my father's bones will soon be clattering in their grave, far away in green Glensheil, where he died for King James, Mhona."

"Beware," continued the old woman, "lest you go for ever, Farquhar."

"It is longer to *for ever* than to Beltane, and by that day I must be at the Birks of Aberfeldy."

Then, seeing that he was determined, the crones muttered among themselves that the *tarvecoill* would fall upon him; but Farquhar Shaw, though far from being free of his native superstitions, laughed aloud; for the tarvecoill is a black cloud, which, if seen on a new-year's eve, is said to portend stormy weather; hence it is a proverb for a misfortune about to happen.

"You were unwise to become a soldier, Farquhar," was their last argument.

"Why?"

"The tongue may tie a knot which the teeth cannot untie."

"As your husbands' tongues did, when they married you all, poor men!" was the good-natured retort of Farquhar. "But fear not for me; ere the snow begins to melt on Ben Nevis, and the sweet wallflower to bloom on the black Castle of Inverlochy, I will be with you all again," he added, while belting his tartan-plaid about him, slinging his target on his shoulder, and whistling upon Bran, his favourite stag-hound; he then set out to join the regiment, by the nearest route, on the skirts of Ben Nevis, resolving to pass the head of Lochlevin, through Larochmohr, and the deep glens that lead towards the Braes of Rannoch, a long, desolate, and perilous journey, but with his sword, his pistols, and gigantic hound to guard him, his plaid for a covering, and the purple heather for a bed wherever he halted, Farquhar feared nothing.

His faithful dog Bran, which had shared his couch and plaid since the time when it was a puppy, was a noble specimen of the Scottish hound, which was used of old in the chase of the white bull, the wolf, and the deer, and which is in reality the progenitor of the common greyhound; for the breed has degenerated in warmer climates than the stern north. Bran (so named from Bran of old) was of such size, strength, and courage, that he was able to drag down the strongest deer; and, in the last encounter with the Caterans of Glen Nevis, he had saved the life of Farquhar, by tearing almost to pieces one who would have slain him, as he lay wounded on the field. His hair was rough and grey; his limbs were muscular and wiry; his chest was broad and deep; his keen eyes were bright as those of an eagle. Such dogs as Bran bear a prominent place in Highland song and story. They were remarkable for their sagacity and love of their master, and their solemn and dirge-like howl was ever deemed ominous and predictive of death and woe.

Bran and his master were inseparable. The noble dog had long been invaluable to him when on hunting expeditions, and now since he had become a soldier in the Reicudan Dhu, Bran was always on guard with him, and the sharer of all his duties; thus Farquhar was wont to assert, "that for watchfulness on sentry, Bran's two ears were worth all the rest in the Black Watch put together."

The sun had set before Farquhar left the green thatched clachan, and already the bases of the purple mountains were dark, though a red glow lingered on their heath-clad summits. Lest some of the Cateran band, of whose malevolence he was now the object, might already have knowledge or suspicion of his departure and be watching him with lynx-like eyes from behind some rock or bracken bush, he pursued for a time a path which led to the westward, until the darkness closed completely in; and then, after casting round him a rapid and searching glance, he struck at once into the old secluded drove-way or Fingalian road, which descended through the deep gorge of Corriehoilzie towards the mouth of Glencoe.

On his left towered Ben Nevis—or "the Mountain of Heaven" —sublime and vast, four thousand three hundred feet and more in height, with its pale summits gleaming in the starlight, under a coating of eternal snow. On his right lay deep glens yawning between pathless mountains that arose in piles above each other, their sides torn and rent by a thousand watercourses, exhibiting rugged banks of rock and gravel, fringed by green waving bracken leaves and black whin bushes, or jagged by masses of stone, lying in piles and heaps, like the black, dreary, and Cyclopean ruins "of an earlier world." Before him lay the wilderness of Larochmohr, a scene of solitary and solemn grandeur, where, under the starlight, every feature of the landscape, every waving bush, or silver birch; every bare scalp of porphyry, and every granite block, torn by storms from the cliffs above; every rugged watercourse, tearing in foam through its deep marl bed between the tufted heather, seemed shadowy, unearthly, and weird—dark and mysterious; and all combined, were more than enough to impress with solemnity the thoughts of any man, but more especially those of a Highlander; for the savage grandeur and solitude of that district at such an hour —the gloaming—were alike, to use a paradox, soothing and terrific.

There was no moon. Large masses of crape-like vapour sailed across the blue sky, and by gradually veiling the stars, made yet darker the gloomy path which Farquhar had to traverse. Even the dog Bran seemed impressed by the unbroken stillness, and trotted close as a shadow by the bare legs of his master.

For a time Farquhar Shaw had thought only of the bloodthirsty Caterans, who in their mood of vengeance at the Black Watch in general, and at him in particular, would have hewn him to pieces without mercy; but now as the distance increased between himself and their haunts by the shores of the Lochy and Eil, other thoughts arose in his mind, which gradually became a prey to the superstition incident alike to his age and country, as all the wild tales he had heard of that sequestered district, and indeed of that identical glen which he was then traversing, crowded upon his memory, until he, Farquhar Shaw, who would have faced any six men sword in hand, or would have charged a grape-shotted battery without fear, actually sighed with apprehension at the waving of a hazel bush on the lone hill side.

Of many wild and terrible things this *locale* was alleged to be the scene, and with some of these the Highland reader may be as familiar as Farquhar.

A party of the Black Watch in the summer of 1738, had marched up the glen, under the command of Corporal Malcolm MacPherson (of whom more anon), with orders to seize a flock of sheep and arrest the proprietor, who was alleged to have "lifted" (*i.e.*, stolen) them from the Camerons of Lochiel. The soldiers found the flock to the number of three hundred, grazing on a hill side, all fat black-faced sheep with fine long wool, and seated near them, crook in hand, upon a fragment of rock, they found the person (one of the Caterans already referred to) who was alleged to have stolen them. He was a strange-looking old fellow, with a long white beard that flowed below his girdle; he was attended by two huge black dogs of fierce and repulsive aspect. He laughed scornfully when arrested by the corporal, and hollowly the echoes of his laughter rang among the rocks, while his giant hounds bayed and erected their bristles, and their eyes flashed as if emitting sparks of fire.

The soldiers now surrounded the sheep and drove them down the hill side into the glen, from whence they proceeded towards Maryburgh, with a piper playing in front of the flock, for it is known that sheep will readily follow the music of the pipe. The Black Watch were merry with their easy capture, but none in MacPherson's party were so merry as the captured shepherd, whom, for security, the corporal had fettered to the left hand of his brother Samuel; and in this order they proceeded for three

miles, until they reached a running stream; when, lo! the whole
of the three hundred fat sheep and the black dogs turned into
clods of brown earth; and, with a wild mocking laugh that seemed
to pass away on the wind which swept the mountain waste, their
shepherd vanished, and no trace of his presence remained but the
empty ring of the fetters which dangled from the left wrist of
Samuel MacPherson, who felt every hair on his head bristle under
his bonnet with terror and affright.

This sombre glen was also the abode of the *Daoine Shie*, or
Good Neighbours, as they are named in the Lowlands; and of this
fact the wife of the pay-sergeant of Farquhar's own company could
bear terrible evidence. These imps are alleged to have a strange
love for abstracting young girls and women great with child, and
leaving in their places bundles of dry branches or withered reeds in
the resemblance of the person thus abstracted, but to all appearance dead or in a trance; they are also exceeding partial to having
their own bantlings nursed by human mothers.

The wife of the sergeant (who was Duncan Campbell of the
family of Duncaves) was without children, but was ever longing to
possess one, and had drunk of all the holy wells in the neighbourhood without finding herself much benefited thereby. On a summer
evening when the twilight was lingering on the hills, she was seated
at her cottage door gazing listlessly on the waters of the Eil, which
were reddened by the last flush of the west, when suddenly a little
man and woman of strange aspect appeared before her—so suddenly that they seemed to have sprung from the ground—and
offered her a child to nurse. Her husband, the sergeant, was absent
on duty at Dumbarton; the poor lonely woman had no one to consult, or from whom to seek permission, and she at once accepted
the charge as one long coveted.

"Take this pot of ointment," said the man, impressively, giving Moina Campbell a box made of shells, "and be careful from
time to time to touch the eyelids of our child therewith."

"Accept this purse of money," said the woman, giving her a
small bag of green silk; "'tis our payment in advance, and anon
we will come again."

The quaint little father and mother then each blew a breath

upon the face of the child and disappeared, or as the sergeant's wife said, seemed to melt away into the twilight haze. The money given by the woman was gold and silver; but Moina knew not its value, for the coins were ancient, and bore the head of King Constantine IV. The child was a strange, pale and wan little creature, with keen, bright, and melancholy eyes; its lean freakish hands were almost transparent, and it was ever sad and moaning. Yet in the care of the sergeant's wife it throve bravely, and always after its eyes were touched with the ointment it laughed, crowed, screamed, and exhibited such wild joy that it became almost convulsed.

This occurred so often that Moina felt tempted to apply the ointment to her own eyes, when lo! she perceived a group of the dwarfish Daoine Shie—little men in trunk hose and sugar-loaf hats, and little women in hoop petticoats and all of a green colour —dancing round her, and making grimaces and antic gestures to amuse the child, which to her horror she was now convinced was a bantling of the spirits who dwelt in Larochmohr!

What was she to do? To offend or seem to fear them was dangerous, and though she was now daily tormented by seeing these green imps about her, she affected unconsciousness and seemed to observe them not; but prayed in her heart for her husband's speedy return, and to be relieved of her fairy charge, to whom she faithfully performed her trust, for in time the child grew strong and beautiful; and when, again on a twilight eve, the parents came to claim it, the woman wept as it was taken from her, for she had learned to love the little creature, though it belonged neither to heaven nor earth.

Some months after, Moina Campbell, more lonely now than ever, was passing through Larochmohr, when suddenly within the circle of a large green fairy ring, she saw thousands, yea myriads of little imps in green trunk house and with sugar-loaf hats, dancing and making merry, and amid them were the child she had nursed and its parents also, and in terror and distress she addressed herself to them.

The tiny voices within the charmed circle were hushed in an instant, and all the little men and women became filled with anger. Their little faces grew red, and their little eyes flashed fire.

"How do *you* see us?" demanded the father of the fairy child, thrusting his little conical hat fiercely over his right eye.

"Did I not nurse your child, my friend!" said Moina, trembling.

"But how do you *see us?*" screamed a thousand little voices.

Moina trembled, and was silent.

"Oho!" exclaimed all the tiny voices, like a breeze of wind, "she has been using our ointment, the insolent mortal!"

"I can alter that," said one fairy man (who being three feet high was a giant among his fellows), as he blew upward in her face, and in an instant all the green multitude vanished from her sight; she saw only the fairy ring and the green bare sides of the silent glen. Of all the myriads she had seen, not one was visible now.

"Fear not, Moina," cried a little voice from the hill side, "for your husband will prosper." It was the fairy child who spoke.

"But his fate will follow him," added another voice, angrily.

Full of fear the poor woman returned to her cottage, from which, to her astonishment, she had been absent ten days and nights; but she saw her husband no more: in the meantime he had embarked for a foreign land, being gazetted to an ensigncy; thus so far the fairy promise of his prospering proved true.

Another story flitted through Farquhar's mind, and troubled him quite as much as its predecessors. In a shieling here a friend of his, when hunting, one night sought shelter. Finding a fire already lighted therein he became alarmed, and clambering into the roof sat upon the cross rafters to wait the event, and ere long there entered a little old man two feet in height. His head, hands, and feet were enormously large for the size of his person; his nose was long, crooked, and of a scarlet hue; his eyes brilliant as diamonds, and they glared in the light of the fire. He took from his back a bundle of reeds, and tying them together, proceeded to blow upon them from his huge mouth and distended cheeks, and as he blew, a skin crept over the dry bundle, which gradually began to assume the appearance of a human face and form.

These proceedings were more than the huntsman on his perch above could endure, and filled by dread that the process below might end in a troublesome likeness of himself, he dropped a sixpence into his pistol (for everything evil is proof to *lead*) and fired straight at the huge head of the spirit or gnome, which vanished with a shriek, tearing away in his wrath and flight the whole of the turf wall on one side of the shieling, which was thus in a moment reduced to ruin.

These memories, and a thousand others of spectral Druids and tall ghastly warriors, through whose thin forms the twinkling stars would shine (but these orbs were hidden now) as they hovered by grey cairns and the grassy graves of old, crowded on the mind of Farquhar; for there were then, and even now *are*, more ghosts, devils, and hobgoblins in the Scottish Highlands than ever were laid of yore in the Red Sea. Nor need we be surprised at this superstition in the early days of the Black Watch, when Dr. Henry tells us, in 1831, that within the last twenty years, when a couple agreed to marry in Orkney, they went to the Temple of the Moon, which was semicircular, and then, on her knees, the woman solemnly invoked the spirit of Woden!

Farquhar, as he strode on, comforted himself with the reflection that those who are born at night—as his mother had a hundred times told him he had been—*never saw spirits*; so he took a good dram from his hunting-flask, and belted his plaid tighter about him, after making a sign of the cross three times, as a protection against all the diablerie of the district, but chiefly against a certain malignant fiend or spirit, who was wont to howl at night among the rocks of Larochmohr, to hurl storms of snow into the deep vale of Corriehoilzie, and toss huge blocks of granite into the deep blue waters of Loch Leven. He shouted on Bran, whistled the march of the Black Watch, "to keep his spirits cheery," and pushed on his way up the mountains, while the broad rain drops of a coming tempest plashed heavily in his face.

He looked up to the "Hill of Heaven." The night clouds were gathering round its awful summit, wheeling, eddying, and floating in whirlwinds from the dark chasms of rock that yawn in its sides. The growling of the thunder among the riven peaks of granite overhead announced that a tempest was at hand; but though Farquhar Shaw had come of a brave and adventurous race, and feared nothing *earthly*, he could not repress a shudder lest the mournful gusts of the rising wind might bear with them the cry of the Tar Uisc, the terrible Water Bull, or the shrieks of the spirit of the storm!

The lonely man continued to toil up that wilderness till he reached the shoulder of the mountain, where, on his right, opened the black narrow gorge, in the deep bosom of which lay Loch Leven, and, on his left, opened the glens that led towards Loch Treig, the haunt of Damh mohr a Vonalia, or Enchanted Stag, which was alleged to live for ever, and be proof to mortal weapons; and now, like a tornado of the tropics, the storm burst forth in all its fury!

The wind seemed to shriek around the mountain summits and to bellow in the gorges below, while the thunder hurtled across the sky, and the lightning, green and ghastly, flashed about the rocks of Loch Leven, shedding, ever and anon, for an instant, a sudden gleam upon its narrow stripe of water, and on the brawling torrents that roared down the mountain sides, and were swelling fast to floods, as the rain, which had long been falling on the frozen summit of Ben Nevis, now descended in a broad and blinding torrent that was swept by the stormy wind over hill and over valley. As Farquhar staggered on, a gleam of lightning revealed to him a little turf shieling under the brow of a pine-covered rock, and making a vigorous effort to withstand the roaring wind, which tore over the bare waste with all the force and might of a solid and palpable body, he reached it on his hands and knees. After securing the rude door, which was composed of three cross bars, he flung himself on the earthen floor of the hut, breathless and exhausted, while Bran, his dog, as if awed by the elemental war without, crept close beside him.

As Farquhar's thoughts reverted to all that he had heard of the district, he felt all a Highlander's native horror of remaining in the *dark* in a place so weird and wild; and on finding near him a quantity of dry wood—bog-pine and oak, stored up, doubtless, by some thrifty and provident shepherd—he produced his flint and tinder-box, struck a light, and, with all the readiness of a soldier and huntsman, kindled a fire in a corner of the shieling, being determined that if it was the place where, about "the hour when churchyards yawn and graves give up their dead," the brownies were alleged to assemble, they should not come upon him unseen or unawares.

Having a venison steak in his haversack, he placed it on the embers to broil, heaped fresh fuel on his fire, and drawing his plaid round Bran and himself, wearied by the toil of his journey on foot in such a night, and over such a country, he gradually dropped asleep, heedless alike of the storm which raved and bellowed in the dark glens below, and round the bare scalps of the vast mountain whose mighty shadows, when falling eastward at eve, darken even the Great Glen of Albyn.

In his sleep, the thoughts of Farquhar Shaw wandered to his comrades, then at the Birks of Aberfeldy. He dreamt that a long time—how long he knew not—had elapsed since he had been in their ranks; but he saw the Laird of Finab, his captain, surveying him with a gloomy brow, while the faces of friends and comrades were averted from him.

"Why is this—how is this?" he demanded.

Then he was told that the Reicudan Dhu were disgraced by the desertion of three of its soldiers, who, on that day, were to die, and the regiment was paraded to witness their fate. The scene with all its solemnity and all its terrors grew vividly before him; he heard the lamenting wail of the pipe as the three doomed men marched slowly past, each behind his black coffin, and the scene of this catastrophe was far, far away, he knew not where; but it seemed to be in a strange country, and then the scene, the sights, and the voices of the people, were foreign to him. In the background, above the glittering bayonets and blue bonnets of the Black Watch, rose a lofty castle of foreign aspect, having a square keep or tower, with four turrets, the vanes of which were shining in the early morning sun. In his ears floated the drowsy hum of a vast and increasing multitude.

Farquhar trembled in every limb as the doomed men passed so near him that he could see their breasts heave as they breathed; but their faces were concealed from him, for each had his head muffled in his plaid, according to the old Highland fashion, when imploring mercy or quarter.

Lots were cast with great solemnity for the firing party or executioners, and, to his horror, Farquhar found himself one of the twelve men chosen for this, to every soldier, most obnoxious duty!

When the time came for firing, and the three unfortunates were kneeling opposite, each within his coffin, and each with his head muffled in a plaid, Farquhar mentally resolved to close his eyes and fire at random against the wall of the castle opposite; but some mysterious and irresistible impulse compelled him to look for a moment, and lo! the plaid had fallen from the face of one of the doomed men, and, to his horror, the dreamer beheld *himself!*

His own face was before him, but ghastly and pale, and his own eyes seemed to be glaring back upon him with affright, while their aspect was wild, sad, and haggard. The musket dropped from his hand, a weakness seemed to overspread his limbs, and writhing in agony at the terrible sight, while a cold perspiration rolled in bead-drops over his clammy brow, the dreamer started, and awoke, when a terrible voice, low but distinct, muttered in his ear—

"Farquhar Shaw, bithidth duil ri fear feachd, ach cha bhi duil ri fear lic!" *

He leaped to his feet with a cry of terror, and found that he was *not* alone, as a little old woman was crouching near the embers of his fire, while Bran, his eyes glaring, his bristles erect, was growling at her with a fierce angry sound, that rivalled the bellowing of the storm, which still continued to rave without.

The aspect of this hag was strange. In the light of the fire which brightened occasionally as the wind swept through the crannies of the shieling, her eyes glittered, or rather glared like fiery sparks; her nose was hooked and sharp; her mouth like an ugly gash; her hue was livid and pale. Her outward attire was a species of yellow mantle, which enveloped her whole form; and her hands, which played or twisted nervously in the generous warmth of the glowing embers, resembled a bundle of freakish knots, or the talons of an aged bird. She muttered to herself at times, and after turning her terrible red eyes twice or thrice covertly and wickedly towards Farquhar, she suddenly snatched the venison steak from amid

* A man may return from an expedition; but there is no hope that he may return from the grave.—*Gaelic Proverb.*

the flames, and, with a chuckle of satisfaction, devoured it steaming hot, and covered as it was with burning cinders.

On Farquhar secretly making a sign of the cross, when beholding this strange proceeding, she turned sharply with a savage expression towards him, and rose to her full stature, which was not more than three feet; and he felt, he knew not why, his heart tremble; for his spirit was already perturbed by the effect of his terrible dream, and clutching the steel collar of Bran (who was preparing to spring at this strange visitor, and seemed to like her aspect as little as his master) he said—

"Woman, who are you?"

"A traveller like yourself, perhaps. But who are *you*?" she asked in a croaking voice.

"Do you know our proverb in Lochaber—

> *What sent the messengers to hell,*
> *But asking what they knew full well?*"

was the reply of Farquhar, as he made a vigorous effort to restrain Bran, whose growls and fury were fast becoming quite appalling; and at this proverb the eyes of the hag seemed to blaze with fresh anger, while her figure became more than ever erect.

"Oich! oich!" grumbled Farquhar, "I would as readily have had the devil as this ugly hag. I have got a shelter, certainly; but with her 'tis out of the cauldron and into the fire. Had she been a brown-eyed lass, to a share of my plaid she had been welcome; but this wrinkled cailloch—down, Bran, down!" he added aloud, as the strong hound strained in his collar, and tasked his master's hand and arm to keep him from springing at the intruder.

"Is this kind or manly of you," she asked, "to keep a wild brute that behaves thus, and to a woman too? Turn him out into the storm; the wind and rain will soon cool his wicked blood."

"Thank you; but in that you must excuse me. Bran and I are as brothers."

"Turn him out, I say," screamed the hag, "or worse may befall him!"

"I shall not turn him out woman," said Farquhar, firmly, while surveying the stranger with some uneasiness; for, to his startled gaze, she seemed to have grown *taller* within the last five minutes. "You have a share of our shelter, and you have had all our supper; but to turn out poor Bran—no, no, that would never do."

To this Bran added a roar of rage, and the fear or fury which blazed in the eyes of the woman fully responded to those of the now infuriated staghound. The glances of each made those of the other more and more fierce.

"Down, Bran; down, I say," said Farquhar. "What the devil hath possessed the dog? I never saw him behave thus before. He must be savage, mother, that you left him none of the savoury venison steak; for all the supper we had was that road-collop from one of MacGillony's brown cattle."

"MacGillony," muttered the hag, spreading her talon-like hands over the embers; "I knew him well."

"You!" exclaimed Farquhar.

"I have said so," she replied with a grin.

"He was a mighty hunter five hundred years ago, who lived and died on the Grampians!"

"And what are five hundred years to me, who saw the waters of the deluge pour through Corriehoilzie, and subside from the slope of Ben Nevis?"

"This is a very good joke, mother," said poor Farquhar, attempting to laugh, while the hideous old woman, who was so small when he first saw her as to be almost a dwarf, was now, palpably, veritably, and without doubt, nearly a head taller than himself; and watchfully he continued to gaze on her, keeping one hand on his dirk and the other on the collar of Bran, whose growls were louder now than the storm that careered through the rocky glen below.

"Woman!" said Farquhar, boldly, "my mind misgives me—there is something about you that I little like; I have just had a dreadful dream."

"A morning dream, too!" chuckled the hag with an elfish grin.

"So I connect your presence here with it."

"Be it so."

"What may that terrible dream foretell?" pondered Farquhar; "for morning dreams are but warnings and presages unsolved.

The blessings of God and all his saints be about me!"

At these words the beldame uttered a loud laugh.

"You are, I presume, a Protestant?" said Farquhar, uneasily.

At this suggestion she laughed louder still, but seemed to grow more and more in stature, till Farquhar became well-nigh sick at heart with astonishment and fear, and began to revolve in his mind the possibility of reaching the door of the shieling and rushing out into the storm, there to commit himself to Providence and the elements. Besides, as her stature grew, her eyes waxed redder and brighter, and her malevolent hilarity increased.

It was a fiend, a demon of the wild, by whom he was now visited and tormented in that sequestered hut.

His heart sank, and as her terrible eyes seemed to glare upon him, and pierce his very soul, a cold perspiration burst over all his person.

"Why do you grasp your dirk, Farquhar—ha! ha!" she asked.

"For the same reason that I hold Bran—to be ready. Am I not one of the King's Reicudan Dhu? But how you know my name?"

" 'Tis a trifle to me, who knew MacGillony."

"From whence came you to-night?"

"From the Isle of Wolves," she replied, with a shout of laughter.

"A story as likely as the rest," said Farquhar, "for that isle is in the Western sea, near unto Coll, the country of the Clan Gillian. You must travel fast."

"Those usually do who travel on the skirts of the wind."

"Woman!" exclaimed Farquhar, leaping up with an emotion of terror which he could no longer control, for her stature now overtopped his own, and ere long her hideous head would touch the rafters of the hut; "thou art either a liar or a fiend! which shall I deem thee?"

"Whichever pleases you most," she replied, starting to her feet.

"Bran, to the proof!" cried Farquhar, drawing his dirk, and preparing to let slip the now maddened hound; "at her, Bran, and hold her down. Good, dog—brave dog! oich, he has a slippery handful that grasps an eel by the tail! at her, Bran, for thou art strong as Cuchullin."

Uttering a roar of rage, the savage dog made a wild bound at

the hag, who, with a yell of spite and defiance, and with a wond-
rous activity, by one spring, left the shieling, and dashing the frail
door to fragments in her passage, rushed out into the dark and
tempestuous night, pursued by the infuriated but baffled Bran—
baffled now, though the fleetest hound on the Braes of Lochaber.

They vanished together in the obscurity, while Farquhar gazed
from the door breathless and terrified. The storm still howled in
the valley, where the darkness was opaque and dense, save when
a solitary gleam of lightning flashed on the ghastly rocks and narrow
defile of Loch Leven; and the roar of the bellowing wind as it
tore through the rocky gorges and deep granite chasms, had in
its sound something more than usually terrific. But, hark! other
sounds came upon the skirts of that hurrying storm.

The shrieks of a fiend, if they could be termed so;—for they
were shrill and high, like cries of pain and laughter mingled. Then
came the loud deep baying, with the yells of a dog, as if in rage
and pain, while a thousand sparks, like those of a rocket, glittered
for a moment in the blackness of the glen, below. The heart of
Farquhar Shaw seemed to stand still for a time, while, dirk in
hand, he continued to peer into the dense obscurity. Again came
the cries of Bran, but nearer and nearer now; and in an instant
more, the noble hound sprang, with a loud whine, to his master's
side, and sank at his feet. It was Bran, the fleet, the strong, the
faithful and the brave; but in what a condition. Torn, lacerated,
covered with blood and frightful wounds—disembowelled and
dying; for the poor animal had only strength to loll out his hot
tongue in an attempt to lick his master's hand before he expired.

"Mother Mary," said Farquhar, taking off his bonnet, inspired
with horror and religious awe, "keep thy blessed hand over me,
for my dog has fought with a demon!"

It may be imagined how Farquhar passed the remainder of that
morning—sleepless and full of terrible thoughts, for the palpable
memory of his dream, and the spisode which followed it, were
food enough for reflection.

With dawn, the storm subsided. The sun arose in a cloudless

sky; the blue mists were wreathed round the brows of Ben Nevis, and a beautiful rainbow seemed to spring from the side of the mountain far beyond the waters of Loch Leven; the dun deer were cropping the wet glistening herbage among the grey rocks; the little birds sang early, and the proud eagle and ferocious gled were soaring towards the rising sun; thus all nature gave promise of a serene summer day.

With his dirk, Farquhar dug a grave for Bran, and lined it with soft and fragrant heather, and there he covered him up and piled a cairn, at which he gave many a sad and backward glance (for it marked where a faithful friend and companion lay) as he ascended the huge mountains of rock, which, on one hand, led to the *Uisc Dhu,* or Vale of the Black Water, and on the other, by the tremendous steep named the Devil's Staircase, to the mouth of Glencoe.

In due time he reached the regiment at its cantonments on the Birks of Aberfeldy, where the independent companies, for the first time were exercised as a battalion by their Lieutenant-Colonel, Sir Robert Munro of Culcairn, who, six years afterwards, was slain at the battle of Falkirk.

Farquhar's terrible dream and adventure in that Highland wilderness were ever before him, and the events subsequent to the formation of the Black Watch into a battalion, with the excitement produced among its soldiers by an unexpected order *to march into England,* served to confirm the gloom that preyed upon his spirits.

The story of how the Black Watch were deceived is well known in the Highlands, though it is only one of the many acts of treachery performed in those days by the British Government in their transactions with the people of that country, when seeking to lessen the adherents of the Stuart cause, and ensnare them into regiments for service in distant lands; hence the many dangerous mutinies which occurred after the enrolment of all the *old* Highland corps.

This unexpected order to march into England caused such a dangerous ferment in the Black Watch, as being a violation of the principles and promise under which it was enrolled, and on which so many Highland gentlemen of good family enlisted in its ranks, that the Lord President, Duncan Forbes of Culloden, warned General Clayton, the Scottish Commander-in-Chief, of the evil effects likely to occur if this breach of faith was persisted in; and to prevent the corps from revolting *en masse,* that officer informed the soldiers that they were to enter England "solely to be seen by King George, who had never seen a highland soldier, and had been graciously pleased to express, or feel great curiosity on the subject".

Cajoled and flattered by this falsehood, the soldiers of the Reicudan Dhu, *all unaware that shipping was ordered to convey them to Flanders,* began their march for England, in the end of March, 1743; and if other proof be wanting that they were deluded, the following announcement in the *Caledonian Mercury* of that year affords it: —

"On Wednesday last, the Lord Sempills Regiment of Highlanders began their march for England, *in order to be reviewed by his Majesty.*"

Everywhere on the march throughout the north of England, they were received with cordiality and hospitality by the people, to whom their garb, aspect, and equipment were a source of interest, and in return, the gentlemen and soldiers of the Reicudan Dhu behaved to the admiration of their officers and of all magistrates; but as they drew nearer to London, according to Major Grose, they were exposed to the malevolent mockery and the national "taunts of the true-bred English clowns, and became gloomy and sullen. Animated even to the humblest private with the feelings of gentlemen," continues this English officer, "they could ill brook the rudeness of boors, nor could they patiently submit to affronts in a country to which they had been called by the *invitation* of their sovereign."

On the 30th April, the regiment reached London, and on the 14th May was reviewed on Finchley Common, by Marshal Wade, before a vast concourse of spectators; but the King, whom they expected to be present, had sailed from Greenwich for Hanover on the same night they entered the English metropolis. Herein they found themselves deceived; for "the King had told them a lie," and the spark thus kindled was soon fanned into a flame.

After the review at Finchley Common, Farquhar Shaw and Corporal Malcolm MacPherson were drinking in a tavern, when three English gentlemen entered, and seating themselves at the same table, entered into conversation, by praising the regiment, their garb, their country, and saying those compliments which are so apt to win the heart of a Scotchman when far from home; and the glens of the Gael seemed then indeed, far, far away, to the imagination of the simple souls who manned the Black Watch in 1743.

Both Farquhar and the corporal being gentlemen, wore the wing of the eagle in their bonnets, and were well educated, and spoke English with tolerable fluency.

"I would that his Majesty had seen us, however," said the corporal; "we have had a long march south from our own country on a bootless errand."

"Can you possibly be so simple as to believe that the King cared a rush on the subject?" asked a gentleman, with an incredulous smile; for he and his companions, like many others who hovered about these new soldiers, were Jacobites and political incendiaries.

"What mean you, sir?" demanded MacPherson, with surprise.

"Why, you simpleton, that story of the King wishing to see you was all a table of a tub—a snare."

"A snare!"

"Yes—a pretext of the ministry to lure you to this distance from your own country, and then transport you bodily for life."

"To where?"

"Oh, that matters little—perhaps to the American plantations."

"Or, to Botany Bay," suggested another, maliciously; "but take another jorum of brandy, and fear nothing; wherever you go, it can't well be a worse place than your own country."

"Thanks, gentlemen," replied Farquhar, loftily, while his hands played nervously with his dirk; "we want no more of your brandy."

"Believe me, sirs," resumed their informant and tormentor, "the real object of the ministry is to get as many fighting men, Jacobites and so forth, out of the Highlands as possible. This is merely part of a new system of government."

"Sirs," exclaimed Farquhar, drawing his dirk with an air of

gravity and determination which caused his new friends at once to put the table between him and them, "will you swear this upon the dirk?"

"How—why?"

"Upon the Holy Iron—we know no oath more binding," continued the Highlander, with an expression of quiet entreaty.

"I'll swear it by the Holy Poker, or anything you please," replied the Englishman, reassured on finding the Celt had no hostile intentions. "'Tis all a fact," he continued, winking to his companions, "for so my good friend Phil Yorke, the Lord Chancellor, who expects soon to be Earl of Hardwick, informed me."

The eyes of the corporal flashed with indignation; and Farquhar struck his forehead as the memory of his terrible dream in the haunted glen rushed upon his memory.

"Oh! yes," said a third gentleman, anxious to add his mite to the growing mischief; "it is all a Whig plot of which you are the victims, as our kind ministry hope that you will all die off like sheep with the rot; or like the Marine Corps; or the Invalids, the old 41st, in Jamaica."

"They dare not deceive us!" exclaimed MacPherson, striking the basket-hilt of his claymore,

"Dare not!"

"No."

"Indeed—why?"

"For in the country of the clans fifty thousand claymores would be on the grindstone to avenge us!"

A laugh followed this outburst.

"King George made you rods to scourge your own countrymen, and now, as useless rods, you are to be flung into the fire," said the first speaker, tauntingly.

"By God and Mary!" began MacPherson, again laying a hand on his sword with sombre fury.

"Peace, Malcolm," interposed Farquhar; "the Saxon is right, and we have been fooled. Bithidh gach ni mar is aill Dhiu. (All things must be as God will have them.) Let us seek the Reicudan Dhu, and woe to the Saxon clowns and to that German churl, their King, if they have deceived us!"

On the march back to London, MacPherson and Farquhar Shaw brooded over what they had heard at Finchley; while to other members of the regiment similar communications had been made, and thus, ere nightfall, every soldier of the Black Watch felt assured that he had been entrapped by a royal falsehood, which the sudden, and to them unaccountable, departure of George II. to Hanover seemed beyond all doubt to confirm.

"In those whom he knows," according to General Stewart, "a Highlander will repose perfect confidence, and if they are his superiors will be obedient and respectful; but ere a stranger can obtain this *confidence*, he must show that he *merits* it. When once it is given, it is constant and unreserved; but if confidence be lost, no man is more suspicious. Every officer of a Highland regiment, on his first joining the corps, must have observed in his little transactions with the men how minute and strict they are in every item; but when once confidence is established, scrutiny ceases, and his word or nod of assent is as good as his bond. In the case in question (the Black Watch), notwithstanding the arts which were practised to mislead the men, they proceeded to no violence, but believing themselves deceived and betrayed, the only remedy that occurred to them was to get back to their own country."

The memory of the commercial ruin at Darien, and of the massacre at Glencoe (the Cawnpore of King William), were too fresh in every Scottish breast not to make the flame of discontent and mistrust spread like wildfire; and thus, long before the bell of St. Paul's had tolled the hour of midnight, the conviction that he had been BETRAYED was firmly rooted in the mind of every soldier of the Black Watch, and measures to baffle those who had deluded and lured them so far from their native mountains were at once proposed, and as quickly acted upon.

At this crisis, the dream of Farquhar was constantly before him, as a foreboding of the terrors to come, and he strove to thrust it from him; but the words of that terrible warning—a man may return from an expedition, but never from the grave—seemed ever in his ears!

On the night after the review, the whole regiment, except its officers, most of whom knew what was on the *tapis*, assembled at twelve o'clock on a waste common near Highgate. The whole were in heavy marching order; and by direction of Corporal Malcolm MacPherson, after carefully priming and loading with ball-cart-ridge, they commenced their march in silence and secrecy and with all speed for Scotland—a wild, daring, and romantic attempt, for they were heedless and ignorant of the vast extent of hostile country that lay between them and their homes, and scarcely knew the route to pursue. They had now but three common ideas;—to keep together, to resist to the last, and to march *north*.

With some skill and penetration they avoided the two great highways, and marched by night from wood to wood, concealing themselves by day so well, that for some time no one knew how or where they had gone, though, by the Lords Justices orders had been issued to all officers commanding troops between London and the Scottish Borders to overtake or intercept them; but the 19th May arrived before tidings reached the metropolis that the Black Watch, one thousand strong, had passed Northampton, and a body of Marshal Wade's Horse (now better known as the 3rd or Prince of Wales's Dragoon Guards) overtook them, when faint by forced and rapid marches, by want of food, of sleep and shelter, the unfortunate regiment had entered Ladywood, about four miles from the market town of Oundle-on-the-Nen, and had, as usual, concealed themselves in a spacious thicket, which, by nine o'clock in the evening, was completely environed by strong columns of English cavalry under General Blakeney.

Captain Ball, of Wade's Horse, approached their bivouac in the dusk, bearer of a flag of truce, and was received by the poor fellows with every respect, and Farquhar Shaw, as interpreter for his com-rades, heard his demands, which were, "that the whole battalion should lay down its arms, and surrender at discretion as mutineers."

"Hitherto we have conducted ourselves quietly and peacefully in the land of those who have deluded and wronged us, even as they wronged and deluded our forefathers," replied Farquhar; "but it may not be so for one day more. Look upon us, sir; we are famished, worn, and desperate. It would move the heart of a stone to know all we have suffered by hunger and thirst, even in this land of plenty."

"The remedy is easy," said the captain.

"Name it, sir."

"Submit."

"We have no such word in our mother-tongue, then how shall I translate it to my comrades, so many of whom are gentlemen?"

"That is your affair, not mine. I give you but the terms dictated by General Blakeney."

"Let the general send us a written promise."

"Written?" reiterated the captain, haughtily.

"By his own hand," continued the Highlander, emphatically; "for here in this land of strangers we know not whom to trust when our King has deceived us."

"And to what must the general pledge himself?"

"That our arms shall not be taken away, and that a free pardon be given to all."

"Otherwise—"

"We will rather be cut to pieces."

"This is your decision?"

"It is," replied Farquhar, sternly.

"Be assured it is a rash one."

"I weigh my words, Saxon, ere I speak them. No man among us will betray his comrade; we are all for one and one for all in the ranks of the Reicudan Dhu!"

The captain reported the result of his mission to the general, who, being well aware that the Highlanders had been entrapped by the Government on one hand, and inflamed to revolt by Jacobite emissaries on the other, was humanely willing to temporize with them, and sent the captain to them once more.

"Surrender yourselves prisoners," said Ball; "lay down your arms, and the general will use all his influence in your favour with the Lords Justices."

"We know of no Lords Justices," they replied. "We acknowledge no authority but the officers who speak our mother-tongue, and our native chiefs who share our blood. To be without arms, in our country, is in itself to be dishonoured."

"Is this still the resolution of your comrades?" asked Captain Ball.

"It is, on my honour as a gentleman and soldier," replied Farquhar.

The English captain smiled at these words, for he knew not the men with whom he had to deal.

"Hitherto, my comrade," said he, "I have been your friend, and the friend of the regiment, and am still anxious to do all I can to save you; but, if you continue in open revolt one hour longer, surrounded as you all are by the King's troops, not a man of you can survive the attack, and be assured that even I, for one, will give quarter to none! Consider well my words—you may survive banishment for a time, but from the grave there is no return."

"The words of my dream!" exclaimed Farquhar, in an agitated tone of voice; "*Bithidh duil ri fear feachd, ach cha bhi duil ri fear lic.* God and Mary, how come they from the lips of this Saxon captain?"

The excitement of the regiment was now so great that Captain Ball requested of Farquhar that two Highlanders should conduct him safely from the wood. Two duinewassals of the Clan Chattan, both corporals, named MacPherson, stepped forward, blew the priming from their pans, and accompanied him to the outposts of his own men—the Saxon *Seidar Dearg*, or Red English soldiers, as the Celts named them.

Here, on parting from them, the good captain renewed his entreaties and promises, which so far won the confidence of the corporals, that, after returning to the regiment, the whole body, in consequence of their statements, agreed to lay down their arms and submit the event to Providence and a court-martial of officers, believing implicitly in the justice of their cause and the ultimate adherence of the Government to the letters of *local* service under which they had enlisted.

Farquhar Shaw and the two corporals of the Clan Chattan nobly offered their own lives as a ransom for the honour and liberties of the regiment, but their offer was declined; for so overwhelming was the force against them, that all in the battalion were alike at the mercy of the ministry. On capitulating, they were at once surrounded by strong bodies of horse, foot, and artillery, with their field-pieces grape-shotted; and the most severe measures were faithlessly and cruelly resorted to by those in authority and those in whom they trusted. While, in defiance of all stipulation and treaty with the Highlanders, the main body of the regiment was marched under escort towards Kent, to embark for Flanders, two hundred privates, chiefly gentlemen or cadets of good family, were selected from its ranks and sentenced to banishment, or service for life in Minorca, Georgia, and the Leeward Isles. The two corporals, Samuel and Malcolm MacPherson, with Farquhar Shaw, were marched back to London, to meet a more speedy, and to men of such spirit as theirs, a more welcome fate.

The examinations of some of these poor fellows prove how they had been deluded into service for the Line.

"I did not desert, sirs," said John Stuart, a gentleman of the House of Urrard, and private in Campbell of Carrick's company. "I repel the insinuation," he continued, with pride; "I wished only to go back to my father's roof and to my own glen, because the inhospitable Saxon churls abused my country and ridiculed my dress. We had no leader; we placed no man over the rest."

"I am neither a Catholic nor a false Lowland Whig," said another private—Gregor Grant, of the family of Rothiemurcus; "but I am a true man, and ready to serve the King, though his actions have proved him a liar! You have said, sirs, that I am afraid to go to Flanders. I am a Highlander, and never yet saw the man I was afraid of. The Saxons told me I was to be transported to the American plantations to work with black slaves. Such was not our bargain with King George. We were but a Watch to serve along the Highland Border, and to keep broken clans from the Braes of Lochaber."

"We were resolved not to be tricked," added Farquhar Shaw. "We will meet the French or Spaniards in any land you please; but we will die, sirs, rather than go, like Saxon rogues, to hoe sugar in the plantations."

"What is your faith?" asked the president of the court-martial.

"The faith of my fathers a thousand years before the hateful sound of the Saxon drum was heard upon the Highland Border!"

"You mean that you have lived—"

"As, please God and the Blessed Mary, I shall die—a Catholic and a Highland gentleman; stooping to none and fearing none—"

"*None*, say you?"

"Save Him who sits upon the right hand of His Father in Heaven."

As Farquhar said this with solemn energy, all the prisoners took off their bonnets and bowed their heads with a religious reverence which deeply impressed the court, but failed to save them.

On the march to the Tower of London, Farquhar was the most resolute and composed of his companions in fetters and misfortune; but on coming in sight of that ancient fortress, his firmness forsook him the blood rushed back upon his heart, and he became deadly pale; for in a moment he recognised the castle of his strange dream—the castle having a square tower, with four vanes and turrets—and then the whole scene of his foreboding vision, when far away in lone Lochaber, came again upon his memory, while the voice of the warning spirit hovered again in his ear, and he knew that the hour of his end was pursuing him!

And now, amid crowds of country clowns and a rabble from the lowest purlieus of London, who mocked and reviled them, the poor Highlanders were marched through the streets of that mighty metropolis (to them, who had been reared in the mountain solitudes of the Gael, a place of countless wonders!) and were thrust into the Tower as prisoners under sentence.

Early on the morning of the 12th July, 1743, when the sun was yet below the dim horizon, and a frowsy fog that lingered on the river was mingling with the city's smoke to spread a gloom over the midsummer morning, all London seemed to be pouring from her many avenues towards Tower Hill, where an episode of no ordinary interest was promised to the sight-loving Cockneys— a veritable military execution, with all its stern terrors and grim solemnity.

All the troops in London were under arms, and long before daybreak had taken possession of an ample space enclosing Tower Hill; and there, conspicuous above all by their high and absurd sugar-loaf caps, were the brilliantly accoutred English and Scots Horse Grenadier Guards, the former under Viscount Cobham,

the latter under Lieutenant-General John Earl of Rothes, K.T.,
and Governor of Duncannon; the Coldstream Guards; the Scots
Fusiliers; and a sombre mass in the Highland garb of dark-green
tartan, whom they surrounded with fixed bayonets.

These last were the two hundred men of the Reicudan Dhu
selected for banishment, previous to which they were compelled
to behold the death, or—as they justly deemed it—the deliberate
murder under trust, of three brave gentlemen, their comrades.

The gates of the Tower revolved, and then the craped and
muffled drums of the Scots Fusilier Guards were heard beating a
dead march before those who were "to return to Lochaber no
more." Between two lines of Yeomen of the Guard, who faced
inwards, the three prisoners came slowly forth, surrounded by an
escort with fixed bayonets, each doomed man marching behind his
coffin, which was borne on the shoulders of four soldiers. On
approaching the parade, each politely raised his bonnet and bowed
to the assembled multitude.

"Courage, gentlemen," said Farquhar Shaw; "I see no gallows
here. I thank God we shall not die a dog's death!"

" 'Tis well," replied MacPherson, "for honour is more precious
than refined gold."

The murmur of the multitude gradually subsided and died
away, like a breeze that passes through a forest, leaving it silent
and still, and then not a sound was heard but the baleful rolling
of the muffled drums and the shrill but sweet cadence of the fifes.
Then came the word, *Halt!* breaking sharply the silence of the
crowded arena, and the hollow sound of the three empty coffins,
as they were laid on the ground, at the distance of thirty paces
from the firing party.

Now the elder brother patted the shoulder of the other, as he
smiled and said—

"Courage—a little time and all will be over—our spirits shall
be with those of our brave forefathers."

"No coronach will be cried over us here, and no cairn will mark
in other times where we sleep in the land of the stranger."

"Brother," replied the other, in the same forcible language, "we
can well spare alike the coronach and the cairn, when to our kins-

men we can bequeath the death task of avenging us!"

"If that bequest be valued, then we shall not die in vain."

Once again they all raised their bonnets and uttered a pious invocation; for now the sun was up, and in the Highland fashion —a fashion old as the days of Baal—they greeted him.

"Are you ready?" asked the provost-marshal.

"All ready," replied Farquhar; *"moch-eirigh 'luain, a ni'n t-suain 'mhairt."* ⋆

This, to them, fatal 12th day of July was a *Monday*; so the proverb was solemnly applicable.

Wan, pale, and careworn they looked, but their eyes were bright, their steps steady, their bearing erect and dignified. They felt themselves victims and martyrs, whose fate would find a terrible echo in the Scottish Highlands; and need I add, that echo *was heard*, when two years afterwards Prince Charles unfurled his standard in Glenfinnan? Thus inspired by pride of birth, of character, and of country—by inborn bravery and conscious innocence, at this awful crisis, they gazed around them without quailing, and exhibited a self-possession which excited the pity and admiration of all who beheld them.

The clock struck the fatal hour at last!

"It is my doom," exclaimed Farquhar; "the hour of my end hath followed me."

They all embraced each other, and declined having their eyes bound up, but stood boldly, each at the foot of his coffin, confronting the levelled muskets of thirty privates of the Grenadier Guards, and they died like the brave men they had lived. One brief paragraph in *St. James's Chronicle* thus records their fate.

"On Monday, the 12th, at six o'clock in the morning, Samuel and Malcolm MacPherson, corporals, and Farquhar Shaw, a private-man, three of the Highland deserters, were shot upon the parade of the Tower pursuant to the sentence of the court-martial. The rest of the Highland prisoners were drawn out to see the execution, and joined in their prayers with great earnestness. They behaved with perfect resolution and propriety. Their bodies were

⋆ Early rising on *Monday* gives a sound sleep on *Tuesday*.—See MacIntosh's *Gaelic Proverbs*.

put into three coffins by three of the prisoners, *their clansmen and namesakes*, and buried in one grave, near the place of execution."

Such is the matter-of-fact record of a terrible fate!

To the slaughter of these soldiers, and the wicked breach of faith perpetrated by the Government, may be traced much of that distrust which characterized the Seaforth Highlanders and other clan regiments in their mutinies and revolts in later years; and nothing inspired greater hatred in the hearts of those who "rose" for Prince Charles in 1745, than the story of the deception and *murder* (for so they named it) of the three soldiers of the Reicudan Dhu by King George at London. "There must have been something more than common in the case and character of these unfortunate men," to quote the good and gallant old General Stewart of Garth, "as Lord John Murray, who was afterwards colonel of the regiment, had portraits of them hung in his dining-room."

This was the first episode in the history of the Black Watch, which soon after covered itself with glory by the fury of its charge at Fontenoy, and on the field of Dettingen exulted that among the dead who lay there was General Clayton, "the Sassenach" whose specious story first lured them from the Birks of Aberfeldy.

GEORGE MACDONALD

THE GOLDEN KEY

THERE WAS a boy who used to sit in the twilight and listen to his great-aunt's stories.

She told him that if he could reach the place where the end of the rainbow stands he would find there a golden key.

"And what is the key for?" the boy would ask. "What is it the key of? What will it open?"

"That nobody knows," his aunt would reply. "He has to find that out."

"I suppose, being gold," the boy once said, thoughtfully, "that I could get a good deal of money for it if I sold it."

"Better never find it than sell it," returned his aunt.

And then the boy went to bed and dreamed about the golden key.

Now all that his great-aunt told the boy about the golden key would have been nonsense, had it not been that their little house stood on the borders of Fairyland. For it is perfectly well known that out of Fairyland nobody ever can find where the rainbow stands. The creature takes such good care of its golden key, always flitting from place to place, lest any one should find it! But in Fairyland it is quite different. Things that look real in this country look very thin indeed in Fairyland, while some of the things that here cannot stand still for a moment, will not move there. So it was not in the least absurd of the old lady to tell her nephew such things about the golden key.

"Did you ever know anybody find it?" he asked, one evening.

"Yes. Your father, I believe, found it."

"And what did he do with it, can you tell me?"

"He never told me."

"What was it like?"

"He never showed it to me."

"How does a new key come there always?"

"I don't know. There it is."

"Perhaps it is the rainbow's egg."

"Perhaps it is. You will be a happy boy if you find the nest."

"Perhaps it comes tumbling down the rainbow from the sky."

"Perhaps it does."

One evening, in summer, he went into his own room, and stood at the lattice-window, and gazed into the forest which fringed the outskirts of Fairyland. It came close up to his great-aunt's garden, and, indeed, sent some straggling trees into it. The forest lay to the east, and the sun, which was setting behind the cottage, looked straight into the dark wood with his level red eye. The trees were all old, and had few branches below, so that the sun could see a great way into the forest and the boy, being keen-sighted, could see almost as far as the sun. The trunks stood like rows of red columns in the shine of the red sun, and he could see down aisle after aisle in the vanishing distance. And as he gazed into the forest he began to feel as if the trees were all waiting for him, and had something they could not go on with till he came to them. But he was hungry, and wanted his supper. So he lingered.

Suddenly, far among the trees, as far as the sun could shine, he saw a glorious thing. It was the end of a rainbow, large and brilliant. He could count all the seven colours, and could see shade after shade beyond the violet; while before the red stood a colour more gorgeous and mysterious still. It was a colour he had never seen before. Only the spring of the rainbow-arch was visible. He could see nothing of it above the trees.

"The golden key!" he said to himself, and darted out of the house, and into the wood.

He had not gone far before the sun set. But the rainbow only glowed the brighter. For the rainbow of Fairyland is not dependent upon the sun, as ours is. The trees welcomed him. The bushes made way for him. The rainbow grew larger and brighter; and at length he found himself within two trees of it.

It was a grand sight, burning away there in silence, with its gorgeous, its lovely, its delicate colours, each distinct, all combining. He could now see a great deal more of it. It rose high into the blue heavens, but bent so little that he could not tell how high the crown of the arch must reach. It was still only a small portion of a huge bow.

He stood gazing at it till he forgot himself with delight—even forgot the key which he had come to seek. And as he stood it grew more wonderful still. For in each of the colours, which was as large as the column of a church, he could faintly see beautiful forms slowly ascending as if by the steps of a winding stair. The forms appeared irregularly—now one, now many, now several, now none —men and women and children—all different, all beautiful.

He drew nearer to the rainbow. It vanished. He started back a step in dismay. It was there again, as beautiful as ever. So he contented himself with standing as near it as he might, and watching the forms that ascended the glorious colours towards the unknown height of the arch, which did not end abruptly, but faded away in the blue air; so gradually that he could not say where it ceased.

When the thought of the golden key returned, the boy very wisely proceeded to mark out in his mind the space covered by the foundation of the rainbow, in order that he might know where to search, should the rainbow disappear. It was based chiefly upon a bed of moss.

Meantime it had grown quite dark in the wood. The rainbow alone was visible by its own light. But the moment the moon rose the rainbow vanished. Nor could any change of place restore the vision to the boy's eyes. So he threw himself down upon the mossy bed, to wait till the sunlight would give him a chance of finding the key. There he fell fast asleep.

When he woke in the morning the sun was looking straight into his eyes. He turned away from it, and the same moment saw a brilliant little thing lying on the moss within a foot of his face. It was the golden key. The pipe of it was of plain gold, as bright as gold could be. The handle was curiously wrought and set with sapphires. In a terror of delight he put out his hand and took it, and had it.

He lay for a while, turning it over and over, and feeding his eyes upon its beauty. Then he jumped to his feet, remembering that the pretty thing was of no use to him yet. Where was the lock to which the key belonged? It must be somewhere, for how could anybody be so silly as make a key for which there was no lock? Where should he go to look for it? He gazed about him, up into the air, down to the earth, but saw no keyhole in the clouds, in the grass, or in the trees.

Just as he began to grow disconsolate, however, he saw something glimmering in the wood. It was a mere glimmer that he saw, but he took it for a glimmer of rainbow, and went towards it.— And now I will go back to the borders of the forest.

Not far from the house where the boy had lived, there was another house, the owner of which was a merchant, who was much away from home. He had lost his wife some years before, and had only one child, a little girl, whom he left to the charge of two servants, who were very idle and careless. So she was neglected and left untidy, and was sometimes ill-used besides.

Now it is well known that the little creatures commonly called fairies, though there are many different kinds of fairies in Fairyland, have an exceeding dislike to untidiness. Indeed, they are quite spiteful to slovenly people. Being used to all the lovely ways of the trees and flowers, and to the neatness of the birds and all woodland creatures, it makes them feel miserable, even in their deep woods and on their grassy carpets, to think that within the same moonlight lies a dirty, uncomfortable, slovenly house. And this makes them angry with the people that live in it, and they would gladly drive them out of the world if they could. They want the whole earth nice and clean. So they pinch the maids black and blue, and play them all manner of uncomfortable tricks.

But this house was quite a shame, and the fairies in the forest could not endure it. They tried everything on the maids without effect, and at last resolved upon making a clean riddance, beginning with the child. They ought to have known that it was not her fault, but they have little principle and much mischief in them, and they thought that if they got rid of her the maids would be sure to be turned away.

So one evening, the poor little girl having been put to bed early, before the sun was down, the servants went off to the village, locking the door behind them. The child did not know she was alone, and lay contentedly looking out of her window towards the forest, of which, however, she could not see much, because of the ivy and other creeping plants which had straggled across her window. All at once she saw an ape making faces at her out of the mirror, and the heads carved upon a great old wardrobe grinning fearfully. Then two old spider-legged chairs came forward into the middle of the room, and began to dance a queer, old-fashioned dance. This set her laughing, and she forgot the ape and the grinning heads. So the fairies saw they had made a mistake, and sent the chairs back to their places. But they knew that she had been reading the story of Silverhair all day. So the next moment she heard the voices of the three bears upon the stairs, big voice, middle voice, and little voice, and she heard their soft, heavy tread, as if they had stockings over their boots, coming nearer and nearer to the door of her room, till she could bear it no longer. She did just as Silverhair did, and as the fairies wanted her to do: she darted to the window, pulled it open, got upon the ivy, and so scrambled to the ground. She then fled to the forest as fast as she could run.

Now, although she did not know it, this was the very best way she could have gone; for nothing is ever so mischievous in its own place as it is out of it; and, besides, these mischievous creatures were only the children of Fairyland, as it were, and there are many other beings there as well; and if a wanderer gets in among them, the good ones will always help him more than the evil ones will be able to hurt him.

The sun was now set, and the darkness coming on, but the child thought of no danger but the bears behind her. If she had looked round, however, she would have seen that she was followed by a very different creature from a bear. It was a curious creature, made like a fish, but covered, instead of scales, with feathers of all colours, sparkling like those of a humming-bird. It had fins, not wings, and swam through the air as a fish does through the water. Its head was like the head of a small owl.

After running a long way, and as the last of the light was disappearing, she passed under a tree with drooping branches. It dropped its branches to the ground all about her, and caught her as in a trap. She struggled to get out, but the branches pressed her closer and closer to the trunk. She was in great terror and distress, when the air-fish, swimming into the thicket of branches, began tearing them with its beak. They loosened their hold at once, and the creature went on attacking them, till at length they let the child go. Then the air-fish came from behind her, and swam on in front, glittering and sparkling all lovely colours; and she followed.

It led her gently along till all at once it swam in at a cottage-door. The child followed still. There was a bright fire in the middle of the floor, upon which stood a pot without a lid, full of water that boiled and bubbled furiously. The air-fish swam straight to the pot and into the boiling water, where it lay quiet. A beautiful woman rose from the opposite side of the fire and came to meet the girl. She took her up in her arms, and said,—

"Ah, you are come at last! I have been looking for you a long time."

She sat down with her on her lap, and there the girl sat staring at her. She had never seen anything so beautiful. She was tall and strong, with white arms and neck, and a delicate flush on her face. The child could not tell what was the colour of her hair, but could not help thinking it had a tinge of dark green. She had not one ornament upon her, but she looked as if she had just put off quantities of diamonds and emeralds. Yet here she was in the simplest, poorest little cottage, where she was evidently at home. She was dressed in shining green.

The girl looked at the lady, and the lady looked at the girl.

"What is your name?" asked the lady.

"The servants always called me Tangle."

"Ah, that was because your hair was so untidy. But that was their fault, the naughty women! Still it is a pretty name, and I will call you Tangle too. You must not mind my asking you questions, for you may ask me the same questions, every one of them, and any others that you like. How old are you?"

"Ten," answered Tangle.

"You don't look like it," said the lady.

"How old are you, please?" returned Tangle.

"Thousands of years old," answered the lady.

"You don't look like it," said Tangle.

"Don't I? I think I do. Don't you see how beautiful I am?"

And her great blue eyes looked down on the little Tangle, as if all the stars in the sky were melted in them to make their brightness.

"Ah! but," said Tangle, "when people live long they grow old. At least I always thought so."

"I have no time to grow old," said the lady. "I am too busy for that. It is very idle to grow old.—But I cannot have my little girl so untidy. Do you know I can't find a clean spot on your face to kiss?"

"Perhaps," suggested Tangle, feeling ashamed, but not too much so to say a word for herself—"perhaps that is because the tree made me cry so."

"My poor darling!" said the lady, looking now as if the moon were melted in her eyes, and kissing her little face, dirty as it was, "the naughty tree must suffer for making a girl cry."

"And what is your name, please?" asked Tangle.

"Grandmother," answered the lady.

"Is it really?"

"Yes, indeed. I never tell stories, even in fun."

"How good of you!"

"I couldn't if I tried. It would come true if I said it, and then I should be punished enough."

And she smiled like the sun through a summer-shower.

"But now," she went on, "I must get you washed and dressed, and then we shall have some supper."

"Oh! I had supper long ago," said Tangle.

"Yes, indeed you had," answered the lady—"three years since you ran away from the bears. You don't know that it is three years since you ran away from the bears. You are thirteen and more now."

Tangle could only stare. She felt quite sure it was true.

"You will not be afraid of anything I do with you—will you?" said the lady.

"I will try very hard not to be; but I can't be certain, you know," replied Tangle.

"I like your saying so, and I shall be quite satisfied," answered the lady.

She took off the girl's night-gown, rose with her in her arms, and going to the wall of the cottage, opened a door. Then Tangle saw a deep tank, the sides of which were filled with green plants, which had flowers of all colours. There was a roof over it like the roof of the cottage. It was filled with beautiful clear water, in which swam a multitude of such fishes as the one that had led her to the cottage. It was the light their colours gave that showed the place in which they were.

The lady spoke some words Tangle could not understand, and threw her into the tank.

The fishes came crowding about her. Two or three of them got under her head and kept it up. The rest of them rubbed themselves all over her, and with their wet feathers washed her quite clean. Then the lady, who had been looking on all the time, spoke again; whereupon some thirty or forty of the fishes rose out of the water underneath Tangle, and so bore her up to the arms the lady held out to take her. She carried her back to the fire, and, having dried her well, opened a chest, and taking out the finest linen garments, smelling of grass and lavender, put them upon her, and over all a green dress, just like her own, shining like hers, and soft like hers, going into just such lovely folds from the waist, where it was tied with a brown cord, to her bare feet.

"Won't you give me a pair of shoes too, grandmother?" said Tangle.

"No, my dear; no shoes. Look here. I wear no shoes."

So saying, she lifted her dress a little, and there were the loveliest white feet, but no shoes. Then Tangle was content to go without shoes too. And the lady sat down with her again, and combed her hair, and brushed it, and then left it to dry while she got the supper.

First she got bread out of one hole in the wall; then milk out of another; then several kinds of fruit out of a third; and then she went to the pot on the fire, and took out the fish now nicely cooked, and, as soon as she had pulled off its feathered skin, ready to be eaten.

"But," exclaimed Tangle. And she stared at the fish, and could say no more.

"I know what you mean," returned the lady. "You do not like to eat the messenger that brought you home. But it is the kindest return you can make. The creature was afraid to go until it saw me put the pot on, and heard me promise it should be boiled the moment it returned with you. Then it darted out of the door at once. You saw it go into the pot of itself the moment it entered, did you not?"

"I did," answered Tangle, "and I thought it very strange; but then I saw you, and forgot all about the fish."

"In Fairyland," resumed the lady, as they sat down to the table, "the ambition of the animals is to be eaten by the people; for that is their highest end in that condition. But they are not therefore destroyed. Out of that pot comes something more than the dead fish, you will see."

Tangle now remarked that the lid was on the pot. But the lady took no further notice of it till they had eaten the fish, which Tangle found nicer than any fish she had ever tasted before. It was as white as snow, and as delicate as cream. And the moment she had swallowed a mouthful of it, a change she could not describe began to take place in her. She heard a murmuring all about her, which became more and more articulate, and at length, as she went on eating, grew intelligible. By the time she had finished her share, the sounds of all the animals in the forest came crowding through the door to her ears; for the door still stood wide open, though it was pitch dark outside; and they were no longer sounds only; they were speech, and speech that she could understand. She could tell what the insects in the cottage were saying to each other too. She had even a suspicion that the trees and flowers all about the cottage were holding midnight communications with each other; but what they said she could not hear.

As soon as the fish was eaten, the lady went to the fire and took the lid off the pot. A lovely little creature in human shape, with large white wings, rose out of it, and flew round and round the roof of the cottage; then dropped, fluttering, and nestled in the lap of the lady. She spoke to it some strange words, carried it to the door, and threw it out into the darkness. Tangle heard the flapping of its wings die away in the distance.

"Now have we done the fish any harm?" she said, returning.

"No," answered Tangle, "I do not think we have. I should not mind eating one every day."

"They must wait their time, like you and me too, my little Tangle."

And she smiled a smile which the sadness in it made more lovely.

"But," she continued, "I think we may have one for supper to-morrow."

So saying she went to the door of the tank, and spoke; and now Tangle understood her perfectly.

"I want one of you," she said,—"the wisest."

Thereupon the fishes got together in the middle of the tank, with their heads forming a circle above the water, and their tails a larger circle beneath it. They were holding a council, in which their relative wisdom should be determined. At length one of them flew up into the lady's hand, looking lively and ready.

"You know where the rainbow stands?" she asked.

"Yes, mother, quite well," answered the fish.

"Bring home a young man you will find there, who does not know where to go."

The fish was out of the door in a moment. Then the lady told Tangle it was time to go to bed; and, opening another door in the side of the cottage, showed her a little arbour, cool and green, with a bed of purple heath growing in it, upon which she threw a large wrapper made of the feathered skins of the wise fishes, shining gorgeous in the firelight. Tangle was soon lost in the strangest, loveliest dreams. And the beautiful lady was in every one of her dreams.

In the morning she woke to the rustling of leaves over her head, and the sound of running water. But, to her surprise, she could find no door—nothing but the moss-grown wall of the cottage. So she crept through an opening in the arbour, and stood in the forest. Then she bathed in a stream that ran merrily through the trees, and felt happier; for having once been in her grandmother's pond, she must be clean and tidy ever after; and, having put on her green dress, felt like a lady.

She spent that day in the wood, listening to the birds and beasts and creeping things. She understood all that they said, though she could not repeat a word of it; and every kind had a different language, while there was a common though more limited understanding between all the inhabitants of the forest. She saw nothing of the beautiful lady, but she felt that she was near all the time; and she took care not to go out of sight of the cottage. It was round, like a snow-hut or a wigwam; and she could see neither door nor window in it. The fact was, it had no windows, and though it was full of doors, they all opened from the inside, and could not even be seen from the outside.

She was standing at the foot of a tree in the twilight, listening to a quarrel between a mole and a squirrel, in which the mole told the squirrel that the tail was the best of him, and the squirrel called the mole Spade-fists, when, the darkness having deepened around her, she became aware of something shining in her face, and looking round, saw that the door of the cottage was open, and the red light of the fire flowing from it like a river through the darkness. She left Mole and Squirrel to settle matters as they might, and darted off to the cottage. Entering, she found the pot boiling on the fire, and the grand, lovely lady sitting on the other side of it.

"I've been watching you all day," said the lady. "You shall have something to eat by-and-by, but we must wait till our supper comes home."

She took Tangle on her knee, and began to sing to her—such songs as made her wish she could listen to them for ever. But at length in rushed the shining fish, and snuggled down in the pot. It was followed by a youth who had outgrown his worn garments. His face was ruddy with health, and in his hand he carried a little jewel, which sparkled in the firelight.

The first words the lady said were,—

"What is that in your hand, Mossy?"

Now Mossy was the name his companions had given him,

because he had a favourite stone covered with moss, on which he used to sit whole days reading; and they said the moss had begun to grow upon him too.

Mossy held out his hand. The moment the lady saw that it was the golden key, she rose from her chair, kissed Mossy on the forehead, made him sit down on her seat, and stood before him like a servant. Mossy could not bear this, and rose at once. But the lady begged him, with tears in her beautiful eyes, to sit, and let her wait on him.

"But you are a great, splendid, beautiful lady," said Mossy.

"Yes, I am. But I work all day long—that is my pleasure; and you will have to leave me so soon!"

"How do you know that, if you please, madam?" asked Mossy.

"Because you have got the golden key."

"But I don't know what it is for. I can't find the key-hole. Will you tell me what to do?"

"You must look for the key-hole. That is your work. I cannot help you. I can only tell you that if you look for it you will find it."

"What kind of box will it open? What is there inside?"

"I do not know. I dream about it, but I know nothing."

"Must I go at once?"

"You may stop here to-night, and have some of my supper. But you must go in the morning. All I can do for you is to give you clothes. Here is a girl called Tangle, whom you must take with you."

"That *will* be nice," said Mossy.

"No, no!" said Tangle. "I don't want to leave you, please, grandmother."

"You must go with him, Tangle. I am sorry to lose you, but it will be the best thing for you. Even the fishes, you see, have to go into the pot, and then out into the dark. If you fall in with the Old Man of the Sea, mind you ask whether he has not got some more fishes ready for me. My tank is getting thin."

So saying, she took the fish from the pot, and put the lid on as before. They sat down and ate the fish, and then the winged creature rose from the pot, circled the roof, and settled on the lady's lap. She talked to it, carried to the door, and threw it out into the dark. They heard the flap of its wings die away in the distance.

The lady then showed Mossy into just such another chamber as that of Tangle; and in the morning he found a suit of clothes laid beside him. He looked very handsome in them. But the wearer of Grandmother's clothes never thinks about how he or she looks, but thinks always how handsome other people are.

Tangle was very unwilling to go.

"Why should I leave you? I don't know the young man," she said to the lady.

"I am never allowed to keep my children long. You need not go with him except you please, but you must go some day; and I should like you to go with him, for he has the golden key. No girl need be afraid to go with a youth that has the golden key. You will take care of her, Mossy, will you not?"

"That I will," said Mossy.

And Tangle cast a glance at him, and thought she should like to go with him.

"And," said the lady, "if you should lose each other as you go through the—the—I never can remember the name of that country,—do not be afraid, but go on and on."

She kissed Tangle on the mouth and Mossy on the forehead, led them to the door, and waved her hand eastward. Mossy and Tangle took each other's hand and walked away into the depth of the forest. In his right hand Mossy held the golden key.

They wandered thus a long way, with endless amusement from the talk of the animals. They soon learned enough of their language to ask them necessary questions. The squirrels were always friendly, and gave them nuts out of their own hoards; but the bees were selfish and rude, justifying themselves on the ground that Tangle and Mossy were not subjects of their queen, and charity must begin at home, though indeed they had not one drone in their poorhouse at the time. Even the blinking moles would fetch them an earth-nut or a truffle now and then, talking as if their mouths, as well as their eyes and ears, were full of cotton wool, or their own velvety fur. By the time they got out of the forest they were very fond of each other, and Tangle was not in the least sorry that her grandmother had sent her away with Mossy.

At length the trees grew smaller, and stood farther apart, and the ground began to rise, and it got more and more steep, till the trees were all left behind, and the two were climbing a narrow path with rocks on each side. Suddenly they came upon a rude doorway, by which they entered a narrow gallery cut in the rock. It grew darker and darker, till it was pitch-dark, and they had to feel their way. At length the light began to return, and at last they came out upon a narrow path on the face of a lofty precipice. This path went winding down the rock to a wide plain, circular in shape, and surrounded on all sides by mountains. Those opposite to them were a great way off, and towered to an awful height, shooting up sharp, blue, ice-enamelled pinnacles. An utter silence reigned where they stood. Not even the sound of water reached them.

Looking down, they could not tell whether the valley below was a grassy plain or a great still lake. They had never seen any space look like it. The way to it was difficult and dangerous, but down the narrow path they went, and reached the bottom in safety. They found it composed of smooth, light-coloured sandstone, undulating in parts, but mostly level. It was no wonder to them now that they had not been able to tell what it was, for this surface was everywhere crowded with shadows. It was a sea of shadows. The mass was chiefly made up of the shadows of leaves innumerable, of all lovely and imaginative forms, waving to and fro, floating and quivering in the breath of a breeze whose motion was unfelt, whose sound was unheard. No forests clothed the mountain-sides, no trees were anywhere to be seen, and yet the shadows of the leaves, branches, and stems of all various trees covered the valley as far as their eyes could reach. They soon spied the shadows of flowers mingled with those of the leaves, and now and then the shadow of a bird with open beak, and throat distended with song. At times would appear the forms of strange, graceful creatures, running up and down the shadow-boles and along the branches, to disappear in the wind-tossed foliage. As they walked they waded knee-deep in the lovely lake. For the shadows were not merely lying on the surface of the ground, but heaped up above it like substantial forms of darkness, as if they had been cast upon a thousand different planes of the air. Tangle and Mossy often lifted their heads and gazed upwards to descry whence the shadows came; but they could see nothing more than a bright mist spread above them, higher than the tops of the mountains, which stood clear against it. No forests, no leaves, no birds were visible.

After a while, they reached more open spaces, where the shadows were thinner; and came even to portions over which shadows only flitted, leaving them clear for such as might follow. Now a wonderful form, half bird-like half human, would float across on outspread sailing pinions. Anon an exquisite shadow group of gambolling children would be followed by the loveliest female form, and that again by the grand stride of a Titanic shape, each disappearing in the surrounding press of shadowy foliage. Sometimes a profile of unspeakable beauty or grandeur would appear for a moment and vanish. Sometimes they seemed lovers that passed linked arm in arm, sometimes father and son, sometimes brothers in loving contest, sometimes sisters entwined in gracefullest community of complex form. Sometimes wild horses would tear across, free, or bestrode by noble shadows of ruling men. But some of the things which pleased them most they never knew how to describe.

About the middle of the plain they sat down to rest in the heart of a heap of shadows. After sitting for a while, each, looking up, saw the other in tears: they were each longing after the country whence the shadows fell.

"We *must* find the country from which the shadows come," said Mossy.

"We must, dear Mossy," responded Tangle. "What if your golden key should be the key to *it*?"

"Ah! that would be grand," returned Mossy. "But we must rest here for a little, and then we shall be able to cross the plain before night."

So he lay down on the ground, and about him on every side, and over his head, was the constant play of wonderful shadows. He could look through them, and see the one behind the other, till they mixed in a mass of darkness. Tangle, too, lay admiring, and wondering, and longing for the country whence the shadows came. When they were rested they rose and pursued their journey.

How long they were in crossing this plain I cannot tell; but before night Mossy's hair was streaked with grey, and Tangle had got wrinkles on her forehead.

As evening drew on, the shadows fell deeper and rose higher. At length they reached a place where they rose above their heads, and made all dark around them. Then they took hold of each other's hand, and walked on in silence and in some dismay. They felt the gathering darkness, and something strangely solemn besides, and the beauty of the shadows ceased to delight them. All at once Tangle found that she had not a hold of Mossy's hand, though when she lost it she could not tell.

"Mossy, Mossy!" she cried aloud in terror.

But no Mossy replied.

A moment after, the shadows sank to her feet, and down under her feet, and the mountains rose before her. She turned towards the gloomy region she had left, and called once more upon Mossy. There the gloom lay tossing and heaving, a dark, stormy, foamless sea of shadows, but no Mossy rose out of it, or came climbing up the hill on which she stood. She threw herself down and wept in despair.

Suddenly she remembered that the beautiful lady had told them, if they lost each other in a country of which she could not remember the name, they were not to be afraid, but to go straight on.

"And besides," she said to herself, "Mossy has the golden key, and so no harm will come to him, I do believe."

She rose from the ground, and went on.

Before long she arrived at a precipice, in the face of which a stair was cut. When she had ascended half-way, the stair ceased, and the path led straight into the mountain. She was afraid to enter, and turning again towards the stair, grew giddy at sight of the depth beneath her, and was forced to throw herself down in the mouth of the cave.

When she opened her eyes, she saw a beautiful little creature with wings standing beside her, waiting.

"I know you," said Tangle. "You are my fish."

"Yes. But I am a fish no longer. I am an aëranth now."

"What is that?" asked Tangle.

"What you see I am," answered the shape. "And I am come to lead you through the mountain."

"Oh, thank you, dear fish—aëranth I mean," returned Tangle, rising.

Thereupon the aëranth took to his wings, and flew on through the long narrow passage, reminding Tangle very much of the way he had swum on before when he was a fish. And the moment his white wings moved, they began to throw off a continuous shower of sparks of all colours, which lighted up the passage before them. —All at once he vanished, and Tangle heard a low, sweet sound, quite different from the rush and crackle of his wings. Before her was an open arch, and through it came light, mixed with the sound of sea-waves.

She hurried out, and fell, tired and happy, upon the yellow sand of the shore. There she lay, half asleep with weariness and rest, listening to the low plash and retreat of the tiny waves, which seemed ever enticing the land to leave off being land, and become sea. And as she lay, her eyes were fixed upon the foot of a great rainbow standing far away against the sky on the other side of the sea. At length she fell fast asleep.

When she awoke, she saw an old man with long white hair down to his shoulders, leaning upon a stick covered with green buds, and so bending over her.

"What do you want here, beautiful woman?" he said.

"Am I beautiful? I am so glad!" answered Tangle, rising. "My grandmother is beautiful."

"Yes. But what do you want?" he repeated, kindly.

"I think I want you. Are not you the Old Man of the Sea?"

"I am."

"Then grandmother says, have you any more fishes ready for her?"

"We will go and see, my dear," answered the old man, speaking yet more kindly than before. "And I can do something for you, can I not?"

"Yes—show me the way up to the country from which the shadows fall," said Tangle.

For there she hoped to find Mossy again.

"Ah! indeed, that would be worth doing," said the old man. "But I cannot, for I do not know the way myself. But I will send you to the Old Man of the Earth. Perhaps he can tell you. He is much older than I am."

Leaning on his staff, he conducted her along the shore to a steep rock, that looked like a petrified ship turned upside down. The door of it was the rudder of a great vessel, ages ago at the bottom of the sea. Immediately within the door was a stair in the rock, down which the old man went, and Tangle followed. At the bottom the old man had his house, and there he lived.

As soon as she entered it, Tangle heard a strange noise, unlike anything she had ever heard before. She soon found that it was the fishes talking. She tried to understand what they said; but their speech was so old-fashioned, and rude, and undefined, that she could not make much of it.

"I will go and see about those fishes for my daughter," said the Old Man of the Sea.

And moving a slide in the wall of his house, he first looked out, and then tapped upon a thick piece of crystal that filled the round opening. Tangle came up behind him, and peeping through the window into the heart of the great deep green ocean, saw the most curious creatures, some very ugly, all very odd, and with especially queer mouths, swimming about everywhere, above and below, but all coming towards the window in answer to the tap of the Old Man of the Sea. Only a few could get their mouths against the glass; but those who were floating miles away yet turned their heads towards it. The Old Man looked through the whole flock carefully for some minutes, and then turning to Tangle, said,—

"I am sorry I have not got one ready yet. I want more time than she does. But I will send some as soon as I can."

He then shut the slide.

Presently a great noise arose in the sea. The Old Man opened the slide again, and tapped on the glass, whereupon the fishes were all as still as sleep.

"They were only talking about you," he said. "And they do speak such nonsense!—To-morrow," he continued, "I must show you the way to the Old Man of the Earth. He lives a long way from here."

"Do let me go at once," said Tangle.

"No. That is not possible. You must come this way first."

He led her to a hole in the wall, which she had not observed before. It was covered with the green leaves and white blossoms of a creeping plant.

"Only white-blossoming plants can grow under the sea," said the Old Man. "In there you will find a bath, in which you must lie till I call you."

Tangle went in, and found a smaller room or cave, in the further corner of which was a great basin hollowed out of a rock, and half-full of the clearest sea-water. Little streams were constantly running into it from cracks in the wall of the cavern. It was polished quite smooth inside, and had a carpet of yellow sand in the bottom of it. Large green leaves and white flowers of various plants crowded up and over it, draping and covering it almost entirely.

No sooner was she undressed and lying in the bath, than she began to feel as if the water were sinking into her, and she were receiving all the good of sleep without undergoing its forgetfulness. She felt the good coming all the time. And she grew happier and more hopeful that she had been since she lost Mossy. But she could not help thinking how very sad it was for a poor old man to live there all alone, and have to take care of a whole seaful of stupid and riotous fishes.

After about an hour, as she thought, she heard his voice calling her, and rose out of the bath. All the fatigue and aching of her long journey had vanished. She was as whole, and strong, and well as if she had slept for seven days.

Returning to the opening that led into the other part of the house, she started back with amazement, for through it she saw the form of a grand man, with a majestic and beautiful face, waiting for her.

"Come," he said; "I see you are ready."

She entered with reverence.

"Where is the Old Man of the Sea?" she asked, humbly.

"There is no one here but me," he answered smiling. "Some people call me the Old Man of the Sea. Others have another name for me, and are terribly frightened when they meet me taking a walk by the shore. Therefore I avoid being seen by them, for they are so afraid, that they never see what I really am. You see me now.—But I must show you the way to the Old Man of the Earth."

He led her into the cave where the bath was, and there she saw, in the opposite corner a second opening in the rock.

"Go down that stair, and it will bring you to him," said the Old Man of the Sea.

With humble thanks Tangle took her leave. She went down the winding-stair, till she began to fear there was no end to it. Still down and down it went, rough and broken, with springs of water bursting out of the rocks and running down the steps beside her. It was quite dark about her, and yet she could see. For after being in that bath, people's eyes always give out a light they can see by. There were no creeping things in the way. All was safe and pleasant, though so dark and damp and deep.

At last there was not one step more, and she found herself in a glimmering cave. On a stone in the middle of it sat a figure with its back towards her—the figure of an old man bent double with age. From behind she could see his white beard spread out on the rocky floor in front of him. He did not move as she entered, so she passed round that she might stand before him and speak to him. The moment she looked in his face, she saw that he was a youth of marvellous beauty. He sat entranced with the delight of what he beheld in a mirror of something like silver, which lay on the floor at his feet, and which from behind she had taken for his white beard. He sat on, heedless of her presence, pale with the joy of his vision. She stood and watched him. At length, all trembling, she spoke. But her voice made no sound. Yet the youth lifted up his head. He showed no surprise, however, at seeing her—only smiled a welcome.

"Are you the Old Man of the Earth?" Tangle had said.

And the youth answered, and Tangle heard him, though not with her ears:

"I am. What can I do for you?"

"Tell me the way to the country whence the shadows fall."

"Ah! That I do not know. I only dream about it myself. I see its shadows sometimes in my mirror: the way to it I do not know. But I think the Old Man of the Fire must know. He is much older than I am. He is the oldest of all."

"Where does he live?"

"I will show you the way to his place. I never saw him myself."

So saying, the young man rose, and then stood for a while gazing at Tangle.

"I wish I could see that country too," he said. "But I must mind my work."

He led her to the side of the cave, and told her to lay her ear against the wall.

"What do you hear?" he asked.

"I hear," answered Tangle, "the sound of a great water running inside the rock."

"That river runs down to the dwelling of the oldest man of all —the Old Man of the Fire. I wish I could go to see him. But I must mind my work. The river is the only way to him."

Then the Old Man of the Earth stooped over the floor of the cave, raised a huge stone from it, and left it leaning. It disclosed a great hole that went plumb-down.

"That is the way," he said.

"But there are no stairs."

"You must throw yourself in. There is no other way."

She turned and looked him full in the face—stood so for a whole minute, as she thought: it was a whole year—then threw herself headlong into the hole.

When she came to herself, she found herself gliding down fast and deep. Her head was underwater, but that did not signify, for, when she thought about it, she could not remember that she had breathed once since her bath in the cave of the Old Man of the Sea. When she lifted up her head a sudden and fierce heat struck her, and she sank it again instantly, and went sweeping on.

Gradually the stream grew shallower. At length she could hardly keep her head under. Then the water could carry her no farther.

She rose from the channel, and went step for step down the burning descent. The water ceased altogether. The heat was terrible. She felt scorched to the bone, but it did not touch her strength. It grew hotter and hotter. She said, "I can bear it no longer." Yet she went on.

At the long last, the stair ended at a rude archway in an all but glowing rock. Through this archway Tangle fell exhausted into a cool mossy cave. The floor and walls were covered with moss—green, soft, and damp. A little stream spouted from a rent in the rock and fell into a basin of moss. She plunged her face into it and drank. Then she lifted her head and looked around. Then she rose and looked again. She saw no one in the cave. But the moment she stood upright she had a marvellous sense that she was in the secret of the earth and all its ways. Everything she had seen, or learned from books; all that her grandmother had said or sung to her; all the talk of the beasts, birds, and fishes; all that had happened to her on her journey with Mossy, and since then in the heart of the earth with the Old man and the Older man—all was plain: she understood it all, and saw that everything meant the same thing though she could not have put it into words again.

The next moment she descried, in a corner of the cave, a little naked child, sitting on the moss. He was playing with balls of various colours and sizes, which he disposed in strange figures upon the floor beside him. And now Tangle felt that there was something in her knowledge which was not in her understanding. For she knew there must be an infinite meaning in the change and sequence and individual forms of the figures into which the child arranged the balls, as well as in the varied harmonies of their colours, but what it all meant she could not tell.* He went on busily, tirelessly, playing his solitary game, without looking up, or seeming to know that there was a stranger in his deep-withdrawn cell. Diligently as a lace-maker shifts her bobbins, he shifted and arranged his balls. Flashes of meaning would now pass from them to Tangle, and now again all would be not merely obscure, but utterly dark. She stood looking for a long time, for there was

*I think I must be indebted to Novalis for these geometrical figures.
G. MACDONALD.

fascination in the sight; and the longer she looked the more an indescribable vague intelligence went on rousing itself in her mind. For seven years she had stood there watching the naked child with his coloured balls, and it seemed to her like seven hours, when all at once the shape the balls took, she knew not why, reminded her of the Valley of Shadows, and she spoke: —

"Where is the Old Man of the Fire?" she said.

"Here I am," answered the child, rising and leaving his balls on the moss. "What can I do for you?"

There was such an awfulness of absolute repose on the face of the child that Tangle stood dumb before him. He had no smile, but the love in his large gray eyes was deep as the centre. And with the repose there lay on his face a shimmer as of moonlight, which seemed as if any moment it might break into such a ravishing smile as would cause the beholder to weep himself to death. But the smile never came, and the moonlight lay there unbroken. For the heart of the child was too deep for any smile to reach from it to his face.

"Are you the oldest man of all?" Tangle at length, although filled with awe, ventured to ask.

"Yes, I am. I am very, very old. I am able to help you, I know. I can help everybody."

And the child drew near and looked up in her face so that she burst into tears.

"Can you tell me the way to the country the shadows fall from?" she sobbed.

"Yes. I know the way quite well. I go there myself sometimes. But you could not go my way; you are not old enough. I will show you how you can go."

"Do not send me out into the great heat again," prayed Tangle.

"I will not," answered the child.

And he reached up, and put his little cool hand on her heart.

"Now," he said, "you can go. The fire will not burn you. Come."

He led her from the cave, and following him through another archway, she found herself in a vast desert of sand and rock. The sky of it was of rock, lowering over them like solid thunderclouds;

and the whole place was so hot that she saw, in bright rivulets, the yellow gold and white silver and red copper trickling molten from the rocks. But the heat never came near her.

When they had gone some distance, the child turned up a great stone, and took something like a egg from under it. He next drew a long curved line in the sand with his finger, and laid the egg on it. He then spoke something Tangle could not understand. The egg broke, a small snake came out, and, lying in the line in the sand, grew and grew till he filled it. The moment he was thus full grown, he began to glide away, undulating like a sea-wave.

"Follow that serpent," said the child. "He will lead you the right way."

Tangle followed the serpent. But she could not go far without looking back at the marvellous Child. He stood alone in the midst of the glowing desert, beside a fountain of red flame that had burst forth at his feet, his naked whiteness glimmering a pale rosy red in the torrid fire. There he stood, looking after her, till, from the lengthening distance, she could see him no more. The serpent went straight on, turning neither to the right nor left.

Meantime Mossy had got out of the lake of shadows, and, following his mournful, lonely way, had reached the sea-shore. It was a dark, stormy evening. The sun had set. The wind was blowing from the sea. The waves had surrounded the rock within which lay the Old Man's House. A deep water rolled between it and the shore, upon which a majestic figure was walking alone.

Mossy went up to him and said,—

"Will you tell me where to find the Old Man of the Sea?"

"I am the Old Man of the Sea," the figure answered.

"I see a strong kingly man of middle age," returned Mossy.

Then the Old Man looked at him more intently, and said,—

"Your sight, young man, is better than that of most who take this way. The night is stormy: come to my house and tell me what I can do for you."

Mossy followed him. The waves flew from before the footsteps of the Old Man of the Sea, and Mossy followed upon dry sand.

When they had reached the cave, they sat down and gazed at each other.

Now Mossy was an old man by this time. He looked much older than the Old Man of the Sea, and his feet were very weary.

After looking at him for moment, the Old Man took him by the hand and led him into his inner cave. There he helped him to undress, and laid him in the bath. And he saw that one of his hands Mossy did not open.

"What have you in that hand?" he asked.

Mossy opened his hand, and there lay the golden key.

"Ah!" said the Old Man, "that accounts for your knowing me. And I know the way you have to go."

"I want to find the country whence the shadows fall," said Mossy.

"I dare say you do. So do I. But meantime, one thing is certain.— What is that key for, do you think?"

"For a keyhole somewhere. But I don't know why I keep it. I never could find the keyhole. And I have lived a good while, I believe," said Mossy, sadly. "I'm not sure that I'm not old. I know my feet ache."

"Do they?" said the Old Man, as if he really meant to ask the question; and Mossy, who was still lying in the bath, watched his feet for a moment before he replied.

"No, they do not," he answered. "Perhaps I am not old either."

"Get up and look at yourself in the water."

He rose and looked at himself in the water, and there was not a gray hair on his head or a wrinkle on his skin.

"You have tasted of death now," said the Old Man. "It is good?"

"It is good," said Mossy. "It is better than life."

"No," said the Old Man: "it is only more life.—Your feet will make no holes in the water now."

"What do you mean?"

"I will show you that presently."

They returned to the outer cave, and sat and talked together for a long time. At length the Old Man of the Sea rose, and said to Mossy,—

"Follow me."

He led him up the stair again, and opened another door. They stood on the level of the raging sea, looking towards the east.

Across the waste of waters, against the bosom of a fierce black cloud, stood the foot of a rainbow, glowing in the dark.

"This indeed is my way," said Mossy, as soon as he saw the rainbow, and stepped out upon the sea. His feet made no holes in the water. He fought the wind, and clomb the waves, and went on towards the rainbow.

The storm died away. A lovely day and a lovelier night followed. A cool wind blew over the wide plain of the quiet ocean. And still Mossy journeyed eastward. But the rainbow had vanished with the storm.

Day after day he held on, and he thought he had no guide. He did not see how a shining fish under the waters directed his steps. He crossed the sea, and came to a great precipice of rock, up which he could discover but one path. Nor did this lead him farther than half-way up the rock, where it ended on a platform. Here he stood and pondered.—It could not be that the way stopped here, else what was the path for? It was a rough path, not very plain, yet certainly a path.—He examined the face of the rock. It was smooth as glass. But as his eyes kept roving hopelessly over it, something glittered, and he caught sight of a row of small sapphires. They bordered a little hole in the rock.

"The keyhole!" he cried.

He tried the key. It fitted. It turned. A great clang and clash, as of iron bolts on huge brazen caldrons, echoed thunderously within. He drew out the key. The rock in front of him began to fall. He retreated from it as far the breadth of the platform would allow. A great slab fell at his feet. In front was still the solid rock, with this one slab fallen forward out of it. But the moment he stepped upon it, a second fell, just short of the edge of the first, making the next step of a stair, which thus kept dropping itself before him as he ascended into the heart of the precipice. It led him into a hall fit for such an approach—irregular and rude in formation, but floor, sides, pillars, and vaulted roof, all of one mass of shining stones of every colour that light can show. In the centre stood seven columns, ranged from red to violet. And on the pedestal of one of them sat a woman, motionless, with her face bowed upon her knees. Seven years had she sat there waiting.

She lifted her head as Mossy drew near. It was Tangle. Her hair
had grown to her feet, and was rippled like the windless sea on
broad sands. Her face was beautiful, like her grandmother's, and
as still and peaceful as that of the Old Man of the Fire. Her form
was tall and noble. Yet Mossy knew her at once.

"How beautiful you are, Tangle!" he said, in delight and
astonishment.

"Am I?" she returned. "Oh, I have waited for you so long! But
you, you are like the Old Man of the Sea. No. You are like the
Old Man of the Earth. No, no. You are like the oldest man of all.
You are like them all. And yet you are my own old Mossy. How
did you come here? What did you do after I lost you? Did you
find the keyhole? Have you got the key still?"

She had a hundred questions to ask him, and he a hundred more
to ask her. They told each other all their adventures, and were as
happy as man and woman could be. For they were younger and
better, and stronger and wiser, than they had ever been before.

It began to grow dark. And they wanted more than ever to
reach the country whence the shadows fall. So they looked about
them for a way out of the cave. The door by which Mossy entered
had closed again, and there was half a mile of rock between them
and the sea. Neither could Tangle find the opening in the floor
by which the serpent had led her thither. They searched till it
grew so dark that they could see nothing, and gave it up.

After a while, however, the cave began to glimmer again. The
light came from the moon, but it did not look like moonlight, for
it gleamed through those seven pillars in the middle, and filled
the place with all colours. And now Mossy saw that there was a
pillar beside the red one, which he had not observed before. And
it was of the same new colour that he had seen in the rainbow
when he saw it first in the fairy forest. And on it he saw a sparkle
of blue. It was the sapphires round the keyhole.

He took his key. It turned in the lock to the sounds of Æolian
music. A door opened upon slow hinges, and disclosed a winding
stair within. The key vanished from his fingers. Tangle went up.
Mossy followed. The door closed behind them. They climbed out
of the earth; and, still climbing, rose above it. They were in the

rainbow. Far abroad, over ocean and land, they could see through its transparent walls the earth beneath their feet. Stairs beside stairs wound up together, and beautiful beings of all ages climbed along with them.

They knew that they were going up to the country whence the shadows fall.

And by this time I think they must have got there.

WILLIAM ALEXANDER

BAUBIE HUIE'S BASTARD GEET

JOCK HUIE'S HOUSEHOLD—BAUBIE ENTERS LIFE

I AM not prepared to say how far Baubie Huie's own up-bringing had been a model of judicious parental nurture. There was ground to fear that it had not been at all times regulated by an enlightened regard to the principle laid down by King Solomon, concerning the training of children. Jock Huie had a muckle sma' faimily, crammed into limited space, in so far as the matter of house accommodation was concerned. It was a little, clay-built, "rape-thackit" cot in which Jock, with Eppie, his wife, and their family dwelt; and the "creaturs" came so thickly, and in such multitude, that Jock, who was a "darger," and did "days' warks" here and there, as he could find them, experienced rather queer sensations when an unusually "coorse" day happened to coop him up at home among the "smatterie" of youngsters.

"Saul o' me, 'oman," would Jock exclaim, when patience had reached its limit; "the din o' that bairns o' yours wud rive a heid o' steen—gar them be quaet, aw'm sayin', or I'll hae to tak' a horse fup to them."

"Haud yer tongue, man; gin ye war amo' them fae screek o' day till gloamin' licht's I am, ye mith speak. Fat can the creaturs dee fan they canna get leuket owre a door?" Eppie would reply.

Notwithstanding his formidable threat, Jock Huie rarely lifted his hand in the way of active correction of his offspring. His wife, who was not indisposed to govern a little more sharply if she could, knew of only one way of enforcing obedience, or some approach thereto, when matters had come to a decided pass of the character indicated, and which may be best described in plain English as indiscriminate chastisement, applied with sufficient heartiness though it might be quite as much in accordance with the dictates of temper as of calm reason. And so it came to pass that, as most of the youthful Huies were gifted with pretty definite wills of their own, the progress of physical development on their part might be taken, in a general way, as indicative, in inverse proportion, of the measure of moral and mental sway which the parental will was able to exercise over them.

All that by the way, however. Jock Huie got his family brought up as he best could, and off his hands mainly; and he, personally, continued his dargin' with perhaps a little less vir than aforetime. Jock was a man of large bones and strong bodily frame; when thirty he had physical strength that seemed equal to any task, and endurance against which no amount of rough usage appeared to tell with evil effect. But after all, men of Jock Huie's class do not wear long. Jock was now a man only a few years past fifty; yet digging in wet drains and ditches, and eating a bit of oat cake, washed down with "treacle ale," to his dinner, day by day, had procured for him a very appreciable touch of "rheumatics," and other indications that he had fairly passed his prime.

And Baubie, his eldest daughter, though not the eldest member of his family, for Jock had various sons older than she—Baubie had grown up—a buxom, ruddy-cheeked "quine" of nineteen. She was servan' lass to the farmer of Brigfit—Briggies in short.

I remember very distinctly a bonnie summer gloamin at that time. It was gey late owre i' the evenin'. Baubie had milket the kye, seyt the milk, and wash'n up her dishes. Her day's work was at last fairly done, and why should not Baubie go out to the Toon Loan to enjoy the quiet scene as the cool dews of evening began to fall upon the landscape around the cosy, old-fashioned farm "steading" of Brigfit.

It matters nothing in this narration where I had been that evening, further than to say that, as I pursued my journey homeward, the road took me past the corner of Briggies' stable, where, altogether unexpectedly to me, I encountered Baubie Huie "in maiden meditation fancy free." Though Baubie's junior by a twelvemonth or so, I had developed since we two had last met from a mere herd loon into a sort of rawish second or third horseman. We had known each other more or less from infancy, Baubie and I, and our talk during the short parley that now ensued had a tinge of the byegone time in it; though, of course, we could not help giving fulfilment, in our own way, to the saying that out of the abundance of the heart, the mouth speaketh; and, naturally enough, at that season of life, that which most occupied our hearts was the present as it bore on our respective positions and prospects.

My own notion (it may be said in confidence) was that I was climbing up the pathway to maturity of life and definiteness of position with creditable alacrity; but in this direction I speedily found that Baubie Huie had fairly out-distanced me. Why, here was the very same "quine" who, almost the last time I saw her, was lugging along a big, sulky bairn, half her own size, wrapped in an old tartan plaid, and her weather-bleached hair hanging loosely about her shoulders—and that bairn her own younger brother—that very quine, giggling and tossing her head knowingly as she spoke, in what seemed a tone of half masculine licence, about the "chiels" that were more or less familiarly known as sweethearts among young women in the neighbourhood of Brigfit. In matters of love and courtship, I was, it must be confessed, an entire novice; whereas in such affairs, it was obvious, Baubie had become an adept; and if I had been somewhat put out by the ready candour with which she criticised the physical appearance and general bearing of this and the other young man—hangers on after Baubie, I was given to understand—I was nothing short of completely "flabbergasted" when, just as we were parting, she said—

"Dinna ye never gae fae hame at even, min? Ye mith come owre the gate some nicht an' see's."

What my confused and stuttering reply amounted to I cannot really say—something grotesquely stupid, no doubt. What it called forth on Baubie's part, at any rate, was another round of giggling and the exclamation, as she turned off toward the dwelling-house of Brigfit—

"Weel, weel, Robbie, a' nicht wi' you; an' a file o' the morn's mornin'."—This was simply the slang form of saying "good night" among persons of Baubie's class. And she added—"I'll need awa' in; for there's Briggies, the aul' snot, at the ga'le o' the hoose— he'll be barrin' 's oot again, eenoo."

Now, far be it from me to say that Baubie was a vicious or immodest young woman. I really am not prepared to say that she was anything of the sort. She had simply got the training that hundreds in her station of life in these northern shires do—home training that is. And after she left the parental roof, her experiences had been the common experiences of her class—that is to associate freely with promiscuous assemblages of farm-servants, male and female; mainly older than herself, without any supervision worth mentioning, as she moved from one situation to another. And how could Baubie, as an apt enough scholar, do other than imbibe the spirit and habits of those in whose companionship she lived day by day? Baubie was simply the natural product of the system under which she had been reared. Her moral tone, as indexed by her speech, might not be very high; and yet, after all, it is very possible to have the mere verbal proprieties fully attended to, where the innate morality is no whit better. Coarseness in the outer form, which is thrust on the view of all, is bad enough; depravity in the inner spirit, which is frequently concealed from many, may be a good deal worse.

Brigfit was a decent man; a very decent man, for he was an elder in the parish kirk, and a bachelor of good repute. He was a careful, industrious farmer, the extent of whose haudin enabled him to "ca' twa pair." Briggies was none of your stylish gentlemen farmers; he needed neither gig nor "shalt" to meet his personal convenience, but did his ordinary business journeys regularly on foot. And he stood on reasonably amicable terms with his servants; but he sought little of their confidence, and as little did he give to them of his own. Only Briggies had certain inflexible rules, and one was that his household should be in bed every night by nine o'clock in winter, and an hour later in summer; when he would himself solemnly put the bar on the door, and then walk as solemnly along to the "horn en'" to seek repose.

Briggies was a very early riser, and as it was his hand that usually put the bar on the door at night, so, honest man, was it his hand that ordinarily took it off in the morning in time to see that the household proper and the occupants of the outside "chaum'er," consisting of the male servants, were stirring to begin the labours of the day in due season. According to Baubie Huie's account, the bar was sometimes tampered with during the interval by the "deems;" only if matters were gone about quietly enough, Briggies, whether or not he might suspect aught in that way, usually said nothing.

"Augh, Robbie, man! Fear't for Briggies kennin? Peer bodie! fan onything comes in's noddle aboot's nowte beasts he canna get rest, but 'll be up an' paumerin aboot the toon' o' the seelence o' the nicht, fan it's as mark 's pick in winter, forbye o' the simmer evenin's. So ae nicht i' the spring time that me an' my neebour hedna been wuntin to gae to oor beds, we pits oot the lamp in gweed time, an' sits still, as quaet 's pussy, till Briggies hed on the bar an' away till 's bed. I'm nae sayin' gin onybody was in ahin that or no, but lang aifter the wee oor hed struck'n, me an' Jinse was thereoot. I suppose the chiels hed made mair noise nor they sud 'a deen, caperin' owre the causeway wi' their muckle tacketie beets. At ony rate in a blink there was Briggies oot an' roon to the byres wi' the booet in 's han'. Fan he hed glampit aboot amo' the beasts till he was satisfeet, he gaes awa' to the hoose again; an' we wusna lang o' bein' aifter 'im. But fudder or no he had leuket ben to the kitchie to see gin we wus there, he hed pitten the bar siccar aneuch on upo' the door this time, I can tell ye; an' nae an in cud we win for near an oor, till we got an aul' ledder an' pat it up to the en' o' the hoose, an' syne I made oot to creep in at the ga'le winnochie—Fat did he say aifterhin? Feint a thing. Briggies never loot on, though he cudna but 'a hed 's ain think, 'cause gin he didna hear huz, he be 't till 'a kent 'gyaun oot' that the bar sudna 'a been aff 'o the door at that time o' nicht."

In this wise did Baubie Huie keep up the colloquy, my own side of which, candour compels me to say, was very badly sustained; for had I been ever so willing to take my part, the requisite fluency and *abandon* had not been attained, to say nothing of the utter absence of knowledge germane to the subject in hand, and personally acquired.

As a matter of course, I did not accept Baubie Huie's invitation to visit Brigfit. If the truth were to be told, I was too much of a greenhorn; one who would have been accurately described by Baubie and her associates as utterly destitute of "spunk." My Mentor of that date, a vigorous fellow of some eight and twenty years, whose habits might be not incorrectly described by the word "haiveless," whose speech was at least as free, as refined, and who occupied the responsible position of first horseman, did not indeed hesitate to characterise my behaviour in relation to such matters, generally, in almost those very words. He knew Baubie Huie, moreover, and his estimate of Baubie was expressed in the words— "Sang, she's a richt quine yon, min; there's nae a deem i' the pairt'll haud 'er nain wi' ye better nor she'll dee; an' she's a fell ticht gweed-leukin hizzie tee," which, no doubt, was a perfectly accurate description according to the notions entertained by the speaker of the qualities desirable in the female sex.

However these things may be, Baubie Huie continued to perform her covenanted duties to the farmer of Brigfit; and, so far as known, yielding the elder average satisfaction as a servant during the summer "half-year."

II

BAUBIE RETURNS HOME

IT WAS nearing the term of Martinmas, and Jock Huie, who had been laid off work for several days by a "beel't thoom," was discussing his winter prospect with Eppie, his wife. Meal was "fell chape," and the potato crop untouched by disease; but Jock's opinion was that, as prices were low for the farmer, feein' would be slack. Cattle were down too, and though the price of beef and mutton was a purely abstract question for him personally—he being a strict vegetarian in practice, not by choice but of necessity —Jock was economist enough to know that the fact bore adversely on the farmer's ability to employ labour; so that, altogether, with a superfluity of regular servants unengaged, and a paucity of work for the common "darger" in the shape of current farming improvements going on, he did not regard the aspect of things as cheering for his class.

"Aw howp neen o' that loons o' ours 'll throw themsel's oot o' a place," said Jock. "Wud ye think ony o' them wud be bidin'?"

"That wud be hard to say, man," replied Eppie.

"That widdifus o' young chiels 's aye sae saucy to speak till," said Jock; whether he meant that the sauciness would be exhibited in the concrete from his own sons toward himself, or if the remark applied to the bearing of servant chiels generally on the point under consideration, was not clear. "But better to them tak' a sma' waage nor lippen to orra wark; an' hae to lie aboot idle the half o' the winter."

"Weel ken we that," said Eppie, with a tolerably lively recollection of her experiences in having previously had one or two of her sons "at hame" during the winter season. "Mere ate-meats till Can'lesmas; I'm seer fowk hae's little need o' that; but creaturs'll tak' their nain gate for a' that."

"Aw howp Baubie's bidin' wi' Briggies, ony wye," added Jock.

"I ken naething aboot it," said Eppie, in a tone that might be described as dry; "Baubie's gey an' gweed at keepin' 'er coonsel till 'ersel."

It was only a fortnight to the term, and Jock would not be kept long in suspense regarding those questions affecting the family arrangements on which he had thus incidentally touched. In point of fact, his mind was set at rest so far when only half the fortnight had run. For the feeing market came in during that period, and as Jock's thumb had not yet allowed him to resume work, he "took a step doon" to the market, where he had the satisfaction of finding that his sons had all formed engagements as regular farm servants. As for Baubie, though Jock learned on sufficient authority that she was present in the market, he failed to "meet in" with her. Concerning Baubie's intended movements, he learnt, too, that she was *not* staying with Briggie's; Briggies himself had indeed told him so; but beyond that Jock's enquiries on the subject did not produce any enlightenment for him.

Subsequently to the feeing market, Jock Huie had once and again reverted to the subject of Baubie's strange behaviour in keeping the family in ignorance of her movements and intentions, but without drawing forth much in the way of response from his wife beyond what she had generally expressed in her previous remark.

The afternoon of the term day had come, and servants who were flittin' were moving here and there. I cannot state the nature of the ruminations that had passed, or were passing, through the mind of either Jock Huie or his wife Eppie concerning their daughter Baubie; but Jock, honest man, had just left his cottage in the grey gloamin to go to the smiddy and get his tramp-pick sharpened with the view of resuming work next day in full vigour, when Baubie dressed in her Sunday garments, and carrying a small bundle, entered. There was a brief pause; and then Baubie's mother, in a distinct and very deliberate tone, said—

"Weel, Baubie, 'oman; an' ye're here neist."

At these words, Baubie, who had just laid aside her bundle, threw herself down beside it, on the top of the family "deece," with the remark,

"Aye; faur ither wud aw gae?"

And then she proceeded silently to untie the strings of her bonnet. Neither Baubie nor her mother was extremely agitated, but there was a certain measure of restrained feeling operating upon both the one and the other. The mother felt that a faithful discharge of the maternal duty demanded that she should give utterance to a reproof as severe as she could properly frame, accompanied by reproaches, bearing on the special wickedness and ingratitude of the daughter; and, on the part of the daughter along with a vague sense of the fitness of all this, in a general way, there were indications of a volcanic state of temper, which might burst out with considerable, if misplaced fierceness, on comparatively slight provocation. And wherefore create a scene of verbal violence; for deep down, below those irascible feelings, did there not lurk in Eppie Huie's bosom a kind of latent sense that if such crises as that which had now emerged were not to be regarded as absolutely certain, they were assuredly to be looked upon as very much in the nature of events inevitable in the ordinary history of the family? And thus it was that Eppie Huie, virtually accepting the situation as part of the common lot, went no further than a general rasping away at details, and the consequences arising out of the main fact.

"Weel, weel, Baubie, 'oman, ye've begun to gae the aul' gate in braw time—ye'll fin't a hard road to yersel', as weel's to them 't 's near conneckit wi' you. Fat gar't ye keep oot o' yer fader's sicht at the market—haudin 'im gyaun like a wull stirk seekin' ye, an' makin' a feel o' 'im?"

"Aw'm seer ye needna speer that—'s gin ye hedna kent to tell 'im yersel'."

"That's a bonnie story to set up noo, ye limmer—that I sud say the like," said Eppie with some heat. "Didnin ye deny't i' my face the vera last time that ye was here?"

"H-mph! an' aw daursay ye believ't 's!"

"Weel, Baubie, 'oman, it's a sair say 't we sud be forc't to tak' for a muckle black lee fat 's been threepit, an' yea-threepit i' oor witters be' them that's sibbest til 's."

To this observation Baubie made no reply: and after a short silence Eppie Huie continued in a dreary monotone—

"Ay, ay! An' this is fat folk get for toilin' themsel's to deith feshin up a faimily! There's little aneuch o' peace or rest for's till oor heid be aneth the green sod—jist oot o' ae tribble in till anither. Little did I or yer peer fader think short syne that ye was to be hame to be a burden till 's."

"Aw ha'ena been a burden yet ony wye," said Baubie with some sharpness, "ye needna be sae ready speakin' that gate."

To this retort Eppie Huie made some reply to the effect that others similarly circumstanced had uttered such brave words, and that time would tell in Baubie's case as it had told in theirs. She then rose and put some water in a small pot, which she hung upon the "crook" over the turf fire, in the light of which Baubie and she had hitherto sat.

"Fa 's the fader o' 't than?" said Eppie Huie, as she turned about from completing the operation just mentioned; but though the words were uttered in a very distinct as well as abrupt tone, there

was no answer till she repeated her question in the form of a sharp
"Aw'm sayin'?"

"Ye'll ken that _a-time_ aneuch," answered Baubie.

"Ken 't a-time aneuch!—an' you here"—

"Ay an' me here—an' fat aboot it? _It_ winna be here the morn,
nor yet the morn's morn," said Baubie in a harder and more
reckless tone than she had yet assumed.

Eppie Huie had, no doubt, a sense of being baffled, more or
less. She resumed her seat, uttering as she did so, something
between a sigh and a groan. There was nothing more said until
the water in the little pot having now got to "the boil," Eppie rose,
and lighting the rush wick in the little black lamp that hung on the
shoulder of the "swye" from which the crook depended, proceeded to "mak' the sowens." When the lamp had been lighted,
Baubie rose from her place on the deece, and lifting her bonnet,
which now lay beside her, and her bundle, said,

"A'm gyaun awa' to my bed."

"Ye better wyte an' get yer sipper—the sowens'll be ready
eenoo."

"Aw'm nae wuntin' nae sipper," said Baubie, turning to go as
she spoke. "There's nae things lyin' i' the mid-hoose bed, is there?"

"Naething; oonless it be the muckle basket, wi' some o' yer
breeders' half-dry't claes. Tak' that bit fir i' yer han'—ye'll need
it, ony wye, to lat ye see to haud aff o' the tubs an' the basket."

And Baubie went off to bed forthwith, notwithstanding a sort of
second invitation, as she was lighting the fir, to wait for some
supper. I rather think that after all she did not relish the comparative light so much as the comparative darkness. And then if
she stayed to get even the first practicable mouthful of "sowens,"
was there not considerable risk that Jock Huie, her father, might
drop in upon her on his return from the smiddy? Not that Baubie
had an unreasonable sensitive dread of facing her father. But
having now got over what she would have called "the warst o' 't,"
with her mother, she felt that her mother, being on the whole so
well "posted up," might be left with advantage to break the ice,
at least, to the old man.

When Jock Huie returned from the smiddy that evening, an event that happened in about half an hour after his daughter Baubie had gone to bed, he seemed to be moody, and in a measure out of temper. He put aside his bonnet, and sat down in his usual corner, while Eppie set the small table for his supper, only one or two remarks of a very commonplace sort having been made up to that point.

"Ye'll better saw awa', man; they've been made this file," said Eppie, as she lifted the dish with the "sowens" to the table from the hearthstone, where it had been placed in order to retain warmth in the mess.

"Aw'm sayin', 'oman," quoth Jock, apparently oblivious to his wife's invitation, "div ye ken onything about that jaud Baubie—there's something or anither nae richt, ere she wud haud oot o' fowk's road this gate?"

"Baubie's here, man," said Eppie Huie; and the brevity of her speech was more than made up by the significance of the words and the tone in which they were uttered.

"Here?" exclaimed Jock in a tone of inquiry, and looking towards his wife as he spoke.

"She's till 'er bed i' the mid-hoose," said Eppie in reply; and, perceiving that Jock's look was only half answered, she added, "Aw daursay she wasna owre fain to see you."

"Fat!" cried Jock, "she'll be wi' a geet to some chiel, is she?"

"Ou ye needna speer," said Eppie in a tone of "dowie" resignation.

"Weel, that does cowe the gowan—a quine o' little mair nor nineteen! But aw mith 'a been seer o' 't. It wasna for naething that she was playin' hide-an'-seek wi' me yon gate. Brawlie kent I that she was i' the market wi' a set o' them. Deil speed them a', weel-a-wat!"

Jock Huie was not a model man exactly in point of moral sentiment; neither was he a man of keen sensibility. But he did nevertheless possess a certain capability of sincere, if it might be uncultured feeling; and he now placed his rough, weather-beaten face against the horny palms of his two hands, and, resting his two elbows on his knees, gave utterance to a prolonged "Hoch-hey!"

Jock maintained this attitude for sometime, and probably would have maintained it a good deal longer, but for the practical view of matters taken by his wife, and the practical advice urgently pressed upon him by her when her patience had got exhausted:—

"Aw'm sayin', man, ye needna connach yer sipper; that'll dee nae gweed to naebody.—Tak' your sowens! Ye're lattin them grow stiff wi' caul', for a' the tribble 't aw was at keepin' them het to you."

Thus admonished, Jock Huie took his supper in silence; and, thereafter, with little more talk beyond one or two questions from Jock of a like nature with those which had been so ineffectually addressed to Baubie by her mother, the husband and wife retired to bed.

III

THE GEET'S ADVENT—INITIAL DIFFICULTIES IN ACQUIRING
AN ECCLESIASTICAL STATUS

THAT JOCK HUIE's daughter, Baubie, had returned home to her father and mother was a fact about which there could be no manner of doubt or equivocation; as to the cause of Baubie's return, there was a general concurrence of opinion in the neighbourhood; indeed, it had been a point settled long before, among elderly and sagacious females who knew her, that Baubie would speedily appear in her true colours. Yet there were a few of this same class of people in whose sides Baubie was still somewhat of a thorn. For when the first few days were over after her return, so far from shrinking out of their sight, Baubie flung herself across their path at the most unexpected times, and exhibited an unmistakeable readiness to meet their friendly criticisms with a prompt retort. Or was it a staring personal scrutiny—well, Baubie was almost ostentatiously ready to stand that ordeal, and stare with the best of her starers in return. Baubie was perfectly able to take care of herself, and if a young woman of her spirit chose to remain six months out of the "hire house," whose business was that but her own? Baubie would like to know that.

It is not to be supposed that this bravado went far in the way of deceiving any but very inexperienced people, if it deceived even them, which is more than doubtful. And in the nature of the case, it would at any rate deceive no one very long.

It was just at Candlemas when it was reported that Jock Huie had become a grandfather; a genealogical dignity the attainment of which did not seem to excite in Jock's breast any particular feeling of elation. Such an idea as that of apprehension lest the line of Huies in his branch should become extinct had certainly never troubled Jock to the extent that would have made him anxious to welcome a grandchild, legitimate or illegitimate; and the belief that this particular bairn was born to be a direct and positive burden upon him hardly tended to make its advent either auspicious or cheering. Jock knew full well the "tyauve" he had had in bringing up his own family proper; and now, ere the obstreperous squalling of the younger of them was well out of his ears, why here was another sample of the race, ready to renew and continue all that turmoil and uproar, by night and by day, from which his small hut had never been free for a good twenty years of his lifetime.

"An' it's a laddie, ye say, that the quine Huie's gotten?"

"A laddie; an' a-wat a richt protty gate-farrin bairnie 's ever ye saw wi' yer twa een."

"Fan came' 't hame no?"

"It was jist the streen, nae langer gane. Aifter 't was weel gloam't, I hears a chap at the window, an' fa sud this be but Eppie 'ersel', peer creatur. I pat my tartan shawl aboot my heid immedantly, an' aifter tellin' the littleans to keep weel ootbye fae the fire, an' biddin' their sister pit them to their beds shortly, I crap my wa's roun' as fest 's aw cud. Jock was nae lang come hame fae 's day's wark, an' was sittin' i' the neuk at 's bit sipper. 'He's jist makin' ready to gae for Mrs. Slorach,' says she. 'Awat I was rael ill-pay't for 'im, peer stock, tir't aneuch nae doot, jist aff o' a sair day's wark. It was a freely immas nicht, wi' byous coorse ploiterie

road; an' it's three mile gweed, but I can asseer ye Jock hed gane
weel, for it wasna muckle passin' twa oors fan he's back an' Mrs.
Slorach wi' 'im."

"Weel, weel, Jock'll get's nain o' 't lickly, honest man. It'll be
a won'er an' they hinna the tsil' to fesh up."

"Ou weel-a-wat that's true aneuch; but there's never a hicht
but there's a howe at the boddom o' 't, as I said to Eppie fan she
first taul' me o' Baubie's misfortune; an' there's never a mou' sen'
but the maet's sen' wi' 't."

"Div they ken yet fa's the fader o' the creatur?"

"Weel, she hed been unco stubborn aboot it no; but aw'm
thinkin' she hed taul' 'er mither at the lang len'th. At a roch
guess, a body mith gae farrer agley, aw daursay, nor licken 't to
ane o' yon chiels 't was aboot the toon wi' 'er at Briggies'—yon
skyeow-fittet breet."

The foregoing brief extract from the conversation of a couple
of those kindly gossips who had all along taken a special interest
in her case will indicate with sufficient distinctness the facts surrounding the birth of Baubie Huie's Geet.

The reputed father of the geet was a sort of nondescript chap,
whose habit it was to figure at one time as an indifferent second
or third "horseman," and next time as an "orra man"; a bullet-
headed bumpkin, with big unshapely feet, spreading considerably
outward as he walked; a decided taste for smoking tobacco; of
somewhat more than average capability in talking bucolic slang
of a gross sort; yet possessing withal a comfortable estimate of his
own graces of person and manner in the eyes of the fair sex. Such
was the—sweetheart, shall we say?—of Baubie Huie.

How one might best define the precise relationship existing
between the nondescript chiel and Baubie, it would not be easy
to say. It was believed that on the feeing market night he had
taken Baubie home to Briggies', he being not greatly the worse
of drink, and that on the term night he had accompanied her part
of the way toward her father's house. There was also a sort of
vague impression that he had since then come once or twice to
visit Baubie, keeping as well out of sight and ken of Jock Huie

and his wife as might be. Be that as it may, now that the child was born, Jock, who was very much of a practical man, desired to know articulately from the man himself whether he was to "tak wi' 't an' pay for't." The idea of asking whether the fellow had any intention of doing the one thing which a man with a shred of honour about him would have felt bound to do in the circumstances—viz., marrying his daughter—had really not occurred to Jock Huie. And so it came to pass, that after a certain amount of rather irritating discussion between himself and the female members of his family, and as the nondescript took very good care not to come to him, Jock "took road" to hunt up the nondescript, who, as he discovered after some trouble, was now serving on a farm some five or six miles off. He found him as third horseman at the plough in a field of "neep-reet," along with his two fellow ploughmen. The nondescript had a sufficient aspect of embarrassment when Jock Huie caught him up at the end rig, where he had been waiting till the ploughs should come out, to indicate that he would not have been disappointed had the visit been omitted; and it seemed not improbable that his two companions might thereafter offer one or two interrogatory remarks on the subject, which would not be a great deal more welcome. At anyrate, Jock Huie had the satisfaction of finding that the nondescript "wasna seekin' to deny't"; nay, that he did not refuse to "pay for't", any backwardness on his part in that respect up to the date of visit, being readily accounted for by the fact that it was the middle of the half-year, when a man was naturally run of cash. Threats about "'reestin' waages," therefore, were perfectly uncalled-for; and, indeed, a sort of unjust aspersion on the general character of the nondescript. It was right that Jock Huie should know that.

"Ye sud hae the civeelity to lat fowk ken faur ye are than; an' ye think ony ill o' that. Bonnie story to haud me trailin' here, lossin' half a day seekin' ye," retorted Jock with some roughness of tone.

Between the date of Jock Huie's visit just mentioned and the term of Whitsunday, the father of Baubie Huie's geet visited the abode of the Huies once at anyrate; and in course of the conference that ensued, it so happened that the subject of getting the geet christened came up—the needful preliminary to that being, as Jock explained, to appear and give satisfaction to that grave Church Court, the Kirk-Session. This was a point which both the paternal and maternal Huie were a good deal more eager to discuss and settle about than either of the immediate parents of the geet. Indeed, the nondescript seemed penetrated with a sort of feeling that that was a part of the business hardly in his line. Not that he objected on principle to the geet being christened; far from it; for when Eppie Huie had stated the necessity of getting themselves "clear't," and having that rite performed, and Jock Huie had vigorously backed up her statement, the nondescript assented with a perfectly explicit "Ou ay"; only he showed a decided tendency always to let the matter drop again. This did not suit Jock Huie's book in the least, however, and he manifested a determination to have the business followed out that was not at all comfortable to the nondescript.

When the nondescript had pondered over the situation for a few days, and all along with the feeling that something must really be done, for he did not in the least relish the idea of further calls from Jock Huie, the happy thought occurred to him of calling on his old master, Briggies, who was one of the elders of the Kirk, and, being after all a humane man, would no doubt be prevailed upon to pave the way for him and Baubie making penitential appearance before the session, and receiving censure and "absolution." So he called on Briggies, and was rather drily told that, neither Baubie nor he being "commeenicants," apart from the censure of the session, which had to be encountered in the first place, he, at anyrate, "as the engaging parent" (and perhaps Baubie too), would have to undergo an examination, at the hands of the minister, as to his knowledge of the cardinal doctrines of the Christian faith, and the significance of the rite of baptism in particular.

"Fat wye cud ye expeck to win throw itherweese, min?" Briggies felt bound to speak as an elder in this case—"Gin fowk winna leern to behave themsel's they maun jist stan' the consequences. The vera Kirk-Session itsel' cudna relieve ye, man, upo' nae ither precunnance."

The nondescript returned much pondering on this disheartening information, which he got opportunity, by and bye, of communicating to Baubie. In private conference, the two agreed that "a scaulin' fae the session," by itself—a thing they had been both accustomed to hear spoken of with extreme jocularity, not less than they had seen those who had undergone the same, regarded as possessing something of the heroism that is rather to be envied—a scaulin' fae the session might well be borne; but to stand a formal examination before the minister in cold blood was another affair. The dilemma having occurred, the two horns were presented to Jock Huie, who was so relentlessly forcing them on to impalement, in the hope of softening his heart, or at anyrate awakening his sympathy; but Jock was just as determined as ever that they must go forward in the performance of their Christian duty, and his one reply was, "Ou, deil care; ye maun jist haud at the Catechis."

IV

THE GEET'S STATUS, ECCLESIASTICAL AND SOCIAL, DEFINED

"Aw'M SAYIN', 'oman, that geet maun be kirsen't some wye or anither; we canna lat the creatur grow up like a haethen."

The speaker in this case was Jock Huie, and the person addressed his wife Eppie. It was a fine Saturday evening toward the latter end of June, and Jock, who had got home from his work at the close of the week, was now in a deliberative mood.

"Weel, man, ye'll need to see fat wye 't's to be manag't," was Eppie's reply.

"They'll jist need 'o tak' her 'er leen; that's a' that I can say aboot it," said Jock.

"Ah-wa, man; wa won'er to her ye speak."

"Weel fat else can ye dee? Aw tell ye the littlean 'll be made a moniment o' i' the kwintra side."

"Ou, weel, ye maun jist gae to the minaister yersel', man, an' tell 'im fat gate her an' huz tee 's been guidet; he's a rael sympatheesin person, an' there's nae doot he'll owreleuk onything as far's he can."

"Sorra set 'im, weel-a-wat!" said Jock Huie emphatically, as he knocked the half-burnt "dottal" of tobacco out of his pipe into the palm of his hand, with a sort of savage thump.

Whether Jock Huie's portentous objurgation on the subject of the Catechism had much or anything to do with the result it would perhaps be difficult to say, but it was a simple matter of fact that after it had been uttered, the father of Baubie's geet exhibited even more than previously a disposition to fight shy of the path of duty on which Jock sought to impel him. The Whitsunday term was drawing on; the Whitsunday term had arrived and the geet still unchristened. Then it was found that the father of the geet had deemed it an expedient thing to seek an appreciable change of air by "flittin'" entirely beyond "kent bounds." True it was, that on the very eve of his departure he had by the hands of a third party transmitted to Baubie for the maintenance of her geet a "paper note" of the value of one pound, and along with it a verbal message to the effect that he was "gyaun to the pairis' o' Birse"; but as it had been a not infrequent practice among the witty to mention the parish named as a sort of mythical region to which one might be condemned to go, for whom no other sublunary use was apparent, Baubie herself was far from assured that the literal Birse was meant; and we may add was equally at a loss as to whether she had further remittances to look for, or if the note was a once and single payment, in full discharge of the nondescript's obligations in respect to the present maintenance, and prospective upbringing of his son—the Bastard Geet.

Baubie Huie's Bastard Geet had now reached the age of fully four months; no wonder if the grand-paternal anxieties should be aroused as to the danger of the "peer innocent" merging into heathenism and becoming a bye-word to the parish. And as Jock Huie had expressed his sense of the importance of kirsenin' as a preventative, so after all, it fell to Jock's lot to take the responsible part in getting the rite performed. The name was a matter of difficulty; had there been an available father, it would have been his duty to confer with the mother on the point, and be fully instructed what name to bestow on the infant; and in the case of his own children, the male part of them at anyrate, Jock Huie had never been much at a loss about the names. Among his sons, Tam, Sawney, and Jock, came in, in orderly succession; but, ponder as he would, the naming of Baubie's geet puzzled him long. Its reputed father bore the name of Samuel—cut down to Samie—Caie, and Jock rejected promptly and with scorn the suggestion, coming from its mother, to inflict upon the bairn any such name, which he, in strong language, declared to be nauseous enough to serve as an emetic to a dog. Indeed, Jock's honest hatred of the nondescript had now reached a pitch that made him resolutely decline to pronounce his name at all; a practice in which, as a rule, he was tacitly imitated by his wife and daughter. Partly from this cause, and partly by reason of the still further delay that occurred in getting the christening over, it came to pass that the poor youngster began to have attached to it, with a sort of permanency, the title of Baubie Huie's Bastard Geet; and when at last the parson had done the official duty in question, and Jock Huie, with a just sense of his position in the matter, had boldly named the bairn after himself, it only led to the idle youth of the neighbourhood ringing the changes on the geet in this fashion—

Aul' Jock, an' young Jock, an' Jock comin' tee;
There'll never be a gweed Jock till aul' Jock dee.

But notwithstanding of all these things the geet throve and grew as only a sturdy scion of humanity could be expected to do.

To say that Baubie Huie was passionately attached to her child, would perhaps be rather an over-statement, yet was she pleased to nurse the poor geet with a fair amount of kindness; and physically the geet seemed to make no ungrateful return. It was edifying to note the bearing of the different members of the family towards the geet. The practical interest taken in its spiritual welfare by old Jock Huie has been mentioned; and despite the trouble it had caused him, Jock was equally prepared now to let the geet have the first and tenderest "bite" from his hard-won daily crust to meet its temporal wants; a measure of self-denial such as many a philanthropist of higher station and greater pretensions has never set before himself. The nature of Eppie Huie's feelings toward the

geet was sufficiently indicated by the skilled and careful nursing
she would expend upon it at those times when Baubie, tired of
her charge, with an unceremonious—"Hae, tak' 'im a file, mither"
—would hand over the geet "body bulk" to the charge of its
grannie. When any of Jock Huie's grown-up sons happened to
visit home, their cue was simply to ignore the geet altogether.
Even when it squalled the loudest they would endeavour to retain
the appearance of stolid obliviousness of its presence; just as they
did when the hapless geet crowed and "walloped" its small limbs
in the superabundance of its joy at being allowed the novel pleasure
of gazing at them. The members of the family who were Baubie's
juniors, did not profess indifference; only their feeling toward the
geet, when it came under their notice on these temporary visits
home, was in the main the reverse of amicable. Her younger sister,
indeed, in Baubie's hearing, designated the unoffending geet a
"nasty brat," whereat Baubie flared up hotly and reminded her
that it was not so very long since she, the sister, was an equally
"nasty brat," to say the very least of it; as she, Baubie, could very
well testify from ample experience of the degrading office of nurse
to her. "Fat ever 't be, ye may haud yer chat ony wye," said Baubie,
and the sister stood rebuked.

When harvest came, the geet being now six months old, was
"spean't," and Baubie "took a hairst." Handed over to the exclusive custody of its grannie for the time being, the geet was destined
thenceforth to share both bed and board, literally, with Eppie and
Jock her husband. The tail of the speaning process when the geet
got "fretty," and especially overnight, brought back to Jock Huie
a lively remembrance of by-gone experiences of a like nature; and
he once or twice rather strongly protested against the conduct of
"that ablich" in "brakin' 's nicht's rest" with its outcries. But, on
the whole, Jock bore with the geet wonderfully.

When her hairst was finished, it was Baubie's luck to get continuous employment from the same master till Martinmas. When
that period had arrived, Baubie, of her own free will and choice,
again stood the feeing market, and found what she deemed a suit-
able engagement at a large farm several miles off, whither she went
in due time; and where, as was to be expected, she found the

domestic supervision of the male and female servants less stringent
on the whole than it had been at the elder's at Brigfit. In so far
as her very moderate wages allowed, after meeting her own needs
in the matter of dress, Baubie Huie was not altogether disinclined
to contribute toward the support of her bastard geet. As a matter
of course, nothing further was heard of or from the nondescript
father of the geet. He had moved sufficiently far off to be well out
of sight at anyrate, and Jock Huie had no means of finding him
out and pressing the claim against him in respect of the child's
maintenance, except by means of the Poor Law Inspector; and
Jock, being a man of independent spirit, had not yet thought of
calling in the services of the "Boord." As time went on, Baubie's
maternal care did not manifest itself in an increasing measure in
this particular of furnishing the means to support the geet more
than it did in any other respect affecting her offspring.

After one or two more flittings from one situation to another,
it became known that Baubie Huie was about to be married. At
another Martinmas term—there had been an interval of two years
—Baubie once more returned home; but this time frankly to
announce to Jock and Eppie Huie that she was "gyaun to be
mairriet" to one Peter Ga', who had been a fellow-servant with
her during a recent half-year. From considerate regard for the
convenience of her parents, and other causes, the happy day would
not be delayed beyond a fortnight; and there would be no extensive "splore" on the occasion, to disturb materially the domestic
arrangements of the Huies.

On this latter point certain of the neighbours were keenly disappointed. Because there were no marriage rejoicings to speak of,
they missed an invitation to join in the same, and they spoke in
this wise:—

"An' there's to be nae mairriage ava, ye was sayin'?"

"Hoot—fat wye cud there? The bridegreem an aul' widow
man 't mith be 'er fader, wi' three-four o' a faimily."

"Na, sirs; a bonny bargaine she'll be to the like o' 'im—three
or four o' a faimily, ye say?"

"So aw b'lieve; an' aw doot it winna be lang ere Baubie gi'e 'im
ane mair to haud it haill wi'."

"Wee, weel! Only fat ither cud ye expeck; but the man maun hae been sair misguidet 't loot 's een see the like o' 'er."

"An' ye may say 't."

"Fat siclike o' a creatur is he, ken ye?"

"Ou weel, he's a byous quate man it wud appear, an' a gweed aneuch servan', but sair haud'n doon naitrally. Only the peer stock maun be willin' to dee the richt gate in a menner, or he wud a never propos't mairryin Baubie."

"Gweed pit 'im wi' the like o' 'er, weel-a-wat—senseless cuttie."

Naturally, and by right, when Baubie had got a home of her own, she ought to have resumed the custody of her Bastard Geet, now a "gangrel bairn" of fully two years; but on the one hand, it was evident that Mr. and Mrs. Ga' had the prospect of finding the available accommodation in a hut, whose dimensions afforded scope for only a very limited but and ben, sufficiently occupied by and bye without the geet; and on the other, Eppie Huie, though abundantly forfough'en for a woman of her years in keeping her house, attending to the wants of her husband, Jock, and meeting such demands as her own family made upon her exertions as general washerwoman, would have rather demurred to parting with the geet, to whom she had become, as far as the adverse circumstances of the case allowed, attached. And thus the geet was left in the undisputed possession of Jock and Eppie Huie, to be trained by them as they saw meet.

Unlucky geet, say you? Well, one is not altogether disposed to admit that without some qualification. Sure enough, Jock Huie, senior, would and did permit Baubie's geet to grow up an uncouth, unkempt, and, in the main, untaught bairn; yet was there from him, even, a sort of genuine, if somewhat rugged affection, flowing out toward little Jock Huie (as the geet was alternatively styled); as when he would dab the shaving brush playfully against the geet's unwhiskered cheek, while sternly refusing him a grip of the gleaming razor, as he lifted the instrument upward for service on his own face; or, at another time, would quench the geet's aspiration after the garments of adult life, manifested in its having managed to thrust its puny arms into a huge sleeved moleskin vest belonging to Jock himself, by dropping his big "wyv'n bonnet" over the toddling creature's head, and down to his shoulders. Bitter memories of Samie Caie had faded into indistinctness more or less. And when the neighbour wives, as they saw the geet with an old black "cutty" in his hand, gravely attempting to set the contents of the same alight with a fiery sod in imitation of its grandfather, would exclaim, admiringly, "Na, but that laddie is a bricht Huie, Jock, man," Jock would feel a sort of positive pride in the youngster, who bade so fairly to do credit to his upbringing.

No; it might be that meagre fare—meagre even to pinching at times—was what the inmates of Jock Huie's cot had to expect; it might be that in a moral and intellectual point of view the nourishment going was correspondingly scanty and insufficient, to say the least of it; but in being merely left to grow up under these negatively unfavourable conditions, a grotesque miniature copy of the old man at whose heels he had learnt to toddle about with such assiduity, I can by no means admit that, as compared with many and many a geet whose destiny it is to come into the world in the like irregular fashion, the lot of Baubie Huie's Bastard Geet could be justly termed unlucky.

WILLIAM BLACK

THE PENANCE OF JOHN LOGAN

I

THE TEMPTATION

THE SUMMER sea was shining fair and calm, a perfect mirror of the almost cloudless heavens overhead, as a small rowing-boat, occupied by a single person, was slowly approaching a lonely little island in the Outer Hebrides. The solitary rower was neither fisherman nor sailor, but merely a holiday-maker—a well-known banker from London, in fact—who was seeking rest and recreation in the West Highlands, and who had rather a fancy for going about all by himself and for exploring out-of-the-way neighbour-hoods. He had heard a good deal of this *Eilean-na-Keal*—the Island of the Burying-place—of its sculptured tombstones, its ancient chapel, its Saints' Well, and other relics and traces of the time when the early Christians made their first settlements in these sea-solitudes; and on this pleasant morning, the water being like a sheet of glass, he thought he could not do better than hire a boat at the little village on the mainland where he chanced to be staying, and pull himself across. It is true that the nearer he got to the island, he found that there was a heavy tide running, and his labour at the oars was a much more arduous task than he had bargained for; but eventually he managed to fight his way through, the boat at last shooting into a small and sheltered bay, well out of the current.

But when he stood up to reconnoitre the shore and select a landing-place, he found to his intense astonishment that the island was not so totally uninhabited as he had been informed it was. A pair of eyes were calmly regarding him; and those eyes belonged to a little old man who was seated on a rock some way along the beach—a little, bent, broad-shouldered old man, with long white hair and tanned and weather-worn face. A further glance showed him a cumbrous and dilapidated rowing-boat hauled up into a kind of creek, and also a number of lobster-traps lying about on the shingle. The new-comer therefore naturally concluded that he had not been forestalled by any such hateful being as a fellow-tourist, but merely by an old lobster-fisherman who had come out to look after his traps.

The Englishman shoved his boat through the seaweed, jumped out, and hauled it up on the beach; and then walked along to the little old man, who had ceased mending his lobster-traps, and was still calmly regarding the stranger.

"Good morning!" the latter said, cheerfully—he was a good-humoured-looking, middle-aged person, who had knocked about the world sufficiently, and who liked to converse with whomsoever he chanced to meet. "This is rather a lonely place for you to be in, isn't it?"

"Ay," said the old man, as he carefully scrutinised the other from head to heel, "there's not many comes here."

"But there used to be people living on the island?" Mr. Ramsden continued, chiefly for the sake of getting his new acquaintance to talk.

The old man paused for a moment or two; then he slowly made answer—

"Ay, I have heard that."

Was he half-witted, then, or was his English defective, or was it his lonely life that had made him thus chary and hesitating of speech? He seemed to ponder over the questions, his eyes all the while taking note of every detail of the stranger's features and dress.

"I saw some seals as I came along: are there many of them about here?"

"Ay, plenty."

"Don't people come and shoot them?"

"No."

"Doesn't anybody ever come here?"

"No."

"Do you ever have to pass the night here?"

"Ay."

"Where do you sleep, then—in your boat?"

He shook his head.

"Where then?"

"In the chaypel."   ? Highland Scots

"Oh, that's the chapel I've heard about: you must come and show me where it is, if you are not too busy. Have you been getting many lobsters lately?"

"Some."

"What do you do with them? You can't have many customers in Harivaig."

"To London," the old man said, laconically.

"Oh, you send them to London? To a fishmonger, or a fish-dealer, perhaps?"

"Ay, do ye know him?" And then old John Logan seemed to wake up a little; indeed, he spoke almost eagerly, though he was continually hesitating for want of the proper word. "Do ye know him?—Corstorphine—Billingsgate—he sends me the boxes. Do ye know him?—bekass—bekass he is not giffing me enough—and if there wass another one now I would go aweh from him. Mebbe you know Corstorphine?"

"No; I'm sorry to say I don't. I should be very glad to help you if I could, but I'm afraid you would run a great risk in giving up a constant customer. I suppose he takes whatever you send?"

"Oh, ay; oh, ay," was the old man's answer, "but he does not gif enough! And—and I hef a young lass at home—she is the daughter of my daughter that's dead—and—and she is going to be married; and the young man—he is for buying a—a part in a herring-smack, and I am for helping him with the money. But Corstorphine should gif more."

"Well, I think so too. So your grand-daughter is going to be married; and you are going to help the young man to buy his share in the herring-smack as a kind of marriage-portion: is that it?"

"Ay, it's something like that," said old Logan—but doubtfully, for perhaps he had not quite understood.

"I should have thought now," Mr. Ramsden resumed—he had a knack of interesting himself in people—"that it would have been worth your while to take the young man into your own business, instead of buying him a share in a smack. You are getting up in years; and this is a very lonely life for you to lead; if the young man came in—with a little capital, perhaps—"

Old Logan shook his head.

"It's not a good business at ahl. There's the coorse weather; and the things brekkin'; and—and then there's Corstorphine. He is not a fair man, Corstorphine. He should gif more—pless me, they hef plenty of money in London, as I wass being told many's the time."

"Yes, but they like to keep it, my friend," the banker replied. "Well, now, if you are not too busy, will you come and show me where the tombstones are, and the other things I have heard about?"

The old man slowly rose, and put aside the trap he had been mending. It was now apparent that, despite his short stature, his white hair, and his glazed eyes, he was a much stronger man— especially about the chest and shoulders—than he had appeared to be when sitting in a crouching position: there was no longer any mystery as to how that big, cumbrous boat had been got over.

"Mebbe you'll not be living in London?" the lobster fisherman asked thoughtfully, as he led the way for his companion along some rising slopes that were thickly matted with bracken.

"Yes, I live in London," was the answer.

"But you are not knowing Corstorphine?" was the next question.

"No, I don't know him; but surely you would not quarrel with him before getting another customer?"

"He is not a fair man; he should be giffing me more"—this was the refrain of the conversation, repeated again and again, as they made their way up to a rude little enclosure, the four-square wall of which had tumbled down until it was nearly level with the grass and the abundant nettles.

And now the banker-traveller found what he had come in search of—all kinds of sculptured gravestones, with memorial figures of knights in armour, lying scattered about among the tall weeds. In most cases he had to clear away this herbage before he could get a proper view of the stones; while his companion stood blankly gazing on, perhaps wondering at this curiosity about such familiar things, but saying nothing. Nor did the stranger apparently expect to get from the old fisherman much information about the Culdees and their haunts, and the Irish princes and knights who were fain to choose for their burial-place one of those sacred islands in the northern seas. He examined tombstone after tombstone, observing the curious emblems—elephants, two-handed swords, rude castles, and such smaller things as pincers and combs—that no doubt would have afforded to anyone sufficiently instructed some hint as to the dignity or office of the now-forgotten dead; and very singular it was to find these memorials of bygone ages in this silent little island set amid these lonely seas. Then they went to the chapel, a small building of hardly any architectural pretensions beyond some sculptured stones over the doorway; while inside the only noticeable feature was a lot of scattered hay—the old fisherman's bed when his business or the weather compelled him to pass a night on the island. Finally, they visited the Saints' Well, a considerable hole bored down through the solid rock; and here the exploration of this isolated little bit of no-man's-territory seemed to have come to an end.

But their last quest had brought them to the top of a ridge, from which they could look down on a tiny bay—a secluded small bay that appeared to be safe from the strong tides that were seen to be running a little further out.

"Not much of a current in here, is there?" the Englishman asked.

"No, not mich," his companion answered.

"Well, look here, my friend, before setting out for home again, I think I should like to have a dip in the sea, and this seems a very nice and likely place. In the meantime, if you go back to your boat, I wish you would pick me out two or three lobsters, and you shall have your own price for them—better than what Corstorphine gives you, I imagine. Do you understand?"

"Oh, ay," said the old man, beginning to move away; "I'll have their claws tied by the time you come."

These were the last words that this hapless traveller was ever to hear on this earth. The old fisherman went slowly back to his boat, to select the lobsters for his unexpected customer. He went leisurely about the task, thinking of nothing, most likely, but the price that would probably be paid for them. Then he lit his pipe, and sat waiting in the silence. An absolute silence it was, save for the noise of certain sea-swallows, that seemed to have been disturbed by the bather, and were now wheeling and darting overhead, uttering screams of alarm and resentment over the intrusion.

Suddenly the old man heard a cry—a call for help, as it seemed to be, from far away. He started up erect, and listened. That faint, boding sound was repeated. Instantly he threw aside the lobster-trap that happened to be in his hand, and, with a speed that could hardly have been expected from one of his age, he made his way up the slopes of bracken, until he stood on a knoll commanding a view of the bay beside which he had left the stranger. The same moment he perceived whence had come that cry of anguish. The swimmer was some way out—perhaps the strong tide had caught him—perhaps cramp had struck him helpless—but just as old John Logan, entirely bewildered and unnerved, was hesitating as to what he ought to do, there was an arm raised from the surface of the water—as if in a last, pitiful appeal to the silent heavens overhead—and then the smooth plain of the sea was blank of any feature whatsoever. Nothing but this wide waste—and the voiceless air—and the warm sun shining abroad over an empty world.

Hardly knowing what he did, the old man rushed down the slopes again, and across the beach, and shoved off the stranger's boat, which was lighter than his own, jumping into it, and setting to work at the oars with a breathless and strenuous haste. But there were two small promontories intervening between this bay and that on the western side of the island; and his hurried pulling was not likely to be of any avail. Old Logan did his best—probably too much alarmed to have any time for the calculation of chances; and ever, as he came within view of the stretch of water where he had seen the drowning man go down, he kept glancing over his shoulder as he tugged away at the oars. There was nothing visible at all—nothing but that wide blue plain of sea, and the lonely shore stretching in successive indentations away to the south. He relaxed his efforts now. He had reached, as well as he could judge, the very spot at which he had seen the stranger disappear. There was no sign of him, nor of any other living thing—even the screaming sea-fowl had departed. He took the oars into the boat, and stood up—looking all around. It was hopeless. If the swimmer had been seized with cramp, as seemed most likely, this strong tide would have swept him away with it long before Logan had come round the point. Indeed, the current was so powerful that the old man had presently to take to the oars again, and pull hard into the quieter waters of the bay, where eventually he landed, dragging the boat a little bit up on the beach.

He was used to loneliness; but this loneliness had never been terrible to him before. That boding cry—that piteous call for aid —seemed still to linger in the air. It was so short a time since he had been familiarly speaking to this fellow-creature, who had been suddenly swept away out of the living and breathing world. In vain the old man, with long-accustomed eyes, swept that vast expanse of water; there was no sign—he knew there could be no sign. It was only a kind of mysterious fascination that kept him gazing on the wide watery plain where he had seen that arm thrown up as in a last despairing appeal for help. Help, he knew, there was none now; the stranger who had sought these solitary shores had vanished for ever from human ken.

There was nothing now for him but to go away back to the village of Harivaig, on the mainland, to acquaint the people there with what had happened; and so, with a parting glance at the empty waste of sea, he set out along the beach. And here, after he had gone some thirty or forty yards, he came upon the drowned man's clothes. He approached them with a morbid curiosity, and yet with a certain reluctance that was akin to fear. They looked strangely like a corpse. They were dead and mute, an unfamiliar and uncanny thing, lying dark on the white beach. And then, as he drew nearer—slowly and cautiously—he noticed that there was some small object there that glittered in the strong sunlight. It was a piece of jewellery, lying on the empty waistcoat. He went close up, his eyes still fixed on those small stones that gleamed in the sun, and, although he did not quite know what this thing was—it was a locket, indeed, of considerable size, with initials on the outside composed of alternate rubies and diamonds—he recognised it as one of those adornments that rich people wore. And then—at what instigation, who can tell?—he bethought him of his grand-daughter, Jeannie, the one sole creature in the world he cared for; she was to be married in the autumn, and she had nothing of this kind to give her value in the eyes of her husband. The young man who was going to marry her had made several voyages to foreign parts, and could talk bravely about the wonderful things he had seen: moreover, he was a smart young fellow and had saved up a little money; the neighbours seemed to consider that the grand-daughter of the poor old lobster-fisherman was making a very good match. But if Jeannie were to wear this pretty thing on her wedding-day, would not the young man prize her the more? For good looks there was none to beat her on mainland or island, and that everyone was ready to say; but her grandfather's hard-earned savings would be drawn upon rather to give the young couple a fair start in life; she would not have fine clothes to wear as a bride. But if she were to appear with this pretty thing at her neck, would not the young man be all the better pleased with her; and Jeannie would be proud to know that he thought something of her; and none of the neighbours would any longer be fancying that as regards the marriage between the two young people she was getting the best of the bargain?

Old John Logan turned slowly round—as if he feared to find someone watching him from afar. But his quick, furtive glance found nothing. The world was empty of all token of life. There were the trending lines of the bay, the placid mirror of the sea, the cloudless heavens; and he was alone with them. And he was alone with this pretty thing that would make his granddaughter of greater importance in the eyes of her husband. Of what use was it now to the drowned man? Doubtless there were other things of value in these clothes if he were to search—money, a gold watch, and so forth; but he would not touch any of these;

for himself he wanted nothing; it was for Jeannie that he coveted this bit of adornment. He could hide it away somewhere. The drowning of the unfortunate man would soon be forgotten. And then the autumn would come; and as the wedding-day drew near he would present Jeannie with this pretty toy; and who could tell that he had not sent to Glasgow for it?

He turned round again towards the bauble that had tempted him, and stood there helpless and motionless for several seconds. Then he knelt down upon the shingle with both knees. But as he took up the locket—with a kind of pretence of only examining it —his hands were shaking as if he had been stricken with palsy. He pushed his scrutiny further. By accident—for he knew nothing of such trinkets—he happened to touch the yielding portion of the gold loop attaching the locket to the watch-chain; he pressed it, and saw how he could take the locket out. The next moment the prize that he had feared almost to look upon lay in the palm of his hand. Then he slowly rose—his knees all shaking beneath him— and furtively his glance searched sea and shore for any sign of any living thing. Then, with many a backward look—for it seemed to him that there must be someone behind him, someone unseen, but watching—he crossed over the grassy ridges and went down to the creek in which his boat lay. His hand was shut now, with a nervous and tremulous grasp.

In the boat there was some old canvas that he sometimes used in patching up the lobster-traps; he cut off a piece, and wrapped up in it that fatal locket, with its glittering jewels; then he made his way up the hill and across to the old chapel. There was no difficulty in finding a hole in which to secrete his treasure; he chose one in the wall, close down to the ground; and then, having deposited the tiny packet there, he went and got some stones and dry earth and closed up the orifice in a rude sort of fashion. But there was little light in this small building; no one could have noticed that the wall had been meddled with.

And then old John Logan went down to the seaside again, and launched his boat. He might have taken the stranger's boat, which was a good deal lighter to pull; but he had left it on the shore of the other bay, and he dreaded to look again on the clothes

lying there. So in his own cumbrous craft he set out for the mainland; and in due course of time he reached the small hamlet of
Harivaig, which was speedily startled by the news that the Englishman who had recently come thither had been drowned, and that
his clothes, and the boat in which he had rowed himself across,
would be found on the beach at Eilean-na-Keal.

II

REMORSE

NOW, THE chief public functionary of Harivaig and its neighbourhood was the parish schoolmaster; and he it was who immediately
took steps to apprise the relatives of the drowned man of what
had happened. There was no difficulty about discovering who he
was. His private address could not be found; but his papers showed
clearly enough that he was a partner in the banking firm of
Ramsden, Holt, and Smith, of London; and it was to them that
the schoolmaster addressed his communication. Then the clothes
of the stranger were brought back from the island, and also the
boat in which he had rowed himself across. Finally, the owner of
the nearest salmon-fishery sent four of his men as a search-party
all along the coast; but although they laboured at their task indus-
triously for the better part of two days, no trace of the missing
man could be found. Indeed, they worked without hope: it was a
matter almost of certainty that the body had been washed out to
sea.

Meanwhile, old John Logan had more than once, and all by
himself, been over to Eilean-na-Keal, and each time he had
stealthily made his way to the small ruined chapel, and taken forth
the locket from its secret repository, and regarded its gleaming
white and red stones. Moreover, he had accidentally discovered
that it would open; and inside he found the portrait of a pale-
faced, delicate-featured lady, apparently of middle age. On making
this discovery, he had hurriedly shut the trinket again—for the
pale face seemed to be looking strangely at him; and he had
formed some dark resolution of removing it, either by gentle means

or force, before the time came for presenting this pretty, bejewelled wedding-gift to his granddaughter. But even when he restricted his contemplation to the outside—to the rich soft golden surface, and the glittering diamonds and rubies—there was not much joy in his heart. For one thing, a nameless terror seemed to seize him the moment he set foot on the island. He felt haunted by some mysterious presence; however his anxious scrutiny might satisfy him that these indented shores were devoid of human life, he appeared to be always expecting someone; when he walked across the lonely little knolls, on his way to the chapel, it was as if there were some living creature following him, close to his shoulder, unseen but felt. And in the dusk of the chapel itself, when he was crouching down, ready to thrust back the locket into the hole in the wall, he would listen intently, as if fearing some footstep without; and then again, when he came forth into the daylight, his dazed eyes would furtively and swiftly look all around, to make sure that he was quite alone. If the time would but pass more quickly! If the days and weeks could be annihilated, and his granddaughter's wedding-morn be reached—then this precious thing would pass into her keeping, and would trouble his rest no more. For old John Logan had got into a perturbed and feverish state; the drowning of the stranger had made a great commotion in this quiet neighbourhood; and Logan, as the last person who had seen him, had to answer innumerable questions—that sometimes seemed to bewilder and frighten him by their unexpectedness.

One morning the old man's granddaughter Jeannie was seated on the rude bench outside the cottage. She had got early finished with her household work, and now she was hemming some handkerchiefs—most likely part of her home-made trousseau—while she sung to herself the cheerful air of "I'll gang nae mair to yon town" without particular regard to the words. She was a good-looking lass of the darker Celtic type—coal-black hair, a complexion as fresh and clear as a June wild rose, dark blue-grey eyes with black lashes, and a pretty and smiling mouth. She was rather neatly dressed, and seemed very well content with herself; indeed, the neighbours were inclined to be indignant among themselves over the fashion in which old John Logan spoiled his pretty granddaughter. Nevertheless, Jeannie Logan (as she was called, though her name was properly Jeannie Carmichael) was a kind of favourite, and that despite the fact of her small house being kept a good deal more trim and tidy than any other in Harivaig.

The old man came out of the cottage, and was going off for the shore, when his granddaughter stopped him.

"Grandfather," said she (but she spoke in Gaelic), "will you not stay at home to-day? Archie is coming over from Usgary."

"What should I stay at home for?" was the answer (also in Gaelic). "When two young people are going to get married they have plenty to talk of by themselves; it does not need the old man of Ross to tell us that."

The young woman's cheeks flushed a little, but she laughed all the same.

"I know," she said, "that everyone thinks we talk of nothing but nonsense. Well, it is not of much consequence what any of them are thinking. But you remember, grandfather, that the valuing of the nets was to be done this week; and Archie was writing to me that he would like to have your opinion."

"My opinion!" the old man said, testily. "What is the use of my opinion? What do I know about herring-nets that I have not seen?"

Their conversation was interrupted. There was a sound of wheels—a most unusual sound in this unfrequented neighbourhood —and presently there came in sight a waggonette and two horses. As the carriage drove past, a clear enough view of the occupants could be obtained; and these were seen to be a young lady of about seventeen or eighteen, fair-complexioned, and in deep mourning, and a tall and elderly gentleman who sat opposite her in the body of the waggonette. The moment they had gone by, Jeannie Logan turned eagerly to her grandfather.

"Do you know who these are?" she said. "For I know. These must be the friends of the gentleman who was drowned. And they will be wanting to see you, grandfather—I am sure of it; so you must go indoors at once, and put on a white collar, and your black coat."

"But for what will they want to see me?" the old man said, with a quick look of apprehension on his face.

"Well, you brought the news over from Eilean-na-Keal; and you were the last that saw the gentleman, and spoke to him. I should not wonder if that was his daughter—poor young lady, this will be a sad day for her. Grandfather, go away and put on your black coat; for they will be coming to see you, or sending for you."

And she was right. Not a quarter of an hour had elapsed when a messenger came from the inn to say that the daughter of the gentleman who had been drowned was there, and that she wished to see John Logan, if he would be so kind as to come along. In the meantime, the old man had taken his granddaughter's advice —indeed, he allowed himself to be governed by her in all such matters—and put on his Sunday clothes. As he was setting out with the messenger, Jeannie Logan placed her hand on his arm for a moment, and said in a low voice,

"Grandfather, I think the young lady will be for going over to Eilean-na-Keal. Well, if the people have any sense, they will not allow her, for it will break her heart."

"Ay, ay!" he said, eagerly. "You are a wise lass, Jeannie; she should not go over to Eilean-na-Keal. No, no; what is the use of her going over to Eilean-na-Keal?"

And this is what he seemed to be pondering over all the way to the inn; for again and again he said in a half-muttering way to his companion.

"Ay, she is a wise lass is Jeannie. She has an old head on young shoulders. Why should the young lady be for going over to Eilean-na-Keal?"

But when at length he reached the inn, and was ushered into the parlour where the strangers were, there was no more speech left in him. This tall, fair-haired girl—whose face was wan and pale, and looked all the paler because of her deep mourning— when she came forward in a pathetic kind of way to take his hand, startled him beyond measure. Had he not seen her before, or someone strangely like her? And then in a bewildered fashion he thought of the face in the locket—the face that he had feared.

This was the daughter, then: that, the mother. And he seemed incapable of meeting the steady glance of those plaintive eyes that regarded him so strangely; he was breathless, irresolute, nervous; he intertwisted his fingers; he had no answer for the questions which the elderly gentleman, the young lady's companion, put to him. The landlady, a placid-looking, middle-aged woman, had taken the liberty of remaining in the room.

"He is not used to the English, sir," she said. "He will tell you when he thinks over it."

"And will you not sit down?" the young lady said very gently to him; and she herself pulled out a chair from the wall. For her the violence of grief seemed over and gone; she was outwardly resigned and calm; it was only at times that tears swam into her eyes, and she appeared anxious to hide her emotion from these strangers.

"Yes, sit down, and take your own time," her companion, who was a Mr. Holt, said to old John Logan. "Just think over it, and tell us at your leisure how Mr. Ramsden came to the island, and what he said to you, and what was the last you saw of him. You can understand that his daughter is very anxious to know."

And then the old man, halting and hesitating at every few words, told his tale. Except for the matter of his English, it ought to have come readily enough to him, for he had narrated it, to the minutest circumstances, again and again among the neighbours. It was noticeable, however, that now he kept his eyes fixed on the ground, and that his narrative was a kind of appeal; he was as a culprit endeavouring to justify himself; and over and over he repeated that no man could have pulled harder than he did to try to reach the drowning swimmer.

"Oh, I am sure of that—I am sure of that!" the girl said, piteously. "And—we will not forget it."

He did not appear to understand what she meant, so anxious was he to exonerate himself.

"There wass the two points to go round," he repeated once more. "When I wass on the top of the land I wass nearer to him —oh, yes—and I could hef run down to the watterside—and—and been nearer—but no use that would be. I hef not been sweeming since I wass a young man; I could not get out to him. And when I went back to the boat there wass the two points to go round—a long weh it was to pull, and the tide running strong—and I pulled as well as I could. I pulled as hard as ever I wass pulling ahl my life——"

"Indeed, I am sure you did your best!" said she—for it seemed pitiable that this old man should think it needful to appeal to her and justify himself.

"Well," said her companion, seeing that Logan's narrative had come to an end, "we have sent for a boat. Miss Ramsden would like to go across to the island; and if you have time to come with us you could show her the place where you last saw her father. Will you add this further obligation to what we already owe you?"

Old Logan was stupefied. In Gaelic he might have remonstrated, and pointed out that it would only be harrowing the feelings of the young lady; but his English was not effective for any such purpose; he had merely to acquiesce in silence; and so it befell that when the salmon fisherman's boat, with a crew of four stalwart rowers, had been brought along, the orphaned girl and her friend, and old John Logan, too, went to the shore, and presently were being taken across the smooth plain of water to Eilean-na-Keal.

She was showing a wonderful fortitude. No sooner had she landed than she began asking the most particular questions— apparently anxious to construct for herself a complete picture of those last minutes of her father's life. Where did he pull his boat up on the beach? Where was he, Logan? What were her father's first words? In what direction did the two of them go to explore the island, and what was the subject of their talk? Thus it was that the old man came to recall and repeat every single sentence that had been uttered between them. He told her of his complaints about Corstorphine. He told her of the approaching marriage of his granddaughter; of the young man who wanted to purchase a share in a herring-smack; of his own wish to help him in that matter; of the small prices he was getting for the lobsters; of his asking her father if he did not know Corstorphine, that perhaps he might remonstrate.

"But you need not let that trouble you," she said, gently; "I will take care you have enough money to buy the share in the boat."

He started somewhat, and stared at her.

"You, Mem? Oh, no, Mem! I could not be thinking of tekking money from you!" he said, with a curious earnestness that seemed to have something of dread in it.

For during all the time that they had been coming over in the boat, and all the time he had been talking to her on the island, the conviction was growing deeper in his heart that he had robbed this grief-stricken girl, and that without the possibility of restitution. When he had originally taken the locket it seemed the property of no one. Its owner was gone away out of this world; he could never come back to reclaim it; it did not belong to him any more. But now the old man knew that it belonged to this gentle-spoken young lady, who was overwhelmed with her sorrow. That was her mother's portrait, sure enough. And here—although he had robbed her of what must be of exceeding value to her—here she was proposing to do him some substantial act of kindness. The mere thought of it terrified him, somehow. It seemed to aggravate his guilt. Had he not done her enough wrong? And what would be the luck of the herring-smack if part of its purchase-money came through his hands that were stained with crime?

They were approaching the ruined chapel—he rather lingering behind her. He was reluctant to go near; he would not enter by the narrow porch; he would have dissuaded her from going further if only he had dared. And yet what could have been more simple, if this anguish of remorse and contrition was becoming unbearable, than for him to have gone courageously forward and taken out the locket from its hiding-place, confessed his fault, and begged for her forgiveness? She seemed a kind and sympathetic creature; she was profoundly grateful to him for the efforts, however futile, he had made to rescue her father. Surely she would accept this, all the reparation he could make, and grant him pardon?

But that was not at all how the matter appeared to old John Logan. In his mind the English were a great and powerful and terrible people. Sailors had told him again and again of the vast men-of-war coming into the Clyde, of their enormous cannon, and of the thunder that shook the world when the huge guns were fired. The dread powers of government were in England; the Queen was there, and Parliament, and the Tower that prisoners were thrown into. And if he confessed that he had robbed an English person, would he not be dragged away to that stranger country, and perhaps hanged? The English were a strong, terrible, and vindictive race—so he had heard many a time, in stories current in his boyhood's day. Not to them dared he appeal for mercy. If he made this confession, her forgiveness would avail him nothing; the inexorable powers of the law would seize him, and how would it be with his granddaughter Jeannie if he was taken away to the south and hanged?

He was less anxious and perturbed when the young lady came out of the chapel, and once more submitted to his guidance. In fact, they were following step by step the careless saunter that her father had little thought to be his last; until, finally, Logan took her to the ridge overlooking the fatal bay, and showed her, as well as he could, the precise spot at which the drowning man had disappeared. It was so lonely, this outlook. She gazed upon it with a kind of shrinking terror. Calm as the sea was, it seemed a cruel, secret, dreadful thing. The silence was awful. She stood there a long while; and it was not until she was coming away that her forced composure entirely broke down. She had turned to cast one long, final, lingering glance towards these empty shores and the voiceless plain of the sea; and it was perhaps some sense of her complete orphanhood that was borne in upon her, or perhaps a feeling that this was a last farewell. But she gave way altogether, and, sinking to the ground, buried her head in her hands, and sobbed and cried passionately and bitterly.

"Edith!" her companion said to her, and he put his hand gently on her shoulder: "Edith, come away now! Indeed, you must come away!"

He assisted her to rise; and then, with bent head and uncertain footsteps, she made her way back to the boat. During the long pull to the mainland, she turned once or twice to regard the small island set amid the calm seas. This was indeed farewell.

Immediately on their arrival at the inn, Mr. Holt began to make preparations for their return to the south; for it was useless allow-ing the girl to remain in this sad neighbourhood. He got his late partner's effects put together, and without much examination; for, finding watch, money, and papers all intact, he did not deem it necessary to make further inquiry, and it certainly never occurred to him at such a time to ask the bereaved daughter about trinkets. The men belonging to the salmon-fishery were liberally rewarded for their two days' search. Then came the question of Logan; and here it was fortunate that Archie MacEachran, who was to marry the old man's granddaughter, happened this very day to have come over from Usgary. Mr. Holt sent for him, and he came: a pleasant-looking, light-haired young fellow he was, with a quick, alert eye, though he was somewhat bashful in manner. Mr. Holt had arranged to see him alone.

"I understand you are to marry John Logan's granddaughter," the banker said to him forthwith, "and there is some question of your buying a share in a herring-smack. Now, Miss Ramsden is very much interested in the old man—and grateful to him for having done what he could to rescue her father when he was drowning; and she would like to do something to show her gratitude. He seemed disturbed when she suggested money; I don't know why that should be so; but it has occurred to me that it might be managed in this way—he intends helping you to buy the share in the boat—"

"Ay, but there's the two ways of it," said this young man eagerly, and he could speak English freely enough, if still with a considerable accent; "he wass wanting me to tek the money ahltogether, and I did not like the look of that, for he has not mich, and the look of it would be that I was being paid for marrying his granddaughter. No, I said, I will tek a loan of the money, and I will pay you back. The Kate and Bella is a lucky boat; the Macdowell brothers that hef her, each one of them hass money in the savings-bank; and now that one of them thinks he can do better by buying sheep and tekking them to the trysts, it is a good chance for me to get his share in the smack. Old John Logan—well, he will be wanting his own savings when he gets too old to look after the lobster-traps; and besides that he will hef to be paying some young girl to mind the house for him, when Jeannie Logan comes to me. But if he will lend me the money, ferry well; and I will pay him back when I can."

"I think you take a very sensible view of the situation," the banker said. "How much is this loan that you require?"

"Well, I hef got ahl the money except about twenty-four pounds."

"Twenty-four pounds," Mr. Holt repeated. "Miss Ramsden thought of giving the old man something bigger than that. However, it can be managed in this way: we will make you a loan of fifty pounds, and you will covenant to pay it back to John Logan, in instalments—extending over three years if you like. We will tell him that we have advanced you this loan on his account—to give you a fair start in your married life—and to preserve his small savings for his own need; and I dare say he won't mind taking the money in that indirect way."

"Not him, sir," the young man said, with a smile. "He knows the value of money as well as anyone. Some of them will be for saying that old John Logan is not ferry wise in the head; but I think he is clever enough about *that*; he can tell you ferry well what is due to him for interest, and how the book stands—that I know fine!"

"That's all right, then," Mr. Holt said, rising—and the other rose too, and stepped towards the door. "There will be some papers for you to sign. Write your full name and address on an envelope, and leave it for me with the landlady before you go. You will hear later on."

"I thank ye, sir; I thank ye," the young man said; but even with the door open he lingered, standing there shamefacedly.

"There's—there's something more," he stammered. "Maybe—I don't know how to say it, but if you were to tell the young lady that we thanked her for her kindness—and—and more than that —that there's not one of us—not one of us—but would rather not hef it at ahl if we could get her father back to her alive."

The banker stepped forward and took the young man's hand for a moment.

"I will give her the message. She is a kind-hearted girl. In this case I think her kindness has been well bestowed."

And so the strangers went away; and the little hamlet of Harivaig returned to its normal condition of slumberous quiet. But this peace brought no comfort to the mind of old John Logan. Ever before him was the remembrance of the grief-stricken young lady, pale and sad-eyed, who had accompanied him over the island; and he knew that the portrait of her mother, that by right belonged to her, was hidden away in the small chapel, and that he dared not bring it forth into the light. He had lost all intention now of giving the jewelled trinket to his granddaughter Jeannie, to adorn her on her wedding day. Even if the portrait were cut out, and deep buried in the earth, there would be something about the locket itself that he could not face. It was no longer flotsam and jetsam; it belonged to the beautiful, gentle-hearted girl who had been so kind to him and his: he had robbed her—as a requital of her bounty towards them.

The neighbours remarked that old John Logan was growing still more strange in his ways. He had hardly a word for anyone now. He seemed morose and depressed; he would not even talk about the purchase of the share in the Kate and Bella—though that was known to be a great thing for young MacEachran and Jeannie Logan; and he did not go over to Eilean-na-Keal as often as he used to do, even when the weather was quite fine. Moreover, in the little Free Church building half-way on the road to Usgary, to which the Harivaig people walked every Sabbath morning, they noticed that, more than once, when the Minister was making a fervent appeal to the consciences of his people, John Logan, with downbent head, would answer with a perfectly audible moan. Some said that the old man was grown older than ever in his ways simply because of the solitary life that he led out at the lobster-baskets. Others hinted that the sight of the stranger drowning had frightened him, and that he had never been quite the same since. While others again maintained that it was merely the going away of his granddaughter that was preying on his mind, and that he would soon get accustomed to it, once the wedding was over.

"Grandfather," said Jeannie Logan to him one night—an open Bible was lying on the table before him, and she had heard him sigh heavily once or twice, as if in great distress or pain, "grandfather, is there anything wrong with you?"

"There is something wrong with me," he answered, in the Gaelic, "that will never be made right in this world."

"What is it, grandfather?" she asked, in sudden alarm.

But he would not speak; and as the days went by matters seemed to grow worse with him. The neighbours wondered; but his grand-daughter could tell them nothing. At last there came one evening —he had got down the Bible, as usual, and as it was almost dark, she was just about to light the lamp.

"Jeannie," said he, "I have something to say to you."

"Yes, grandfather?"

"You have been a good lass to me in this house; and you will make a good wife. I could not wish to see you better married. The lad will do well. And you will say nothing to anyone to-night, nor yet in the morning; but to-morrow morning I am going away."

"Going away, grandfather!" she exclaimed. "Why, where are you going?"

"I am going away," he said—and as she lit the lamp at this moment, she was startled to find that there were tears running down the old man's face. "I am going away—to—to Greenock— and maybe further than that, and maybe I will never come back to Harivaig. But you have been a good lass—and you will make a good wife."

"Grandfather," said she, suddenly, "are you going away on my account? Is it because I am going to be married?"

"No, no; it is not that. I am glad that you will have a house of your own and a husband to look after you. It is not that; it is of no use for you to know; and if any of them ask you where I have gone you can say I am away by the Dunara Castle to the south. Be a good lass, Jeannie, be a good lass; you will have a house of your own now; and the lad will do well."

All her prayers and entreaties and expostulations were of no avail; she could get no further answer from him; nay, he enjoined her to silence; and early in the morning—long before the hamlet of Harivaig was awake—she heard him open the door and set out. He had started on his long and weary tramp to the nearest port at which the Dunara Castle called.

III

A PILGRIMAGE

During that long sea-voyage to Greenock old John Logan saw many strange things, but nothing so strange as the termination of it, when, just after nightfall, the steamer slowly glided into its appointed berth alongside the quay. He had never beheld a large town before; and although this town was invisible, the amazing extent of it could be guessed from its bewildering glare—rows of points of yellow fire gleaming afar, as if along unknown hills, fiercer white lights, and green lamps, and red lamps, down here in the harbour, while the very heavens overhead were irradiated by a dull, sombre, steady glow. When Logan, with his small bundle in his hand, left the gangway, and found himself stranded on the quay—amid these hurrying black figures, and the bewildering gas-lamps, and general confusion and noise—he knew not which way to turn. What he had in his mind was to find out the steamer that would carry him on to London; but how was he to discover her whereabouts in the dark? He had been told on board the Dunara Castle that there was such a steamer—the Anchor Line, they said. But he knew not where nor whom to ask; indeed, he was somewhat dazed, not to say frightened; he stood there irresolute, watching men and things pass by him as in some black and appalling nightmare.

And then, cautiously and fearfully, he began his quest, wandering like a ghost round the dimly-lit basins and docks. But all these vessels seemed dead He made bold to ask one or two of the solitary passers-by; but they did not stay to answer this old man with his hesitating speech and unintelligible questions. At last one of them, more civil than his predecessors, did stop for a second to ascertain what the old man wanted; and then, with a curt "She'll be doon the morn," he went on his way again.

So there was the long night to be passed in this terrible place. He began to look at the houses, wondering whether he dared ask at any of them for a night's lodging. His stock of money was small; and he wished to hoard it; for what was yet before him was all unknown. Moreover, a night in the open was nothing to him— had it been on the sea, that is, or on the shores of an island; what a night in the streets of a town might be, he knew not. He wandered on. He came upon a wider thoroughfare, where there was an amazing concourse of people—a double stream of people, passing along the pavement, under the gas-lamps, in front of the blazing windows of the shops. There were shouts and cries; there was a roar and rattle of wheels; the lights fell on all kinds of strange faces, many of them grimy and disfigured, some with unkempt hair and dissolute features, others loud-laughing with a ghastly mirth. It was like some kind of Pandemonium, into which he might fall, and be swept away; he shrank back from it; he hid himself in the gloom of one of the by-streets, and gazed forth upon it with an insatiable, terrified curiosity. And then he thought the neighbourhood of the docks would be safer for him. He would feel more at his ease if he were near the water; so he turned his back upon that flaming, roaring, turbulent highway, and set out through the silence of the dark little thoroughfare to reach the harbour and the quays.

He had proceeded some way down this little by-street when the prevailing quietude was broken in upon by the distant raucous voice of someone bawling "Ye Banks and Braes" to the discordant accompaniment of a concertina. Presently two figures loomed in sight—one of them flinging his arms about as he made this hideous din with the concertina; the other growling and cursing at his companion for the noise he was making. They proved to be two great hulking fellows—loafers about the docks, most likely; and as they came up to old John Logan, one of them, a beetle-browed, surly-looking dog, angrily knocked the concertina out of his neighbour's hand, so as to ensure some kind of silence, while he proceeded, apparently from mere ill-temper, to cross-question John Logan as to how he came to be there and what he wanted. The old man, suspecting no ill, told him in his hesitating English that he was waiting for the steamer that was next day going to London, and that he was not sure whether to ask somewhere for a bed. By this time the brawling musician had quieted down, and seemed much interested in the stranger.

"Ye auld gomeril," said he, with rough jocularity, "what are ye aboot? Do ye no ken that my freen' here's the captain o' the verra steamer ye're gaun' in—ay, as sure 's death: what for would I tell ye a lee? And dinna ye ken that she's already cam' doon frae Glesca—she's lying in the harbour, man, and what's to prevent yer ganging on board and getting a nicht's rest in yer ain berth?"

"Ay, could I do that?" old Logan said, eagerly: here was just the fulfilment of his most anxious wishes—to get on board the vessel at once, and know that he was safe bound for London.

"Of course ye can!" the other said, gaily; while the heavy-browed ruffian stood silently by and watched. "There's my freen' the captain: speak him fair, and he'll put ye on board directly, and ye'll have yer ain bunk. Ye've got yer passage-money!"

"Ay," answered the old man.

"And maybe something ower?"

"Ay, ay—maybe," Logan said, with some hesitation.

"Ye'll have to pay yer passage-money afore ye gang on board —that's the rule in this line o' steamers," said the musician, who was gradually losing his boisterously facetious tone, and attending to this matter in a strictly business fashion. "And the best thing for ye will be to step round to the captain's house—it's no very far frae here—and we'll just settle up at once, and then ye'll gang strecht on board. It's no safe for an auld man like you to be wanderin' about Greenock streets: ye'll be far better on board the ship. Come on!"

Old Logan suspected nothing. He had seen captains of coasting-vessels no better dressed than either of these men; and he was not likely to know the difference between the master of a trading-smack and the master of an Anchor Liner. But, indeed, it was his extreme anxiety to get at once on board the steamer that induced him to consent. Without further scruple he accompanied the two strangers—down this street, across another, and along a third, until they stopped at a certain "close." This close or entrance was pitch-dark; but the concertina-player led the way, old Logan following, and groping with his hands along the wall, the surly-browed scoundrel bringing up the rear. Then they had to ascend a stair, also in absolute darkness; but at the second landing a door was opened, and that gave some small indication of their whereabouts. They entered the house. It seemed empty, for there was not a sound of any kind; however, by the dull light of a small lamp in the lobby the old Highlander was ushered into a room, and there the leader of the party struck a match and lit a candle that was on the chimney-piece. It was a dingy little den; but Logan was not thinking of his surroundings: it was the steamer that concerned him.

The door was made fast behind them: the candle was placed on the table.

"Now, my decent old freen'," the concertina-player began, resuming his jocular manner, "we'll jist settle this business at once. Out wi' the little bits o' dibs. And ye may just as weel hand us over the lot: ye'll no want any money till ye get to London. Come on!—let's see what ye've got. Is't in a stocking? I'm vexed I canna offer ye a dram to croon the bargain; but never mind—just hand us ower what ye've got, and I'll gie ye a receipt at Marti'mas."

And now it was that old John Logan began to realise the position in which he found himself; and it was impossible to say which was the more disquieting—this bantering that was growing near to bullying, or the sinister silence with which the other confederate stood and looked on.

"I'll—I'll pay when I get on board the steamer," the old man said, and instinctively he turned and glanced towards the door.

"Will ye now?" the concertina-player rejoined, with a burst of laughter. "Weel, that's a guid ane! Ye're a funny auld deevle!" He put both elbows on the table, rested his head in his hands, and stared mockingly at old Logan. "Do ye no think this is a fine, quate place to do our wee bit o' business? We wadna disappoint the captain? If ye speak him fair, maybe he'll leave ye the price o' a dram. I'm getting awfu' dry mysel'; and I wish ye'd bring out they bonnie pound-notes—or is it a' in half-croons and shillins, in a nice wee bag?"

But here his accomplice broke in impatiently.

"Oh, stop your jaw!" he said; and then he turned to Logan: "Here, oot wi' that money!"

"Ay, that's it, Tam," the other said, complacently, "you get the money, and I'll just hae a look at the bundle—maybe there's a braw saytin waistcoat that'll dae for my weddin'."

He reached across, and would have seized the bundle, but that the old man—now thoroughly alarmed—snatched it out of his grasp and made forthwith for the door. Instantly the more taciturn of the two scoundrels placed himself in his way; whereupon Logan, wild with fright, dropped his bundle, and gripped the man with both hands, to hurl him on one side. The attack was so sudden—the strength of the old man so unexpected—that this heavy-built brute was taken aback—his one foot tripped over the other—he staggered a step or two and fell headlong before he had time to clutch at anything but the useless wall. Logan turned in haste to pick up his bundle, only to find that the other bully was rushing at him with an uplifted poker. The blow would have fallen on his head, but that he warded it off with his arm; and then, in desperation, he drove at this fellow as he had driven at the other—with the whole weight of his heavy shoulders—sending him crashing against the table. In an instant everything was in blackness. The candle had been knocked over. And now, for a moment, it was just possible that the old man might have got safely away if he could have found the door at once; but instead of the door he stumbled against the more burly of the two ruffians, who seized and tried to hold him, while the other, with the most horrible threats and imprecations, was endeavouring to find a match to light the candle. And no sooner was the room lit again than the scrimmage recommenced; for the old man fought with the fury of a wild cat. It was not his money he was fighting for, nor yet his little bundle of clothes, but for the safety of a certain treasure sewn up in the lining of his coat, of the existence of which they little dreamed. Of course, such an unequal struggle could have but one end. A blow on the head with the poker knocked him senseless; and he knew no more.

When he came to himself—he had no idea how long thereafter —there was a fierce glare of yellow light striking into his dazed

eyes. It was a policeman's lantern. He was lying on the pavement
outside; and when the policeman helped him up to a sitting position, it was seen that his white hair was bedabbled with blood.

"Ye're an auld chap to hae been fechtin'," the policeman said,
in no unkindly way. "How came ye to be in such a state as this?
Ye're no drunk, too! Weel, ye'll hae to get up and gang wi' me to
the office, and gie an account of yoursel'."

But the first thing that old John Logan did on regaining consciousness was quickly to put his hand to his side. It was enough.
He felt the hard substance there under the cloth. They had robbed
him of his little bundle of clothes, and plundered him of every
penny, but they had not discovered the jewelled trinket, the restitution of which would make such reparation as was now possible,
and perchance mitigate in some measure the remorse and anguish
of his soul. Obediently, like a child, he did what the policeman told
him. He gave him what account he could of the circumstances
leading up to the robbery, and of the robbery itself; but he could
not say which of the "closes" in this dark little thoroughfare was
the one he had been induced to enter, for the thieves had taken
the precaution of dragging him some little way along the pavement after fetching him out. And obediently, if somewhat slowly
—for he was faint and weak from want of blood—he accompanied
the policeman to the station. Here he told his story over again, and
had the wounds on his head dressed; and the inspector on duty,
finding that the old man had been left without a farthing, would
have allowed him to pass the night in one of the cells. But John
Logan would not hear of that; nor would he listen to the proposal
that he should remain in Greenock for a time to see whether the
detectives could not discover the thieves who had robbed him, and
perhaps get back some of the stolen property. His mind was set
on London. The steamer was coming down the Clyde the next
day. If he had no money, perhaps they would let him work his
passage as a deck hand. So, as well as he was able, he thanked the
people at the police-office for their kind treatment of him, and went
forth again into the night.

But this time, while he was still anxious to get down to the
harbour, with the vague instinct that he would somehow be safer

near the water, he kept to the thoroughfares where he saw plenty of people. In this wise he made his way along Cathcart Street, and down the lane leading to the Custom House, until at length he found himself on the quay. Out there was the black water; and afar he could see the red and green sailing-lights of the steamers passing up and down the estuary. There was hardly anyone on this wide, open breadth of stone; so he wandered along, looking for some corner of a shed where he might rest for the night. For it was getting late; and the old man was weak and exhausted; moreover, there was a singing in his head that seemed to stupefy him; so that, when he happened in his wandering search to come upon a barrow that was chained to a post—it was dark here, and he thought no one would disturb him—he crept on to it, and lay down with his arm for a pillow, and with his other hand clasped over the jewelled toy that had brought him so much tribulation.

IV

A FRIEND IN NEED

BUT THERE was not much sleep for old John Logan. His circumstances were too desperate. He gave up the hope of being able to work his passage to London; they would not take an old whitehaired man. Nor did he think of going by road; the distance, to his imagination, was immeasurable; he would die of hunger by the way. And if that were to be the end, there would be no restitution and atonement; his secret would be buried with him; there would be no chance of begging for forgiveness from the gentlevoiced, sad-eyed young lady who had been so kind to them all. Nay, on the awful day of Judgment, when he was arraigned as a thief, would she not be there, summoned to confront him as his accuser? How could he make known then what his contrition had been? She would stand opposite him; she would recognise him as the man for whose granddaughter she had done so much; and she would know him to be a thief. London seemed the width of worlds away. And so was Harivaig, too, to one who was penniless. He could not get back, if he had wished to get back. But he did not wish it. His life contained but one burning desire, and all things else were unregarded. So the night passed, in fruitless longings; in wild, pathetic visions of fulfilment; in the contemplation of failure, and leaden despair; and as he lay there, worn out and sleepless, with an aching head and a heavy heart, there gradually came into the eastern heavens a wan grey light that broadened and widened up until the new day was shining over land and sea.

He rose from his hard and restless couch, and looked around him with dazed eyes. The wide waters of the <u>Firth</u> were all of a shimmering grey; far away on the other side was the wooded promontory of Roseneath, with the big castle on a clearance between the trees; there were white villages along the further shores, under the low-lying hills. The business of the work-a-day world had already begun; there were vessels going up and down—here a small tug towing after it a mass of floating timber, there a larger steamer taking a big three-master away up the river. Along the quays, too, near at hand, signs of life were becoming visible; so in case anyone should complain of his having appropriated this not very desirable bed, he got on his feet again and began to wander back in the direction of the town. He had no thought of finding the two men who had robbed him—still less of recovering what they had taken from him. Indeed, he hardly knew what he was doing; only, the inspector at the police-office had spoken kindly to him, and he seemed to be drawn back thither, if he could but hit upon the way. There might be some word of advice. Anyhow, he wandered on.

He could not, however, discover the whereabouts of the police-station, and his hopes in that direction were too vague to prompt him to ask his way of a stranger. But now that the activities of the streets were declaring themselves in every direction—the shops being opened, the passers-by increasing in number—each moment seemed to add to his dismay at the thought that the steamer would soon be arriving, and would leave the quay again and set forth on its long voyage to London, while he was left in this unknown town, among all these unknown people. The more he considered this probability, the more terrible it seemed. If only he could send to Harivaig for the money to pay his passage! It was impossible. Days—he knew not how many—would have to elapse before an answer could be got; and in the meantime how was he to live? But it was the thought of the steamer coming into the quay within the next few hours that rendered him almost desperate. He began to look at the passers-by individually, wondering whether there was not some friendly soul amongst them who would lend him what he wanted. He had money at home. He would pay the loan twice over—if only he could get on at once to London. Even if he never returned to Harivaig—for as to what might befall him he was all uncertain—there were those there who would see that the money was honourably repaid.

But, as it chanced, Dame Fortune was bent this morning on making amends to old John Logan for her evil treatment of him on the previous night. As he was wandering along, regarding this one and that, he came upon a corner public-house that had just been opened, the proprietor of which was standing at the door, with his hands behind his back. He was a tall, thin man, with an aquiline nose, keen grey eyes, and light reddish-brown hair—in short, a Sutherlandshire-looking man; while there was an expression of easy good-nature about his features that was calculated to invite confidence. Old Logan hesitated—turned away—went back again—and finally, when this tall Highland-looking man retired into the shop, he followed, after a moment's pause. But when he entered, he could see no one but a young fellow who was busy polishing up the brass of the bar. Logan waited in silence. The young man turned to him.

"Weel, what is't?"

"I—I wass going to London," Logan began, in a breathless kind of way, "and—and—they hef stolen ahl my money; and I wass thinking that if I could get the loan of the money to tek me to London, I would pay it back—"

"Money to tak ye to London!" the barkeeper retorted, scornfully. "Yer heed's in a creel! Get oot o' this!"

John Logan was turning hopelessly away when the proprietor of the public-house came forth from the back premises.

"What's that, Jimmy?"

His assistant told him, with a laugh of derision. John Logan was still lingering there: the new-comer, with keen but not unkindly eyes, was scanning him from head to heel.

"Where do ye come from?" he asked.

"From Harivaig," Logan answered; "that is across the point from Usgary."

"Usgary?" the tall man repeated. "Then I suppose you have the Gaelic."

"Oh, yes, indeed—yes, indeed!" old Logan exclaimed, eagerly; and then, to his unspeakable surprise and rejoicing, he found this stranger talking to him in his native tongue.

"Tell me what has happened to you, and why you have come all the way from Usgary to Greenock, an old man like you."

There was no impediment now; with a sort of feverish haste old Logan told the story of what had befallen him—though he said nothing of the aim of his journey to London—and described his present straits; and if he did not directly beg for money to carry him on, he was eager to point out that the loan would be assuredly repaid.

"Well," said the other, continuing to talk in the Gaelic, "you are a foolish man to go into a house that you did not know; and if I were to lend you the money how should I be sure you would not fling it away in the same fashion?"

"But if I get enough to pay for the steamer, that is all I want," Logan said, with anxious eyes. "If I can get to London that is all I want. There is one Corstorphine there who knows me."

"If it comes to that, and you are so anxious to get to London, why do you not go in the train? You can leave Greenock to-night and be in London in the morning."

"The train?—I have heard about that, but I do not know it."

"Have you never seen a railway train?"

"No."

The tall, good-natured-looking publican seemed amused. He took down his Glengarry cap, and put it on his head.

"Come," said he, "and I will show you what a train is like."

Then, as they walked along the street, he said:

"And perhaps I will lend you the money, and you will find yourself in London to-morrow morning. For blood is thicker than water, as everyone knows; and I am sorry that one from the north, and a Highlander like myself, should have been robbed by these Lowland devils. It is a good thing to have the Gaelic when you meet with a Highlander; and that is the truth."

However, the publican's intentions were of no avail, in this direction at least. When they had climbed up the long flight of stairs, and entered the wide, hollow-sounding station, a train was just arriving at the platform—the huge black engine coming along with its ponderous clink-clank; and then, when it stopped, there was a sudden rush and roar of escaped steam, that caused old Logan to start back with terror on his face.

"Well, now you have seen a train," his companion said; "and do you know that it can take you to London in a dozen hours?"

Logan was silent for a moment or two; then he said—

"God knows that I am anxious to go to London; and if it is on foot I must go, then it is on foot that I will be going; but it is not in *that* that I am going."

Nor would anything shake his resolution; and his newly-found friend, seeing that the old man could not be reasoned out of this unconquerable dread, good-naturedly assented to his taking the longer route by steamer, and said he should have enough money to pay his passage. Not only that, but, discovering that Logan had had no breakfast, he took him into a coffee-shop and gave him a substantial meal; he presented him with a supply of tobacco for the voyage; altogether, he played the part of good Samaritan; and the only receipt he took for the money he advanced was the address of Logan's relatives in the north. Moreover, he came down to the wharf to see the old man away; and as the big steamer stood out to the rippling waters of the Firth, he waved his Glengarry cap once or twice before turning and going back to his shop. That was the last of him that John Logan ever saw; but the old man did not forget his countryman, nor the help he had got from him in time of sore need.

The long voyage southward proved to be quite uneventful; and he was looking forward without any great apprehension to his

landing in London, for he had been told that the St. Katharine
Dock, where the steamer would reach her berth, was not far from
Billingsgate. He received this information from a wily-looking little
foreign sailor, who, like himself, was one of the steerage-passengers,
and who had attached himself to the old man, professing great
friendship soon after their leaving Greenock. He was a small,
yellow-faced, crop-haired creature, who wore rings in his ears,
who had a sleek, insinuating manner, and looked of southern birth,
though what English he knew sounded rather as if it had been
picked up in the north of Europe. He had been all over the world,
according to his own account; and was returning to London after
having been summoned to Scotland to give evidence in a salvage
case. He had a pack of cards with him, and would have beguiled
the time in playing these with this new acquaintance, only that he
found the old man had a superstitious horror of the "devil's books."
Logan's refusal did not interrupt their intimacy; on the contrary,
Vedroz, as he called himself, became more and more friendly, and
showed his sympathetic concern by asking innumerable questions,
that John Logan sometimes answered, and sometimes did not
answer.

On day, the shifty-eyed, dusky-faced little sailor said, in an off-
hand kind of fashion—

"My vrent, yo 'ave pain—no?—in your left side?"

John Logan, looking somewhat alarmed, said that he had no pain
there.

"No?—vy you put up your hant so often? No pain? You 'ave
no rheumatics dare? No? Vell, I vas make mistake. Das its nod-
ings. Ver glad you 'ave no pain."

And then again, the same afternoon, he began to talk to the old
Highlander about the best way of concealing valuables about one's
person; and the straits he, Vedroz, had been put to in protecting
himself against rogues and thieves. The waistband of his trousers
seemed to be his favourite hiding-place. If you sewed the money
into the lining of your coat—so he said, watching the old man's face
the while—the coat might be torn off in a scuffle, or stolen when
you were asleep. The subject seemed to interest him; he returned
to it again and again; but John Logan, though he looked more and

more anxious, only held his peace. He made no confession; but sometimes he would ask, as if to be reassured, how far the St. Katherine's Docks were from Billingsgate.

When at last, after a voyage so long that it appeared to him that he had been carried away out of the world altogether, they arrived at their destination, and were free to leave the ship, Vedroz undertook to show the old man the way to Billingsgate Market, and would take no refusal. And indeed Logan was not a little terrified at the sight of the vastness of the place into which he was about to plunge; and was glad of this friendly escort. It was as yet early morning when they made their way into Upper East Smithfield; though already there were heavy vans and lorries, making a dull, continuous, distant roar through the solitude of the half-sleeping city. Vedroz bent his steps eastward, talking lightly all the while. Old John Logan kept looking out for Billingsgate, which he expected to recognise by its piles of fish-boxes; but he saw nothing of the kind. Soon they had got into one of the lowest districts in Shadwell; and Vedroz was airily explaining, in his broken English, that the distances in London were so great that one had to exercise patience.

"And 'ere is my 'ouse," said he, "up this court 'ere. You vill come up vid me?—No?—Why no?—one moment?—I keep you no one moment—den we go on to Billingsgate."

Logan followed him; but he was resolved upon entering no house. When they had got a little way up this narrow court, Vedroz knocked at a certain door; and that was immediately opened by a colossally tall, broad-shouldered, muscular-looking woman of hideous aspect, who glanced quickly from the one to the other of them.

"My vrent, dis is my vife," Vedroz said, leading the way into the passage. "Anna, dis is a vrent of mine from Scotland. Come in! No? No for one second? My Gott, why you no come in?"

But old John Logan resolutely declined; and for a moment Vedroz seemed disconcerted. Then he said—

"Ver' well. You stay there; I come back directly. You talk to my vife : Anna, see if my goot vrent will no come into the 'ouse."

He left, and was absent for several minutes, while the huge-limbed virago, instead of repeating the invitation, merely stood and stared at the old man in a stony silence. Then Vedroz made his appearance again, bearing in his hand a pewter tankard.

"'Ere, my vrent," said he, still standing within the passage; "'ere is a drink for you—oh, ver' good drink!—ver' good drink in the morning!"

But again John Logan declined, and firmly; and the little sallow-faced sailor's eyes began to burn with concealed rage.

"My Gott, why you no drink? You dink it will do 'arm?—no 'arm!—ver' good for you—'ere, drink!"

And he held out the tankard again—inviting the old man to step into the passage. But John Logan was resolved. He would not drink—he would not enter the house. Then Vedroz, his eyes sparkling with anger, came to the door; he glanced up and down the court to see that there was no one about: then he said, in a low voice,

"Anna—quick—bring him in!"

With a bound like a tigress the huge creature sprang upon the old man, and fixed both hands on his coat-collar; and the next moment he would have been dragged off his feet and into the house, but that with an extraordinary effort he pitched the whole weight of his shoulders against her chest so that they both reeled against the half-opened door. He sent up loud shouts of alarm; he fought and tore to get out of this terrible grip; and all at once he found himself thrown violently backwards—free as air—and the door shut in his face! He made instant use of his liberty. He did not stay to ask what had frightened his assailants; he hastily picked up his cap, that had been knocked off in the struggle, ran down the court and out into the street, and looked wildly around for help. Well; there was plenty, if need were. But he was not pursued; and he had no wish to go back to that den, even with assistance; so he hurriedly walked on—he knew not in what direction; but only anxious to get away from this dreadful neighbourhood. As it chanced, he took pretty much the same route that he had come; and presently he was in the High-street of Shadwell, where, there being now plenty of people about, he could breathe a little more freely, and consider as to what he should do. His heart was beating with a frightful violence; but the treasure sewn in the lining of his coat was safe.

Well, it took him a considerable time to find his way from Shadwell to Billingsgate Market, for he walked slowly, and he carefully scanned the appearance of anyone whom he approached to ask his simple question. But he did get there in the end, without further peril or adventure; and to his own surprise—for the roar of traffic, the number of people, the mass of houses, and shops, and yards, and waggons were all bewildering to him—he was not long in finding out the place of his search. And then it was—in a small counting-house at the back of some wide premises —that old John Logan found himself at last face to face with the actual Corstorphine, who had for so many years been to him but a name.

V

ABSOLUTION

MR. CORSTORPHINE was a jovial-looking, stout, rotund person, with a florid face, and bright, twinkling, small blue eyes.

"So you're John Logan?" said he, in a very friendly fashion. "Take a seat—take a seat. And what's brought ye to London? To collect your accounts? I dare say there's something in your favour in our books—I'll just see—"

"No," said the old man, "it is not that at ahl. I—I hef come to London to—to speak to Mr. Holt—that wass the name—and I wass thinking you would tell me where to find him."

"Holt?" said Mr. Corstorphine. "Holt? Oh, yes; by-the-bye, that was a sad business that happened up your way; I saw it all in the papers. You mean Holt, of Ramsden, Holt, don't you? Is it about the drowning of Mr. Ramsden you've come up to London?"

John Logan looked at the other straight in the face; he was not sure what to answer. Certain speeches of his own he had in a measure prepared; but he was not ready with replies to questions.

"Ay," said he, with deliberation, "it hass something to do with that."

Mr. Corstorphine waited for a moment, but the old man was silent; so, not caring to be too curious, he good-naturedly said:

"Oh, well, if you want to see Mr. Holt, I don't suppose there will be any difficulty. Their office is in Lombard-street."

"Ay?" said the old man, looking rather downcast. "Is it far aweh?"

"Not at all; a few minutes' walk. Are you going on there now?"

Logan hesitated; he hardly knew how to formulate the request that was in his mind.

"I am not knowing mich about towns," said he, slowly.

"Oh, but I'll send one of my lads with you," Corstorphine said at once.

"Ay, will ye do that?" the old man answered, looking up quickly and gratefully. "I wass thinking of it many's the time—maybe ye would do that. For I am not knowing mich about towns—and—and—my head is not quite right since they struck me in Greenock—and if there wass a young lad now to tek me to Mr. Holt—I would pay the young lad—"

"You will do nothing of the kind," Corstorphine said, good-humouredly. "Come along, and I'll see you safe on the way to Lombard-street."

Thus it was that old John Logan found himself plunged into the very heart of the great city, in the busiest time of the forenoon. His guide soon discovered that he was a total stranger, and was so civil as to point out the Monument to him; but Logan took little notice of that—it was the dense, hurrying mass of people that overawed him. The lad with difficulty got him to cross to the western side of Gracechurch-street—he was afraid of venturing into that roaring Maelström; and, indeed he had to take the old man by the arm and haul him this way and that, or they would never have got safely through the surging stream of cabs and waggons and omnibuses. Old Logan was quite breathless when they got to Lombard-street—not from physical exertion, but from the excitement caused by this strange, bewildering spectacle, and the mental contagion of all this eager haste. Indeed, when they reached the bank, and when his companion briefly informed him that this was Ramsden, Holt's, he hesitated about entering, for in this distracting whirl he had forgotten the speeches he had prepared during those idle days on board the steamer.

But here a fortunate circumstance happened. A brougham drove up, and there stepped from it no other than Mr. Holt himself, whose eye instantly fell on this unwonted figure that was near the door of the bank.

"Bless me!" he said, going up to Logan, "how have you come here? Do you bring any news? Has the body been found?"

John Logan was startled by so sudden an encounter; he regarded this tall, keen-looking man with a troubled eye.

"No," he managed to say at last, and he shook his head.

"But you have come to see me?" the other asked, promptly.

"Ay, ay," Logan made answer. "I—I wass wanting—"

"But come in, first of all," the banker said. "Come up to my room—then we'll hear what you've got to say," and he led the way into the bank, and upstairs to his own room, where he shut the door, and asked John Logan to be seated.

"Well, now, what can I do for you?" said he, pleasantly enough. "Was not that arrangement about the boat satisfactory? I thought the young man was very well content; and he seems an honest fellow—I think you may count on the instalments being paid."

Old John Logan was looking all around him: this place in which he found himself was like a house; had he arrived at the goal of his long journey already!

"It's the young lady," said he, turning vaguely inquiring eyes upon the banker.

"What young lady? Miss Ramsden?"

"Ay, ay," the old man said, with a kind of breathless eagerness. "It's to see her I hef come ahl the way—and—and I wass thinking you would tell me where to find her. If it is only for a moment—she was ferry, ferry kind to us—and—and if she would not think it trouble—only for a moment—"

"But what do you want to see her about?" Mr. Holt naturally asked: then directly something in the old man's face told him he had been indiscreet. "Ah, I see it is something you have got to say to herself. Very well; there can be no objection. I dare say it must be something of importance to have brought you so far; and I dare say, too, she will tell me all about it later on. However, if you want to see her, you will almost certainly find her at home this morning. If she is out, wait till she returns—she is pretty sure to be back by lunch-time. I will give you a card, and you will show it to the man who opens the door; and I will send a commissionaire with you to take you to the house, for I suppose you'd never make your way to Cornwall-gardens by yourself."

As well as he was able, the old man expressed his grateful thanks; and presently he was out once more in the wild Babel of confusion, under the guidance of this taciturn commissionaire. But now he felt that every step was taking him nearer and nearer to the end and aim of his journey. His heart shook within him as he thought of the ordeal before him; and his only wish was that it were well over and done with. He did not care what happened to him after that. The atonement once made to *her*, they might take him away and put him in gaol or hang him if they wished. It was of no consequence whether he ever went back to Harivaig. He was an old man; his days were about done anyway; and his granddaughter Jeannie would be well provided for and comfortably settled with her husband in their new home in Usgary.

Meanwhile the commissionaire who was acting as his guide had met with the same difficulty that the Greenock publican had experienced: old John Logan could not be induced to enter a train. Indeed, his dismay on being asked to go by an underground tunnel was even greater than before; so the commissionaire had to sacrifice the tickets he had purchased at the Mansion House Station, had to ascend to the upper air again, and take his charge down to Kensington on the top of an omnibus. Even that method of travelling seemed to the old fisherman to be fraught with imminent danger; but no doubt his fear of falling off helped in a measure to distract his mind from thinking of the trying interview that was now drawing near.

When they reached the large mansion in Cornwall-gardens to which they had been directed, the servant who opened the door stared with surprise and even resentment at this old man who

had dared to ring the visitors' bell; but his manner changed somewhat when he was shown Mr. Holt's card. He said that Miss
Ramsden was out riding just then, but that she would be back
in half an hour or so; and would he step in and wait? The commissionaire, having seen his task accomplished, left; and old John
Logan entered the house. The man-servant hesitated as to whether
he should ask this odd-looking visitor, whose clothes and cap had
suffered a good deal in his rough experiences of travel, to go any
further than the hall. But Logan settled that matter for himself;
he sat down on a chair that happened to be handy, and the footman, with another curious glance, disappeared, and left the old
man alone.

The moment he had departed, John Logan whipped off his coat,
took out his sailor's jackknife, and slit open a sewed patch in the
inside lining. The locket that had cost him so much was in his
hand. He undid the piece of canvas in which it was wrapped, and
placed that in his pocket. He hastily put on his coat again, and
then he sat still, waiting with the trinket that he had hardly dared
to look on, clasped and hidden in his trembling fingers.

He heard the sound of horses' hoofs without. The servant who
had let him in came along the hall and opened the door. There
was a tall, fair-haired young lady in a black riding-habit coming
up the steps. A young man, rather older than herself, immediately
followed. The groom was leading away the horses. John Logan
rose to his feet, though his heart was beating and his legs were
shaking so that he could hardly stand. The world seemed to swim
round him. He did not know that she turned very pale on catch-
ing sight of him, and came quickly forward, and asked him what
he had come to tell her?

"Is is about my father?" she said, hurriedly.

For a moment he could not speak, he was all trembling so; then
he said:

"No, no, Mem. I wass come to gif you back something—something that wass yours—and it is a long weh I have come to—to—"

She saw that he was strongly agitated—and also that he glanced
in a timorous fashion at her cousin, who was standing by.

"Mem," said the old man, in a sort of desperation, "will you be that kind—I wass thinking to see you by yourself—"

"Fred, wait for me in the drawing-room," she said instantly. And then, quickly laying aside her hat and riding-whip, she took the old man gently by the hand. "Come in here," she said, leading him into the dining-room, and shutting the door behind them. "I see you are greatly distressed. What is it about? Can I help you? It is not about your granddaughter, is it, that was to be married? If I can help you, I'm sure I will!"

The old man stood helpless, bewildered, shaking from head to foot—his English was all gone from him—he could not explain: then, with a half-stifled cry of anguish, he threw himself at her feet, his two clenched hands on the floor, tears streaming from his eyes, his white head bowed with the violence of his sobbing.

"*Má-an-nus!—má-an-nus!—má-an-nus!*" * was all he could say, in this overwhelming grief, in the despair of his appeal to her.

"But what is it?" she asked, in great alarm and commiseration, for it seemed so pitiable to see this white-haired old man so utterly stricken down.

He unclasped one of his hands, and put the locket at her feet.

"I hef brought it," he said—though his voice was so broken with his sobs that she could only make out a word or two here and there; "if you hef no pardon for me—I cannot tell what that will be for me—when I took it, I wass not thinking it wass anybody's—I had neffer seen you, Mem—God knows, I would not hef taken anything from you—but—but the clothes they were lying on the shore—and—and there wass no one—and I wass thinking of my lass Jeannie, and of her getting married, and not with the things that some of the young lasses hef for their wedding-day—it—it is your pardon, Mem, I am asking—it is your pardon I am praying for—and if you hef no pardon for me, then God help me—for I—for I—"

But here he broke into another fit of passionate crying and sobbing, so that he could not proceed with his appeal to her for forgiveness. As for her, the tears were running down her own cheeks; this seemed so piteous a thing. She knelt down on one knee, and took up the locket.

---

* Properly *mathanas*—compassion, mercy, forgiveness.

"I think I understand you," she said, very gently. "Well; you have brought it back—what more could you do? I do forgive you —indeed, indeed I do forgive you!"

He seized the hem of her dress, and kissed it again and again.

"I wass not thinking," he continued, between his sobs, "that it belonged to any one. And there wass Jeannie, she wass going to be married—and—and I thought the young lad would be prouder of her. Mem, I did not know it wass yours—I did not; and when you wass coming to Harivaig—after that, there wass no peace for me, day or night; and I wass asking myself, day and night, if the young lady would gif me her pardon, if I went aweh to London—"

"And, indeed, indeed I do!" the girl said, in deep commiseration. "Come!" she said, putting her hand on his shoulder. "Come and tell me how you made such a long journey. I did miss the locket, and could not imagine where it had gone. But now you have brought it back—and come such a long way to restore it— well, now, you must not say a word more about it."

Old John Logan rose and wiped his wet cheeks with the back of his hand, and took a step towards the door.

"The long weh I hef come, Mem," said he, pausing now and again to gather his speech, "wass to gif back what I had taken—and —and to ask for your pardon. Now you hef been kind to me— more kind to me as I deserve—and—and that is ofer now—and God bless you for it, Mem. That is ofer now—but there's the other people—and I will tell them what I hef done—and if it is to be hanged I am, then it will not matter so much to be hanged now, since I hef your pardon. And now I will say good-bye to you, Mem; and God bless you as you hef been merciful to me this day."

She guessed his meaning directly; and in an instant she had interposed herself between him and the door.

"No," said she, courageously, "you are not going like that, or with any such intention. What has been done has been settled and forgiven between you and me; and no one else has the right to interfere. *No one else* has got anything to do with it. If you like, it will be a secret between you and me: not a word to be said. And I am not going to let you leave the house like this." She put her hand on his arm. "Come," she said, quite cheerfully, so as to reassure him, and calm down his violent distress and agitation. "I want you to tell me all about your coming here, and I want to know what you are going to do before you go back. I suppose you have no friends in London—unless you will call me your friend? I want you to tell me about your granddaughter, and the marriage, and what you are going to buy in London to take to her for her wedding-day. If she would not be offended, I should like to send her some things; and perhaps she would rather be pleased to have them come all the way from London."

Her calm and soothing tones prevailed; he suffered himself to be led towards the window, and he took a seat there, she sitting opposite him in the embrasure. He understood that he was asked for the story of his adventures since leaving Harivaig, and he began and in the most simple fashion related the various incidents as well as his halting speech would allow. She was greatly concerned when he told her about the fighting in the Greenock den; and declared he must see a surgeon in London, to make sure his wounds had been properly dressed, and were healing satisfactorily; and then, when he brought his narrative down to this very day, and when she discovered that he had had nothing to eat or drink since very early that morning, she went promptly to the mantel-piece and rang the bell.

The footman appeared.

"Luncheon, Richard—and tell Mrs. Moulseley and Mr. Hare." She turned to the old man.

"You will stay and have some lunch with me?" she said.

"Oh, no, Mem!" said he, glancing nervously at the table—which was already laid.

"But you must! Why, how many hours is it since you left the steamer this morning?"

Presently an elderly lady appeared, followed by the young man who had been out riding with Miss Ramsden—a tall young Englishman of the familiar blonde type. The moment young Hare perceived that the old fisherman was still in the dining-room, and apparently was going to stay to lunch, he said to his cousin—

"Edith!"

It was a kind of summons: she followed out into the hall.

"Why, what are you going to do now?" he said, by way of friendly remonstrance.

She stepped into the morning-room opposite, to be out of the way of the servants, and he accompanied her.

"This is an old man who has come a long way," she said to him; "and I am interested in him; and I have asked him to take lunch with me—that is all."

"How silly you are!" he said. "Why—"

She flushed up a little.

"You need not come in to luncheon unless you like!" she said, somewhat stiffly.

He looked at her, and smiled, and made bold to take her hand.

"So you want to quarrel, do you? My dear Edith, you don't know how. You haven't got it in you. You can't fight—you haven't got the weapons—what is it?—

> *Un sourire qui dit: Bataille!*
> *Un soupir qui dit: Je me rends!*

that's the way *you* would fight, if you were to try."

She withdrew her hand none the less.

"You don't know how I am interested in this old man," she said, "and you don't know what a pitiable story he has just told me. But it is of no consequence. As I say, you need not come in to luncheon unless you like."

"Edith, don't be stupid!" he made answer, quite good-naturedly. "I was not thinking of myself at all; I was thinking of your ancient friend—whom you will make extremely uncomfortable. Do you imagine you are doing him any kindness? He would be a great deal happier if you would let him have his dinner in the servants' hall."

"Well, then, he is not going down to the servants' hall," was her reply.

"And I," said he, with a bit of a laugh, "am not going to be debarred from sitting next to you at luncheon simply because you choose to be cantankerous. Come along; if you keep Mrs. Moulse-

ley waiting another minute she'll snap your head off," and with
that he put his hand lightly on her shoulder and shoved her out
of the room before him.

But old John Logan was far too preoccupied to be in any way
embarrassed or uncomfortable when the young lady insisted on
his taking a place next to her at table; nor did he seem to perceive
how assiduous she was in paying him little friendly attentions. His
mind was intently fixed on quite other things. The servants placed
various dishes before him; he paid no heed. The butler filled his
glass; he did not look at it.

"But you are not eating anything!" his young hostess said.

"I wass not thinking of it," he answered, simply; and then he
relapsed into a brooding silence, as if there was no outward world
for him at all.

She began to wonder what this was that was weighing so heavily
on his thoughts. Had she not fully satisfied him of her forgiveness?
Had she not been explicit enough? Or was there still in his mind
some dark imagining that quite outside the sphere of her acquittal
there dwelt unknown terrors of punishment and vengeance? The
moment that luncheon was over, she allowed her other two companions to leave, and desired the old man to remain with her.
And then an adroit question or two soon made the matter more
or less clear.

"It is you, Mem, who hef been kind to me," said he, fixing his
eyes on the table before him, as if to seek out this that was troub-
ling him; while she listened to him patiently and in silence, as he
slowly constructed sentence after sentence. "And when I wass
leaving Harivaig, I did not know whether I would ever be finding
you; and now you wass giffing me your pardon; and what more
is to happen to me, that I do not heed now, since you had mercy
for me. But—but you said a secret. If I wass to go back to Harivaig, I would be thinking—ahl the day long, sometimes in the
night too. I would be thinking there would be some one coming.
He would say to me, 'You hef a secret, and that iss good as between
the young lady and you; but the judges are not satisfied—there
iss more to be done yet.' And now I am here in this town, where
the judges are, I—I would sooner go to them. If they hef no pardon

for me—well, I am an old man; it is not much matter now; and Jeannie would neffer know anything about it. When I wass coming through the streets I looked for them; but I wass not seeing them anywhere. And now, Mem, I will go. Whateffer happens there iss my thanks to you for your goodness to me; and I had no right to expect so mich from you. But I am not thinking of going back to Harivaig with a secret—and be waiting and waiting for the judges."

She was quick to perceive what all this meant.

"But you don't understand!" she said, with an almost pathetic eagerness. "It need not be a secret unless you like—that must be just as you wish—but I mentioned a secret merely because it is nobody else's business but yours and mine. No one can interfere now; it is settled. Surely you have suffered enough—surely you have made sufficient atonement: and if I say that—if I tell you that—who can interfere? The judges would not think of harming you. You might live all the rest of your life in London—you might walk through the streets every day—and nobody would think of meddling with you. Indeed," she said—for it suddenly occurred to her that the best way of assuring him of his safety would be to familiarise him with the London streets and the sight of the great official buildings and the repositories of power and authority, "I'm going to ask you to remain in London for a day or two, and go about, and see what the place is like. That is, until I can find some little presents for you to take home to your granddaughter, for the wedding. And there are a lot of things you have to do," she continued, in a brisk and matter-of-fact way, "before you can set out again for the North. You ought at once to send your friend in Greenock, who was so kind to you, the money he lent you—and if you haven't got it—"

"But, ay, ay!" he said, quickly; "there's Corstorphine! There's some money that Corstorphine is owing to me—"

"Well, we'll arrange about that later on," said she. "In the meantime I want you to see a little of London, and I'll get you some one who will take you about."

For so gentle-mannered and smooth-spoken a young lady she had a prompt and businesslike way of going about things. She rang the bell. The footman appeared.

"Tell Kemp I want to see him at once," she said. "If he is round at the stables send for him."

"Yes, Miss."

A few minutes thereafter she was told that Kemp was in the hall; and immediately she left the room, shutting the door behind her.

"I sha'n't want the carriage this afternoon, Kemp," she said to this grave, stout, elderly person, who, in fact, was her coachman.

"Very well, Miss."

"But there is an old fisherman here, who has come from the North to see me, and you must look after him, and find lodgings for him for a night or two. Has your wife let that room that is next to yours?"

"No, Miss."

"That will do very well. You will see that the old man is comfortable. And in the meantime I want you to take him out now, and show him some of the sights of London—take him to see Buckingham Palace, and the Houses of Parliament, and the Horse Guards, and so on. And first of all you must persuade him to go somewhere and have some dinner; he has had nothing since early morning; be sure he has a good dinner; and when he comes back in the evening he must have some tea in his own room; and perhaps I may come round for a moment to see how he is getting on."

She took a sovereign from her purse.

"Mind you make him cheerful and comfortable, and talk to him, and get everything he needs. Is there any Highland whiskey to be got in London refreshment-rooms?"

"They says so, Miss," the coachman answered, with grave caution.

"You must see what he would like with his dinner. His name is Mr. Logan. You must call him 'Mr.' Now I will give him over into your hands; and I hope to hear at night that he has spent a very pleasant afternoon."

And, strangely enough, this mere girl had hit upon the right way of going about this thing. Old John Logan, during the two or three days he spent in London, got to be convinced that he had nothing to fear—that no one wanted to harm him—that he was a free man—that the young lady's forgiveness of him was all-sufficient. For one thing, Miss Ramsden took very good care not to say anything of what she had done or was doing to Mr. Holt. She had heard of such a phrase as "compounding a felony;" and while she felt in her heart that she was justified in assuring this old man that he had suffered enough and made ample expiation, she did not quite know how her conduct might strike a legal or commercial mind. She thought she would tell Mr. Holt all about it—after John Logan had gone home.

In the meantime, the old man's gratitude towards her was some-thing extraordinary to witness. It was like the dumb gratitude of a dog, for he could not say much of what he felt. And when she showed him the pretty bits of finery that she had bought for his granddaughter, and that were to help to deck out the bride, tears rose to the old man's eyes, and he said—

"If you had the Gaelic, Mem, I could tell you what I wass thinking of you, Mem, and—and your kindness—but I will never be able to tell you that."

His last speech to her, when the time came for his bidding her farewell, was of the same apologetic nature. She did not go down to the St. Katherine's Docks with him; but she put him in safe hands; and Mr. Holt, at her intercession, had made arrangements with one of the sub-officers on board the Anchor Liner, by which the old man would be taken care of if he had any time to wait in Greenock for the Dunara Castle. John Logan, as he was being driven down to St. Katherine's Docks in a four-wheeled cab, saw, amongst the other things they passed, the Tower of London; and he beheld it without a qualm; the gentle-voiced young lady had successfully banished all his fears.

But what was he to say to the people when, after the long, and, as it chanced, uneventful voyage, he got back to Harivaig again—as one returned from the dead? Well; he said nothing at all. If anyone asked him, he answered that he had been away to the south, and had seen many strange sights. But when Jeannie Logan, in mingled shyness and pride, began to show to her intimate friends the beautiful things that the English young lady had sent her for her wedding-day, then the bruit got abroad that old John Logan was so insensately fond of his spoiled granddaughter that he had gone all the way to London to purchase adornments for her. Jeannie protested against this misapprehension, and even showed them the very grateful letter she was going to send to Miss Ramsden; but all was of no use.

Moreover, they made still another mistake when the wedding-day came round. The marriage took place in the inn, as the custom holds in those parts; and in the evening all the people—some of them very remote kinsfolk, who had come from long distances—assembled at supper. It was a protracted feast; and there was a mighty babblement of laughter, and talking, and joking, to say nothing of the piper up at the fireplace end of the room, who was screaming away with "Hoop her and gird her" and "Follow her over the border;" so that, towards the end of the banquet, it was with difficulty the roaring guests could be got to understand that old John Logan—old John Logan, of all people in the world—was going to propose a health, with Highland honours too. Perhaps it was the excitement of the moment, perhaps it was an extra drop of Glendarroch that had put the idea into the old man's head; however, there was silence when he mounted on his chair, and raised his glass in his trembling hand.

"We are all friends here," said he, in the Gaelic, "and I ask all friends of me and mine to drink this: Blessings on her—and a hundred thousand blessings!—and long life and happiness to the *Roa-nam-bân!*" *

He put his right foot on the table.

"*Nish—nish! Suasa—suasa!*" † he called; and therewith he tossed off the whiskey, and dashed the glass down to the floor, so that it should never be drunk out of again.

"*Roa-nam-bân!—Roa-nam-bân!*" they cried; but they were all laughing at him; they thought it was a foolish thing for the infatuated old man to call his granddaughter the best of women, even on her wedding-day. For not one of them (except, perhaps, the

---

* Properly *Rogha-nam-ban.*—The best, the choicest among women.
† *Nish—nish! Suasa—suasa!*—Now—now! Up with it—up with it!

granddaughter herself—who was not offended) guessed who it was whom old John Logan had in his mind, when he called on his friends to drink long life and happiness to the *Roa-nam-bân*.

MARGARET OLIPHANT

THE LIBRARY WINDOW

I

I WAS not aware at first of the many discussions which had gone on about that window. It was almost opposite one of the windows of the large old-fashioned drawing-room of the house in which I spent that summer, which was of so much importance in my life. Our house and the library were on opposite sides of the broad High Street of St Rule's, which is a fine street, wide and ample, and very quiet, as strangers think who come from noisier places; but in a summer evening there is much coming and going, and the stillness is full of sound—the sound of footsteps and pleasant voices, softened by the summer air. There are even exceptional moments when it is noisy: the time of the fair, and on Saturday night sometimes, and when there are excursion trains. Then even the softest sunny air of the evening will not smooth the harsh tones and the stumbling steps; but at these unlovely moments we shut the windows, and even I, who am so fond of that deep recess where I can take refuge from all that is going on inside, and make myself a spectator of all the varied story out of doors, withdraw from my watch-tower. To tell the truth, there never was very much going on inside. The house belonged to my aunt, to whom (she says, Thank God!) nothing ever happens. I believe that many things have happened to her in her time; but that was all over at the period of which I am speaking, and she was old, and very quiet. Her life went on in a routine never broken. She got up at the same hour every day, and did the same things in the same rotation, day by day the same. She said that this was the greatest support in the world, and that routine is a kind of salvation. It may be so; but it is a very dull salvation, and I used to feel that I would rather have incident, whatever kind of incident it might be. But then at that time I was not old, which makes all the difference.

At the time of which I speak the deep recess of the drawing-room window was a great comfort to me. Though she was an old lady (perhaps because she was so old) she was very tolerant, and had a kind of feeling for me. She never said a word, but often gave me a smile when she saw how I had built myself up, with my books and my basket of work. I did very little work, I fear—now and then a few stitches when the spirit moved me, or when I had got well afloat in a dream, and was more tempted to follow it out than to read my book, as sometimes happened. At other times, and if the book were interesting, I used to get through volume after volume sitting there, paying no attention to anybody. And yet I did pay a kind of attention. Aunt Mary's old ladies came in to call, and I heard them talk, though I very seldom listened; but for all that, if they had anything to say that was interesting, it is curious how I found it in my mind afterwards, as if the air had blown it to me. They came and went, and I had the sensation of their old bonnets gliding out and in, and their dresses rustling, and now and then had to jump up and shake hands with some one who knew me, and asked after my papa and mamma. Then Aunt Mary would give me a little smile again, and I slipped back to my window. She never seemed to mind. My mother would not have let me do it, I know. She would have remembered dozens of things there were to do. She would have sent me upstairs to fetch some-thing which I was quite sure she did not want, or downstairs to carry some quite unnecessary message to the housemaid. She liked to keep me running about. Perhaps that was one reason why I was so fond of Aunt Mary's drawing-room, and the deep recess of the window, and the curtain that fell half over it, and the broad window-seat, where one could collect so many things without being found fault with for untidiness. Whenever we had anything the matter with us in these days, we were sent to St Rule's to get up our strength. And this was my case at the time of which I am going to speak.

Everybody had said, since ever I learned to speak, that I was fantastic and fanciful and dreamy, and all the other words with which a girl who may happen to like poetry, and to be fond of thinking, is so often made uncomfortable. People don't know what they mean when they say fantastic. It sounds like Madge Wildfire or something of that sort. My mother thought I should always be busy, to keep nonsense out of my head. But really I was not at all fond of nonsense. I was rather serious than otherwise. I would have been no trouble to anybody if I had been left to myself. It was only that I had a sort of second-sight, and was conscious of things to which I paid no attention. Even when reading the most interesting book, the things that were being talked about blew in to me; and I heard what the people were saying in the streets as they passed under the window. Aunt Mary always said I could do two or indeed three things at once—both read and listen, and see. I am sure that I did not listen much, and seldom looked out, of set purpose—as some people do who notice what bonnets the ladies in the street have on; but I did hear what I couldn't help hearing, even when I was reading my book, and I did see all sorts of things, though often for a whole half-hour I might never lift my eyes.

This does not explain what I said at the beginning, that there were many discussions about that window. It was, and still is, the last window in the row, of the College Library which is opposite my aunt's house in the High Street. Yet it is not exactly opposite, but a little to the west, so that I could see it best from the left side of my recess. I took it calmly for granted that it was a window like any other till I first heard the talk about it which was going on in the drawing-room. "Have you never made up your mind, Mrs Balcarres," said old Mr Pitmilly, "whether that window opposite is a window or no?" He said Mistress Balcarres—and he was always called Mr Pitmilly, Morton: which was the name of his place.

"I am never sure of it, to tell the truth," said Aunt Mary, "all these years."

"Bless me!" said one of the old ladies, "and what window may that be?"

Mr Pitmilly had a way of laughing as he spoke, which did not please me; but it was true that he was not perhaps desirous of pleasing me. He said, "Oh, just the window opposite," with his laugh running through his words; "our friend can never make up her mind about it, though she has been living opposite it since—"

"You need never mind the date," said another; "the Leebrary window! Dear me, what should it be but a window? up at that height it could not be a door."

"The question is," said my aunt, "if it is a real window with glass in it, or if it is merely painted, or if it once was a window, and has been built up. And the oftener people look at it, the less they are able to say."

"Let me see this window," said old Lady Carnbee, who was very active and strong-minded; and then they all came crowding upon me—three or four old ladies, very eager, and Mr Pitmilly's white hair appearing over their heads, and my aunt sitting quiet and smiling behind.

"I mind the window very well," said Lady Carnbee; "ay: and so do more than me. But in its present appearance it is just like any other window; but has not been cleaned, I should say, in the memory of man."

"I see what ye mean," said one of the others. "It is just a very dead thing without any reflection in it; but I've seen as bad before."

"Ay, it's dead enough," said another, "but that's no rule; for these hizzies of women-servants in this ill age—"

"Nay, the women are well enough," said the softest voice of all, which was Aunt Mary's. "I will never let them risk their lives cleaning the outside of mine. And there are no women-servants in the Old Library: there is maybe something more in it than that."

They were all pressing into my recess, pressing upon me, a row of old faces, peering into something they could not understand. I had a sense in my mind how curious it was, the wall of old ladies in their old satin gowns all glazed with age, Lady Carnbee with her lace about her head. Nobody was looking at me or thinking of me; but I felt unconsciously the contrast of my youngness to their oldness, and stared at them as they stared over my head at the Library window. I had given it no attention up to this time.

I was more taken up with the old ladies than with the thing they were looking at.

"The framework is all right at least, I can see that, and pented black—"

"And the panes are pented black too. It's no window, Mrs Balcarres. It has been filled in, in the days of the window duties: you will mind, Lady Carnbee."

"Mind!" said that oldest lady. "I mind when your mother was marriet, Jeanie: and that's neither the day nor yesterday. But as for the window, it's just a delusion: and that is my opinion of the matter, if you ask me."

"There's a great want of light in that muckle room at the college," said another. "If it was a window, the Leebrary would have more light."

"One thing is clear," said one of the younger ones, "it cannot be a window to see through. It may be filled in or it may be built up, but it is not a window to give light."

"And who ever heard of a window that was no to see through?" Lady Carnbee said. I was fascinated by the look on her face, which was a curious scornful look as of one who knew more than she chose to say: and then my wandering fancy was caught by her hand as she held it up, throwing back the lace that drooped over it. Lady Carnbee's lace was the chief thing about her—heavy black Spanish lace with large flowers. Everything she wore was trimmed with it. A large veil of it hung over her old bonnet. But her hand coming out of this heavy lace was a curious thing to see. She had very long fingers, very taper, which had been much admired in her youth; and her hand was very white, or rather more than white, pale, bleached, and bloodless, with large blue veins standing up upon the back; and she wore some fine rings, among others a big diamond in an ugly old claw setting. They were too big for her, and were wound round and round with yellow silk to make them keep on: and this little cushion of silk, turned brown with long wearing, had twisted round so that it was more conspicuous than the jewels; while the big diamond blazed underneath in the hollow of her hand, like some dangerous thing hiding and sending out darts of light. The hand, which seemed to come almost to a point, with this strange ornament underneath, clutched at my half-terrified imagination. It too seemed to mean far more than was said. I felt as if it might clutch me with sharp claws, and the lurking, dazzling creature bite—with a sting that would go to the heart.

Presently, however, the circle of the old faces broke up, the old ladies returned to their seats, and Mr Pitmilly, small but very erect, stood up in the midst of them, talking with mild authority like a little oracle among the ladies. Only Lady Carnbee always contradicted the neat, little old gentleman. She gesticulated, when she talked, like a Frenchwoman, and darted forth that hand of hers with the lace hanging over it, so that I always caught a glimpse of the lurking diamond. I thought she looked like a witch among the comfortable little group which gave such attention to everything Mr Pitmilly said.

"For my part, it is my opinion there is no window there at all," he said. "It's very like the thing that's called in scienteefic language an optical illusion. It arises generally, if I may use such a word in the presence of ladies, from a liver that is not just in the perfitt order and balance that organ demands—and then you will see things—a blue dog, I remember, was the thing in one case, and in another—"

"The man has gane gyte," said Lady Carnbee; "I mind the windows in the Auld Leebrary as long as I mind anything. Is the Leebrary itself an optical illusion too?"

"Na, na," and "No, no," said the old ladies; "a blue dogue would be a strange vagary: but the Library we have all kent from our youth," said one. "And I mind when the Assemblies were held there one year when the Town Hall was building," another said.

"It is just a great divert to me," said Aunt Mary: but what was strange was that she paused there, and said in a low tone, "now": and then went on again, "for whoever comes to my house, there are aye discussions about that window. I have never just made up my mind about it myself. Sometimes I think it's a case of these wicked window duties, as you said, Miss Jeanie, when half the windows in our houses were blocked up to save the tax. And then,

I think, it may be due to that blank kind of building like the great
new buildings on the Earthen Mound in Edinburgh, where the
windows are just ornaments. And then whiles I am sure I can see
the glass shining when the sun catches it in the afternoon."

"You could so easily satisfy yourself, Mrs Balcarres, if you
were to—"

"Give a laddie a penny to cast a stone, and see what happens,"
said Lady Carnbee.

"But I am not sure that I have any desire to satisfy myself,"
Aunt Mary said. And then there was a stir in the room, and I had
to come out from my recess and open the door for the old ladies
and see them downstairs, as they all went away following one
another. Mr Pitmilly gave his arm to Lady Carnbee, though she
was always contradicting him; and so the tea-party dispersed.
Aunt Mary came to the head of the stairs with her guests in an
old-fashioned gracious way, while I went down with them to see
that the maid was ready at the door. When I came back Aunt
Mary was still standing in the recess looking out. Returning to
my seat, she said, with a kind of wistful look, "Well, honey: and
what is your opinion?"

"I have no opinion. I was reading my book all the time," I said.

"And so you were, honey, and no' very civil; but all the same
I ken well you heard every word we said."

II

It was a night in June; dinner was long over, and had it been
winter the maids would have been shutting up the house, and my
Aunt Mary preparing to go upstairs to her room. But it was still
clear daylight, that daylight out of which the sun has been long
gone, and which has no longer any rose reflections, but all has
sunk into a pearly neutral tint—a light which is daylight yet is
not day. We had taken a turn in the garden after dinner, and now
we had returned to what we called our usual occupations. My
aunt was reading. The English post had come in, and she had got
her "Times", which was her great diversion. The "Scotsman"

was her morning reading, but she liked her "Times" at night.

As for me, I too was at my usual occupation, which at that time was doing nothing. I had a book as usual, and was absorbed in it: but I was conscious of all that was going on all the same. The people strolled along the broad pavement, making remarks as they passed under the open window which came up into my story or my dream, and sometimes made me laugh. The tone and the faint sing-song, or rather chant, of the accent, which was "a wee Fifish," was novel to me, and associated with holiday, and pleasant; and sometimes they said to each other something that was amusing, and often something that suggested a whole story; but presently they began to drop off, the footsteps slackened, the voices died away. It was getting late, though the clear soft daylight went on and on. All through the lingering evening, which seemed to consist of interminable hours, long but not weary drawn out as if the spell of the light and the outdoor life might never end, I had now and then, quite unawares, cast a glance at the mysterious window which my aunt and her friends had discussed, as I felt, though I dared not say it even to myself, rather foolishly. It caught my eye without any intention on my part, as I paused, as it were, to take breath, in the flowing and current of undistinguishable thoughts and things from without and within which carried me along. First it occurred to me, with a little sensation of discovery, how absurd to say it was not a window, a living window, one to see through! Why, then, had they never *seen* it, these old folk? I saw as I looked up suddenly the faint greyness as of visible space within—a room behind, certainly—dim, as it was natural a room should be on the other side of the street—quite indefinite: yet so clear that if some one were to come to the window there would be nothing surprising in it. For certainly there was a feeling of space behind the panes which these old half-blind ladies had disputed about whether they were glass or only fictitious panes marked on the wall. How silly! when eyes that could see could make it out in a minute. It was only a greyness at present, but it was unmistakable, a space that went back into gloom, as every room does when you look into it across a street. There were no curtains to show whether it was inhabited or not; but a room—

oh, as distinctly as ever room was! I was pleased with myself, but said nothing, while Aunt Mary rustled her paper, waiting for a favourable moment to announce a discovery which settled her problem at once. Then I was carried away upon the stream again, and forgot the window, till something threw unawares a word from the outer world, "I'm goin' hame; it'll soon be dark." Dark! what was the fool thinking of? it never would be dark if one waited out, wandering in the soft air for hours longer; and then my eyes, acquiring easily that new habit, looked across the way again.

Ah, now! nobody indeed had come to the window; and no light had been lighted, seeing it was still beautiful to read by—a still, clear, colourless light; but the room inside had certainly widened. I could see the grey space and air a little deeper, and a sort of vision, very dim, of a wall, and something against it; something dark, with the blackness that a solid article, however indistinctly seen, takes in the lighter darkness that is only space—a large, black, dark thing coming out into the grey. I looked more intently, and made sure it was a piece of furniture, either a writing-table or perhaps a large bookcase. No doubt it must be the last, since this was part of the old library. I never visited the old College Library, but I had seen such places before, and I could well imagine it to myself. How curious that for all the time these old people had looked at it, they had never seen this before!

It was more silent now, and my eyes, I suppose, had grown dim with gazing, doing my best to make it out, when suddenly Aunt Mary said, "Will you ring the bell, my dear? I must have my lamp."

"Your lamp?" I cried, "when it is still daylight." But then I gave another look at my window, and perceived with a start that the light had indeed changed: for now I saw nothing. It was still light, but there was so much change in the light that my room, with the grey space and the large shadowy bookcase, had gone out, and I saw them no more: for even a Scotch night in June, though it looks as if it would never end, does darken at the last. I had almost cried out, but checked myself, and rang the bell for Aunt Mary, and made up my mind I would say nothing till next morning, when to be sure naturally it would be more clear.

Next morning I rather think I forgot all about it—or was busy: or was more idle than usual: the two things meant nearly the same. At all events I thought no more of the window, though I still sat in my own, opposite to it, but occupied with some other fancy. Aunt Mary's visitors came as usual in the afternoon; but their talk was of other things, and for a day or two nothing at all happened to bring back my thoughts into this channel. It might be nearly a week before the subject came back, and once more it was old Lady Carnbee who set me thinking; not that she said anything upon that particular theme. But she was the last of my aunt's afternoon guests to go away, and when she rose to leave she threw up her hands, with those lively gesticulations which so many old Scotch ladies have. "My faith!" said she, "there is that bairn there still like a dream. Is the creature bewitched, Mary Balcarres? and is she bound to sit there by night and by day for the rest of her days? You should mind that there's things about, uncanny for women of our blood."

I was too much startled at first to recognise that it was of me she was speaking. She was like a figure in a picture, with her pale face the colour of ashes, and the big pattern of the Spanish lace hanging half over it, and her hand held up, with the big diamond blazing at me from the inside of her uplifted palm. It was held up in surprise, but it looked as if it were raised in malediction; and the diamond threw out darts of light and glared and twinkled at me. If it had been in its right place it would not have mattered; but there, in the open of the hand! I started up, half in terror, half in wrath. And then the old lady laughed, and her hand dropped. "I've wakened you to life, and broke the spell," she said, nodding her old head at me, while the large black silk flowers of the lace waved and threatened. And she took my arm to go down-stairs, laughing and bidding me be steady, and no' tremble and shake like a broken reed. "You should be as steady as a rock at your age. I was like a young tree," she said, leaning so heavily that my willowy girlish frame quivered—"I was a support to virtue, like Pamela, in my time."

"Aunt Mary, Lady Carnbee is a witch!" I cried, when I came back.

"Is that what you think, honey? well: maybe she once was," said Aunt Mary, whom nothing surprised.

And it was that night once more after dinner, and after the post came in, and the "Times", that I suddenly saw the Library window again. I had seen it every day—and noticed nothing; but to-night, still in a little tumult of mind over Lady Carnbee and her wicked diamond which wished me harm, and her lace which waved threats and warnings at me, I looked across the street, and there I saw quite plainly the room opposite, far more clear than before. I saw dimly that it must be a large room, and that the big piece of furniture against the wall was a writing-desk. That in a moment, when first my eyes rested upon it, was quite clear: a large old-fashioned escritoire, standing out into the room: and I knew by the shape of it that it had a great many pigeon-holes and little drawers in the back, and a large table for writing. There was one just like it in my father's library at home. It was such a surprise to see it all so clearly that I closed my eyes, for the moment almost giddy, wondering how papa's desk could have come here —and then when I reminded myself that this was nonsense, and that there were many such writing-tables besides papa's, and looked again—lo! it had all become quite vague and indistinct as it was at first; and I saw nothing but the blank window, of which the old ladies could never be certain whether it was filled up to avoid the window-tax, or whether it had ever been a window at all.

This occupied my mind very much, and yet I did not say anything to Aunt Mary. For one thing, I rarely saw anything at all in the early part of the day; but then that is natural: you can never see into a place from outside, whether it is an empty room or looking-glass, or people's eyes, or anything else that is mysterious, in the day. It has, I suppose, something to do with the light. But in the evening in June in Scotland—then is the time to see. For it is daylight, yet it is not day, and there is a quality in it which I cannot describe, it is so clear, as if every object was a reflection of itself.

I used to see more and more of the room as the days went on. The large escritoire stood out more and more into the space: with sometimes white glimmering things, which looked like papers, lying on it: and once or twice I was sure I saw a pile of books on the floor close to the writing-table, as if they had gilding upon them in broken specks, like old books. It was always about the time when the lads in the street began to call to each other that they were going home, and sometimes a shriller voice would come from one of the doors, bidding somebody to "cry upon the laddies" to come back to their suppers. That was always the time I saw best, though it was close upon the moment when the veil seemed to fall and the clear radiance became less living, and all the sounds died out of the street, and Aunt Mary said in her soft voice, "Honey! will you ring for the lamp?" She said honey as people say darling: and I think it is a prettier word.

Then finally, while I sat one evening with my book in my hand, looking straight across the street, not distracted by anything, I saw a little movement within. It was not any one visible—but everybody must know what it is to see the stir in the air, the little disturbance—you cannot tell what it is, but that indicates some one there, even though you can see no one. Perhaps it is a shadow making just one flicker in the still place. You may look at an empty room and the furniture in it for hours, and then suddenly there will be the flicker, and you know that something has come into it. It might only be a dog or a cat; it might be, if that were possible, a bird flying across; but it is some one, something living, which is so different, so completely different, in a moment from the things that are not living. It seemed to strike right through me, and I gave a little cry. Then Aunt Mary stirred a little, and put down the huge newspaper that almost covered her from sight, and said, "What is it honey?" I cried "Nothing," with a little gasp, quickly, for I did not want to be disturbed just at this moment when somebody was coming! But I suppose she was not satisfied, for she got up and stood behind to see what it was, putting her hand on my shoulder. It was the softest touch in the world, but I could have flung it off angrily: for that moment everything was still again, and the place grew grey and I saw no more.

"Nothing," I repeated, but I was so vexed I could have cried. "I told you it was nothing, Aunt Mary. Don't you believe me, that you come to look—and spoil it all!"

I did not mean of course to say these last words; they were forced out of me. I was so much annoyed to see it all melt away like a dream: for it was no dream, but as real as—as real as—myself or anything I ever saw.

She gave my shoulder a little pat with her hand. "Honey," she said, "were you looking at something? Is't that? is't that?" "Is it what?" I wanted to say, shaking off her hand, but something in me stopped me: for I said nothing at all, and she went quietly back to her place. I suppose she must have rung the bell herself, for immediately I felt the soft flood of the light behind me, and the evening outside dimmed down, as it did every night, and I saw nothing more.

It was next day, I think, in the afternoon that I spoke. It was brought on by something she said about her fine work. "I get a mist before my eyes," she said; "you will have to learn my old lace stitches, honey—for I soon will not see to draw the threads."

"Oh, I hope you will keep your sight," I cried, without thinking what I was saying. I was then young and very matter-of-fact. I had not found out that one may mean something, yet not half or a hundredth part of what one seems to mean: and even then probably hoping to be contradicted if it is anyhow against one's self.

"My sight!" she said, looking up at me with a look that was almost angry; "there is no question of losing my sight—on the contrary, my eyes are very strong. I may not see to draw fine threads, but I see at a distance as well as ever I did—as well as you do."

"I did not mean any harm, Aunt Mary," I said. "I thought you said— But how can your sight be as good as ever when you are in doubt about that window? I can see into the room as clear as—" My voice wavered, for I had just looked up and across the street, and I could have sworn that there was no window at all, but only a false image of one painted on the wall.

"Ah!" she said, with a little tone of keenness and of surprise: and she half rose up, throwing down her work hastily, as if she meant to come to me: then, perhaps seeing the bewildered look on my face, she paused and hesitated—"Ay, honey!" she said, "have you got so far ben as that?"

What did she mean? Of course I knew all the old Scotch phrases as well as I knew myself; but it is a comfort to take refuge in a little ignorance, and I know I pretended not to understand whenever I was put out. "I don't know what you mean by 'far ben,'" I cried out, very impatient. I don't know what might have followed, but some one just then came to call, and she could only give me a look before she went forward, putting out her hand to her visitor. It was a very soft look, but anxious, and as if she did not know what to do: and she shook her head a very little, and I thought, though there was a smile on her face, there was something wet about her eyes. I retired into my recess, and nothing more was said.

But it was very tantalising that it should fluctuate so; for sometimes I saw that room quite plain and clear—quite as clear as I could see papa's library, for example, when I shut my eyes. I compared it naturally to my father's study, because of the shape of the writing-table, which, as I tell you, was the same as his. At times I saw the papers on the table quite plain, just as I had seen his papers many a day. And the little pile of books on the floor at the foot—not ranged regularly in order, but put down one above the other, with all their angles going different ways, and a speck of the old gilding shining here and there. And then again at other times I saw nothing, absolutely nothing, and was no better than the old ladies who had peered over my head, drawing their eyelids together, and arguing that the window had been shut up because of the old long-abolished window tax, or else that it had never been a window at all. It annoyed me very much at those dull moments to feel that I too puckered up my eyelids and saw no better than they.

Aunt Mary's old ladies came and went day after day while June went on. I was to go back in July, and I felt that I should be very unwilling indeed to leave until I had quite cleared up—as I was indeed in the way of doing—the mystery of that window which changed so strangely and appeared quite a different thing, not only to different people, but to the same eyes at different times. Of course I said to myself it must simply be an effect of the light.

And yet I did not quite like that explanation either, but would have been better pleased to make out to myself that it was some superiority in me which made it so clear to me, if it were only the great superiority of young eyes over old—though that was not quite enough to satisfy me, seeing it was a superiority which I shared with every little lass and lad in the street. I rather wanted, I believe, to think that there was some particular insight in me which gave clearness to my sight—which was a most impertinent assumption, but really did not mean half the harm it seems to mean when it is put down here in black and white. I had several times again, however, seen the room quite plain, and made out that it was a large room, with a great picture in a dim gilded frame hanging on the farther wall, and many other pieces of solid furniture making a blackness here and there, besides the great escritoire against the wall, which had evidently been placed near the window for the sake of the light. One thing became visible to me after another, till I almost thought I should end by being able to read the old lettering on one of the big volumes which projected from the others and caught the light; but this was all preliminary to the great event which happened about Midsummer Day—the day of St John, which was once so much thought of as a festival, but now means nothing at all in Scotland any more than any other of the saints' days: which I shall always think a great pity and loss to Scotland, whatever Aunt Mary may say.

III

It was about midsummer, I cannot say exactly to a day when, but near that time, when the great event happened. I had grown very well acquainted by this time with that large dim room. Not only the escritoire, which was very plain to me now, with the papers upon it, and the books at its foot, but the great picture that hung against the farther wall, and various other shadowy pieces of furniture, especially a chair which one evening I saw had been moved into the space before the escritoire,—a little change which made my heart beat, for it spoke so distinctly of some one who had already

made me start, two or three times before, by some vague shadow of
him or thrill of him which made a sort of movement in the silent
space: a movement which made me sure that next minute I must
see something or hear something which would explain the whole
—if it were not that something always happened outside to stop
it, at the very moment of its accomplishment. I had no warning
this time of movement or shadow. I had been looking into the
room very attentively a little while before, and had made out everything almost clearer than ever; and then had bent my attention
again on my book, and read a chapter or two at a most exciting
period of the story: and consequently had quite left St Rule's,
and the High Street, and the College Library, and was really in a
South American forest, almost throttled by the flowery creepers,
and treading softly lest I should put my foot on a scorpion or a
dangerous snake. At this moment something suddenly calling my
attention to the outside, I looked across, and then, with a start,
sprang up, for I could not contain myself. I don't know what I
said, but enough to startle the people in the room, one of whom
was old Mr Pitmilly. They all looked round upon me to ask what was
the matter. And when I gave my usual answer of "Nothing," sitting
down again shamefaced but very much excited, Mr Pitmilly got
up and came forward, and looked out, apparently to see what was
the cause. He saw nothing, for he went back again, and I could
hear him telling Aunt Mary not to be alarmed, for Missy had
fallen into a doze with the heat, and had startled herself waking
up, at which they all laughed: another time I could have killed
him for his impertinence, but my mind was too much taken up
now to pay any attention. My head was throbbing and my heart
beating. I was in such high excitement, however, that to restrain
myself completely, to be perfectly silent, was more easy to me
then than at any other time of my life. I waited until the old
gentleman had taken his seat again, and then I looked back. Yes,
there he was! I had not been deceived. I knew then, when I looked
across, that this was what I had been looking for all the time—
that I had known he was there, and had been waiting for him,
every time there was that flicker of movement in the room—him
and no one else. And there at last, just as I had expected, he was.

I don't know that in reality I ever had expected him, or any one: but this was what I felt when, suddenly looking into that curious dim room, I saw him there.

He was sitting in the chair, which he must have placed for himself, or which some one else in the dead of night when nobody was looking must have set for him, in front of the escritoire— with the back of his head towards me, writing. The light fell upon him from the left hand, and therefore upon his shoulders and the side of his head, which, however, was too much turned away to show anything of his face. Oh, how strange that there should be some one staring at him as I was doing, and he never to turn his head, to make a movement! If any one stood and looked at me, were I in the soundest sleep that ever was, I would wake, I would jump up, I would feel it through everything. But there he sat and never moved. You are not to suppose, though I said the light fell upon him from the left hand, that there was very much light. There never is in a room you are looking into like that across the street; but there was enough to see him by—the outline of his figure dark and solid, seated in the chair, and the fairness of his head visible faintly, a clear spot against the dimness. I saw this outline against the dim gilding of the frame of the large picture which hung on the farther wall.

I sat all the time the visitors were there, in a sort of rapture, gazing at this figure. I knew no reason why I should be so much moved. In an ordinary way, to see a student at an opposite window quietly doing his work might have interested me a little, but certainly it would not have moved me in any such way. It is always interesting to have a glimpse like this of an unknown life —to see so much and yet know so little, and to wonder, perhaps, what the man is doing, and why he never turns his head. One would go to the window—but not too close, lest he should see you and think you were spying upon him—and one would ask, Is he still there? is he writing, writing always? I wonder what he is writing! And it would be a great amusement: but no more. This was not my feeling at all in the present case. It was a sort of breathless watch, an absorption. I did not feel that I had eyes for anything else, or any room in my mind for another thought. I no longer heard, as I generally did, the stories and the wise remarks (or foolish) of Aunt Mary's old ladies or Mr Pitmilly. I heard only a murmur behind me, the interchange of voices, one softer, one sharper; but it was not as in the time when I sat reading and heard every word, till the story in my book, and the stories they were telling (what they said almost always shaped into stories), were all mingled into each other, and the hero in the novel became somehow the hero (or more likely heroine) of them all. But I took no notice of what they were saying now. And it was not that there was anything very interesting to look at, except the fact that he was there. He did nothing to keep up the absorption of my thoughts. He moved just so much as a man will do when he is very busily writing, thinking of nothing else. There was a faint turn of his head as he went from one side to another of the page he was writing; but it appeared to be a long long page which never wanted turning. Just a little inclination when he was at the end of the line, outward, and then a little inclination inward when he began the next. That was little enough to keep one gazing. But I suppose it was the gradual course of events leading up to this, the finding out of one thing after another as the eyes got accustomed to the vague light: first the room itself, and then the writing-table, and then the other furniture, and last of all the human inhabitant who gave it all meaning. This was all so interesting that it was like a country which one had discovered. And then the extraordinary blindness of the other people who disputed among themselves whether it was a window at all! I did not, I am sure, wish to be disrespectful, and I was very fond of my Aunt Mary, and I liked Mr Pitmilly well enough, and I was afraid of Lady Carnbee. But yet to think of the—I know I ought not to say stupidity—the blindness of them, the foolishness, the insensibility! discussing it as if a thing that your eyes could see was a thing to discuss! It would have been unkind to think it was because they were old and their faculties dimmed. It is so sad to think that the faculties grow dim, that such a woman as my Aunt Mary should fail in seeing, or hearing, or feeling, that I would not have dwelt on it for a moment, it would have seemed so cruel! And then such a clever old lady as Lady Carnbee, who could see through a millstone, people said—and Mr Pitmilly, such an old man of the world. It did indeed bring tears to my eyes to think that all those clever people, solely by reason of being no longer young as I was, should have the simplest things shut out from them; and for all their wisdom and their knowledge be unable to see what a girl like me could see so easily. I was too much grieved for them to dwell upon that thought, and half ashamed, though perhaps half proud too, to be so much better off than they.

All those thoughts flitted through my mind as I sat and gazed across the street. And I felt there was so much going on in that room across the street! He was so absorbed in his writing, never looked up, never paused for a word, never turned round in his chair, or got up and walked about the room as my father did. Papa is a great writer, everybody says: but he would have come to the window and looked out, he would have drummed with his fingers on the pane, he would have watched a fly and helped it over a difficulty, and played with the fringe of the curtain, and done a dozen other nice, pleasant, foolish things, till the next sentence took shape. "My dear, I am waiting for a word," he would say to my mother when she looked at him, with a question why he was so idle, in her eyes; and then he would laugh, and go back again to his writing-table. But He over there never stopped at all. It was like a fascination. I could not take my eyes from him and that little scarcely perceptible movement he made, turning his head. I trembled with impatience to see him turn the page, or perhaps throw down his finished sheet on the floor, as somebody looking into a window like me once saw Sir Walter do, sheet after sheet. I should have cried out if this Unknown had done that. I should not have been able to help myself, whoever had been present; and gradually I got into such a state of suspense waiting for it to be done that my head grew hot and my hands cold. And then, just when there was a little movement of his elbow, as if he were about to do this, to be called away by Aunt Mary to see Lady Carnbee to the door! I believe I did not hear her till she had called me three times, and then I stumbled up, all flushed and hot, and nearly crying. When I came out from the recess to give the old lady my arm (Mr Pitmilly had gone away some time before), she put up her hand and stroked my cheek. "What ails the bairn!" she said; "she's fevered. You must not let her sit her lane in the window, Mary Balcarres. You and me know what comes of that." Her old fingers had a strange touch, cold like something not living, and I felt that dreadful diamond sting me on the cheek.

I do not say that this was not just a part of my excitement and suspense; and I know it is enough to make any one laugh when the excitement was all about an unknown man writing in a room on the other side of the way, and my impatience because he never came to an end of the page. If you think I was not quite as well aware of this as any one could be! but the worst was that this dreadful old lady felt my heart beating against her arm that was within mine. "You are just in a dream," she said to me, with her old voice close at my ear as we went downstairs. "I don't know who it is about, but it's bound to be some man that is not worth it. If you were wise you would think of him no more."

"I am thinking of no man!" I said, half crying. "It is very unkind and dreadful of you to say so, Lady Carnbee. I never thought of—any man, in all my life!" I cried in a passion of indignation. The old lady, clung tighter to my arm, and pressed it to her, not unkindly.

"Poor little bird," she said, "how it's strugglin' and flutterin'! I'm not saying but what it's more dangerous when it's all for a dream."

She was not at all unkind; but I was very angry and excited, and would scarcely shake that old pale hand which she put out to me from her carriage window when I had helped her in. I was angry with her, and I was afraid of the diamond, which looked up from under her finger as if it saw through and through me; and whether you believe me or not, I am certain that it stung me again—a sharp malignant prick, oh full of meaning! She never wore gloves, but only black lace mittens, through which that horrible diamond gleamed. I ran upstairs—she had been the last to go—and Aunt Mary too had gone to get ready for dinner, for it was late. I hurried to my place, and looked across, with my heart beating more than ever. I made quite sure I should see the finished sheet lying white upon the floor. But what I gazed at was only the dim blank of that window which they said was no window. The light had changed in some wonderful way during that five minutes I had been gone, and there was nothing, nothing, not a reflection, not a glimmer. It looked exactly as they all said, the blank form of a window painted on the wall. It was too much: I sat down in my excitement and cried as if my heart would break. I felt that they had done something to it, that it was not natural, that I could not bear their unkindness—even Aunt Mary. They thought it not good for me! not good for me! and they had done something—even Aunt Mary herself—and that wicked diamond that hid itself in Lady Carnbee's hand. Of course I knew all this was ridiculous as well as you could tell me; and I was exasperated by the disappointment and the sudden stop to all my excited feelings, and I could not bear it. It was more strong than I.

I was late for dinner, and naturally there were some traces in my eyes that I had been crying when I came into the full light in the dining-room, where Aunt Mary could look at me at her pleasure, and I could not run away. She said, "Honey, you have been shedding tears. I'm loth, loth that a bairn of your mother's should be made to shed tears in my house."

"I have not been made to shed tears," cried I; and then, to save myself another fit of crying, I burst out laughing and said, "I am afraid of that dreadful diamond on old Lady Carnbee's hand. It bites—I am sure it bites! Aunt Mary, look here."

"You foolish lassie," Aunt Mary said; but she looked at my cheek under the light of the lamp, and then she gave it a little pat with her soft hand. "Go away with you, you silly bairn. There is no bite; but a flushed cheek, my honey, and a wet eye. You must just read out my paper to me after dinner when the post is in: and we'll have no more thinking and no more dreaming for to-night."

"Yes, Aunt Mary," said I. But I knew what would happen; for when she opens up her "Times," all full of the news of the world, and the speeches and things which she takes an interest in, though I cannot tell why—she forgets. And as I kept very quiet and made not a sound, she forgot to-night what she had said, and the curtain hung a little more over me than usual, and I sat down in my recess as if I had been a hundred miles away. And my heart gave a great jump, as if it would have come out of my breast; for he was there. But not as he had been in the morning—I suppose the light, perhaps, was not good enough to go on with his work without a lamp or candles—for he had turned away from the table and was fronting the window, sitting leaning back in his chair, and turning his head to me. Not to me—he knew nothing about me. I thought he was not looking at anything; but with his face turned my way. My heart was in my mouth: it was so unexpected, so strange! though why it should have seemed strange I know not, for there was no communication between him and me that it should have moved me; and what could be more natural than that a man, wearied of his work, and feeling the want perhaps of more light, and yet that it was not dark enough to light a lamp, should turn round in his own chair, and rest a little, and think—perhaps of nothing at all? Papa always says he is thinking of nothing at all. He says things blow through his mind as if the doors were open, and he has no responsibility. What sort of things were blowing through this man's mind? or was he thinking, still thinking, of what he had been writing and going on with it still? The thing that troubled me most was that I could not make out his face. It is very difficult to do so when you see a person only through two windows, your own and his. I wanted very much to recognise him afterwards if I should chance to meet him in the street. If he had only stood up and moved about the room, I should have made out the rest of his figure, and then I should have known him again; or if he had only come to the window (as papa always did), then I should have seen his face clearly enough to have recognised him. But, to be sure, he did not see any need to do anything in order that I might recognise him, for he did not know I existed; and probably if he had known I was watching him, he would have been annoyed and gone away.

But he was as immovable there facing the window as he had been seated at the desk. Sometimes he made a little stir with a hand or a foot, and I held my breath, hoping he was about to rise from his chair—but he never did it. And with all the efforts I made I could not be sure of his face. I puckered my eyelids together as old Miss Jeanie did who was shortsighted, and I put my hands on each side of my face to concentrate the light on him: but it was all in vain. Either the face changed as I sat staring, or else it was the light that was not good enough, or I don't know what it was. His hair seemed to me light—certainly there was no dark line about his head, as there would have been had it been very dark—and I saw, where it came across the old gilt frame on the wall behind, that it must be fair: and I am almost sure he had no beard. Indeed I am sure that he had no beard, for the outline of his face was distinct enough; and the daylight was still quite clear out of doors, so that I recognised perfectly a baker's boy who was on the pavement opposite, and whom I should have known again whenever I had met him: as if it was of the least importance to recognise a baker's boy! There was one thing, however, rather curious about this boy. He had been throwing stones at something or somebody. In St Rule's they have a great way of throwing stones at each other, and I suppose there had been a battle. I suppose also that he had one stone in his hand left over from the battle, and his roving eye took in all the incidents of the street to judge where he could throw it with most effect and mischief. But apparently he found nothing worthy of it in the street, for he suddenly turned round with a flick under his leg to show his cleverness, and aimed it straight at the window. I remarked without remarking that it struck with a hard sound and without any breaking of glass, and fell straight down on the pavement. But I took no notice of this even in my mind, so intently was I watching the figure within, which moved not nor took the slightest notice, and remained just as dimly clear, as perfectly seen, yet as indistinguishable, as before. And then the light began to fail a little, not diminishing the prospect within, but making it still less distinct than it had been.

Then I jumped up, feeling Aunt Mary's hand upon my shoulder. "Honey," she said, "I asked you twice to ring the bell; but you did not hear me."

"Oh, Aunt Mary!" I cried in great penitence, but turning again to the window in spite of myself.

"You must come away from there: you must come away from there," she said, almost as if she were angry: and then her soft voice grew softer, and she gave me a kiss: "never mind about the lamp, honey; I have rung myself, and it is coming; but, silly bairn, you must not aye be dreaming—your little head will turn."

All the answer I made, for I could scarcely speak, was to give a little wave with my hand to the window on the other side of the street.

She stood there patting me softly on the shoulder for a whole minute or more, murmuring something that sounded like, "She must go away, she must go away." Then she said, always with her hand soft on my shoulder, "Like a dream when one awaketh." And when I looked again, I saw the blank of an opaque surface and nothing more.

Aunt Mary asked me no more questions. She made me come into the room and sit in the light and read something to her. But I did not know what I was reading, for there suddenly came into my mind and took possession of it, the thud of the stone upon the window, and its descent straight down, as if from some hard substance that threw it off: though I had myself seen it strike upon the glass of the panes across the way.

IV

I AM afraid I continued in a state of great exaltation and commotion of mind for some time. I used to hurry through the day till the evening came, when I could watch my neighbour through the window opposite. I did not talk much to any one, and I never said a word about my own questions and wonderings. I wondered who he was, what he was doing, and why he never came till the evening (or very rarely); and I also wondered much to what house the room belonged in which he sat. It seemed to form a portion of the old College Library, as I have often said. The window was one of the line of windows which I understood lighted the large hall; but whether this room belonged to the library itself, or how its occu-

pant gained access to it, I could not tell. I made up my mind that
it must open out of the hall, and that the gentleman must be the
Librarian or one of the assistants, perhaps kept busy all the day
in his official duties, and only able to get to his desk and do his
own private work in the evening. One has heard of so many things
like that—a man who had to take up some other kind of work for
his living, and then when his leisure-time came, gave it all up to
something he really loved—some study or some book he was writing. My father himself at one time had been like that. He had been
in the Treasury all day, and then in the evening wrote his books,
which made him famous. His daughter, however little she might
know of other things, could not but know that! But it discouraged
me very much when somebody pointed out to me one day in the
street an old gentleman who wore a wig and took a great deal of
snuff, and said, That's the Librarian of the old College. It gave
me a great shock for a moment; but then I remembered that an
old gentleman has generally assistants, and that it must be one
of them.

Gradually I became quite sure of this. There was another small
window above, which twinkled very much when the sun shone,
and looked a very kindly bright little window, above that dullness
of the other which hid so much. I made up my mind this was the
window of his other room, and that these two chambers at the
end of the beautiful hall were really beautiful for him to live in,
so near all the books, and so retired and quiet, that nobody knew
of them. What a fine thing for him! and you could see what use
he made of his good fortune as he sat there, so constant at his
writing for hours together. Was it a book he was writing, or
could it be perhaps Poems? This was a thought which made my
heart beat; but I concluded with much regret that it could not
be Poems, because no one could possibly write Poems like that,
straight off, without pausing for a word or a rhyme. Had they
been Poems he must have risen up, he must have paced about
the room or come to the window as papa did—not that papa wrote
Poems: he always said, "I am not worthy even to speak of such
prevailing mysteries," shaking his head—which gave me a wonderful admiration and almost awe of a Poet who was thus much greater

even than papa. But I could not believe that a poet could have kept
still for hours and hours like that. What could it be then? perhaps
it was history; that is a great thing to work at, but you would not
perhaps need to move nor to stride up and down, or look out
upon the sky and the wonderful light.

He did move now and then, however, though he never came to
the window. Sometimes, as I have said, he would turn round in
his chair and turn his face towards it, and sit there for a long
time musing when the light had begun to fail, and the world was
full of that strange day which was night, that light without colour,
in which everything was so clearly visible, and there were no
shadows. "It was between the night and the day, when the fairy
folk have power." This was the after-light of the wonderful, long,
long summer evening, the light without shadows. It had a spell
in it, and sometimes it made me afraid: and all manner of strange
thoughts seemed to come in, and I always felt that if only we had
a little more vision in our eyes we might see beautiful folk walking
about in it, who were not of our world. I thought most likely he
saw them, from the way he sat there looking out: and this made
my heart expand with the most curious sensation, as if of pride
that, though I could not see, he did, and did not even require to
come to the window, as I did, sitting close in the depth of the
recess, with my eyes upon him, and almost seeing things through
his eyes.

I was so much absorbed in these thoughts and in watching him
every evening—for now he never missed an evening, but was
always there—that people began to remark that I was looking
pale and that I could not be well, for I paid no attention when
they talked to me, and did not care to go out, nor to join the other
girls for their tennis, nor to do anything that others did; and some
said to Aunt Mary that I was quickly losing all the ground I had
gained, and that she could never send me back to my mother
with a white face like that. Aunt Mary had begun to look at me
anxiously for some time before that, and, I am sure, held secret
consultations over me, sometimes with the doctor, and sometimes
with her old ladies, who thought they knew more about young girls
than even the doctors. And I could hear them saying to her that

I wanted diversion, that I must be diverted, and that she must take me out more, and give a party, and that when the summer visitors began to come there would perhaps be a ball or two, or Lady Carnbee would get up a picnic. "And there's my young lord coming home," said the old lady whom they called Miss Jeanie, "and I never knew the young lassie yet that would not cock up her bonnet at the sight of a young lord."

But Aunt Mary shook her head. "I would not lippen much to the young lord," she said. "His mother is sore set upon siller for him; and my poor bit honey has no fortune to speak of. No, we must not fly so high as the young lord; but I will gladly take her about the country to see the old castles and towers. It will perhaps rouse her up a little."

"And if that does not answer we must think of something else," the old lady said.

I heard them perhaps that day because they were talking of me, which is always so effective a way of making you hear—for latterly I had not been paying any attention to what they were saying; and I thought to myself how little they knew, and how little I cared about even the old castles and curious houses, having something else in my mind. But just about that time Mr Pitmilly came in, who was always a friend to me, and, when he heard them talking, he managed to stop them and turn the conversation into another channel. And after a while, when the ladies were gone away, he came up to my recess, and gave a glance right over my head. And then he asked my Aunt Mary if ever she had settled her question about the window opposite, "that you thought was a window sometimes, and then not a window, and many curious things," the old gentleman said.

My Aunt Mary gave me another very wistful look; and then she said, "Indeed, Mr Pitmilly, we are just where we were, and I am quite as unsettled as ever; and I think my niece she has taken up my views, for I see her many a time looking and wondering, and I am not clear now what her opinion is."

"My opinion!" I said, "Aunt Mary." I could not help being a little scornful, as one is when one is very young. "I have no opinion. There is not only a window but there is a room, and I

could show you—" I was going to say, "show you the gentleman who sits and writes in it," but I stopped, not knowing what
they might say, and looked from one to another. "I could tell you
—all the furniture that is in it," I said. And then I felt something like a flame that went over my face, and that all at once
my cheeks were burning. I thought they gave a little glance at
each other, but that may have been folly. "There is a great picture,
in a big dim frame," I said, feeling a little breathless, "on the wall
opposite the window—"

"Is there so?" said Mr Pitmilly, with a little laugh. And he
said, "Now I will tell you what we'll do. You know that there is a
conversation party, or whatever they call it, in the big room
to-night, and it will be all open and lighted up. And it is a handsome room, and two-three things well worth looking at. I will
just step along after we have all got our dinner, and take you over
to the pairty, madam—Missy and you—"

"Dear me!" said Aunt Mary. "I have not gone to a pairty for
more years than I would like to say—and never once to the
Library Hall." Then she gave a little shiver, and said quite low, "I
could not go there."

"Then you will just begin again to-night, madam," said Mr Pitmilly, taking no notice of this, "and a proud man will I be leading
in Mistress Balcarres that was once the pride of the ball."

"Ah, once!" said Aunt Mary, with a low laugh and then a
sigh. "And we'll not say how long ago;" and after that she made
a pause, looking always at me: and then she said, "I accept your
offer, and we'll put on our braws; and I hope you will have no
occasion to think shame of us. But why not take your dinner
here?"

That was how it was settled, and the old gentleman went away
to dress, looking quite pleased. But I came to Aunt Mary as soon
as he was gone, and besought her not to make me go. "I like the
long bonnie night and the light that lasts so long. And I cannot
bear to dress up and go out, wasting it all in a stupid party. I
hate parties, Aunt Mary!" I cried, "and I would far rather stay
here."

"My honey," she said, taking both my hands, "I know it will

maybe be a blow to you,—but it's better so."

"How could it be a blow to me?" I cried; "but I would far rather not go."

"You'll just go with me, honey, just this once: it is not often I go out. You will go with me this one night, just this one night, my honey sweet."

I am sure there were tears in Aunt Mary's eyes, and she kissed me between the words. There was nothing more that I could say; but how I grudged the evening! A mere party, a conversazione (when all the College was away, too, and nobody to make conversation!), instead of my enchanted hour at my window and the soft strange light, and the dim face looking out, which kept me wondering and wondering what was he thinking of, what was he looking for, who was he? all one wonder and mystery and question, through the long, long, slowly fading night!

It occurred to me, however, when I was dressing—though I was so sure that he would prefer his solitude to everything—that he might perhaps, it was just possible, be there. And when I thought of that, I took out my white frock—though Janet had laid out my blue one—and my little pearl necklace which I had thought was too good to wear. They were not very large pearls, but they were real pearls, and very even and lustrous though they were small; and though I did not think much of my appearance then, there must have been something about me—pale as I was but apt to colour in a moment, with my dress so white, and my pearls so white, and my hair all shadowy—perhaps, that was pleasant to look at: for even old Mr Pitmilly had a strange look in his eyes, as if he was not only pleased but sorry too, perhaps thinking me a creature that would have troubles in this life, though I was so young and knew them not. And when Aunt Mary looked at me, there was a little quiver about her mouth. She herself had on her pretty lace and her white hair very nicely done, and looked her best. As for Mr Pitmilly, he had a beautiful fine French cambric frill to his shirt, plaited in the most minute plaits, and with a diamond pin in it which sparkled as much as Lady Carnbee's ring; but this was a fine frank kindly stone, that looked you straight in the face and sparkled, with the light dancing in

it as if it were pleased to see you, and to be shining on that old
gentleman's honest and faithful breast: for he had been one of
Aunt Mary's lovers in their early days, and still thought there
was nobody like her in the world.

I had got into quite a happy commotion of mind by the time
we set out across the street in the soft light of the evening to
the Library Hall. Perhaps, after all, I should see him, and see the
room which I was so well acquainted with, and find out why he
sat there so constantly and never was seen abroad. I thought I
might even hear what he was working at, which would be such a
pleasant thing to tell papa when I went home. A friend of mine
at St Rule's—oh, far, far more busy than you ever were, papa!—
and then my father would laugh as he always did, and say he was
but an idler and never busy at all.

The room was all light and bright, flowers wherever flowers
could be, and the long lines of the books that went along the walls
on each side, lighting up wherever there was a line of gilding or
an ornament, with a little response. It dazzled me at first all that
light: but I was very eager, though I kept very quiet, looking
round to see if perhaps in any corner, in the middle of any group,
he would be there. I did not expect to see him among the ladies.
He would not be with them,—he was too studious, too silent:
but perhaps among that circle of grey heads at the upper end of
the room—perhaps—

No: I am not sure that it was not half a pleasure to me to make
quite sure that there was not one whom I could take for him, who
was at all like my vague image of him. No: it was absurd to
think that he would be here, amid all that sound of voices, under
the glare of that light. I felt a little proud to think that he was in
his room as usual, doing his work, or thinking so deeply over it,
as when he turned round in his chair with his face to the light.

I was thus getting a little composed and quiet in my mind, for
now that the expectation of seeing him was over, though it was a
disappointment, it was a satisfaction too—when Mr Pitmilly came
up to me, holding out his arm. "Now," he said, "I am going to
take you to see the curiosities." I thought to myself that after I
had seen them and spoken to everybody I knew, Aunt Mary

would let me go home, so I went very willingly, though I did not care for the curiosities. Something, however, struck me strangely and we walked up the room. It was the air, rather fresh and strong, from an open window at the east end of the hall. How should there be a window there? I hardly saw what it meant for the first moment, but it blew in my face as if there was some meaning in it, and I felt very uneasy without seeing why.

Then there was another thing that startled me. On that side of the wall which was to the street there seemed no windows at all. A long line of bookcases filled it from end to end. I could not see what that meant either, but it confused me. I was altogether confused. I felt as if I was in a strange country; not knowing where I was going, not knowing what I might find out next. If there were no windows on the wall to the street, where was my window? My heart, which had been jumping up and calming down again all the time, gave a great leap at this, as if it would have come out of me—but I did not know what it could mean.

Then we stopped before a glass case, and Mr Pitmilly showed me some things in it. I could not pay much attention to them. My head was going round and round. I heard his voice going on, and then myself speaking with a queer sound that was hollow in my ears; but I did not know what I was saying or what he was saying. Then he took me to the very end of the room, the east end, saying something that I caught—that I was pale, that the air would do me good. The air was blowing full on me, lifting the lace of my dress, lifting my hair, almost chilly. The window opened into the pale daylight, into the little lane that ran by the end of the building. Mr Pitmilly went on talking, but I could not make out a word he said. Then I heard my own voice speaking through it, though I did not seem to be aware that I was speaking. "Where is my window?—where, then, is my window?" I seemed to be saying, and I turned right round, dragging him with me, still holding his arm. As I did this my eye fell upon something at last which I knew. It was a large picture in a broad frame, hanging against the farther wall.

What did it mean? Oh, what did it mean? I turned round again to the open window at the east end, and to the daylight, the strange light without any shadow, that was all round about this lighted hall, holding it like a bubble that would burst, like something that was not real. The real place was the room I knew, in which that picture was hanging, where the writing-table was, and where he sat with his face to the light. But where was the light and the window through which it came? I think my senses must have left me. I went up to the picture which I knew, and then I walked straight across the room, always dragging Mr Pitmilly, whose face was pale, but who did not struggle but allowed me to lead him, straight across to where the window was—where the window was not;—where there was no sign of it. "Where is my window?—where is my window?" I said. And all the time I was sure that I was in a dream, and these lights were all some theatrical illusion, and the people talking; and nothing real but the pale, pale, watching, lingering day standing by to wait until that foolish bubble should burst.

"My dear," said Mr Pitmilly, "my dear! Mind that you are in public. Mind where you are. You must not make an outcry and frighten your Aunt Mary. Come away with me. Come away, my dear young lady! and you'll take a seat for a minute or two and compose yourself; and I'll get you an ice or a little wine." He kept patting my hand, which was on his arm, and looking at me very anxiously. "Bless me! bless me! I never thought it would have this effect," he said.

But I would not allow him to take me away in that direction. I went to the picture again and looked at it without seeing it: and then I went across the room again, with some kind of wild thought that if I insisted I should find it. "My window—my window!" I said.

There was one of the professors standing there, and he heard me. "The window!" said he. "Ah, you've been taken in with what appears outside. It was put there to be in uniformity with the window on the stair. But it never was a real window. It is just behind that bookcase. Many people are taken in by it," he said.

His voice seemed to sound from somewhere far away, and as if it would go on for ever; and the hall swam in a dazzle of shining and of noises round me; and the daylight through the open window grew greyer, waiting till it should be over and the bubble burst.

V

IT WAS Mr Pitmilly who took me home; or rather it was I who took him, pushing him on a little in front of me, holding fast by his arm, not waiting for Aunt Mary or any one. We came out into the daylight again outside, I, without even a cloak or a shawl, with my bare arms, and uncovered head, and the pearls round my neck. There was a rush of the people about, and a baker's boy, that baker's boy, stood right in my way and cried, "Here's a braw ane!" shouting to the others: the words struck me somehow, as his stone had struck the window, without any reason. But I did not mind the people staring, and hurried across the street, with Mr Pitmilly half a step in advance. The door was open, and Janet standing at it, looking out to see what she could see of the ladies in their grand dresses. She gave a shriek when she saw me hurrying across the street; but I brushed past her, and pushed Mr Pitmilly up the stairs, and took him breathless to the recess, where I threw myself down on the seat, feeling as if I could not have gone another step farther, and waved my hand across to the window. "There! there!" I cried. Ah! there it was—not that senseless mob—not the theatre and the gas, and the people all in a murmur and clang of talking. Never in all these days had I seen that room so clearly. There was a faint tone of light behind, as if it might have been a reflection from some of those vulgar lights in the hall, and he sat against it, calm, wrapped in his thought, with his face turned to the window. Nobody but must have seen him. Janet could have seen him had I called her upstairs. It was like a picture, all the things I knew, and the same attitude, and the atmosphere, full of quietness, not disturbed by anything. I pulled Mr Pitmilly's arm before I let him go,—"You see, you see!" I cried. He gave me the most bewildered look, as if he would have liked to cry. He saw nothing! I was sure of that from his eyes. He was an old man, and there was no vision in him. If I had called up

Janet, she would have seen it all. "My dear!" he said. "My dear!" waving his hands in a helpless way.

"He has been there all these nights," I cried, "and I thought you could tell me who he was and what he was doing; and that he might have taken me in to that room, and showed me, that I might tell papa. Papa would understand, he would like to hear. Oh, can't you tell me what work he is doing, Mr Pitmilly? He never lifts his head as long as the light throws a shadow, and then when it is like this he turns round and thinks, and takes a rest!"

Mr Pitmilly was trembling, whether it was with cold or I know not what. He said, with a shake in his voice, "My dear young lady—my dear—" and then stopped and looked at me as if he were going to cry. "It's peetiful, it's peetiful," he said; and then in another voice, "I am going across there again to bring your Aunt Mary home; do you understand, my poor little thing, my— I am going to bring her home—you will be better when she is here." I was glad when he went away, as he could not see anything: and I sat alone in the dark which was not dark, but quite clear light—a light like nothing I ever saw. How clear it was in that room! not glaring like the gas and the voices, but so quiet, everything so visible, as if it were in another world. I heard a little rustle behind me, and there was Janet, standing staring at me with two big eyes wide open. She was only a little older than I was. I called to her, "Janet, come here, come here, and you will see him,—come here and see him!" impatient that she should be shy and keep behind. "Oh, my bonnie young leddy!" she said, and burst out crying. I stamped my foot at her, in my indignation that she would not come, and she fled before me with a rustle and swing of haste, as if she were afraid. None of them, none of them! not even a girl like myself, with the sight in her eyes, would understand. I turned back again, and held out my hands to him sitting there, who was the only one that knew. "Oh," I said, "say something to me! I don't know who you are, or what you are: but you're lonely and so am I; and I only—feel for you. Say something to me!" I neither hoped that he would hear, nor expected any answer. How could he hear, with the street between us, and his window shut, and all the murmuring of the voices and the people standing about? But for one moment it seemed to me that there was only him and me in the whole world.

But I gasped with my breath, that had almost gone from me, when I saw him move in his chair! He had heard me, though I knew not how. He rose up, and I rose too, speechless, incapable of anything but this mechanical movement. He seemed to draw me as if I were a puppet moved by his will. He came forward to the window, and stood looking across at me. I was sure that he looked at me. At last he had seen me: at last he had found out that somebody, though only a girl, was watching him, looking for him, believing in him. I was in such trouble and commotion of mind and trembling, that I could not keep on my feet, but dropped kneeling on the window-seat, supporting myself against the window, feeling as if my heart were being drawn out of me. I cannot describe his face. It was all dim, yet there was a light on it: I think it must have been a smile; and as closely as I looked at him he looked at me. His hair was fair, and there was a little quiver about his lips. Then he put his hands upon the window to open it. It was stiff and hard to move; but at last he forced it open with a sound that echoed all along the street. I saw that the people heard it, and several looked up. As for me, I put my hands together, leaning with my face against the glass, drawn to him as if I could have gone out of myself, my heart out of my bosom, my eyes out of my head. He opened the window with a noise that was heard from the West Port to the Abbey. Could any one doubt that?

And then he leaned forward out of the window, looking out. There was not one in the street but must have seen him. He looked at me first, with a little wave of his hand, as if it were a salutation—yet not exactly that either, for I thought he waved me away; and then he looked up and down in the dim shining of the ending day, first to the east, to the old Abbey towers, and then to the west, along the broad line of the street where so many were coming and going, but so little noise, all like enchanted folk in an enchanted place. I watched him with such a melting heart, with such a deep satisfaction as words could not say; for nobody could tell me now that he was not there,—nobody could say I was

dreaming any more. I watched him as if I could not breathe—my
heart in my throat, my eyes upon him. He looked up and down,
and then he looked back to me. I was the first, and I was the
last, though it was not for long: he did know, he did see, who
it was that had recognised him and sympathised with him all the
time. I was in a kind of rapture, yet stupor too; my look went with
his look, following it as if I were his shadow; and then suddenly
he was gone, and I saw him no more.

I dropped back again upon my seat, seeking something to support me, something to lean upon. He had lifted his hand and
waved it once again to me. How he went I cannot tell, nor where
he went I cannot tell; but in a moment he was away, and the
window standing open, and the room fading into stillness and
dimness, yet so clear, with all its space, and the great picture in
its gilded frame upon the wall. It gave me no pain to see him
go away. My heart was so content, and I was so worn out and
satisfied—for what doubt or question could there be about him
now? As I was lying back as weak as water, Aunt Mary came
in behind me, and flew to me with a little rustle as if she had
come on wings, and put her arms round me, and drew my head
on to her breast. I had begun to cry a little with sobs like a child.
"You saw him, you saw him!" I said. To lean upon her, and feel
her voice saying "Honey, my honey!"—as if she were nearly crying too. Lying there I came back to myself, quite sweetly, glad of
everything. But I wanted some assurance from them that they had
seen him too. I waved my hand to the window that was still standing open, and the room that was stealing away into the faint dark.
"This time you saw it all?" I said, getting more eager. "My
honey!" said Aunt Mary, giving me a kiss: and Mr Pitmilly
began to walk about the room with short little steps behind, as if
he were out of patience. I sat straight up and put away Aunt
Mary's arms. "You cannot be so blind, so blind!" I cried. "Oh, not
to-night, at least not to-night!" But neither the one nor the other
made any reply. I shook myself quite free, and raised myself up.
And there, in the middle of the street, stood the baker's boy like a
statue, staring up at the open window, with his mouth open and
his face full of wonder—breathless, as if he could not believe

what he saw. I darted forward, calling to him, and beckoned him to come to me. "Oh, bring him up! bring him, bring him to me!" I cried.

Mr Pitmilly went out directly, and got the boy by the shoulder. He did not want to come. It was strange to see the little old gentleman, with his beautiful frill and his diamond pin, standing out in the street, with his hand upon the boy's shoulder, and the other boys round, all in a little crowd. And presently they came towards the house, the others all following, gaping and wondering. He came in unwilling, almost resisting, looking as if we meant him some harm. "Come away, my laddie, come and speak to the young lady," Mr Pitmilly was saying. And Aunt Mary took my hands to keep me back. But I would not be kept back.

"Boy," I cried, "you saw it too: you saw it: tell them you saw it! It is that I want, and no more."

He looked at me as they all did, as if he thought I was mad. "What's she wantin' wi' me?" he said; and then, "I did nae harm, even if I did throw a bit stane at it—and it's nae sin to throw a stane."

"You rascal!" said Mr Pitmilly, giving him a shake; "have you been throwing stones? You'll kill somebody some of these days with your stones." The old gentleman was confused and troubled, for he did not understand what I wanted, nor anything that had happened. And then Aunt Mary, holding my hands and drawing me close to her, spoke. "Laddie," she said, "answer the young lady, like a good lad. There's no intention of finding fault with you. Answer her, my man, and then Janet will give ye your supper before you go."

"Oh speak, speak!" I cried; "answer them and tell them! you saw that window opened, and the gentleman look out and wave his hand?"

"I saw nae gentleman," he said, with his head down, "except this wee gentleman here."

"Listen, laddie," said Aunt Mary. "I saw ye standing in the middle of the street staring. What were ye looking at?"

"It was naething to make a wark about. It was just yon windy yonder in the library that is nae windy. And it was open—as sure's death. You may laugh if you like. Is that a' she's wantin' wi' me?"

"You are telling a pack of lies, laddie," Mr Pitmilly said.

"I'm tellin' nae lees—it was standin' open just like ony ither windy. It's as sure's death. I couldna believe it mysel'; but it's true."

"And there it is," I cried, turning round and pointing it out to them with great triumph in my heart. But the light was all grey, it had faded, it had changed. The window was just as it had always been, a sombre break upon the wall.

I was treated like an invalid all that evening, and taken upstairs to bed, and Aunt Mary sat up in my room the whole night through. Whenever I opened my eyes she was always sitting there close to me, watching. And there never was in all my life so strange a night. When I would talk in my excitement, she kissed me and hushed me like a child. "Oh, honey, you are not the only one!" she said. "Oh whisht, whisht, bairn! I should never have let you be there!"

"Aunt Mary, Aunt Mary, you have seen him too?"

"Oh whisht, whisht, honey!" Aunt Mary said: her eyes were shining—there were tears in them. "Oh whisht, whisht! Put it out of your mind, and try to sleep. I will not speak another word," she cried.

But I had my arms round her, and my mouth at her ear. "Who is he there?—tell me that I will ask no more—"

"Oh honey, rest, and try to sleep! It is just—how can I tell you?—a dream, a dream! Did you not hear what Lady Carnbee said?—the women of our blood—"

"What? what? Aunt Mary, oh Aunt Mary—"

"I canna tell you," she cried in her agitation, "I canna tell you! How can I tell you, when I know just what you know and no more? It is a longing of your life after—it is a looking—for what never comes."

"He will come," I cried. "I shall see him to-morrow—that I know, I know!"

She kissed me and cried over me, her cheek hot and wet like mine. "My honey, try if you can sleep—try if you can sleep: and we'll wait to see what to-morrow brings."

"I have no fear," said I; and then I suppose, though it is strange to think of, I must have fallen asleep—I was so worn-out, and young, and not used to lying in my bed awake. From time to time I opened my eyes, and sometimes jumped up remembering everything; but Aunt Mary was always there to soothe me, and I lay down again in her shelter like a bird in its nest.

But I would not let them keep me in bed next day. I was in a kind of fever, not knowing what I did. The window was quite opaque, without the least glimmer in it, flat and blank like a piece of wood. Never from the first day had I seen it so little like a window. "It cannot be wondered at," I said to myself, "that seeing it like that, and with eyes that are old, not so clear as mine, they should think what they do." And then I smiled to myself to think of the evening and the long light, and whether he would look out again, or only give me a signal with his hand. I decided I would like that best: not that he should take the trouble to come forward and open it again, but just a turn of his head and a wave of his hand. It would be more friendly and show more confidence,—not as if I wanted that kind of demonstration every night.

I did not come down in the afternoon, but kept at my own window upstairs alone, till the tea-party should be over. I could hear them making a great talk; and I was sure they were all in the recess staring at the window, and laughing at the silly lassie. Let them laugh! I felt above all that now. At dinner I was very restless, hurrying to get it over; and I think Aunt Mary was restless too. I doubt whether she read her "Times" when it came; she opened it up so as to shield her, and watched from a corner. And I settled myself in the recess, with my heart full of expectation. I wanted nothing more than to see him writing at his table, and to turn his head and give me a little wave of his hand, just to show that he knew I was there. I sat from half-past seven o'clock to ten o'clock: and the daylight grew softer and softer, till at last it was as if it was shining through a pearl, and not a shadow to be seen. But the window all the time was as black as night, and there was nothing, nothing there.

Well: but other nights it had been like that; he would not be there every night only to please me. There are other things in a man's life, a great learned man like that. I said to myself I was not disappointed. Why should I be disappointed? There had been other nights when he was not there. Aunt Mary watched me, every movement I made, her eyes shining, often wet, with a pity in them that almost made me cry: but I felt as if I were more sorry for her than for myself. And then I flung myself upon her, and asked her, again and again, what it was, and who it was, imploring her to tell me if she knew? and when she had seen him, and what had happened? and what it meant about the women of our blood? She told me that how it was she could not tell, nor when: it was just at the time it had to be; and that we all saw him in our time—"that is," she said, "the ones that are like you and me." What was it that made her and me different from the rest? but she only shook her head and would not tell me. "They say," she said, and then stopped short. "Oh, honey, try and forget all about it—if I had but known you were of that kind! They say—that once there was one that was a Scholar, and liked his books more than any lady's love. Honey, do not look at me like that. To think I should have brought all this on you!"

"He was a Scholar?" I cried.

"And one of us, that must have been a light woman, not like you and me— But maybe it was just in innocence; for who can tell? She waved to him and waved to him to come over: and yon ring was the token: but he would not come. But still she sat at her window and waved and waved—till at last her brothers heard of it, that were stirring men; and then—oh, my honey, let us speak of it no more!"

"They killed him!" I cried, carried away. And then I grasped her with my hands, and gave her a shake, and flung away from her. "You tell me that to throw dust in my eyes—when I saw him only last night: and he is living as I am, and as young!"

"My honey, my honey!" Aunt Mary said.

After that I would not speak to her for a long time; but she kept close to me, never leaving me when she could help it, and always with that pity in her eyes. For the next night it was the same;

and the third night. That third night I thought I could not bear
it any longer. I would have to do something—if only I knew what
to do! If it would ever get dark, quite dark, there might be something to be done. I had wild dreams of stealing out of the house
and getting a ladder, and mounting up to try if I could not open
that window, in the middle of the night—if perhaps I could get
the baker's boy to help me; and then my mind got into a whirl,
and it was as if I had done it; and I could almost see the boy put
the ladder to the window, and hear him cry out that there was
nothing there. Oh, how slow it was, the night! and how light it
was, and everything so clear—no darkness to cover you, no
shadow, whether on one side of the street or on the other side! I
could not sleep, though I was forced to go to bed. And in the
deep midnight, when it is dark dark in every other place, I
slipped very softly downstairs, though there was one board on
the landing-place that creaked—and opened the door and stepped
out. There was not a soul to be seen, up or down, from the Abbey
to the West Port: and the trees stood like ghosts and the silence
was terrible, and everything as clear as day. You don't know what
silence is till you find it in the light like that, not morning but
night, no sun-rising, no shadow, but everything as clear as the
day.

It did not make any difference as the slow minutes went on:
one o'clock, two o'clock. How strange it was to hear the clocks
striking in that dead light when there was nobody to hear them!
But it made no difference. The window was quite blank; even the
marking of the panes seemed to have melted away. I stole up again
after a long time, through the silent house, in the clear light, cold
and trembling, with despair in my heart.

I am sure Aunt Mary must have watched and seen me coming
back, for after a while I heard faint sounds in the house; and very
early, when there had come a little sunshine into the air, she came
to my bedside with a cup of tea in her hand; and she, too, was
looking like a ghost. "Are you warm, honey—are you comfortable?" she said. "It doesn't matter," said I. I did not feel as if anything mattered; unless if one could get into the dark somewhere
—the soft, deep dark that would cover you over and hide you—

but I could not tell from what. The dreadful thing was that there was nothing, nothing to look for, nothing to hide from—only the silence and the light.

That day my mother came and took me home. I had not heard she was coming; she arrived quite unexpectedly, and said she had no time to stay, but must start the same evening so as to be in London next day, papa having settled to go abroad. At first I had a wild thought I would not go. But how can a girl say I will not, when her mother has come for her, and there is no reason, no reason in the world, to resist, and no right! I had to go, whatever I might wish or any one might say. Aunt Mary's dear eyes were wet; she went about the house drying them quietly with her handkerchief, but she always said, "It is the best thing for you, honey—the best thing for you!" Oh, how I hated to hear it said that it was the best thing, as if anything mattered, one more than another! The old ladies were all there in the afternoon, Lady Carnbee looking at me from under her black lace, and the diamond lurking, sending out darts from under her finger. She patted me on the shoulder, and told me to be a good bairn. "And never lippen to what you see from the window," she said. "The eye is deceitful as well as the heart." She kept patting me on the shoulder, and I felt again as if that sharp wicked stone stung me. Was that what Aunt Mary meant when she said yon ring was the token? I thought afterwards I saw the mark on my shoulder. You will say why? How can I tell why? If I had known, I should have been contented, and it would not have mattered any more.

I never went back to St Rule's and for years of my life I never looked out of a window when any other window was in sight. You ask me did I ever see him again? I cannot tell: the imagination is a great deceiver, as Lady Carnbee said: and if he stayed there so long, only to punish the race that had wronged him, why should I ever have seen him again? for I had received my share. But who can tell what happens in a heart that often, often, and so long as that, comes back to do its errand? If it was he whom I have seen again, the anger is gone from him, and he means good and no longer harm to the house of the woman that loved him. I have seen his face looking at me from a crowd. There was one time when I came home a widow from India, very sad, with my little children: I am certain I saw him there among all the people coming to welcome their friends. There was nobody to welcome me,—for I was not expected: and very sad was I, without a face I knew: when all at once I saw him, and he waved his hand to me. My heart leaped up again: I had forgotten who he was, but only that it was a face I knew, and I landed almost cheerfully, thinking here was some one who would help me. But he had disappeared, as he did from the window, with that one wave of his hand.

And again I was reminded of it all when old Lady Carnbee died —an old, old woman—and it was found in her will that she had left me that diamond ring. I am afraid of it still. It is locked up in an old sandal-wood box in the lumber-room in the little old country-house which belongs to me, but where I never live. If any one would steal it, it would be a relief to my mind. Yet I never knew what Aunt Mary meant when she said, "Yon ring was the token," nor what it could have to do with that strange window in the old College Library of St Rule's.

ROBERT LOUIS STEVENSON

THE MERRY MEN

I

EILEAN AROS

It was a beautiful morning in the late July when I set forth on foot for the last time for Aros. A boat had put me ashore the night before at Grisapol; I had such breakfast as the little inn afforded, and, leaving all my baggage till I had an occasion to come round for it by sea, struck right across the promontory with a cheerful heart.

I was far from being a native of these parts, springing, as I did, from an unmixed lowland stock. But an uncle of mine, Gordon Darnaway, after a poor, rough youth, and some years at sea, had married a young wife in the islands; Mary Maclean she was called, the last of her family; and when she died in giving birth to a daughter, Aros, the sea-girt farm, had remained in his possession. It brought him in nothing but the means of life, as I was well aware; but he was a man whom ill-fortune had pursued; he feared, cumbered as he was with the young child, to make a fresh adventure upon life; and remained in Aros, biting his nails at destiny. Years passed over his head in that isolation, and brought neither help nor contentment. Meantime our family was dying out in the lowlands; there is little luck for any of that race; and perhaps my father was the luckiest of all, for not only was he one of the last to die, but he left a son to his name and a little money to support it. I was a student of Edinburgh University, living well enough at my own charges, but without kith or kin; when some news of me found its way to Uncle Gordon on the Ross of Grisapol; and he, as he was a man who held blood thicker than water, wrote to me the day he heard of my existence, and taught me to count Aros as my home. Thus it was that I came to spend my vacations in that part of the country, so far from all society and comfort, between the codfish and the moorcocks; and thus it was that now, when I had done with my classes, I was returning thither with so light a heart that July day.

The Ross, as we call it, is a promontory neither wide nor high, but as rough as God made it to this day; the deep sea on either hand of it, full of rugged isles and reefs most perilous to seamen —all overlooked from the eastward by some very high cliffs and the great peak of Ben Kyaw. *The Mountain of the Mist*, they say the words signify in the Gaelic tongue; and it is well named. For that hill-top, which is more than three thousand feet in height, catches all the clouds that come blowing from the sea-ward; and, indeed, I used often to think that it must make them for itself; since when all heaven was clear to the sea level, there would ever be a streamer on Ben Kyaw. It brought water, too, and was mossy to the top in consequence. I have seen us sitting in broad sunshine on the Ross, and the rain falling black like crape upon the mountain. But the wetness of it made it often appear more beautiful to my eyes; for when the sun struck upon the hill-sides there were many wet rocks and watercourses that shone like jewels even as far as Aros, fifteen miles away.

The road that I followed was a cattle-track. It twisted so as nearly to double the length of my journey; it went over rough boulders so that a man had to leap from one to another, and through soft bottoms where the moss came nearly to the knee. There was no cultivation anywhere, and not one house in the ten miles from Grisapol to Aros. Houses of course there were—three at least; but they lay so far on the one side or the other that no stranger could have found them from the track. A large part of the Ross is covered with big granite rocks, some of them larger than a two-roomed house, one beside another, with fern and deep heather in between them where the vipers breed. Any way the wind was, it was always sea air, as salt as on a ship; the gulls were as free as moorfowl over all the Ross; and whenever the way rose a little, your eye would kindle with the brightness of the sea. From the very midst of the land, on a day of wind and a high spring, I have heard the Roost roaring like a battle where it runs by Aros, and the great and fearful voices of the breakers that we call the Merry Men.

Aros itself—Aros Jay, I have heard the natives call it, and they say it means *the House of God*—Aros itself was not properly a piece of the Ross, nor was it quite an islet. It formed the south-west corner of the land, fitted close to it, and was in one place only separated from the coast by a little gut of the sea, not forty feet across the narrowest. When the tide was full, this was clear and still, like a pool on a land river; only there was a difference in the weeds and fishes, and the water itself was green instead of brown; but when the tide went out, in the bottom of the ebb, there was a day or two in every month when you could pass dry-shod from Aros to the mainland. There was some good pasture, where my uncle fed the sheep he lived on; perhaps the feed was better because the ground rose higher on the islet than the main level of the Ross, but this I am not skilled enough to settle. The house was a good one for that country, two stories high. It looked westward over a bay, with a pier hard by for a boat, and from the door you could watch the vapours blowing on Ben Kyaw.

On all this part of the coast, and especially near Aros, these great granite rocks that I have spoken of go down together in troops into the sea, like cattle on a summer's day. There they stand, for all the world like their neighbours ashore; only the salt water sobbing between them instead of the quiet earth, and clots of sea-pink blooming on their sides instead of heather; and the great sea-conger to wreathe about the base of them instead of the poisonous viper of the land. On calm days you can go wandering between them in a boat for hours, echoes following you about the labyrinth; but when the sea is up, Heaven help the man that hears that caldron boiling.

Off the south-west end of Aros these blocks are very many, and much greater in size. Indeed, they must grow monstrously bigger out to sea, for there must be ten sea miles of open water sown with them as thick as a country place with houses, some standing thirty feet above the tides, some covered, but all perilous to ships; so that on a clear, westerly blowing day, I have counted, from

the top of Aros, the great rollers breaking white and heavy over
as many as six-and-forty buried reefs. But it is nearer in shore
that the danger is worst; for the tide, here running like a mill-
race, makes a long belt of broken water—a *Roost* we call it—
at the tail of the land. I have often been out there in a dead calm
at the slack of the tide; and a strange place it is, with the sea
swirling and combing up and boiling like the caldrons of a linn,
and now and again a little dancing mutter of sound as though the
Roost were talking to itself. But when the tide begins to run again,
and above all in heavy weather, there is no man could take a boat
within half a mile of it, nor a ship afloat that could either steer or
live in such a place. You can hear the roaring of it six miles away.
At the seaward end there comes the strongest of the bubble; and
it's here that these big breakers dance together—the dance of
death, it may be called—that have got the name, in these parts, of
the Merry Men. I have heard it said that they run fifty feet high;
but that must be the green water only, for the spray runs twice
as high as that. Whether they got the name from their movements,
which are swift and antic, or from the shouting they make about
the turn of the tide, so that all Aros shakes with it, is more than
I can tell.

The truth is, that in a south-westerly wind, that part of our
archipelago is no better than a trap. If a ship got through the
reefs, and weathered the Merry Men, it would be to come ashore
on the south coast of Aros, in Sandag Bay, where so many dismal
things befell our family, as I propose to tell. The thought of all
these dangers, in the place I knew so long, makes me particularly
welcome the works now going forward to set lights upon the head-
lands and buoys along the channels of our iron-bound, inhospitable islands.

The country people had many a story about Aros, as I used to
hear from my uncle's man, Rorie, an old servant of the Mac-
leans, who had transferred his services without afterthought on
the occasion of the marriage. There was some tale of an unlucky
creature, a sea-kelpie, that dwelt and did business in some fearful manner of his own among the boiling breakers of the Roost.
A mermaid had once met a piper on Sandag beach, and there sang

to him a long, bright midsummer's night, so that in the morning he was found stricken crazy, and from thenceforward, till the day he died, said only one form of words; what they were in the original Gaelic I cannot tell, but they were thus translated: "Ah, the sweet singing out of the sea." Seals that haunted on that coast have been known to speak to man in his own tongue, presaging great disasters. It was here that a certain saint first landed on his voyage out of Ireland to convert the Hebrideans. And, indeed, I think he had some claim to be called saint; for, with the boats of that past age, to make so rough a passage, and land on such a ticklish coast, was surely not far short of the miraculous. It was to him, or to some of his monkish underlings who had a cell there, that the islet owes its holy and beautiful name, the House of God.

Among these old wives' stories there was one which I was inclined to hear with more credulity. As I was told, in that tempest which scattered the ships of the Invincible Armada over all the north and west of Scotland, one great vessel came ashore on Aros, and before the eyes of some solitary people on a hill-top, went down in a moment with all hands, her colours flying even as she sank. There was some likelihood in this tale; for another of that fleet lay sunk on the north side, twenty miles from Grisapol. It was told, I thought, with more detail and gravity than its companion stories, and there was one particularity which went far to convince me of its truth: the name, that is, of the ship was still remembered, and sounded, in my ears, Spanishly. The *Espirito Santo* they called it, a great ship of many decks of guns, laden with treasure and grandees of Spain, and fierce soldadoes, that now lay fathom deep to all eternity, done with her wars and voyages, in Sandag Bay, upon the west of Aros. No more salvos of ordnance for that tall ship, the "Holy Spirit," no more fair winds or happy ventures; only to rot there deep in the sea-tangle and hear the shoutings of the Merry Men as the tide ran high about the island. It was a strange thought to me first and last, and only grew stranger as I learned the more of Spain, from which she had set sail with so proud a company, and King Philip, the wealthy king, that sent her on that voyage.

And now I must tell you, as I walked from Grisapol that day, the *Espirito Santo* was very much in my reflections. I had been favourably remarked by our then Principal in Edinburgh College, that famous writer, Dr. Robertson, and by him had been set to work on some papers of an ancient date to rearrange and sift of what was worthless; and in one of these, to my great wonder, I found a note of this very ship, the *Espirito Santo*, with her captain's name, and how she carried a great part of the Spaniards' treasure, and had been lost upon the Ross of Grisapol; but in what particular spot the wild tribes of that place and period would give no information to the king's enquiries. Putting one thing with another, and taking our island tradition together with this note of old King Jamie's perquisitions after wealth, it had come strongly on my mind that the spot for which he sought in vain could be no other than the small bay of Sandag on my uncle's land; and being a fellow of a mechanical turn, I had ever since been plotting how to weigh that good ship up again with all her ingots, ounces, and doubloons, and bring back our house of Darnaway to its long-forgotten dignity and wealth.

This was a design of which I soon had reason to repent. My mind was sharply turned on different reflections; and since I became the witness of a strange judgment of God's, the thought of dead men's treasures has been intolerable to my conscience. But even at that time I must acquit myself of sordid greed; for if I desired riches, it was not for their own sake, but for the sake of a person who was dear to my heart—my uncle's daughter, Mary Ellen. She had been educated well, and had been a time to school upon the mainland; which, poor girl, she would have been happier without. For Aros was no place for her, with old Rorie the servant, and her father, who was one of the unhappiest men in Scotland, plainly bred up in a country place among Cameronians, long a skipper sailing out of the Clyde about the islands, and now, with infinite discontent, managing his sheep and a little 'long shore fishing for the necessary bread. If it was sometimes weariful to me, who was there but a month or two, you may fancy what it was to her who dwelt in that same desert all the year round, with the sheep and flying sea-gulls, and the <u>Merry Men</u> singing and dancing in the Roost!

↳ Northern lichts?
N/a - see p. 312

II

WHAT THE WRECK HAD BROUGHT TO AROS

IT WAS half-flood when I got the length of Aros; and there was nothing for it but to stand on the far shore and whistle for Rorie with the boat. I had no need to repeat the signal. At the first sound, Mary was at the door flying a handkerchief by way of answer, and the old long-legged serving-man was shambling down the gravel to the pier. For all his hurry, it took him a long while to pull across the bay; and I observed him several times to pause, go into the stern, and look over curiously into the wake. As he came nearer, he seemed to me aged and haggard, and I thought he avoided my eye. The coble had been repaired, with two new thwarts and several patches of some rare and beautiful foreign wood, the name of it unknown to me.

"Why, Rorie," said I, as we began the return voyage, "this is fine wood. How came you by that?"

"It will be hard to cheesel," Rorie opined reluctantly; and just then, dropping the oars, he made another of those dives into the stern which I had remarked as he came across to fetch me, and, leaning his hand on my shoulder, stared with an awful look into the waters of the bay.

"What is wrong?" I asked, a good deal startled.

"It will be a great feesh," said the old man, returning to his oars; and nothing more could I get out of him but strange glances and an ominous nodding of the head. In spite of myself, I was infected with a measure of uneasiness; I turned also, and studied the wake. The water was still and transparent, but, out here in the middle of the bay, exceeding deep. For some time I could see naught; but at last it did seem to me as if something dark—a great fish, or perhaps only a shadow—followed studiously in the track of the moving coble. And then I remembered one of Rorie's superstitions: how in a ferry in Morven, in some great, exterminating feud among the clans, a fish, the like of it unknown in all our waters, followed for some years the passage of the ferry-boat, until no man dared to make the crossing.

"He will be waiting for the right man," said Rorie.

Mary met me on the beach, and led me up the brae and into the house of Aros. Outside and inside there were many changes. The garden was fenced with the same wood that I had noted in the boat; there were chairs in the kitchen covered with strange brocade; curtains of brocade hung from the window; a clock stood silent on the dresser; a lamp of brass was swinging from the roof; the table was set for dinner with the finest of linen and silver; and all these new riches were displayed in the plain old kitchen that I knew so well, with the high-backed settle, and the stools, and the closet bed for Rorie; with the wide chimney the sun shone into, and the clear-smouldering peats; with the pipes on the mantelshelf and the three-cornered spittoons, filled with seashells instead of sand, on the floor; with the bare stone walls and the bare wooden floor, and the three patchwork rugs that were of yore its sole adornment—poor man's patchwork, the like of it unknown in cities, woven with homespun, and Sunday black, and sea-cloth polished on the bench of rowing. The room, like the house, had been a sort of wonder in that country-side, it was so neat and habitable; and to see it now, shamed by these incongruous additions, filled me with indignation and a kind of anger. In view of the errand I had come upon to Aros, the feeling was baseless and unjust; but it burned high, as the first moment, in my heart.

"Mary, girl," said I, "this is the place I had learned to call my home, and I do not know it."

"It is my home by nature, not by the learning," she replied; "the place I was born and the place I'm like to die in; and I neither like these changes, nor the way they came, nor that which came with them. I would have liked better, under God's pleasure, they had gone down into the sea, and the Merry Men were dancing on them now."

Mary was always serious; it was perhaps the only trait that she shared with her father; but the tone with which she uttered these words was even graver than of custom.

"Ay," said I, "I feared it came by wreck, and that's by death; yet when my father died I took his goods without remorse."

"Your father died a clean-strae death, as the folk say," said Mary.

"True," I returned; "and a wreck is like a judgment. What was she called?"

"They ca'd her the *Christ-Anna*," said a voice behind me; and, turning round, I saw my uncle standing in the doorway.

He was a sour, small bilious man, with a long face and very dark eyes; fifty-six years old, sound and active in body, and with an air somewhat between that of a shepherd and that of a man following the sea. He never laughed, that I heard; read long at the Bible; prayed much, like the Cameronians he had been brought up among; and, indeed, in many ways, used to remind me of one of the hill-preachers in the killing times before the Revolution. But he never got much comfort, nor even, as I used to think, much guidance, by his piety. He had his black fits when he was afraid of hell; but he had led a rough life, to which he would look back with envy, and was still a rough, cold, gloomy man.

As he came in at the door out of the sunlight, with his bonnet on his head and a pipe hanging in his button-hole, he seemed, like Rorie, to have grown older and paler, the lines were deeplier ploughed upon his face, and the whites of his eyes were yellow, like old stained ivory, or the bones of the dead.

"Ay," he repeated, dwelling upon the first part of the word, "the *Christ-Anna*. It's an awfu' name."

I made him my salutations, and complimented him upon his look of health; for I feared he had perhaps been ill.

"I'm in the body," he replied, ungraciously enough; "aye in the body and the sins of the body, like yoursel'. Denner," he said abruptly to Mary, and then ran on, to me: "They're grand braws, thir that we hae gotten, are they no'? Yon's a bonny knock, but it'll no gang; and the naper's by ordnar. Bonny, bairnly braws; it's for the like o' them folk sells the peace of God that passeth understanding; it's for the like o' them, an' maybe no' even sae muckle worth, folk daunton God to His face and burn in muckle hell; and it's for that reason the Scripture ca's them, as I read the passage, the accursed thing.—Mary, ye girzie," he interrupted himself to cry with some asperity, "what for hae ye no' put out the twa candlesticks?"

"Why should we need them at high noon?" she asked.

But my uncle was not to be turned from his idea. "We'll bruik them while we may," he said; and so two massive candlesticks of wrought silver were added to the table equipage, already so unsuited to that rough seaside farm.

"She cam' ashore Februar' 10, about ten at nicht," he went on to me. "There was nae wind, and a sair run o' sea; and she was in the sook o' the Roost, as I jaloose. We had seen her a' day, Rorie and me, beating to the wind. She wasna a handy craft, I'm thinking, that Christ-Anna; for she would neither steer nor stey wi' them. A sair day they had of it; their hands was never aff the sheets, and it perishin' cauld—ower cauld to snaw; and aye they would get a nip o' wind, and awa' again, to pit the emp'y hope into them. Eh, man! but they had a sair day for the last o't! He would have had a prood, prood heart that won ashore upon the back o' that."

"And were all lost?" I cried. "God help them!"

"Wheesht!" he said sternly. "Nane shall pray for the deid on my hearth-stane."

I disclaimed a Popish sense for my ejaculation; and he seemed to accept my disclaimer with unusual facility, and ran on once more upon what had evidently become a favourite subject.

"We fand her in Sandag Bay, Rorie an' me, and a' thae braws in the inside of her. There's a kittle bit, ye see, about Sandag; whiles the sook rins strong for the Merry Men; an' whiles again, when the tide's makin' hard an' ye can hear the Roost blawin' at the far-end of Aros, there comes a back-spang of current straucht into Sandag Bay. Weel, there's the thing that got the grip on the Christ-Anna. She but to have come in ram-stam an' stern forrit; for the bows of her are aften under, and the back-side of her is clear at hie-water o' neaps. But, man! the dunt that she cam doon wi' when she struck! Lord save us a'! but it's an unco life to be a sailor—a cauld, wan-chancy life. Mony's the gliff I got myself' in the great deep; and why the Lord should hae made yon unco water is mair than ever I could win to understand. He made the vales and the pastures, the bonny green yaird, the halesome, canty land—

And now they shout and sing to Thee,
For Thou hast made them glad,

as the Psalms say in the metrical version. No' that I would preen my faith to that clink neither; but it's bonny, and easier to mind. 'Who go to sea in ships,' they hae't again—

and in
Great waters trading be,
Within the deep these men God's works
And His great wonders see.

Weel, it's easy sayin' sae. Maybe Dauvit wasna very weel acquant wi' the sea. But, troth, if it wasna prentit in the Bible, I wad whiles be temp'it to think it wasna the Lord, but the muckle, black deil that made the sea. There's naething good comes oot o't but the fish; an' the spentacle o' God riding on the tempest, to be shüre, whilk would be what Dauvit was likely ettling at. But, man, they were sair wonders that God showed to the *Christ-Anna* —wonders, do I ca' them? Judgments, rather: judgments in the mirk nicht among the draygons o' the deep. And their souls—to think o' that—their souls, man, maybe no' prepared! The sea— a muckle yett to hell!"

I observed, as my uncle spoke, that his voice was unnaturally moved and his manner unwontedly demonstrative. He leaned forward at these last words, for example, and touched me on the knee with his spread fingers, looking up into my face with a certain pallor, and I could see that his eyes shone with a deep-seated fire, and that the lines about his mouth were drawn and tremulous.

Even the entrance of Rorie, and the beginning of our meal, did not detach him from his train of thought beyond a moment. He condescended, indeed, to ask me some questions as to my success at college, but I thought it was with half his mind; and even in his extempore grace, which was, as usual, long and wandering, I could find the trace of his preoccupation, praying, as he did, that God would "remember in mercy fower puir, feckless, fiddling, sinful creatures here by their lee-lane beside the great and dowie waters."

Soon there came an interchange of speeches between him and Rorie.

"Was it there?" asked my uncle.

"Ou, ay!" said Rorie.

I observed that they both spoke in a manner of aside, and with some show of embarrassment, and that Mary herself appeared to colour, and looked down on her plate. Partly to show my knowledge, and so relieve the party from an awkward strain, partly because I was curious, I pursued the subject.

"You mean the fish?" I asked.

"Whatten fish?" cried my uncle. "Fish, quo' he! Fish! Your een are fu' o' fatness, man; your heid dozened wi' carnal leir. Fish! it's a bogle!"

He spoke with great vehemence, as though angry; and perhaps I was not very willing to be put down so shortly, for young men are disputatious. At least I remember I retorted hotly, crying out upon childish superstitions.

"And ye come frae the College!" sneered Uncle Gordon. "Gude kens what they learn folk there; it's no' muckle service onyway. Do ye think, man, that there's naething in a' yon saut wilderness o' a world oot wast there, wi' the sea-grasses growin', an' the sea-beasts fechtin', an' the sun glintin' down into it, day by day? Na; the sea's like the land, but fearsomer. If there's folk ashore, there's folk in the sea—deid they may be, but they're folk whatever; and as for deils, there's nane that's like the sea-deils. There's no sae muckle harm in the land-deils, when a's said and done. Lang syne, when I was a callant in the south country, I mind there was an auld, bald bogle in the Peewie Moss. I got a glisk o' him mysel', sittin' on his hunkers in a hag, as grey's a tombstane. An', troth, he was a fearsome-like taed. But he steered naebody. Nae doobt, if ane that was a reprobate, ane the Lord hated, had gane

by there wi' his sin still upon his stamach, nae doobt the creature
would hae lowped upo' the likes o' him. But there's deils in the
deep sea would yoke on a communicant! Eh, sirs, if ye had gane
doon wi' the puir lads in the *Christ-Anna,* ye would ken by now
the mercy o' the seas. If ye had sailed it for as lang as me, ye would
hate the thocht of it as I do. If ye had but used the een God gave
ye, ye would hae learned the wickness o' that fause, saut, cauld,
bullering creature, and of a' that's in it by the Lord's permission: labsters an' partans, an' sic-like, howking in the deid;
muckle, gutsy, blawing whales; an' fish—the hale clan o' them—
cauld-wamed, blind-ee'd uncanny ferlies. Oh, sirs," he cried, "the
horror—the horror o' the sea!"

We were all somewhat staggered by this outburst; and the
speaker himself, after that last hoarse apostrophe, appeared to sink
gloomily into his own thoughts. But Rorie, who was greedy of
superstitious lore, recalled him to the subject by a question.

"You will not ever have seen a teevil of the sea?" he asked.

"No' clearly," replied the other. "I misdoobt if a mere man
could see ane clearly and conteenue in the body. I hae sailed wi'
a lad—they ca'd him Sandy Gabart; he saw ane, shüre eneuch,
an' shüre eneuch it was the end of him. We were seeven days oot
frae the Clyde—a sair wark we had had—gaun north wi' seeds
an' braws an' things for the Macleod. We had got in ower near
under the Cutchull'ns, an' had just gane about by Soa, an' were
off on a long tack, we thocht would maybe hauld as far's Copna-
how. I mind the nicht weel; a mune smoored wi' mist; a fine-gaun
breeze upon the water, but no steedy; an'—what nane o' us likit
to hear—anither wund gurlin' owerheid, amang thae fearsome,
auld stane craigs o' the Cutchull'ns. Weel, Sandy was forrit wi'
the jib sheet; we couldna see him for the mains'l, that had just
begude to draw, when a' at ance he gied a skirl. I luffed for my
life, for I thocht we were ower near Soa; but na, it wasna that,
it was puir Sandy Gabart's deid skreigh, or near-hand, for he was
deid in half an hour. A't he could tell was that a sea-deil, or sea-
bogle, or sea-spenster, or sic-like, had clum up by the bowsprit,
an' gi'en him ae cauld, uncanny look. An', or the life was oot o'
Sandy's body, we kent weel what the thing betokened, and why

the wund girled in the taps o' the Cutchull'ns; for doon it cam'
—a wund do I ca' it! it was the wund o' the Lord's anger—an a'
that nicht we focht like men dementit, and the neist that we kenned
we were ashore in Loch Uskevagh, an' the cocks were crawin' in
Benbecula."

"It will have been a merman," Rorie said.

"A merman!" screamed my uncle with immeasurable scorn.
"Aauld wives' clavers! There's nae sic things as mermen."

"But what was the creature like?" I asked.

"What like was it? Gude forbid that we sul ken what like it
was! It had a kind of a heid upon it—man could say nae mair."

Then Rorie, smarting under the affront, told several tales of
mermen, mermaids, and sea-horses that had come ashore upon
the islands and attacked the crews of boats upon the sea; and my
uncle, in spite of his incredulity, listened with uneasy interest.

"Aweel, aweel," he said, "it may be sae; I may be wrang; but
I find nae word o' mermen in the Scriptures."

"And you will find nae word of Aros Roost, maybe," objected
Rorie, and his argument appeared to carry weight.

When dinner was over, my uncle carried me forth with him
to a bank behind the house. It was a very hot and quiet afternoon;
scarce a ripple anywhere upon the sea, nor any voice but the
familiar voice of sheep and gulls; and perhaps in consequence of
this repose in nature, my kinsman showed himself more rational
and tranquil than before. He spoke evenly and almost cheerfully
of my career, with every now and then a reference to the lost ship
or the treasures it had brought to Aros. For my part, I listened
to him in a sort of trance, gazing with all my heart on that remembered scene, and drinking gladly the sea-air and the smoke of
peats that had been lit by Mary.

Perhaps an hour had passed when my uncle, who had all the
while been covertly gazing on the surface of the little bay, rose
to his feet and bade me follow his example. Now I should say
that the great run of tide at the south-west end of Aros exercises
a perturbing influence round all the coast. In Sandag Bay, to the
south, a strong current runs at certain points of the flood and ebb
respectively; but in this northern bay—Aros Bay, as it is called—

where the house stands and on which my uncle was now gazing, the only sign of disturbance is towards the end of the ebb, and even then it is too slight to be remarkable. When there is any swell, nothing can be seen at all; but when it is calm, as it often is, there appear certain strange, undecipherable marks—sea-runes, as we may name them—on the glassy surface of the bay. The like is common in a thousand places on the coast; and many a boy must have amused himself as I did, seeking to read in them some reference to himself or those he loved. It was to these marks that my uncle now directed my attention, struggling, as he did so, with an evident reluctance.

"Do you see yon scart upo' the water?" he inquired; "yon ane wast the grey stane? Ay? Weel, it'll no' be like a letter, wull it?"

"Certainly it is," I replied. "I have often remarked it. It is like a C."

He heaved a sigh as if heartily disappointed with my answer, and then added below his breath: "Ay, for the *Christ-Anna*."

"I used to suppose, sir, it was for myself," said I; "for my name is Charles."

"And so ye saw't afore?" he ran on, not heeding my remark. "Weel, weel, but that's unco strange. Maybe, it's been there waitin', as a man wad say, through a' the weary ages. Man, but that's awfu'." And then, breaking off: "Ye'll no' see anither, will ye?" he asked.

"Yes," said I. "I see another very plainly, near the Ross side, where the road comes down—an M."

"An M," he repeated very low; and then, again after another pause: "An' what wad ye make o' that?" he inquired.

"I had always thought it to mean Mary, sir," I answered, growing somewhat red, convinced as I was in my own mind that I was on the threshold of a decisive explanation.

But we were each following his own train of thought to the exclusion of the other's. My uncle once more paid no attention to my words; only hung his head and held his peace; and I might have been led to fancy that he had not heard me, if his next speech had not contained a kind of echo from my own.

"I would say naething o' thae clavers to Mary," he observed, and began to walk forward.

There is a belt of turf along the side of Aros Bay where walking is easy; and it was along this that I silently followed my silent kinsman. I was perhaps a little disappointed at having lost so good an opportunity to declare my love; but I was at the same time far more deeply exercised at the change that had befallen my uncle. He was never an ordinary, never, in the strict sense, an amiable man; but there was nothing in even the worst that I had known of him before, to prepare me for so strange a transformation. It was impossible to close the eyes against one fact; that he had, as the saying goes, something on his mind; and as I mentally ran over the different words which might be represented by the letter M—misery, mercy, marriage, money, and the like—I was arrested with a sort of start by the word murder. I was still considering the ugly sound and fatal meaning of the word, when the direction of our walk brought us to a point from which a view was to be had to either side, back towards Aros Bay and homestead, and forward on the ocean, dotted to the north with isles, and lying to the southward blue and open to the sky. There my guide came to a halt, and stood staring for awhile on that expanse. Then he turned to me and laid a hand on my arm.

"Ye think there's naething there?" he said, pointing with his pipe; and then cried out aloud, with a kind of exultation: "I'll tell ye, man! The deid are down there—thick like rattons!"

He turned at once, and, without another word, we retraced our steps to the house of Aros.

I was eager to be alone with Mary; yet it was not till after supper, and then but for a short while, that I could have a word with her. I lost no time beating about the bush, but spoke out plainly what was on my mind.

"Mary," I said, "I have not come to Aros without a hope. If that should prove well founded, we may all leave and go somewhere else, secure of daily bread and comfort; secure, perhaps, of something far beyond that, which it would seem extravagant in me to promise. But there's a hope that lies nearer to my heart than money." At that I paused. "You can guess fine what that is, Mary," I said. She looked away from me in silence, and that was small encouragement, but I was not to be put off. "All my days I have thought the world of you," I continued; "the time goes on and I think always the more of you; I could not think to be happy or hearty in my life without you: you are the apple of my eye." Still she looked away, and said never a word; but I thought I saw that her hands shook. "Mary," I cried in fear, "do ye no' like me?"

"Oh, Charlie man," she said, "is this a time to speak of it? Let me be a while; let me be the way I am; it'll not be you that loses by the waiting!"

I made out by her voice that she was nearly weeping, and this put me out of any thought but to compose her. "Mary Ellen," I said, "say no more; I did not come to trouble you: your way shall be mine, and your time too; and you have told me all I wanted. Only just this one thing more: what ails you?"

She owned it was her father, but would enter into no particulars, only shook her head, and said he was not well and not like himself, and it was a great pity. She knew nothing of the wreck. "I havena been near it," said she. "What for would I go near it, Charlie lad? The poor souls are gone to their account long syne; and I would just have wished they had ta'en their gear with them —poor souls!"

This was scarcely any great encouragement for me to tell her of the *Espirito Santo*; yet I did so, and at the very first word she cried out in surprise. "There was a man at Grisapol," she said, "in the month of May—a little, yellow, black-avised body, they tell me, with gold rings upon his fingers, and a beard; and he was speiring high and low for that same ship."

It was towards the end of April that I had been given these papers to sort out by Dr. Robertson: and it came suddenly back upon my mind that they were thus prepared for a Spanish historian, or a man calling himself such, who had come with high recommendations to the Principal, on a mission of inquiry as to the dispersion of the great Armada. Putting one thing with another, I fancied that the visitor "with the gold rings upon his fingers" might be the same with Dr. Robertson's historian from Madrid. If that were so, he would be more likely after treasure for himself than information for a learned society. I made up my mind, I should lose no time over my undertaking; and if the ship lay sunk in Sandag Bay, as perhaps both he and I supposed, it should not be for the advantage of this ringed adventurer, but for Mary and myself, and for the good, old, honest, kindly family of the Darnaways.

III

LAND AND SEA IN SANDAG BAY

I WAS early afoot next morning; and as soon as I had a bite to eat, set forth upon a tour of exploration. Something in my heart distinctly told me that I should find the ship of the Armada; and although I did not give way entirely to such hopeful thoughts, I was still very light in spirits and walked on air. Aros is a very rough inlet, its surface strewn with great rocks and shaggy with fern and heather; and my way lay almost north and south across the highest knoll; and though the whole distance was inside of two miles, it took more time and exertion than four upon a level road. Upon the summit, I paused. Although not very high—not three hundred feet, as I think—it yet outtops all the neighbouring lowlands of the Ross, and commands a great view of sea and islands. The sun, which had been up for some time, was already hot upon my neck; the air was listless and thundery, although purely clear; away over the north-west, where the isles lie thickliest congregated, some half a dozen small and ragged clouds hung together in a covey; and the head of Ben Kyaw wore, not merely a few streamers, but a solid hood of vapour. There was a threat in the weather. The sea, it is true, was smooth like glass: even the Roost was but a seam on that wide mirror, and the Merry Men no more than caps of foam; but to my eye and ear, so long familiar with these places, the sea also seemed to lie uneasily; a sound of it, like a long sigh, mounted to me where I stood; and, quiet as it was, the Roost itself appeared to be revolving mischief. For I ought to say that all we dwellers in these parts attributed, if not prescience, at least a quality of warning, to that strange and dangerous creature of the tides.

I hurried on, then, with the greater speed, and had soon descended the slope of Aros to the part that we call Sandag Bay. It is a pretty large piece of water compared with the size of the isle; well sheltered from all but the prevailing wind; sandy and shoal and bounded by low sand-hills to the west, but to the eastward lying several fathoms deep along a ledge of rocks. It is upon that side that, at a certain time each flood, the current mentioned by my uncle sets so strong into the bay; a little later, when the Roost begins to work higher, an undertow runs still more strongly in the reverse direction; and it is the action of this last, as I suppose, that has scoured that part so deep. Nothing is to be seen out of Sandag Bay but one small segment of the horizon and, in heavy weather, the breakers flying high over a deep-sea reef.

From half-way down the hill I had perceived the wreck of February last, a brig of considerable tonnage, lying, with her back broken, high and dry on the east corner of the sands; and I was making directly towards it, and already almost on the margin of the turf, when my eyes were suddenly arrested by a spot, cleared of fern and heather, and marked by one of those long, low, and almost human-looking mounds that we see so commonly in graveyards. I stopped like a man shot. Nothing had been said to me of any dead man or interment on the island; Rorie, Mary, and my uncle had all equally held their peace; of her at least, I was certain that she must be ignorant; and yet here, before my eyes, was proof indubitable of the fact. Here was a grave; and I had to ask myself, with a chill, what manner of man lay there in his last sleep, awaiting the signal of the Lord in that solitary, sea-beat resting-place? My mind supplied no answer but what I feared to entertain. Shipwrecked, at least, he must have been; perhaps, like the old Armada mariners, from some far and rich land over-sea; or perhaps one of my own race, perishing within eyesight of the smoke of home. I stood awhile uncovered by his side, and I could have desired that it had lain in our religion to put up some prayer for that unhappy stranger, or, in the old classic way, outwardly to honour his misfortune. I knew, although his bones lay there, a part of Aros, till the trumpet sounded, his imperishable soul was forth

and far away, among the raptures of the everlasting Sabbath or
the pangs of hell; and yet my mind misgave me even with a fear,
that perhaps he was near me where I stood, guarding his sepulchre,
and lingering on the scene of his unhappy fate.

Certainly it was with a spirit somewhat overshadowed that I
turned away from the grave to the hardly less melancholy spectacle of the wreck. Her stem was above the first arc of the flood;
she was broken in two a little abaft the foremast—though indeed
she had none, both masts having broken short in her disaster;
and as the pitch of the beach was very sharp and sudden, and
the bows lay many feet below the stern, the fracture gaped widely
open, and you could see right through her poor hull upon the
farther side. Her name was much defaced, and I could not make
out clearly whether she was called *Christiania*, after the Nor-
wegian city, or *Christiana*, after the good woman, Christian's wife,
in that old book the "Pilgrim's Progress." By her build she was
a foreign ship, but I was not certain of her nationality. She had
been painted green, but the colour was faded and weathered, and
the paint peeling off in strips. The wreck of the mainmast lay
alongside, half-buried in sand. She was a forlorn sight, indeed,
and I could not look without emotion at the bits of rope that still
hung about her, so often handled of yore by shouting seamen; or
the little scuttle where they had passed up and down to their
affairs; or that poor noseless angel of a figurehead that had dipped
into so many running billows.

I do not know whether it came most from the ship or from the
grave, but I fell into some melancholy scruples, as I stood there,
leaning with one hand against the battered timbers. The home-
lessness of men, and even of inanimate vessels, cast away upon
strange shores, came strongly in upon my mind. To make a profit
of such pitiful misadventures seemed an unmanly and a sordid
act; and I began to think of my then quest as of something sacri-
legious in its nature. But when I remembered Mary I took heart
again. My uncle would never consent to an imprudent marriage,
nor would she, as I was persuaded, wed without his full approval.
It behoved me, then, to be up and doing for my wife; and I thought
with a laugh how long it was since that great sea-castle, the

Espirito Santo, had left her bones in Sandag Bay, and how weak it would be to consider rights so long extinguished and misfortunes so long forgotten in the process of time.

I had my theory of where to seek for her remains. The set of the current and the soundings both pointed to the east side of the bay under the ledge of rocks. If she had been lost in Sandag Bay, and if, after these centuries, any portion of her held together, it was there that I should find it. The water deepens, as I have said, with great rapidity, and even close alongside the rocks several fathoms may be found. As I walked upon the edge I could see far and wide over the sandy bottom of the bay; the sun shone clear and green and steady in the deeps; the bay seemed rather like a great transparent crystal, as one sees them in a lapidary's shop; there was naught to show that it was water but an internal trembling, a hovering within of sun-glints and netted shadows, and now and then a faint lap and a dying bubble round the edge. The shadows of the rocks lay out for some distance at their feet, so that my own shadow, moving, pausing, and stooping on the top of that, reached sometimes half across the bay. It was above all in this belt of shadows that I hunted for the *Espirito Santo*; since it was there the undertow ran strongest, whether in or out. Cool as the whole water seemed this broiling day, it looked, in that part, yet cooler, and had a mysterious invitation for the eyes. Peer as I pleased, however, I could see nothing but a few fishes or a bush of sea-tangle, and here and there a lump of rock that had fallen from above and now lay separate on the sandy floor. Twice did I pass from one end to the other of the rocks, and in the whole distance I could see nothing of the wreck, nor any place but one where it was possible for it to be. This was a large terrace in five fathoms of water, raised off the surface of the sand to a considerable height, and looking from above like a mere outgrowth of the rocks on which I walked. It was one mass of great sea-tangles like a grove, which prevented me judging of its nature, but in shape and size it bore some likeness to a vessel's hull. At least it was my best chance. If the *Espirito Santo* lay not there under the tangles, it lay nowhere at all in Sandag Bay; and I prepared to put the question to the proof, once and for all, and either go back to Aros a rich man or cured for ever of my dreams of wealth.

I stripped to the skin, and stood on the extreme margin with my hands clasped, irresolute. The bay at that time was utterly quiet; there was no sound but from a school of porpoises some-where out of sight behind the point; yet a certain fear withheld me on the threshold of my venture. Sad sea-feelings, scraps of my uncle's superstitions, thoughts of the dead, of the grave, of the old broken ships, drifted through my mind. But the strong sun upon my shoulders warmed me to the heart, and I stooped forward and plunged into the sea.

It was all that I could do to catch a trail of the sea-tangle that grew so thickly on the terrace; but once so far anchored I secured myself by grasping a whole armful of these thick and slimy stalks, and, planting my feet against the edge, I looked around me. On all sides the clear sand stretched forth unbroken; it came to the foot of the rocks, scoured into the likeness of an alley in a garden by the action of the tides; and before me, for as far as I could see, nothing was visible but the same many-folded sand upon the sun-bright bottom of the bay. Yet the terrace to which I was then holding was as thick with strong sea-growths as a tuft of heather, and the cliff from which it bulged hung draped below the water-line with brown lianas. In this complexity of forms, all swaying together in the current, things were hard to be distinguished; and I was still uncertain whether my feet were pressed upon the natural rock or upon the timbers of the Armada treasure-ship, when the whole tuft of tangle came away in my hand, and in an instant I was on the surface, and the shores of the bay and the bright water swam before my eyes in a glory of crimson.

I clambered back upon the rocks, and threw the plant of tangle at my feet. Something at the same moment rang sharply, like a falling coin. I stooped, and there, sure enough, crusted with the red rust, there lay an iron shoe-buckle. The sight of this poor human relic thrilled me to the heart, but not with hope nor fear, only with a desolate melancholy. I held it in my hand, and the thought of its owner appeared before me like the presence of an actual man. His weather-beaten face, his sailor's hands, his sea-

voice hoarse with singing at the capstan, the very foot that had
once worn that buckle and trod so much along the swerving decks
—the whole human fact of him, as a creature like myself, with
hair and blood and seeing eyes, haunted me in that sunny, solitary
place, not like a spectre, but like some friend whom I had basely
injured. Was the great treasure-ship indeed below there, with her
guns and chain and treasure, as she had sailed from Spain; her
decks a garden for the seaweed, her cabin a breeding-place for
fish, soundless but for the dredging water, motionless but for the
waving of the tangle upon her battlements—that old, populous,
sea-riding castle, now a reef in Sandag Bay? Or, as I thought it
likelier, was this a waif from the disaster of the foreign brig—was
this shoe-buckle bought but the other day and worn by a man
of my own period in the world's history, hearing the same news
from day to day, thinking the same thoughts, praying, perhaps,
in the same temple with myself? However it was, I was assailed
with dreary thoughts; my uncle's words, "the dead are down
there," echoed in my ears; and though I determined to dive once
more, it was with a strong repugnance that I stepped forward to
the margin of the rocks.

A great change passed at that moment over the appearance of
the bay. It was no more that clear, visible interior, like a house
roofed with glass, where the green, submarine sunshine slept so
stilly. A breeze, I suppose, had flawed the surface, and a sort of
trouble and blackness filled its bosom, where flashes of light and
clouds of shadow tossed confusedly together. Even the terrace
below obscurely rocked and quivered. It seemed a graver thing to
venture on this place of ambushes; and when I leaped into the
sea a second time it was with a quaking in my soul.

I secured myself as at first, and groped among the waving tangle.
All that met my touch was cold and soft and gluey. The thicket
was alive with crabs and lobsters, trundling to and fro lopsidedly,
and I had to harden my heart against the horror of their carrion
neighbourhood. On all sides I could feel the grain and the clefts
of hard, living stone; no planks, no iron, not a sign of any wreck;
the *Espirito Santo* was not there. I remember I had almost a sense
of relief in my disappointment, and I was about ready to leave

go, when something happened that sent me to the surface with my heart in my mouth. I had already stayed somewhat late over my explorations; the current was freshening with the change of the tide, and Sandag Bay was no longer a safe place for a single swimmer. Well, just at the last moment there came a sudden flush of current, dredging through the tangles like a wave. I lost one hold, was flung sprawling on my side, and, instinctively grasping for a fresh support, my fingers closed on something hard and cold. I think I knew at that moment what it was. At least I instantly left hold of the tangle, leaped for the surface, and clambered out next moment on the friendly rock with the bone of a man's leg in my grasp.

Mankind is a material creature, slow to think and dull to perceive connections. The grave, the wreck of the brig, and the rusty shoe-buckle were surely plain advertisements. A child might have read their dismal story, and yet it was not until I touched that actual piece of mankind that the full horror of the charnel ocean burst upon my spirit. I laid the bone beside the buckle, picked up my clothes, and ran as I was along the rocks towards the human shore. I could not be far enough from the spot; no fortune was vast enough to tempt me back again. The bones of the drowned dead should henceforth roll undisturbed by me, whether on tangle or minted gold. But as soon as I trod the good earth again, and had covered my nakedness against the sun, I knelt down over against the ruins of the brig, and out of the fulness of my heart prayed long and passionately for all poor souls upon the sea. A generous prayer is never presented in vain; the petition may be refused, but the petitioner is always, I believe, rewarded by some gracious visitation. The horror, at least, was lifted from my mind; I could look with calm of spirit on that great bright creature, God's ocean; and as I set off homeward up the rough sides of Aros, nothing remained of my concern beyond a deep determination to meddle no more with the spoils of wrecked vessels or the treasures of the dead.

I was already some way up the hill before I paused to breathe and look about me. The sight that met my eyes was doubly strange.

For, first, the storm that I had foreseen was now advancing with almost tropical rapidity. The whole surface of the sea had been dulled from its conspicuous brightness to an ugly hue of corrugated lead; already in the distance the white waves, the "skipper's daughters," had begun to flee before a breeze that was still insensible on Aros; and already along the curve of Sandag Bay there was a splashing run of sea that I could hear from where I stood. The change upon the sky was even more remarkable. There had begun to arise out of the south-west a huge and solid continent of scowling cloud; here and there, through rents in its contexture, the sun still poured a sheaf of spreading rays; and here and there, from all its edges, vast inky streamers lay forth along the yet unclouded sky. The menace was express and imminent. Even as I gazed, the sun was blotted out. At any moment the tempest might fall upon Aros in its might.

The suddenness of this change of weather so fixed my eyes on heaven that it was some seconds before they alighted on the bay, mapped out below my feet, amphitheatre of lower hillocks sloping towards the sea, and beyond that the yellow arc of beach and the whole extent of Sandag Bay. It was a scene on which I had often looked down, but where I had never before beheld a human figure. I had but just turned my back upon it and left it empty, and my wonder may be fancied when I saw a boat and several men in that deserted spot. The boat was lying by the rocks. A pair of fellows, bareheaded, with their sleeves rolled up, and one with a boat-hook, kept her with difficulty to her moorings, for the current was growing brisker every moment. A little way off upon the ledge two men in black clothes, whom I judged to be superior in rank, laid their heads together over some task which at first I did not understand, but a second after I had made it out—they were taking bearings with the compass; and just then I saw one of them unroll a sheet of paper and lay his finger down, as though identifying features in a map. Meanwhile a third was walking to and fro, poking among the rocks and peering over the edge into the water. While I was still watching them with the stupefaction of surprise, my mind hardly yet able to work on what my eyes reported, this third person suddenly stooped and summoned his companions with a cry so loud that it reached my ears upon the hill. The others ran to him, even dropping the compass in their hurry, and I could see the bone and the shoe-buckle going from hand to hand, causing the most unusual gesticulations of surprise and interest. Just then I could hear the seamen crying from the boat, and saw them point westward to that cloud continent which was ever the more rapidly unfurling its blackness over heaven. The others seemed to consult; but the danger was too pressing to be braved, and they bundled into the boat, carrying my relics with them, and set forth out of the bay with all speed of oars.

I made no more ado about the matter, but turned and ran for the house. Whoever these men were, it was fit my uncle should be instantly informed. It was not then altogether too late in the day for a descent of the Jacobites; and maybe Prince Charlie, whom I knew my uncle to detest, was one of the three superiors whom I had seen upon the rock. Yet as I ran, leaping from rock to rock, and turned the matter loosely in my mind, this theory grew ever the longer the less welcome to my reason. The compass, the map, the interest awakened by the buckle, and the conduct of that one among the strangers who had looked so often below him in the water, all seemed to point to a different explanation of their presence on that outlying, obscure islet of the western sea. The Madrid historian, the search instituted by Dr. Robertson, the bearded stranger with the rings, my own fruitless search that very morning in the deep water of Sandag Bay, ran together, piece by piece, in my memory, and I made sure that these strangers must be Spaniards in quest of ancient treasure and the lost ship of the Armada. But the people living in outlying islands, such as Aros, are answerable for their own security; there is none near by to protect or even to help them; and the presence in such a spot of a crew of foreign adventurers—poor, greedy, and most likely lawless—filled me with apprehensions for my uncle's money, and even for the safety of his daughter. I was still wondering how we were to get rid of them when I came, all breathless, to the top of Aros. The whole world was shadowed over; only in the extreme east, on a hill of the mainland, one last gleam of sunshine lingered like a jewel; rain had begun to fall, not heavily, but in drops; the sea was rising with each moment, and already a band of white encircled Aros and the nearer coasts of Grisapol. The boat was still pulling seaward, but I now became aware of what had been hidden from me lower down—a large, heavily sparred, handsome schooner lying-to at the south end of Aros. Since I had not seen her in the morning when I had looked around so closely at the signs of the weather, and upon these lone waters where a sail was rarely visible, it was clear she must have lain last night behind the uninhabited Eilean Gour, and this proved conclusively that she was manned by strangers to our coast, for that anchorage, though good enough to look at, is little better than a trap for ships. With such ignorant sailors upon so wild a coast, the coming gale was not unlikely to bring death upon its wings.

IV

THE GALE

I FOUND my uncle at the gable-end, watching the signs of the weather, with a pipe in his fingers.

"Uncle," said I, "there were men ashore at Sandag Bay—"

I had no time to go further; indeed, I not only forgot my words, but even my weariness, so strange was the effect on Uncle Gordon. He dropped his pipe and fell back against the end of the house with his jaw fallen, his eyes staring, and his long face as white as paper. We must have looked at one another silently for a quarter of a minute, before he made answer in this extraordinary fashion: "Had he a hair kep on?"

I knew as well as if I had been there that the man who now lay buried at Sandag had worn a hairy cap, and that he had come ashore alive. For the first and only time I lost toleration for the man who was my benefactor and the father of the woman I hoped to call my wife.

"These were living men," said I, "perhaps Jacobites, perhaps the French, perhaps pirates, perhaps adventurers come here to seek the Spanish treasure-ship; but, whatever they may be, dangerous at least to your daughter and my cousin. As for your own guilty terrors, man, the dead sleeps well where you have laid him. I stood this morning by his grave; he will not wake before the trump of doom."

My kinsman looked upon me, blinking, while I spoke; then he fixed his eyes for a little on the ground, and pulled his fingers foolishly; but it was plain that he was past the power of speech.

"Come," said I. "You must think for others. You must come up the hill with me and see this ship."

He obeyed without a word or a look, following slowly after my impatient strides. The spring seemed to have gone out of his body, and he scrambled heavily up and down the rocks, instead of leaping, as he was wont, from one to another. Nor could I, for all my cries, induce him to make better haste. Only once he replied to me complainingly, and like one in bodily pain: "Ay, ay, man, I'm coming." Long before we had reached the top I had no other thought for him but pity. If the crime had been monstrous, the punishment was in proportion.

At last we emerged above the sky-line of the hill, and could see around us. All was black and stormy to the eye; the last gleam of sun had vanished; a wind had sprung up, not yet high, but gusty and unsteady to the point; the rain, on the other hand, had ceased. Short as was the interval, the sea already ran vastly higher than when I had stood there last; already it had begun to break over some of the outward reefs, and already it moaned aloud in the sea-caves of Aros. I looked, at first, in vain for the schooner.

"There she is," I said at last. But her new position, and the course she was now lying, puzzled me. "They cannot mean to beat to sea," I cried.

"That's what they mean," said my uncle, with something like joy; and just then the schooner went about and stood upon another tack, which put the question beyond the reach of doubt. These strangers, seeing a gale on hand, had thought first of sea-room. With the wind that threatened, in these reef-sown waters and contending against so violent a stream of tide, their course was certain death.

"Good God!" said I, "they are all lost."

"Ay," returned my uncle, "a'—a' lost. They hadna a chance but to rin for Kyle Dona. The gate they're gaun the noo, they couldna win through an the muckle deil were there to pilot them. Eh, man," he continued, touching me on the sleeve, "it's a braw nicht for a shipwreck! Twa in ae twalmonth! Eh, but the Merry Men'll dance bonny!"

I looked at him, and it was then that I began to fancy him no longer in his right mind. He was peering up to me, as if for sympathy, a timid joy in his eyes. All that had passed between us was already forgotten in the prospect of this fresh disaster.

"If it were not too late," I cried with indignation, "I would take the coble and go out to warn them."

"Na, na," he protested, "ye maunna interfere; ye maunna meddle wi' the like o' that. It's His"—doffing his bonnet—"His wull. And, eh, man! but it's a braw nicht for't!"

Something like fear began to creep into my soul; and, reminding him that I had not yet dined, I proposed we should return to the house. But no; nothing would tear him from his place of outlook.

"I maun see the hail thing, man Charlie," he explained; and then as the schooner went about a second time, "Eh, but they han'le her bonny!" he cried. "The *Christ-Anna* was naething to this."

Already the men on board the schooner must have begun to realise some part, but not yet the twentieth, of the dangers that environed their doomed ship. At every lull of the capricious wind they must have seen how fast the current swept them back. Each tack was made shorter, as they saw how little it prevailed. Every moment the rising swell began to boom and foam upon another sunken reef; and ever and again a breaker would fall in sounding ruin under the very bows of her, and the brown reef and streaming tangle appear in the hollow of the wave. I tell you, they had to stand to their tackle: there was no idle man aboard that ship, God knows. It was upon the progress of a scene so horrible to any human-hearted man that my misguided uncle now pored and gloated like a connoisseur. As I turned to go down the hill, he was lying on his belly on the summit, with his hands stretched forth and clutching in the heather. He seemed rejuvenated, mind and body.

When I got back to the house already dismally affected, I was still more sadly downcast at the sight of Mary. She had her sleeves rolled up over her strong arms, and was quietly making bread. I got a bannock from the dresser and sat down to eat it in silence.

"Are ye wearied, lad?" she asked after a while.

"I am not so much wearied, Mary," I replied, getting on my feet, "as I am weary of delay, and perhaps of Aros too. You know me well enough to judge me fairly, say what I like. Well, Mary, you may be sure of this: you had better be anywhere but here."

"I'll be sure of one thing," she returned: "I'll be where my duty is."

"You forget, you have a duty to yourself," I said.

"Ay, man," she replied, pounding at the dough; "will you have found that in the Bible, now?"

"Mary," I said solemnly, "you must not laugh at me just now. God knows I am in no heart for laughing. If we could get your father with us, it would be best; but with him or without him, I want you far away from here, my girl; for your own sake, and for mine, ay, and for your father's too, I want you far—far away from here. I came with other thoughts; I came here as a man comes home; now it is all changed, and I have no desire nor hope but to flee—for that's the word—flee, like a bird out of the fowler's snare, from this accursed island."

She had stopped her work by this time.

"And do you think, now," said she, "do you think, now, I have neither eyes nor ears? Do ye think I havena broken my heart to have these braws (as he calls them, God forgive him!) thrown into the sea? Do ye think I have lived with him, day in, day out, and not seen what you saw in an hour or two? No," she said, "I know there's wrong in it; what wrong, I neither know nor want to know. There was never an ill thing made better by meddling, that I could hear of. But, my lad, you must never ask me to leave my father. While the breath is in his body, I'll be with him. And he's not long for here, either: that I can tell you, Charlie—he's not long for here. The mark is on his brow; and better so—maybe better so."

I was a while silent, not knowing what to say; and when I roused my head at last to speak, she got before me.

"Charlie," she said, "what's right for me needna be right for you. There's sin upon this house and trouble; you are a stranger; take your things upon your back and go your ways to better places and to better folk, and if you were ever minded to come back, though it were twenty years syne, you would find me aye waiting."

"Mary Ellen," I said, "I asked you to be my wife, and you said as good as yes. That's done for good. Wherever you are, I am; as I shall answer to my God."

As I said the words the wind suddenly burst out raving, and then seemed to stand still and shudder round the house of Aros. It was the first squall, or prologue, of the coming tempest, and as we started and looked about us, we found that a gloom, like the approach of evening, had settled round the house.

"God pity all poor folks at sea!" she said. "We'll see no more of my father till the morrow's morning."

And then she told me, as we sat by the fire and hearkened to the rising gusts, of how this change had fallen upon my uncle. All last winter he had been dark and fitful in his mind. Whenever the Roost ran high, or, as Mary said, whenever the Merry Men were dancing, he would lie out for hours together on the Head, if it were night, or on the top of Aros by day, watching the tumult of the sea, and sweeping the horizon for a sail. After February the 10th, when the wealth-bringing wreck was cast ashore at Sandag, he had been at first unnaturally gay, and his excitement had never fallen in degree, but only changed in kind from dark to darker. He neglected his work, and kept Rorie idle. They two would speak together by the hour at the gable-end, in guarded tones and with an air of secrecy, and almost of guilt; and if she questioned either, as at first she sometimes did, her inquiries were put aside with confusion. Since Rorie had first remarked the fish that hung about the ferry, his master had never set foot but once upon the mainland of the Ross. That once—it was in the

height of the springs—he had passed dryshod while the tide was
out; but, having lingered overlong on the far side, found himself
cut off from Aros by the returning waters. It was with a shriek of
agony that he had leaped across the gut, and he had reached home
thereafter in a fever-fit of fear. A fear of the sea, a constant haunt-
ing thought of the sea, appeared in his talk and devotions, and
even in his looks when he was silent.

Rorie alone came in to supper; but a little later my uncle
appeared, took a bottle under his arm, put some bread in his
pocket, and set forth again to his outlook, followed this time by
Rorie. I heard that the schooner was losing ground, but the crew
were still fighting every inch with hopeless ingenuity and courage;
and the news filled my mind with blackness.

A little after sundown the full fury of the gale broke forth,
such a gale as I have never seen in summer, nor, seeing how
swiftly it had come, even in winter. Mary and I sat in silence,
the house quaking overhead, the tempest howling without, the
fire between us sputtering with raindrops. Our thoughts were far
away with the poor fellows on the schooner, or my not less unhappy
uncle, houseless on the promontory; and yet ever and again we
were startled back to ourselves, when the wind would rise and
strike the gable like a solid body, or suddenly fall and draw
away, so that the fire leaped into flame and our hearts bounded
in our sides. Now the storm in its might would seize and shake
the four corners of the roof, roaring like Leviathan in anger. Anon,
in a lull, cold eddies of tempest moved shudderingly in the room,
lifting the hair upon our heads and passing between us as we sat.
And again the wind would break forth in a chorus of melancholy
sounds, hooting low in the chimney, wailing with flutelike soft-
ness round the house.

It was perhaps eight o'clock when Rorie came in and pulled me
mysteriously to the door. My uncle, it appeared, had frightened
even his constant comrade; and Rorie, uneasy at his extravagance,
prayed me to come out and share the watch. I hastened to do as I
was asked; the more readily as, what with fear and horror, and
the electrical tension of the night, I was myself restless and disposed for action. I told Mary to be under no alarm, for I should

be a safeguard on her father; and wrapping myself warmly in a plaid, I followed Rorie into the open air.

That night, though we were so little past midsummer, was as dark as January. Intervals of a groping twilight alternated with spells of utter blackness; and it was impossible to trace the reason of these changes in the flying horror of the sky. The wind blew the breath out of a man's nostrils; all heaven seemed to thunder overhead like one huge sail; and when there fell a momentary lull on Aros, we could hear the gusts dismally sweeping in the distance. Over all the lowlands of the Ross the wind must have blown as fierce as on the open sea; and God only knows the uproar that was raging around the head of Ben Kyaw. Sheets of mingled spray and rain were driven in our faces. All round the isle of Aros the surf, with an incessant, hammering thunder, beat upon the reefs and beaches. Now louder in one place, now lower in another, like the combinations of orchestral music, the constant mass of sound was hardly varied for a moment. And loud above all this hurly-burly I could hear the changeful voices of the Roost and the intermittent roaring of the Merry Men. At that hour, there flashed into my mind the reason of the name that they were called. For the noise of them seemed almost mirthful, as it outtopped the other noises of the night; or if not mirthful, yet instinct with a portentous joviality. Nay, and it seemed even human. As when savage men have drunk away their reason, and, discarding speech, bawl together in their madness by the hour; so, to my ears, these deadly breakers shouted by Aros in the night.

Arm in arm, and staggering against the wind, Rorie and I won every yard of ground with conscious effort. We slipped on the wet sod, we fell together sprawling on the rocks. Bruised, drenched, beaten, and breathless, it must have taken us near half an hour to get from the house down to the Head that overlooks the Roost. There, it seemed, was my uncle's favourite observatory. Right in the face of it, where the cliff is highest and most sheer, a hump of earth, like a parapet, makes a place of shelter from the common winds, where a man may sit in quiet and see the tide and the mad billows contending at his feet. As he might look down from the window of a house upon some street disturbance, so, from this post, he looks down upon the tumbling of the Merry Men. On such a night, of course, he peers upon a world of blackness, where the waters wheel and boil, where the waves joust together with the noise of an explosion, and the foam towers and vanishes in the twinkling of an eye. Never before had I seen the Merry Men thus violent. The fury, height, and transiency of their spoutings was a thing to be seen and not recounted. High over our heads on the cliff rose their white columns in the darkness; and the same instant, like phantoms, they were gone. Sometimes three at a time would thus aspire and vanish; sometimes a gust took them, and the spray would fall about us, heavy as a wave. And yet the spectacle was rather maddening in its levity than impressive by its force. Thought was beaten down by the confounding uproar; a gleeful vacancy possessed the brains of men, a state akin to madness; and I found myself at times following the dance of the Merry Men as it were a tune upon a jigging instrument.

I first caught sight of my uncle when we were still some yards away in one of the flying glimpses of twilight that chequered the pitch darkness of the night. He was standing up behind the parapet, his head thrown back and the bottle to his mouth. As he put it down, he saw and recognised us with a toss of one hand fleeringly above his head.

"Has he been drinking?" shouted I to Rorie.

"He will aye be drunk when the wind blaws," returned Rorie in the same high key, and it was all that I could do to hear him.

"Then—was he so—in February?" I inquired.

Rorie's "Ay" was a cause of joy to me. The murder, then, had not sprung in cold blood from calculation; it was an act of madness no more to be condemned than to be pardoned. My uncle was a dangerous madman, if you will, but he was not cruel and base as I had feared. Yet what a scene for a carouse, what an incredible vice, was this that the poor man had chosen! I have always thought drunkenness a wild and almost fearful pleasure, rather demoniacal than human; but drunkenness, out here in the roaring blackness, on the edge of a cliff above that hell of waters, the man's head spinning like the Roost, his foot tottering on the edge of death, his ear watching for the signs of shipwreck, surely that, if it were credible in any one, was morally impossible in a man like my uncle, whose mind was set upon a damnatory creed and haunted by the darkest superstitions. Yet so it was; and, as we reached the bight of shelter and could breathe again, I saw the man's eyes shining in the night with an unholy glimmer.

"Eh, Charlie man, it's grand!" he cried. "See to them!" he continued, dragging me to the edge of the abyss from whence arose that deafening clamour and those clouds of spray; "see to them dancin', man! Is that no wicked?"

He pronounced the word with gusto, and I thought it suited with the scene.

"They're yowlin' for thon schooner," he went on, his thin, insane voice clearly audible in the shelter of the bank, "an' she's comin' aye nearer, aye nearer, aye nearer an' nearer an' nearer; an' they ken't, the folk kens it, they ken weel it's by wi' them. Charlie lad, they're a' drunk in yon schooner, a' dozened wi' drink. They were a' drunk in the *Christ-Anna*, at the hinder end. There's nane could droon at sea wantin' the brandy. Hoot awa, what do you ken?" with a sudden blast of anger. "I tell ye, it canna be; they daurna droon withoot it. Hae," holding out the bottle, "tak' a sowp."

I was about to refuse, but Rorie touched me as if in warning; and indeed I had already thought better of the movement. I took the bottle, therefore, and not only drank freely myself, but contrived to spill even more as I was doing so. It was pure spirit, and almost strangled me to swallow. My kinsman did not observe the loss, but, once more throwing back his head, drained the remainder to the dregs. Then, with a loud laugh, he cast the bottle forth among the Merry Men, who seemed to leap up, shouting to receive it.

"Hae, bairns!" he cried, "there's your hansel. Ye'll get bonnier nor that or morning."

Suddenly, out in the black night before us, and not two hundred yards away, we heard, at a moment when the wind was silent, the clear note of a human voice. Instantly the wind swept howling down upon the Head, and the Roost bellowed, and churned, and danced with a new fury. But we had heard the sound, and we

knew, with agony, that this was the doomed ship now close on
ruin, and that what we had heard was the voice of her master
issuing his last command. Crouching together on the edge, we
waited, straining every sense, for the inevitable end. It was long,
however, and to us it seemed like ages, ere the schooner suddenly
appeared for one brief instant, relieved against a tower of glimmering foam. I still see her reefed mainsail flapping loose, as the boom
fell heavily across the deck; I still see the black outline of the hull,
and still think I can distinguish the figure of a man stretched upon
the tiller. Yet the whole sight we had of her passed swifter than
lightning; the very wave that disclosed her fell burying her for
ever; the mingled cry of many voices at the point of death rose
and was quenched in the roaring of the Merry Men. And with
that the tragedy was at an end. The strong ship, with all her gear,
and the lamp perhaps still burning in the cabin, the lives of so
many men, precious surely to others, dear, at least, as heaven to
themselves, had all, in that one moment, gone down into the
surging waters. They were gone like a dream. And the wind still
ran and shouted, and the senseless waters in the Roost still leaped
and tumbled as before.

How long we lay there together, we three, speechless and
motionless, is more than I can tell, but it must have been for long.
At length, one by one, and almost mechanically, we crawled back
into the shelter of the bank. As I lay against the parapet, wholly
wretched and not entirely master of my mind, I could hear my
kinsman maundering to himself in an altered and melancholy
mood. Now he would repeat to himself with maudlin iteration,
"Sic a fecht as they had—sic a sair fecht as they had, puir lads, puir
lads!" and anon he would bewail that "a' the gear was as gude's
tint," because the ship had gone down among the Merry Men
instead of stranding on the shore; and throughout, the name—
the *Christ-Anna*—would come and go in his divagations, pronounced with shuddering awe. The storm all this time was rapidly
abating. In half an hour the wind had fallen to a breeze, and the
change was accompanied or caused by a heavy, cold, and plump-
ing rain. I must then have fallen asleep, and when I came to
myself, drenched, stiff, and unrefreshed, day had already broken,

grey, wet, discomfortable day; the wind blew in faint and shifting capfuls, the tide was out, the Roost was at its lowest, and only the strong beating surf round all the coasts of Aros remained to witness of the furies of the night.

V

A MAN OUT OF THE SEA

RORIE SET out for the house in search of warmth and breakfast; but my uncle was bent upon examining the shores of Aros, and I felt it a part of duty to accompany him throughout. He was now docile and quiet, but tremulous and weak in mind and body; and it was with the eagerness of a child that he pursued his exploration. He climbed far down upon the rocks; on the beaches he pursued the retreating breakers. The merest broken plank or rag of cordage was a treasure in his eyes to be secured at the peril of his life. To see him, with weak and stumbling footsteps, expose himself to the pursuit of the surf, or the snares and pitfalls of the weedy rock, kept me in a perpetual terror. My arm was ready to support him, my hand clutched him by the skirt, I helped him to draw his pitiful discoveries beyond the reach of the returning wave; a nurse accompanying a child of seven would have had no different experience.

Yet, weakened as he was by the reaction from his madness of the night before, the passions that smouldered in his nature were those of a strong man. His terror of the sea, although conquered for the moment, was still undiminished; had the sea been a lake of living flames, he could not have shrunk more panically from its touch; and once, when his foot slipped and he plunged to the mid-leg into a pool of water, the shriek that came up out of his soul was like the cry of death. He sat still for a while, panting like a dog, after that; but his desire for the spoils of shipwreck triumphed once more over his fears; once more he tottered among the curded foam; once more he crawled upon the rocks among the bursting bubbles; once more his whole heart seemed to be set on driftwood, fit, if it was fit for anything, to throw upon the fire. Pleased as he was with what he found, he still incessantly grumbled at his ill-fortune.

"Aros," he said, "is no' a place for wrecks ava'—no' ava'. A' the years I've dwalt here, this ane maks the second; and the best o' the gear clean tint!"

"Uncle," said I, for we were now on a stretch of open sand, where there was nothing to divert his mind, "I saw you last night, as I never thought to see you—you were drunk."

"Na, na," he said, "no' as bad as that. I had been drinking, though. And to tell ye the God's truth, it's a thing I canna mend. There's nae soberer man than me in my ordnar; but when I hear the wind blaw in my lug, it's my belief that I gang gyte."

"You are a religious man," I replied, "and this is sin."

"Ou," he returned, "if it wasna sin, I dinna ken that I would care for't. Ye see, man, it's defiance. There's a sair spang o' the auld sin o' the warld in yon sea; it's an unchristian business at the best o't; an' whiles when it gets up, an' the wind skreighs— the wind an' her are a kind of sib, I'm thinkin'—an' thae Merry Men, the daft callants, blawin' and lauchin', and puir souls in the deid-thraws warstlin' and leelang nicht wi' their bit ships— weel, it comes ower me like a glamour. I'm a deil, I ken't. But I think naething o' the puir sailor lads; I'm wi' the sea, I'm just like ane o' her ain Merry Men."

I thought I should touch him in a joint of his harness. I turned me towards the sea; the surf was running gaily, wave after wave, with their manes blowing behind them, riding one after another up the beach, towering, curving, falling one upon another on the trampled sand. Without, the salt air, the scared gulls, the wide-spread army of the sea-chargers, neighing to each other, as they gathered together to the assault of Aros; and close before us, that line on the flat sands, that, with all their number and their fury, they might never pass.

"Thus far shalt thou go," said I, "and no farther." And then I quoted as solemnly as I was able a verse that I had often before fitted to the chorus of the breakers:

> *But yet the Lord, that is on high,*
> *Is more of might by far*
> *Than noise of many waters is,*
> *Or great sea-billows are.*

"Ay," said my kinsman, "at the hinder end, the Lord will triumph; I dinna misdoobt that. But here on earth, even silly men-folk daur Him to His face. It is no' wise; I am no' sayin' that it's wise; but it's the pride of the eye, and it's the lust o' life, an' it's the wale o' pleesures."

I said no more, for we had now begun to cross a neck of land that lay between us and Sandag; and I withheld my last appeal to the man's better reason till we should stand upon the spot associated with his crime. Nor did he pursue the subject; but he walked beside me with a firmer step. The call that I had made upon his mind acted like a stimulant, and I could see that he had forgotten his search for worthless jetsam, in a profound, gloomy, and yet stirring train of thought. In three or four minutes we had topped the brae and began to go down upon Sandag. The wreck had been roughly handled by the sea; the stem had been spun round and dragged a little lower down; and perhaps the stern had been forced a little higher, for the two parts now lay entirely separate on the beach. When we came to the grave I stopped, uncovered my head in the thick rain, and, looking my kinsman in the face, addressed him.

"A man," said I, "was in God's providence suffered to escape from mortal dangers; he was poor, he was naked, he was wet, he was weary, he was a stranger; he had every claim upon the bowels of your compassion; it may be that he was the salt of the earth, holy, helpful, and kind; it may be he was a man laden with iniquities to whom death was the beginning of torment. I ask you in the sight of Heaven: Gordon Darnaway, where is the man for whom Christ died?"

He started visibly at the last words; but there came no answer, and his face expressed no feeling but a vague alarm.

"You were my father's brother," I continued; "you have taught me to count your house as if it were my father's house; and we are both sinful men walking before the Lord among the sins and dangers of this life. It is by our evil that God leads us into good; we sin, I dare not say by His temptation, but I must say with His consent; and to any but the brutish man his sins are the beginning of wisdom. God has warned you by this crime; He warns you still by the bloody grave between our feet; and if there shall follow no repentance, no improvement, no return to Him, what can we look for but the following of some memorable judgment?"

Even as I spoke the words, the eyes of my uncle wandered from my face. A change fell upon his looks that cannot be described; his features seemed to dwindle in size, the colour faded from his cheeks, one hand rose waveringly and pointed over my shoulder into the distance, and the oft-repeated name fell once more from his lips: "The *Christ-Anna!*"

I turned; and if I was not appalled to the same degree, as I return thanks to Heaven that I had not the cause, I was still startled by the sight that met my eyes. The form of a man stood upright on the cabin-hutch of the wrecked ship; his back was towards us; he appeared to be scanning the offing with shaded eyes, and his figure was relieved to its full height, which was plainly very great, against the sea and sky. I have said a thousand times that I am not superstitious; but at that moment, with my mind running upon death and sin, the unexplained appearance of a stranger on that sea-girt, solitary island filled me with a surprise that bordered close on terror. It seemed scarce possible that any human soul should have come ashore alive in such a sea as had raged last night along the coast of Aros; and the only vessel within miles had gone down before our eyes among the Merry Men. I was assailed with doubts that made suspense unbearable, and, to put the matter to the touch at once, stepped forward and hailed the figure like a ship.

He turned about, and I thought he started to behold us. At this my courage instantly revived, and I called and signed to him to draw near, and he, on his part, dropped immediately to the sands, and began slowly to approach, with many stops and hesitations. At each repeated mark of the man's uneasiness I grew the more confident myself; and I advanced another step, encourag-

ing him as I did so with my head and hand. It was plain the
castaway had heard indifferent accounts of our island hospitality;
and indeed, about this time, the people farther north had a sorry
reputation.

"Why," I said, "the man is black!"

And just at that moment, in a voice that I could scarce have
recognised, my kinsman began swearing and praying in a mingled
stream. I looked at him; he had fallen on his knees, his face was
agonised; at each step of the castaway's the pitch of his voice
rose, the volubility of his utterance and the fervour of his language
redoubled. I call it prayer, for it was addressed to God; but surely
no such ranting incongruities were ever before addressed to the
Creator by a creature: surely if prayer can be a sin, this mad
harangue was sinful. I ran to my kinsman, I seized him by the
shoulders, I dragged him to his feet.

"Silence, man," said I, "respect your God in words, if not in
action. Here, on the very scene of your transgressions, He sends
you an occasion of atonement. Forward and embrace it: welcome
like a father yon creature who comes trembling to your mercy."

With that, I tried to force him towards the black; but he felled
me to the ground, burst from my grasp, leaving the shoulder of
his jacket, and fled up the hillside towards the top of Aros like
a deer. I staggered to my feet again, bruised and somewhat
stunned; the negro had paused in surprise, perhaps in terror, some
half-way between me and the wreck; my uncle was already far
away, bounding from rock to rock; and I thus found myself torn
for a time between two duties. But I judged, and I pray Heaven
that I judged rightly, in favour of the poor wretch upon the sands;
his misfortune was at least not plainly of his own creation; it was
one, besides, that I could certainly relieve; and I had begun by
that time to regard my uncle as an incurable and dismal lunatic.
I advanced accordingly towards the black, who now awaited my
approach with folded arms, like one prepared for either destiny.
As I came nearer, he reached forth his hand with a great gesture,
such as I had seen from the pulpit, and spoke to me in something
of a pulpit voice, but not a word was comprehensible. I tried him
first in English, then in Gaelic, both in vain; so that it was clear we

must rely upon the tongue of looks and gestures. Thereupon I signed to him to follow me, which he did readily and with a grave obeisance like a fallen king; all the while there had come no shade of alteration in his face, neither of anxiety while he was still waiting, nor of relief now that he was reassured; if he were a slave, as I supposed, I could not but judge he must have fallen from some high place in his own country, and, fallen as he was, I could not but admire his bearing. As we passed the grave, I paused and raised my hands and eyes to heaven in token of respect and sorrow for the dead; and he, as if in answer, bowed low and spread his hands abroad; it was a strange motion, but done like a thing of common custom; and I supposed it was ceremonial in the land from which he came. At the same time he pointed to my uncle, whom we could just see perched upon a knoll, and touched his head to indicate that he was mad.

We took the long way round the shore, for I feared to excite my uncle if we struck across the island; and as we walked, I had time enough to mature the little dramatic exhibition by which I hoped to satisfy my doubts. Accordingly, paused on a rock, I proceeded to imitate before the negro the action of the man whom I had seen the day before taking bearings with the compass at Sandag. He understood me at once, and, taking the imitation out of my hands, showed me where the boat was, pointed out seaward as if to indicate the position of the schooner, and then down along the edge of the rock with the words "Espirito Santo," strangely pronounced, but clear enough for recognition. I had thus been right in my conjecture; the pretended historical inquiry had been but a cloak for treasure-hunting; the man who had played on Dr. Robertson was the same as the foreigner who visited Grisapol in spring, and now, with many others, lay dead under the Roost of Aros: there had their greed brought them, there should their bones be tossed for evermore. In the meantime the black continued his imitation of the scene, now looking up skyward as though watching the approach of the storm; now, in the character of a seaman, waving the rest to come aboard; now as an officer, running along the rock and entering the boat; and anon bending over imaginary oars with the air of a hurried boatman; but all with the same solemnity of manner, so that I was never even moved to smile. Lastly, he indicated to me, by a pantomime not to be described in words, how he himself had gone up to examine the stranded wreck, and, to his grief and indignation, had been deserted by his comrades; and thereupon folded his arms once more, and stooped his head, like one accepting fate.

The mystery of his presence being thus solved for me, I explained to him by means of a sketch the fate of the vessel and of all aboard her. He showed no surprise nor sorrow, and, with a sudden lifting of his open hand, seemed to dismiss his former friends or masters (whichever they had been) into God's pleasure. Respect came upon me and grew stronger, the more I observed him; I saw he had a powerful mind and a sober and severe character, such as I loved to commune with; and before we reached the house of Aros I had almost forgotten, and wholly forgiven him, his uncanny colour.

To Mary I told all that had passed without suppression, though I own my heart failed me; but I did wrong to doubt her sense of justice.

"You did the right," she said. "God's will be done." And she set out meat for us at once.

As soon as I was satisfied, I bade Rorie keep an eye upon the castaway, who was still eating, and set forth again myself to find my uncle. I had not gone far before I saw him sitting in the same place, upon the very topmost knoll, and seemingly in the same attitude as when I had last observed him. From that point, as I have said, the most of Aros and the neighbouring Ross would be spread below him like a map; and it was plain that he kept a bright look-out in all directions, for my head had scarcely risen above the summit of the first ascent before he had leaped to his feet and turned as if to face me. I hailed him at once, as well as I was able, in the same tones and words as I had often used before, when I had come to summon him to dinner. I passed on a little farther, and again tried parley, with the same result. But when I began a second time to advance, his insane fears blazed up again, and still in dead silence, but with incredible speed, he began to flee from before me along the rocky summit of the hill. An hour before he had been dead weary, and I had been comparatively active. But now his strength was recruited by the fervour of insanity, and it would have been vain for me to dream of pursuit. Nay, the very attempt, I thought, might have inflamed his terrors, and thus increased the miseries of our position. And I had nothing left but to turn homeward and make my sad report to Mary.

She heard it, as she had heard the first, with a concerned composure, and, bidding me lie down and take that rest of which I stood so much in need, set forth herself in quest of her misguided father. At that age it would have been a strange thing that put me from either meat or sleep; I slept long and deep; and it was already long past noon before I awoke and came downstairs into the kitchen. Mary, Rorie, and the black castaway were seated about the fire in silence; and I could see that Mary had been weeping. There was cause enough, as I soon learned, for tears. First she, and then Rorie, had been forth to seek my uncle; each in turn had found him perched upon the hill-top, and from each in turn he had silently and swiftly fled. Rorie had tried to chase him, but in vain; madness lent a new vigour to his bounds; he sprang from rock to rock over the widest gullies; he scoured like the wind along the hill-tops; he doubled and twisted like a hare before the dogs; and Rorie at length gave in; and the last that he saw, my uncle was seated as before upon the crest of Aros. Even during the hottest excitement of the chase, even when the fleet-footed servant had come, for a moment, very near to capture him, the poor lunatic had uttered not a sound. He fled, and he was silent, like a beast; and this silence had terrified his pursuer.

There was something heart-breaking in the situation. How to capture the madman, how to feed him in the meanwhile, and what to do with him when he was captured, were the three difficulties that we had to solve.

"The black," said I, "is the cause of this attack. It may even be his presence in the house that keeps my uncle on the hill. We have done the fair thing; he has been fed and warmed under this roof; now I propose that Rorie put him across the bay in the coble, and take him through the Ross as far as Grisapol."

In this proposal Mary heartily concurred; and bidding the black follow us, we all three descended to the pier. Certainly, Heaven's will was declared against Gordon Darnaway; a thing had happened, never paralleled before in Aros: during the storm, the coble had broken loose, and, striking on the rough splinters of the pier, now lay in four feet of water with one side stove in. Three days of work at least would be required to make her float. But I was not to be beaten. I led the whole party round to where the gut was narrowest, swam to the other side, and called to the black to follow me. He signed, with the same clearness and quiet as before, that he knew not the art; and there was truth apparent in his signals, it would have occurred to none of us to doubt his truth; and that hope being over, we must all go back even as we came to the house of Aros, the negro walking in our midst without embarrassment.

All we could do that day was to make one more attempt to communicate with the unhappy madman. Again he was visible on his perch; again he fled in silence. But food and a great cloak were at least left for his comfort; the rain, besides, had cleared away, and the night promised to be even warm. We might compose ourselves, we thought, until the morrow; rest was the chief requisite, that we might be strengthened for unusual exertions; and as none cared to talk, we separated at an early hour.

I lay long awake, planning a campaign for the morrow. I was to place the black on the side of Sandag, whence he should head my uncle towards the house; Rorie in the west, I on the east, were to complete the cordon, as best we might. It seemed to me, the more I recalled the configuration of the island, that it should be possible, though hard, to force him down upon the low ground along Aros Bay; and once there, even with the strength of his madness, ultimate escape was hardly to be feared. It was on his terror of the black that I relied; for I made sure, however he might run, it would not be in the direction of the man whom he supposed to have returned from the dead, and thus one point of the compass at least would be secure.

When at length I fell asleep, it was to be awakened shortly after by a dream of wrecks, black men, and submarine adventure; and I found myself so shaken and fevered that I arose, descended the stair, and stepped out before the house. Within, Rorie and the black were asleep together in the kitchen; outside was a wonderful night of stars, with here and there a cloud still hanging, last stragglers of the tempest. It was near the top of the flood, and the Merry Men were roaring in the windless quiet of the night. Never, not even in the height of the tempest, had I heard their song with greater awe. Now, when the winds were gathered home, when the deep was dandling itself back into its summer slumber, and when the stars rained their gentle light over land and sea, the voice of these tide-breakers was still raised for havoc. They seemed, indeed, to be part of the world's evil and the tragic side of life. Nor were their meaningless vociferations the only sounds that broke the silence of the night. For I could hear, now shrill and thrilling and now almost drowned, the note of a human voice that accompanied the uproar of the Roost. I knew it for my kinsman's; and a great fear fell upon me of God's judgments, and the evil in the world. I went back again into the darkness of the house as into a place of shelter, and lay long upon my bed, pondering these mysteries.

It was late when I again woke, and I leaped into my clothes and hurried to the kitchen. No one was there; Rorie and the black had both stealthily departed long before; and my heart stood still at the discovery. I could rely on Rorie's heart, but I placed no trust in his discretion. If he had thus set out without a word, he was plainly bent upon some service to my uncle. But what service could he hope to render even alone, far less in the company of the man in whom my uncle found his fears incarnated? Even if I were not already too late to prevent some deadly mischief, it was plain I must delay no longer. With the thought I was out of the house; and often as I have run on the rough sides of Aros, I never ran as I did that fatal morning. I do not believe I put twelve minutes to the whole ascent.

My uncle was gone from his perch. The basket had indeed been torn open and the meat scattered on the turf; but, as we found afterwards, no mouthful had been tasted; and there was not another trace of human existence in that wide field of view. Day had already filled the clear heavens; the sun already lighted in a rosy bloom upon the crest of Ben Kyaw; but all below me the rude knolls of Aros and the shield of sea lay steeped in the clear darkling twilight of the dawn.

"Rorie!" I cried; and again "Rorie!" My voice died in the silence, but there came no answer back. If there were indeed an enterprise afoot to catch my uncle, it was plainly not in fleetness of foot, but in dexterity of stalking, that the hunters placed their trust. I ran on farther, keeping the higher spurs, and looking right and left, nor did I pause again till I was on the mount above Sandag. I could see the wreck, the uncovered belt of sand, the waves idly beating, the long ledge of rocks, and on either hand the tumbled knolls, boulders, and gullies of the island. But still no human thing.

At a stride the sunshine fell on Aros, and the shadows and colours leaped into being. Not half a moment later, below me to the west, sheep began to scatter as in a panic. There came a cry. I saw my uncle running. I saw the black jump up in hot pursuit; and before I had time to understand, Rorie also had appeared, calling directions in Gaelic as to a dog herding sheep.

I took to my heels to interfere, and perhaps I had done better to have waited where I was, for I was the means of cutting off the madman's last escape. There was nothing before him from that moment but the grave, the wreck, and the sea in Sandag Bay. And yet Heaven knows that what I did was for the best.

My Uncle Gordon saw in what direction, horrible to him, the chase was driving him. He doubled, darting to the right and left; but high as the fever ran in his veins, the black was still the swifter. Turn where he could, he was still forestalled, still driven toward the scene of his crime. Suddenly he began to shriek aloud, so that the coast re-echoed; and now both I and Rorie were calling on the black to stop. But all was vain, for it was written otherwise. The pursuer still ran, the chase still sped before him screaming; they avoided the grave, and skimmed close past the timbers of the wreck; in a breath they had cleared the sand; and still my kinsman did not pause, but dashed straight into the surf; and the black, now almost within reach, still followed swiftly behind him. Rorie and I both stopped, for the thing was now beyond the hands of men, and these were the decrees of God that came to pass before our eyes. There was never a sharper ending. On that steep beach they were beyond their depth at a bound; neither could swim; the black rose once for a moment with a throttling cry; but the current had them, racing seaward; and if ever they came up again, which God alone can tell, it would be ten minutes after, at the far end of Aros Roost, where the sea-birds hover fishing.

GLOSSARY

ablich insignificant person, good-for-nothing

agley wrong, off course

ahin behind

argolbargoling quarrelling

atemeets oatmeal

aught anything; possessions, property

ay, aye ever

back-spang (lit.) backward leap; in *The Merry Men*, a counter-current

bardy bold

barley-hoods fits of obstinacy, ill humour

barming churning

barns-breaking breaking of heads; any injurious action

baudrons puss, cat

beel't poisoned, festering

begude began

behoof behalf

bein thriving, comfortable

ben into

bidin' remaining, staying at home

billie companion, comrade

bink kitchen shelves

birl drill, drive among

birkie lively fellow

blear blind; *to blear one's e'e* to blind by flattery

bogle hobgoblin, ghost

booet lantern

bra' or *braw* fine; *braws* fine clothes, best clothes

braid broad; plain, intelligible

bratch dog

breet brute

brockit black and white mixture, streaked

bruik enjoy

brunt burnt

buckie reckless person

bullering roaring, bellowing

but to must, as in *she but to have come in,* in *The Merry Men*

but-and-ben cottage of two apartments, an outer and inner room

by ordnar exceptional

byous extraordinary

ca twa pair boast two pairs (of horses)

canny cautious

cantrips spells, magic tricks

canty cheerful

carle little old man

carlines old women

causeway paved yard, paved part of street

chape, chaep cheap

chat conversation, talk; *haud yer chat* hold your tongue

chaumer chamber, applied to sleeping quarters for farm-servants in outhouses

cheena metal crockery

chiels, chields fellows, servants

chumly lug fireside

clanjamfray collection, bunch; riff-raff

clavers frivolous talk

cleuch precipice; hollow between steep banks

clootie devil

coalheugh shafthead of coalpit

cod pillow

comported behaved

conceit o' me fancy for me

connach spoil

coorse harsh, rough

couthy agreeable, kind

cowe the gowan (lit.) pulls the daisy-beats all
crap crept
crook chain with hooks above fire
crunkly rough
cummer godmother; female gossip
curch head covering
cuttie silly girl
cutty tobacco pipe

daddles fists
darger day labourer
dauded struck, knocked
daunton terrify, intimidate
dawty daughter, darling
dead-thraws death-throes
deece sofa-shaped, unpadded wooden seat
deel devil
deems dames, lassies
dirige funeral feast
doddy cow without horns
doit coin worth a penny Scots
dooms very, absolutely
dowie dismal
dozened set in one's ways; stupefied
droich dwarf
dule, dole woe, lamentation; hardship
dun-faced sallow
dunne wassel highland gentleman who gets title from land he occupies, though held at will of a chieftain
dunt blow, stroke with a hollow sound

een eyes
eildrich weird, unearthly
ettling aiming, attempting

fain glad
fash to bother, trouble
fashous troublesome
fashery troublesome matter
faur ither wud aw gae? Where else would I go?

feckless weak, poor-spirited
feein', feeing hiring for a term's work
fell extremely
ferlies wonders
feshin up bringing up
fiky fussy
file while
fitted matched
fleeringly contemptuously
forbye as well as, let alone
forenent opposite
foresman head servant
forfochten, forfoughten weary, exhausted
forrit forward
fower four
freats superstitious observances
freely very
fudder whether

gae go
gade went
gade ae best aff always came off best
gaun, gawn, gyaun going; *he'd be't till a kent gyaun oot* he'd know for a sure thing
gangrel vagrant
gar cause to; *gar me speak* cause me to speak
gate way, road; manner
gate-farrin' presentable
gowk cuckoo
gear possessions
geet child
genie natural talent
gey, geyan very
gin if
girzie maidservant; familiar, slightly contemptuous address to young girl
glaikit stupid
glamour enchantment, influence of spell
glampit sprained
gliff sudden fear
glisk glance
glunamie rough fellow

gou'd gold
gousty desolate, dreary
gowan daisy
grumph grunt
Gude God
gudeman head of family; *gude-man and gudewife* husband and wife
gurlin' growling
gutsy gluttonous
gweed good
gyte enraged, delirious

hagg moss ground that has formerly been broken up
hairst harvest
hansel first payment in bargain; guarantee of what's to follow
hantle considerable number, much
haud hold; *haud her nain* hold her own; *haudin' him gyaun* keeping him going
haiveless unmannerly, slovenly; reckless
hind servant, farm worker
hinder-end last, very end
hire-house farm in which "fee'd" servant works
hooly slowly, cautiously
hope sloping hollow between two hills
horn en' the last room in a *but and ben*; where horn spoons used
howkin' digging
howdie midwife
howp hope
humdudgeon needless fuss
hunkers squatting

immas changeable
instanter right away
ill faured, ill fa'ard ugly, ill favoured
ill pay't very sorry, ill pleased
it that

jaloose suspect

jaud jade
jaup weary; muddy water, dregs
jo sweetheart

kenning knowing
kithe show
knock clock
kye cattle
kyloes highland cattle

lamiter lame person
lave rest, remainder
lang-headed having much foresight
latchets shoelaces
leir to teach; learning
leuch, leugh laugh
lift sky
limmer scoundrel
linn waterfall, or pool beneath
lippen trust to, put confidence in
loan piece of uncultivated ground about a croft or *toun*
long-keepit long standing
loon, lown lad; *herd loon* boy who watches cattle
lopper ripple
lowped leapt
lugging dragging
lugs ears

main moan
maun must; *maunna* mustn't
messes portions; measures
mirk dark; *mirk's pick in winter* as dark as pitch
misleart misguided, wrongly taught
mith might
morning if he had not had his *morning* in his head, in *The Two Drovers*, refers to the eighteenth century custom of a mid-morning refreshment, and its effect on brain.
muckle, meikle much, great

neaps turnips
neep-reet turnip root

neist next
neuk corner
nowte beasts, cattle

orra exceptional, odd; *orra wark* odd jobs

paction agreement
partan crab
paumerin' aboot wandering
pickthank a toady, parasitical informer
pikery pilfering
ploiterie muddy
pluffy flabby, chubby
precunnance understanding
preen pin
protty tricky

quine, quean young girl (sometimes used in derogation)

raff worthless character
ram-stam precipitately
rape rope, especially one made of straw
rape-thacket thatched with straw
rashe rush; large number; violent rush
rattons rats
reestin wages resting wages, wages withheld
rive break, burst

saughing rushing sound, churning
saut salt
scaulin' scolding; in *Baubie Huie* it means a public reprimand from the church session
scarting scratching
scarts cormorants
scouts pour out forcibly
screek o' day dawn
seer sure
seyt strain
shalt pony
shone, shoon shoes
sib related by blood; *sibbest* closest related to

siccar eneough sure, secure enough
sin-syne since
skreigh screech
skirl a shrill cry
skyeow-fittet splay-footed
slays pulverised mess
smatterie trifles
smiddy smithy
smoored smothered
sneeshing snuff
snot dolt
soncy healthy, strapping
sook suck, suction
sorra sorrow
soup mouthful
sowens oatmeal mixture
sowp measure of liquid
spaewife fortune teller
spang leap
spean wean
speer, speir ask
speuing vomiting
splore fuss
sprack spruce, sprightly
spunk spirit
stank pool, pond, drain
steen, stane stone
steered disturbed
stey steep
stock good-natured fellow
stots bullocks of two-three years old
strae straw; *a clean strae death* a peaceful death in (straw) bed
stramash, straemash uproar, riotous disorder
strath valley
straucht straight
streen, the streen yesterday night, yestreen
sune soon
swye influence

tacksman one who holds a lease, tenant
taed toad
thole endure
thraws agonies

threepit insisted on repeatedly
ticht tight, plump
toon, toun farm steading
tramp pick kind of narrow spade for turning hard soil
tribble trouble
tyauve to make rough by working with hands; tease out, or wrestle with

unco strange

vir energy
vogie proud

wad would
wanchancy unlucky, dangerous
warstlin wresting

wast west
wat know; *weel a wat* well I know, indeed
waur worse
wean child
whatten what kind of
widdifus wild; worthless bunch
winnockie window
witters throats (withers)
wode insane, outrageous
wulcats wildcats
wull wild
wyte responsibility

yerking beating
yett gate
yoke quarrel, attack
yowlin' caterwauling

BIOGRAPHICAL NOTES

THE TWO DROVERS
The text is from the author's, or "Magnum" edition of 1829-33. The story first appeared in *Chronicles of the Canongate*, 2 vols., 1827.

THE BROWNIE OF THE BLACK HAGGS
The text is from the 1837 edition of Hogg's prose, *Tales and Sketches by the Ettrick Shepherd*, 6 vols. (containing the stories of which Hogg approved, with his revisions, just before his death). The story first appeared in Blackwood's Edinburgh Magazine, vol. XXIV, 1828; then again in *The Shepherd's Calendar*, 1829.

THE GUDEWIFE
The text is from Frazer's Magazine, December 1833.

THE WIDOW OF DUNSKAITH
The text is from *Tales and Sketches by Hugh Miller*, edited by Mrs. Miller, 1863. The story first appeared in Wilson's *Tales of the Borders*, in the later series edited by Alexander Leighton after Wilson's death in 1836, till 1841, to which Miller contributed eight stories in 1837-38.

HOW WE GOT UP THE GLENMUTCHKIN RAILWAY AND HOW WE GOT OUT OF IT
The text is from Blackwood's Magazine, October 1845.

THE STORY OF FARQUHAR SHAW
The text is from *Legends of the Black Watch*, 1859.

THE GOLDEN KEY
The text is from *Dealings with the Fairies*, 1867.

BAUBIE HUIE'S BASTARD GEET
The text is from *Sketches of Life Among my Ain Folk,* 1875.

THE PENANCE OF JOHN LOGAN
The text is from the volume of short stories called *The Penance of John Logan,* 1889. The "new and revised" edition reprints it unchanged.

THE LIBRARY WINDOW
The text is from Blackwood's Magazine, January 1896; the story was reprinted in *Stories of the Seen and Unseen,* 1902.

THE MERRY MEN
The text is from the volume of stories called *The Merry Men,* 1887. The story first appeared in Cornhill Magazine, June and July 1882. But Stevenson altered it drastically for the 1887 collection.